# Blood Fever

# Blood Fever

*Simone Beaudelaire*

# Acknowledgments

I want to thank Julie.

With all your many hats... friend, critique partner, editor, and so much more.

I couldn't do it without you.

# Dedication

For my wonderful husband,

## Edwin Stark

You taught me not to fear the darkness inside me,

and you were right, as usual.

# Prologue

New Orleans, 1903

Night tightened its claws around the city, choking life and light to sullen, crouching terror. In the penetrating blackness, a cat screamed, a child wailed. A man, his face at once youthful and mature, as though in his prime and yet ancient, leaned his arm against a windowsill. Behind him, revelers chased away the dark in wild laughter. He ignored them all, staring as though his eyes could penetrate beyond the pool of yellow streetlights near the courtyard and into the invisible street beyond.

"I know you're out there," he growled beneath his breath. "I know you're there. Stay where you are. Come no closer. We do not need to do this."

The night offered no reply, not that he had expected one.

"Philippe," a woman breathed, her exhalation hot on his ear as her fingers closed around his arm.

He whirled to face his hostess. "Camille." His pounding heart slowed at the sight of her familiar face, her dark hair piled loosely into a careless knot on the back of her head, and her scarlet gown clinging scandalously low on her ample breasts.

"Philippe, my love, why are you looking out into that gloomy court-yard," she demanded in English, delicately accented with her native

French, "when all the beautiful flowers of Louisiana bloom just over your shoulder?"

Philippe spared a glance at the painted prostitutes. Though he found them lovely, their allure could not fully distract him from the knowledge that somewhere beyond the torches' light, a creature hunted him. *But not yet, Lord,* he begged silently. *I'm so tired. So tired of all this.* "I'm sorry to be a bad guest, Camille," he said with all due humility.

"Silly." She waved her hand, accepting the apology while pretending to dismiss it. "Don't worry for me, but I fear Geneviève would be heartbroken if you did not visit her. She has a new dress she wants to show you." She extended a bare arm from which a mere scrap of a sleeve dangled, its scarlet hue drawing his eye to the enticing fullness of her pale bosom.

Philippe took the offer, laying his hand on her elbow and allowing her to lead him back into the crowded parlor. There, ladies fanned themselves against the sultry evening, black lace fluttering over faces ranging in hues from cream to coffee.

Philippe adored them all. A woman's beauty never escaped him, whether white, black or some mixture thereof. He scanned each face, recalling an evening spent with one, an hour with another, and felt for each a surge of affection. Then a rustle of taffeta drew his attention to the stairs. Clad in icy white, Geneviève descended, arm-in-arm with a portly gentleman, a false smile plastered on her full lips.

Philippe ran his gaze over her lovely face from her hair—brown and lushly curly, tendrils escaping their thick, ornate knot—to her broad high forehead, eyes too dark and nose too wide to provide evidence of the European ancestry she claimed. Their eyes locked, and she blushed.

"Thank you, my dear," the portly gentleman wheezed, patting her hand. She turned, curved her lips at the fellow, and then dropped his arm and scampered away. She caught Philippe's eyes again with a teasing, sideways glance, and acted as though she meant to sneak past him.

"No, you don't, m'mselle," Philippe growled, grabbing her arm.

"Why, sir!" her hand fluttered around her bosom. "Unhand me this minute." She wrinkled her nose at him.

"Not without a kiss." Philippe dropped the pseudo-aggressive tone and added, "I've missed you, Gen."

She stilled, smile fading. Then she led him toward the door.

"Geneviève," Camille barked.

"Never fear, my lady," Philippe said, interceding, "I'll be buying her entire evening."

A mercenary grin flashed across the madam's face, and she waved to the couple as they passed beyond the doorway into breathless darkness.

Geneviève stepped into Philippe's arms. He enfolded her. She lifted her face and he claimed her plump lips with hungry urgency. Geneviève clung to his neck and mouth. He curved one hand around the back of her neck and splayed the other along her spine.

"I'm still amazed you allow this," he murmured.

She smiled against his lips. "You're special, Philippe."

"Do you say that to everyone?" he asked, eyes probing hers. They never discussed her profession, but tonight he had to know.

Her eyebrows drew together, staring into him as though reading his intentions. Then she slowly twisted her head to one side and then the other. "This is special, at least to me. The others... they don't have anything to do with my heart, my feelings. I do my work, nothing more."

"And me?" he demanded, hope flaring.

Her smile turned wistful. "You stopped being work to me long ago, Philippe." Then she broke eye contact, gaze skirting away. "But for naught. I'm... I am what I am. What could a *putain* like me mean to someone like you?"

"To someone like me?" He chuckled without humor. "What do you imagine I am, Gen? Rich? Powerful? I am all those things and you're right. Someone like me should want an innocent virgin to keep his manor and bear his *enfants*."

She swallowed hard. The working of her throat revealed her sorrow.

3

Philippe tucked a finger under her chin and lifted her face. "But, *minette*, I am not like those men. What I have seen... what I have endured..." he allowed the faintest scrap of his shame and rage to bleed into his expression.

Her eyes bulged. He waited for her to withdraw, but instead, she ran her fingers into his hair. Emboldened, he pressed on. "What have I to do with youth and innocence? I would frighten a young maiden out of her wits. Only one who has walked through the fire can match me. So, to answer your question, *minette*; to a man like me, you might only seem good for an evening, but as for myself..." he stroked the curve of her cheek. "You mean hope, and I have not hoped in so long."

Geneviève laid her forehead against his lips, rubbing like the kitten he had named her. "What are you saying, Philippe?"

"I'm saying," he began, tenderly stroking his fingers over her silky skin, "that I would like to take you away from this life. I'd rather you remain with me. Are you willing?"

"As your mistress?" Again, her gaze slid away from his, but not before he saw the conflicted thoughts she sought to conceal.

"Perhaps you could call it that," he said, "but remember, the future contains many mysteries, and the world is large. I must be honest with you, *minette*. Being with me will not be easy for you. I am not what you think, and I am constantly in danger. If you agree, you will share that risk. We must always be on the run, never staying long in any place, never making connections because they might betray us. You would be trading one shadow life for another. I cannot offer you more."

Geneviève caught her lip between her teeth. "You give me much to consider," she admitted. "I do like the thought of having only one man, a man who says such nice, caring things to me, instead of a crew of clients who pat my head like a good dog." She traced her hand down Philippe's back. He shivered as her fingers stimulated his skin. "What kind of trouble keeps a man of wealth and power on the run?"

She lifted her eyes to his, and he wondered what she saw in his face—in his too-black eyes that should have been blue, given the paleness of his skin. *Can you see what I am? Can you understand at all, minette? How can I expect that you would? Half legend, half monster, I shouldn't exist, and yet I fight not only to survive, but to live, really live.* His heart hurt even as it surged with hope, knowing eventually he would lose her. *Even if we make a perfect future together, it will someday come to an end. By staving off loneliness now, you're purchasing grief later.* And yet, the heavy perfume of jasmine and magnolia rising from her hair, the baby softness of her tawny skin, the bright hope in her dark eyes lured him past sense and reason into a place that felt perilously like... love.

"I wish I could offer you more, *minette.* I wish I could buy you a plantation with a beautiful home and servants to attend to your every desire. I wish I could set you up as the belle of every ball. It cannot be. I can only offer you shadows, and danger... and every corner of my battered heart. Will you accept it, Geneviève?"

Her fingers fluttered over her mouth. "Do you mean that, Philippe?" she breathed, exhaling a scent of peppermint and exotic spices.

He leaned down and touched his lips to her forehead. "I do." The word carried the weight of a vow, a vow he could never make, but was making nonetheless.

She met his eyes with steady certainty. "I will."

Joy swelled Philippe's heart at her simple declaration. "Then come, my lady. Your home awaits."

"Oh!" she blinked. "But what about Madame Camille? She will be angry if I disappear. She always says I can't leave, that none of us may, because we owe her money." She lowered her eyes, skin coloring. "Because I'm... mixed, I owe her more than most."

*Did she think I didn't know?* "My love, I do not believe one person may own another, and not long ago, this nation fought a war to prove it. Now, all people are free, save that one heart permits the other ownership. If it worries you, I can pay her... not to buy you, but to free you from any claim she might have."

Geneviève studied his boots as she gave a curt nod. *How humiliating it must be to think your very existence causes someone to claim ownership. Her African blood only makes her special.*

To speak such thoughts aloud, even in private, invited trouble, and so he set out to prove to her how much he cared by lifting her chin and claiming her lips in a kiss of aching tenderness. It struck him how very sacred their conversation felt, as though their relationship, anathema to society and unsanctioned by the Church, carried the weight of a priest's blessing. "Come, love. I will settle accounts tomorrow with Camille. Tonight, we feast."

Geneviève's expression lightened into one of radiant joy, so her dusky complexion glowed like topaz under the flickering streetlights.

Suddenly feeling exposed, Philippe turned partly away from his beloved's face and led her through the gate and out into the street.

Here, the darkness turned palpable and threatening—not the vague sense of foreboding he had experienced inside the whorehouse, but a more visceral danger that made him want to run for the river and board the first boat away... or charter one.

It seemed Philippe's tension translated itself to Geneviève. She crept closer to his body, wrapping his cloak around her overly revealing dress as though to hide herself from view. She seemed to tug at him, urging him to hurry, but with no clear understanding of where they headed.

"Come now, *minette*," he urged, trying to lighten their flight with a jest, "you needn't rush so. There remains plenty of night for your ravishment."

She laughed, her usual bell-like giggle, though he could hear that she didn't truly mean it. "Oh, and should I act like a blushing bride?" she teased back. "Should I hide under the bedclothes in my thickest nightgown?"

"Nay, my lady. The heat is too dense. You would melt away and I would be left to ravish a puddle." He swept her around a gloomy corner. In the distance, the soft lapping of water over stone gave way to the mournful shriek of a paddle wheeler as it rocked in its moorings. Something small swooped down at them, barely visible in the moonlight. Geneviève dodged with a squeak as leathery wings flapped past her head.

"Something feels wrong tonight, Philippe," she commented, her bravado faltering on every word.

"It does," he agreed. "I fear the danger that stalks me must be drawing near. They always bring such a sense of dread. We will not be able to linger long in the city."

"Will we leave soon, then?" she asked, a little breathlessly. "I've never been outside of New Orleans."

"First thing in the morning," he replied tersely. "I'm afraid Madame Camille will have to make do without payment. She's earned a fortune on your debasement. She's had enough."

"I suppose," Geneviève agreed, "but, oh, Philippe, I feel afraid. Afraid of Camille, the night, even the dark, and I'm a creature of darkness."

He laughed, low and humorless. "*Minette*, you are pure sunshine, and have nothing in common with true creatures of darkness. I know."

She drew to a halt in a beam of silvery moonlight. "Philippe, are you able to move about in the daytime?"

He froze, arrested by her sudden movement and unexpected words. "How do you know such things?" he demanded harshly.

"My grandmother," Geneviève stated, meeting his eyes without fear. "Her ancestors came from Senegal, but before that, who knows? She never stated her origin, I don't know if she even knew it, but somewhere in that faraway land, they spoke a legend of creatures, neither alive nor dead, who rose from the earth to feed on the living and turn them also into shades. Are you such a creature, Philippe? Are you what my French father called... *vampyr?*"

"You are far smarter than you give yourself credit for," he muttered, and then shook his head. "*Non, minette*, I am not a vampire, but you have truly named my enemy."

Geneviève gulped, turning ashen as the realization of what she faced—what she had agreed to—dawned on her.

"Do you wish to return to the *bordel?*" he asked. "You are far safer there. Indeed, it was selfish of me to bring you away. Perhaps, in time, you could buy your freedom. Do I take you home, Geneviève?"

She considered for a long, silent moment. "Home, Philippe? Do you really think that place is my home? Non, *mon amour*. My only home... is you."

A poignant blend of love and guilt swirled through Philippe. "As long as there is breath in my body, *minette*, as long as I live, I will give my life to protect yours."

She nodded, accepting what feeble protection he could give. *I pray you never know how feeble it truly is.*

Again, the bat swooped over the couple, intent on its nightly feast of insects, and Geneviève flinched away from it. Unfrozen at last, Philippe moved his mistress forward, racing through the darkened streets to the door of his townhouse, a building in dark burgundy brick with a wrought-iron railing, around which ivy twined. Quickly turning the key in the lock did not prevent a thrill of nervous tension from creeping up Philippe's neck. He pulled Geneviève closer to his side. At last, the door consented to swing inward, and they ducked through, slamming it shut to keep dark things in the night.

Philippe sighed with relief and set a match to the wick of an oil lamp on a table near the door. The tiny ray of light chased back the breathless darkness in the room, until it sulked in the corners and peered out from beneath tables and sofas.

"This was supposed to be so different," Philippe complained. "I had such a romantic evening planned for you, *minette*."

She smiled, full lips curving into an expression of true happiness. "Don't worry, *mon amour*. We're safe now."

He grasped the lamp in one hand, his lady in the other and led her into the parlor. "I wish this could be your home forever."

She shrugged. "I like the idea of going somewhere new, to a place where I most likely will not come across former clients at dinner parties and have to look their wives in the eye."

"I see your point." He dipped his chin in a sympathetic nod. "Well then, my dear, shall we retire, since we successfully navigated the streets? I feel we ought to celebrate." Then, dropping his teasing formality, he added, "Are you able to enjoy it, *minette,* or has your work left you jaded... or afraid?"

She bit her lip. "I'm not certain. I don't usually pay close attention, *tu vois?* I try to tune it out, to think on other things. Perhaps we should... practice?" The hope in her eyes resurrected his own.

Words seemed superfluous, so he simply moved toward the stairs, leading her to his second-floor bedroom. He had sparsely furnished the spacious room with a bed, from which netting served a dual purpose of adornment and protection from the constantly whining mosquitos, an oversized bureau, a wardrobe, and a chair. Of tables, lamps and other fripperies, there were none. *Perhaps Gen can help me turn my abode into a home. I hope so.*

Her pulse throbbed visibly in her throat, drawing his eye, despite the dim light provided only by a smiling sliver of a moon that peered through the window. *She's nervous,* he realized. *I wonder if it's because she's afraid of her employer... or because she's afraid I'm going to continue treating her like a whore.* The thought bothered him, deep down. He'd made peace with her profession long since, but it suddenly dawned on him that he hadn't addressed his own willingness to use her that way. *I was her client. How do you go from client to lover?* Though he cared deeply for Geneviève, he realized her past—their shared past—might interfere with their future.

"*Minette,* do you actually want to do this?" he asked softly.

She lowered dark eyebrows and regarded him, her lips screwed to the side in a quizzical expression.

"I mean," he clarified, "do you want to 'practice,' as you say, tonight? We can wait, let the memories fade for a time, if you'd rather."

The questioning expression faded to a look of startled tenderness. "Philippe, I understand what it means to be your mistress. I'm not unwilling." Her fingers began to work the buttons on the back of her dress.

He closed his hand over hers, arresting the movement, more certain than ever that this would be a misstep. "No, *minette,* not this way. We would be better off to come together another time, when you're as ready and eager as I am. I cannot bear to be a client to you anymore. I'm not asking you to trade many for one."

He stroked his thumb over her hand and made a suggestion that hurt, even though he knew it was right. "If you cannot accept this between us, then I will make you a different offer. Let us travel together, away from this place, as we said. We will travel, and when we find a place you think you'd like, you stay there. I'll provide you the means to care for yourself."

Geneviève's eyes widened. "You would do such a thing for me?" Then suspicion closed down her expression. "Why?"

He extended one hand and stroked down her cheek. "I love you," he said simply. "I want you to be happy. Of course, I would prefer to be the one who provides that happiness, but if you cannot accept it from me, you can still live a meaningful life, far from all this. That would be enough." His heart twisted as he voiced the words, but he would in no way retract them. *Her happiness is all that matters.*

Geneviève stared. Her eyes grew brilliant as stars, and a crystal tear rolled down her cheek. Her fingers came to rest on the front of his snowy-white shirt and then slid upward, until she caressed the stubble-roughened paleness of his cheek. He waited, not understanding what her gesture meant, and she drew him forward, claiming his lips in a kiss that shocked him with its innocent sweetness.

"Gen?" he mumbled against her lips.

"I..." she paused for another smudge of her lips on his. "I love you. I didn't think it was possible, but I see I'm capable of it after all and..." Geneviève's impassioned speech ended abruptly as Philippe took charge of the kiss, turning it sensual with a swipe of his tongue. "Hmmm," she hummed.

"Sweet girl." His lips slid down her chin and onto her throat. She tilted her head back, trusting him to kiss that pulse that tempted him. He trailed his tongue over the artery. The scent of her, warm and alive, teased the feral beast that lived within him, but her trust, especially in light of all the suffering the recent years of her life had brought, fought it back down. He clamped his mouth over her throat, not to bite, but to apply suction, claiming her as his own with a passion mark.

Geneviève's back arched, thrusting plump breasts against his chest.

Philippe released her throat before the temptation could overwhelm his nobility. He stared down at the dark loveliness of his woman. *My woman. How long has it been since I had someone love me?*

He shuddered at the dark memories his thought provoked. *That wasn't love. This is. Geneviève, my darling kitten, resting eagerly against my heart. Maybe it's selfish to claim her. Maybe I should take her somewhere safe and move on, but how can I?*

Her dark eyes shone in the faint moonlight. Her lips glistened with moisture, full and tempting. He lowered his head, tasting the heady, pillowy softness. *Can it be wrong to love someone? Someone who needs love as badly as I do? I know what it is to be used, and to use others. How I pray we can overcome that and forge something real.*

In her kiss, he could taste her growing desire. It gave him hope. "Gen," he murmured softly against her lips, "have you ever been loved by a man before?"

She looked askance at him, eyes narrowing.

"I mean loved, truly loved, *minette*, not work."

"Not in a long, long time," she admitted, looking up at him through thick, enticing eyelashes. "Even then, I'm not sure. It might have been love... or it might have been a naïve young girl succumbing to a casual seducer. Who knows? At the time, it felt real. Since then, there has only been work... though you've strained the boundaries for quite some time now."

Guilt pierced his heart. "Can you forgive me for using you in such a way? I knew better, and yet..."

"And yet, I was, up until a few moments ago, a woman of a certain profession. How could you have seen me as anything other than a body to be used? It was my job."

"I know what it is to be a possession," Philippe admitted, heat flaring on his cheekbones. Geneviève's eyes widened. "I know what it is not to own my own body. I'm sorry I did it to you. Forgive me, my love? And please, don't say it's all right. It isn't."

She nodded. "I forgive you," she said, her voice taking on the serious tone he'd hoped for. "Come now, my darling. Let us lie down, shall we? Begin again?"

At her words, Philippe felt fresh, newly born of innocent love and tender affection. The dark bonds of abuse fell away with each step as they approached the bed, pulled back the lush blue brocade covering, and revealed snowy sheets beneath. Geneviève bit her lip, the picture of a nervous young bride, despite the scandalous gown she wore. Her expression grew unguarded, and he could see the nervous excitement glowing in her eyes. "Start fresh," Philippe agreed. "Together, my love, we can make all things new. Leave the past behind with the dead in the cemetery and make a new life, just for us."

Her lips curved into a luscious smile that warmed him to the depths of his frozen soul. Her gaze broke contact with his and a suspicious color flared along her cheekbones, as once again, her fingers went to the fastenings of her gown. This time, he allowed it. He helped her, working as one with her to release the ties and buttons until the fabric fell into a crumpled pool at her feet. Beneath it, she wore her shoes—white satin pumps with little bows on top—and nothing more. Her skin glowed like amber in the flickering lamplight.

Though he'd bedded her so many times before, tonight she looked like a stranger; the curves of her body unfamiliar to his eyes. He traced gentle fingers over the fullness of her bosom, the soft dip of her waist, the slender plumpness of her thigh.

She stood, frozen yet quivering before him, accepting his touch. Her nostrils flared on a shuddering inhalation.

He admired her feminine beauty as he busied himself removing his own clothing. Shirt, trousers, and undergarments joined the pile on the floor. In his long life, Philippe had lain with hundreds of women, but he could not recall ever having felt so vulnerable. That vulnerability reflected back to him in his beloved's eyes. She reached out a tentative hand and traced the muscles of his chest. He captured her fingers, trapping them against his heart so she could feel the pulse.

Philippe drew Geneviève to him, aligning their bodies. He ran a caressing hand down her back and cupped her bottom. She embraced him again, drawing him down for a kiss. Philippe marveled how, even as his body burned with readiness, his heart could only dwell on the purity of their unexpected love. She shifted in his embrace. The erect tips of her breasts dragged through the coarse hairs on his chest. His thickened sex caressed the softness surrounding her navel.

Philippe allowed his hands to wander over Geneviève's body, marveling at the softness of the skin on her back, the firm curve of her rear, the full plumpness of her breasts, the soft roundness of her lower belly. Her breath caught and grew harsh as he pleasured her with delicate touches. She squirmed in his grasp. "Too much?" he breathed against her lips.

"No," she whispered back. "More, please, Philippe."

Grinning to himself, Philippe lowered his lady back onto the bed and knelt, straddling her. "This is for you, my love. Tell me what pleases you."

Grasping the fullness of her breasts, he pushed them together and nuzzled into the deep cleft. Her nipples touched his cheeks and he turned to suckle one and then the other, listening carefully to her breathing in hopes of hearing a reaction.

Geneviève did not disappoint. Gasps and soft vocalizations rewarded his efforts. Pulling back, Philippe stared down at his beloved's glistening breasts. "So lovely," he murmured. He took hold of one brown peak and tugged gently. Geneviève moaned. *She enjoys a firm touch,* he noted, and realized he'd guessed that before. Philippe savored his lady's pleasure, teasing gasps and sighs from her, until her body relaxed, and her thighs fell open between his. Reasoning this cue meant she was ready for greater intimacy, he moved down her body, savoring caramel curves like fine sweets. Lifting her thighs in his hands, he positioned her, laid out and open. She tensed, and he could nearly hear her thinking how she dreaded the sudden surge that signaled the move from her pleasure to his own. Philippe had no such plan. Lowering his head, he kissed her low, far below her navel, at the uppermost edge of the dark hairs that guarded her sex. The scent of her arousal teased him. Unable to resist, he dragged his lips over the center of her pleasure. She squeaked in surprise, her thighs closing around his shoulders.

Genevieve's reaction puzzled Philippe. *Surely a woman of such experience would not be surprised by such a simple pleasure technique.*

Then the nature of her previous encounters dawned on him. *She existed for the pleasure of others, and no one gave any thought to hers. That ends now.*

Easing his tongue over the tender, swollen bud, Philippe set out to arouse his lady. He spread the lips of her sex back from his target, holding her open to his plundering.

His own sex clamored for release, but he knew his time would come soon enough, and so he pushed the thought into the background and focused entirely on his woman.

Her surprise gave way to ecstatic moaning. Her hands fisted in the sheets and her head tossed on the pillow, but Philippe gave no quarter. With infinite care and patience, he escorted her to the summit. She poised on the brink, shuddering and tense, and then Genevieve took flight. A wild cry tore from her lips, and her hips bucked.

Philippe watched her orgasm, entranced. Then he surged over her, capturing her whimpering mouth with his own. Without prompting, her heels came to rest on his back, allowing him easier access to her clenching heat. He eased in, slow and steady, until their bodies merged as one.

"Oh, Philippe," Genevieve moaned. He responded with a throaty growl. They poised, frozen, for an endless moment, basking in the transformation from dirty lust to tender passion. Then Philippe eased back and surged into Genevieve again. He watched her closely, noting her reaction to his possession. Her eyes soft and dreamy, her hands clutched on his shoulders, she arched her hips, meeting him thrust for thrust. *She likes this. I'm so thankful.* Philippe braced his forearms on the mattress, raining kisses onto Genevieve's face as he surged deep, eased back and returned. The tide of their pleasure rose in tandem, tensing their bodies. The rhythm of their joining grew urgent and wild. Genevieve's fingernails scored Philippe's shoulders.

One final thrust ignited the fuse. Philippe and Genevieve succumbed, the ecstasy of their joining seeming to sink deep into their hearts and bind them as one.

Love welled in Philippe's heart, deeper and stronger than he'd believed himself capable of feeling. With all care and gentleness, he slipped from her body. Her eyes met his.

"Je t'aime, minette," he told her solemnly. She smiled.

He rose to his feet. Genevieve scooted back along the mattress and leaned against the headboard of the bed, reaching out one hand to Philippe.

"Yes, my love?" he asked, laying his palm against hers.

"I had no idea it could be like that," she informed him with soft intensity.

He nodded. "Neither did I, but I am so glad."

He bent over her hand and touched his lips to the pulse in her wrist. *There are many things she will need to know, and all of them are hard, ugly and painful, but for tonight, this connection suffices.* "Would you care for a glass of wine?"

Genevieve's smile warmed Philippe's heart as they gazed into one another's eyes for an endless, tender moment. Then she squeezed his hand and released him. "I would love a glass of wine," she said.

Philippe smiled and moved, naked and unembarrassed, through the room, to a silver tray containing a bottle and two clean glasses. *Did I know she would agree? I hoped, but the reality is so much more than I ever would have expected. Soon we will have to leave this city. I like it here, but the danger is too great. I must keep Gen safe.*

He pulled the cork from the bottle, and rich, red liquid flowed into the antique glass. *I'd better wait a bit on my own mixture. She might not be ready for that.*

The bed creaked as Genevieve rose to her feet. She padded away from him towards the bureau, with its wood-framed mirror.

"What are you doing, my darling?" he asked.

She giggled. "I feel different. I wanted to see if I look it as well."

"You had best look happy," he admonished.

A flash of white in the vicinity of the wardrobe caught his eye; the movement almost too fast to follow. A familiar, unwanted sensation flared in his mind. *We are not alone.* Philippe's breath caught. *Oh, dear God, no!*

Genevieve squeaked and began to struggle.

The antique glass slipped from Philippe's fingers to shatter unnoticed on the floor as he raced forward.

Genevieve screamed, hands scrabbling at the side of her neck.

"Nooo!" he shouted, laying his hands on the tiny, dark-haired woman who seemed to have sprung from his nightmares. "Ragonde, no!"

With every bit of his strength, he managed to drag the woman away from Genevieve and throw her aside. He hurried forward, heart clenching at the sight of blood spraying from his beloved's torn artery.

"Philippe," she wept, meeting his eyes in the mirror.

He reached for her. *I must try to stanch the bleeding,* he thought. Though he knew a hopeless injury when he saw one, he could no more resist trying to help than he could tear out his own heart. In the corner, the intruder hissed with laughter.

Genevieve regarded Philippe as he approached her. A great shudder shook her frame. She withdrew toward the window. "Gen, please, let me help you," he urged.

"It's too late," Ragonde informed him, her voice filled with cold humor. She made no move to approach him. "She's already dead. She just doesn't know it yet."

"Shut up, you," he snapped, not even sparing a glance, knowing the evil creature would remain still to watch the suffering she had caused. "Gen, Gen... please."

"Stay away," she whispered. "You did this."

She backed up onto the balcony. Again, Philippe advanced.

Her spine pressed to the wrought iron railing, Genevieve met Philippe's eyes. The hurt and betrayal within them twisted like a knife in his heart. "Gen..."

"I trusted you," she whispered, one hand clutching her injured neck. Blood surged like the tide between her fingers.

"Wait, don't. Gen!"

She sagged, seeming close to losing consciousness, and then drew herself up one last time for a wild, shrieking leap from the balcony.

"Nooooo!" Philippe shouted, seconds before her body slammed into the street below.

Behind him, Ragonde murmured, "You know why I am here, and you know what you must do. Our master will never rest until he has you back in his harem. Return willingly, and all will be forgiven, but do not make us fight you. You will lose, and you know what that means."

"Never!" Philippe snarled.

Shouts pierced the night, and the sound of approaching footsteps drove Philippe back into the shadows.

"Dear God," an unfamiliar voice shouted. "What happened?"

Somehow, despite the distance and her waning strength, Genevieve's soft whisper reached him. "Philippe St. Pierre. He... bit me."

Philippe's eyes closed in despair. *She didn't see Ragonde somehow. She thinks I betrayed her.*

"What's happening?" another voice broke into Philippe's misery.

"Get a physician," the first voice shouted. "She's injured... No! Wait, never mind. She's gone."

"But what happened?"

"I don't know, but I think the fellow who lives in this house is going to have to explain."

In agony, Philippe withdrew into his bedroom. Just as he expected, Ragonde had vanished. Concealing himself in one of the many secret places within his home, Philippe waited for the furor to begin. Hot tears burned his throat and eyes. *I should never have dared to hope. There is no happiness for one such as me. Rest in peace, my beloved.*

"I will never go back," he whispered to the night. It seemed as though a mocking laugh responded, taunting him.

# Chapter One

St. Mary Parish, Louisiana. 1945

"You're nuts, Pops," Donny said around a mouthful of andouille.

"Chew with your mouth closed," Mrs. Delaney nagged, shoving her own food around on her plate, "and don't talk to your father that way."

"But, Ma," the young man complained, resting one elbow on the red-checked tablecloth, "he wants to grow wheat. We live in a floodplain. There's no lettuce in that."

"Lettuce?" Mr. Delaney peeked over the top of his newspaper at his son. "No one said anything about lettuce."

"He means money, Pa," Daphne explained, taking a dainty bite of her grits. The explosion of flavor on her tongue forced her eyes shut for a moment. *Yum. Ma does make the best grits in Louisiana. I'm sure of that.*

Mr. Delaney glared at his daughter, his sunburned skin crinkling. "Lettuce is money? Holy Moses, how these kids talk."

"Son, can't you use normal words, like anyone could understand?" Mrs. Delaney begged.

Donny shrugged, shoveling a huge bite of toast into his mouth. "Just because you and Pa are fuddy duddies doesn't mean I have to be," Donny argued, spraying crumbs over the table.

"Your mouth, son," his mother fretted. "Didn't you learn anything after all these years? Oh, it was a mistake to send you to college."

"Whack him with the spoon, Mother," Mr. Delaney urged, returning his gaze to the newspaper.

Though Mrs. Delaney made no move to comply, her son glared. Hastily swallowing his toast, he choked, gagged, and took a large swallow of tepid coffee. "I'm not kidding though," he continued. "Don't flip your lid, but the war is almost over. The government ain't interested in any new contracts. I asked. Growing wheat is a waste of money. Now if we cultivate sugar cane or maybe tobacco in our new field, we'll really be cooking with gas."

With a sigh, Mr. Delaney lowered his newspaper again. "Translation, please?" he asked his daughter.

Daphne tucked a forkful of egg into her mouth, chewed and swallowed. "He thinks we should grow sugar cane or tobacco." *That's the heart of the message after all. No need to get tangled up trying to explain slang.*

"What? Why?" He turned to his son, blinked, and then returned his faded, gray-green eyes to Daphne. "Did he say he thinks the war is almost over? Victory in Europe doesn't mean anything. The Pacific could rage on for years."

"No way," Donny insisted, this time without the juicy mouthful of food to accompany his tirade. "The aces all agree. The Japs are done for. It won't be a year, not even enough to extract some hen fruits from the Arsenaults."

"Hen fruits?" Mrs. Delany exclaimed, horrified. "Son, that's so... vulgar!"

Daphne hid her grin behind her coffee cup. *Donny's really rolling out the slang today.*

"Even if the war is almost over, which I don't believe," Mr. Delaney grumbled, "I don't know why you would argue with growing chicken feed. Once we join our operation with the Arsenaults', we'll have one of the largest farms in St. Mary Parish. It makes sense for us to grow grain instead of buying it."

"It's all about lettuce," Donny explained. "Eggs are too dad-blamed cheap. The boys coming back from overseas have a taste for smokes, and they'll want more. Or candy. If we give people stuff they want, but don't need, they'll pay more for it, see?"

"Are we talking about lettuce again?" Mr. Delaney demanded.

Daphne swallowed fast to avoid spraying coffee over her family. Then she recalled the letter she'd received earlier in the week and her amusement withered like the lettuce her father kept obsessing over. *I didn't know how to explain this to them. A week later, I still don't.* The delicious breakfast she'd been dreaming about since September suddenly tasted like ashes. Daphne pushed her plate away and lifted her eyes to the kitchen ceiling, tracing dark wooden beams from one end of the spacious room to the other, where a new, sparkly, top-of-the-line stove had been purchased with the proceeds of war contracts.

*Amazing how things change. When I was a baby, we were barely surviving, scrabbling on the edge of bankruptcy, despite the farm's prosperity. I remember Ma and Pa talking about losing everything, but we never quite did. The war changed our fortunes. Once it's over, I wonder what will happen. Will we go back to being poor, or will the investments my parents have made in land, equipment and crop diversification mean they remain prosperous?*

She glanced from her father to her brother. *They're thinking differently. Dad's so old-fashioned, he and Donny almost can't communicate anymore, and... I'm different too. Three years in the city, attending Newcomb Memorial College—and sometimes Tulane—has changed me in ways I can scarcely understand, let alone explain.*

"Daphne," Mrs. Delaney turned to her daughter and frowned to see her pushing food around on her plate. "Finish that, would you?"

"I'm not hungry, Ma," Daphne said softly. "I'll put this in the icebox until later, okay?"

"It will be disgusting if you reheat it," Mrs. Delaney pointed out.

"I don't mind." *I'll probably sneak it out to the pigs when no one is looking. They won't mind either.*

Mrs. Delaney eyed her daughter, a disapproving frown plastered on her weathered, angular face. Her thin hair, heavily streaked with gray, had once again resisted the pin curls she'd laboriously placed last night and straggled, bumpy and lank in the coastal humidity, around her shoulders as though in mockery of fashion. Daphne's own light brown hair had been tucked into a simple, smooth bun she knew would hold all day. As always, Mrs. Delaney's eyes lingered on the roundness of Daphne's cheeks, the plumpness of her shoulders, which pushed her shoulder pads and the puffs of her short sleeves into a strange configuration, the fullness of her bosom that strained the buttons of her blouse, and then sighed. Years of deprivation had graced Mrs. Delaney with the perfect, slim figure, and despite her haggard appearance, she felt lovely, and so exuded just such an air. Daphne, plump, plain, and uninterested in fashion, seemed to mock her mother with her very existence. *Not that I mean to. I am who I am, that's all.*

"Perhaps it's just as well," Mrs. Delaney said at last. "You could certainly do with smaller portions. But never mind the ice box. There will be lunch at lunchtime, as always. Take your plate out to Chester and Otto, and then you may wash the dishes."

"Yes, Mama," Daphne agreed. Rising, leaving her father and brother to their mutually unintelligible debate about crop selection, Daphne hurried to obey.

Outside, temperatures seemed to be flirting with the shady side of sixty, typical for winter on the southern coast, though Daphne didn't feel the cold nearly as painfully as slimmer girls.

Chickens, their feathers puffed, clucked and scratched in the yard behind the house. *Though we only have eight, not like the neighbors' commercial egg production facility.* "Pardon me, Betty," she said to a plump red hen, who hopped out of her way, and took the opportunity to peck at her shoelace as she passed. "Silly bird."

The yard of the house stretched a good distance to the back, filled with Ma's vegetable garden, now mostly dormant for the winter. Past the first fence, the rice field stretched far into the horizon. The new plot, purchased from a neighbor who'd moved away, lay on the west side of the property, fallow and empty, waiting for Mr. Delaney and his son to decide what to grow.

To the east, between the Delaney and Arsenault properties, a pen had been erected. Two fat sows, ironically called Chester and Otto, oinked at her approach. They rooted around the empty trough in hopes of finding some tidbit left from their breakfast. At her approach, two sets of pink ears pricked up. "Yes, ladies, I've brought you a snack—from one pig to another. I hope you enjoy it. It's delicious, but I have no appetite."

The pigs tilted their heads in unison and stared at the gloomy human before them, but the moment the food landed in their trough, they turned their attention to eggs, grits, sausage and toast. For reasons she couldn't quite put her finger on, seeing the animals enjoying the breakfast she no longer cared to eat made her moody. She meandered back into the kitchen, where a sink full of warm water and suds awaited her dishes... along with everyone else's. From the next room, she could hear her father and brother, still debating the relative merits of various crops. With a sigh, Daphne began to wash. The egg clung to the plates and the grease in the pan resisted her efforts. She scrubbed hard while her fingers turned pruny. *I can wash test tubes all day, but the sight of a sink full of breakfast dishes makes me want to cry.* Of course, she'd been crying quite a bit lately, and no surprise. *I can't wait to get out of here.*

"I'm serious," her father's voice filtered into the kitchen. "Once we consolidate the two operations, it will make all kinds of sense to grow feed and—"

Donny interrupted in a rapid gush of semi-comprehensible slang, and Daphne's shoulders sagged in relief. *I don't want to think about feed, chickens, or the Arsenaults for a long, long time.* Quickly finishing the last grimy pot, she scooted outside again. This time the barn, her refuge from childhood, called her with the promise of comfort.

Inside, the scents of hay and horses wrapped around her, and the half-light filtering between gaps in the boards checkered the floor with irregular bars of light. Glad for the long pants she had purchased for laboratory safety, since they kept scratchy bits of straw away from her legs, she climbed the ladder to the hayloft and perched on a square bale. Reaching into her pocket, she drew out two envelopes. *Amazing how these two sheets of paper changed my future completely.* She carefully slipped the first from its envelope and regarded the contents with a smile, before easing it back in again and tucking it away for a later time. The second she stared at with sightless eyes for long moments while she built up her stamina.

*I have to feel this, if I want to put it behind me,* she told herself. Her heart began to pound, and her stomach clenched, threatening to expel the bit of breakfast she'd eaten. Then she began to read.

> **Dear Daphne,**
>
> **I know this is a rotten thing to do, and I'm sorry. I never meant for you to be hurt. I do care about you, believe it or not. Care too much to let you think, for another moment, that we have a future together. I know our parents have always wanted this, and for a while, I agreed with them, but... I can't. I have to be honest. Daphne, I've met someone here in France. I'm staying. Our engagement is over. You can keep the ring, or sell it, or return it to my parents. Whatever you feel is fitting. Again, I'm very sorry. I know this must hurt you, but it's better than living the rest of your life with a husband who's in love with someone else. Take care, Daphne. I wish you all the best.**
>
> **Bob**

A sob climbed up from Daphne's chest. Her eyes burned, and she wiped furiously at her cheek. "Goodbye, Bob," she whispered, clutching the letter to her chest.

"What's up, Daph?" Donny's head appeared at the top of the ladder.

Daphne started violently. "Nothing." She wiped her eyes again.

"Don't give me that line, baby-doll," Donny urged. "I'm no fat-head, so come on, gimme the dope."

"It's a good thing I've gone to college in the city," she said dryly, "or I'd be as lost as Pa. What's up with all the slang, Donny? You never used to talk like that."

He shrugged. "It's my dame," he explained. "Actually, she's a bit of a call-girl, you know? Just for practice. She makes a pass at everyone, and she won't ration herself for no fuddy-duddy. But we're talking about you. What's eating you?" He climbed the rest of the way into the hayloft and sat cross-legged beside his sister.

Daphne made a face, opened her mouth and closed it again. Then she silently extended the note.

Donny grabbed it and as he read, his firm jaw went slack, and his hazel eyes widened. "Now don't that beat all? I'd like to give that guy a knuckle sandwich." His fist balled, crushing the note into trash. He laid a free hand on Daphne's shoulder. "Pa's gonna flip his lid," he informed her solemnly. "If you want my two cents' worth, you'd better take a powder."

Daphne nodded. "That's why I haven't said anything yet. I don't want to cause a big fuss. Thing is, I think I have a great future, one that has nothing to do with my arranged marriage to Bob Arsenault and his chicken farm. I mean, I was willing, when I thought we... well, I loved him a little, but only just a little. I'm not going to wither and die. I mean, look at me, Donny. Why would someone stay true to a fat little farm girl like me? I'm not surprised, and only a little disappointed... but it does sting."

"Quit busting your own chops, sis," Donny said with an impatient wave of the hand. "You're... well, you're just a cookie. I think Bob might be a bit of a wolf, you know, on the lookout for dames. You could do better. Just be yourself, and you'll be hitched before you know it."

Daphne rolled her eyes. "Thanks, Donny, but I have a feeling my future is in the workplace, not the kitchen. I'm actually excited about it. I just needed a minute to let Bob go, you know? Pa's going to take it a lot harder than I am."

Donny made a face that expressed both regret and disappointment, and then ran his fingers through his sandy hair.

Shaking off her disappointment, Daphne added, "And as for you, mister, don't settle for any gold diggers. You're a dreamboat. Find a dolly who's not so corny, and you'll have a gas."

Donny rocked back at her rapid delivery of slang. Daphne took the opportunity to scuttle down the ladder and rush to her bedroom, shutting the door behind her.

*He's right about one thing,* she thought as she examined the bold blue stripes in the wallpaper. *I need to get out of here. I'm not going to marry Bob and be a rich farmwife. I'm not sure if I actually wanted to. For as long as I can remember, that was the path I followed, but is it what I really want.*

She examined her life without the frame of her family's plans. *Bob and I didn't actually fit that well. I was worried how everything would work out. This is better.*

Despite the rational knowledge that losing her fiancé wouldn't hurt her in the long run, the pain of rejection did not lessen one iota. "I want to go home," she said aloud, and then her eyes widened as she realized her family's farm no longer felt like her safe place. "Ah, well," she added. "I guess it means I'm growing up. But what kind of home do I want?"

"I hope you answer that question with the farm next door," her mother's voice cut into her moody daydream.

"Ma." Daphne rolled over and sat up on the edge of the bed, smoothing a strand of straight, light brown hair away from her face.

Her mother bustled into the room, her sparse, gray-streaked hair seeming on the verge of floating away in her great agitation. In her hand, she waved a sheet of crumpled paper.

*Oh, dad blame it.* "Is anything the matter?" Daphne asked sweetly, playing dumb.

"Stop it," her mother growled. The paper made a snapping noise as she gave it a hard shake. "What is the meaning of this?"

Daphne sagged. "I suppose it's fairly obvious. Bob went away to war and met someone. It happens. Our arrangement was always more familial than personal, you know. I'm glad he didn't get blown up or anything."

Her mother lavished a sour look on her but remained silent.

"Well, what do you want me to do, Ma?" He's made his decision, and he's in *France*. It's not as if I could do anything about it. Even if you and Pa spend the money to send me to France, he never loved me that much. It would embarrass us all, and for nothing."

If anything, Mrs. Delaney's frown deepened.

"Stop scowling, Ma. Say something. What do you want?"

"What do I want, Daphne?" her mother repeated, narrowing her eyes until wrinkles wreathed her face. "I want a daughter who's not an embarrassment to the family."

Daphne gulped. Heat climbed up her face. Her fingers fluttered around her lips, and her mouth opened and closed several times as tiny croaks emerged.

"I want a daughter who can understand her family's needs and make them her goals, instead of pursuing her own selfish desires... Education? Bah! Who needs it? You're going to be a farmer's wife—or at least you were. And another thing. You might try eating a bit less, so you can improve your figure. You look like you're made of..."

*Don't say it,* Daphne pleaded with her eyes.

"...pumpkins."

Sobs chased the heat up into her throat. "Ma," she whimpered. "Ma, I can't help it."

"You can," her mother refuted. "You're a selfish little pig. No wonder Bob left you. You don't deserve a man like that."

Daphne bit down on her trembling lip. Then she drew a shuddering breath, released it, and dragged the note out of her pocket. "Listen, Ma, Bob is gone. For whatever reason, he's not coming back, so Pa will have to find a different way to merge farms with the Arsenaults. You should know, though, that I had another option arise."

Mrs. Delaney crossed her arms over her chest and raised one eyebrow.

"Well, um, Newcomb College has been increasing its interest in the sciences, so I took a couple of classes, and I loved them. Ma, I want to be a scientist, like Marie Curie. I want to challenge boundaries like Amelia Earhart, and I want to do it by studying diseases. I want to discover cures so fewer families have to mourn children."

As Daphne described her dreams, her excitement grew. Her mother's familiar disapproval faded from her attention in the face of all she'd learned, all she wanted to learn. "I got a notice from the college that a prominent scientist was offering a one-time chance to work as his laboratory assistant. Ma, he's studying yellow fever, trying to learn more about it, maybe even find a cure. There's already a vaccine, but what about people who can't use it, or who already have the disease? The need is great! So, I applied. If I'm going to be taken seriously, I need lab experience, not just classes. And guess what? I got it. I was selected, even though a whole bunch of boys applied. I'll get paid and everything. Not enough to buy the Arsenault farm, but more than enough to cover my living expenses and tuition, so I won't be a burden anymore.

"Just think, Ma... Someday, *your daughter* might be remembered as one of the discoverers of the yellow fever cure. Wouldn't that be an honor?"

Mrs. Delaney rolled her eyes. "Scientists? Vaccines? This is supposed to be an honor? This is supposed to be better than you marrying well? You must be joking. Are you sure you're a girl at all?"

For the briefest of moments, Daphne couldn't breathe. Her throat closed completely as though she'd received a physical blow. Her belly clenched and threatened to invert itself. *Well, girl,* a sour voice in her head drawled, *what do you expect, really? You know what she wants and you're not giving it to her. You knew she would be unhappy, and how nasty she can be when she doesn't get her way. There's no surprise in any of this.* Her windpipe unsealed itself and air rushed into her lungs in a gasp. She panted in distress. *What now? You have a choice... do you stay here and endure her verbal beatings, or do you go back to the* *city, where your contributions are appreciated, and you can make your* *own way?*

Her mother's voice inserted itself into her internal monologue. "Besides, if a man invites a woman to work in a small, private space with him, do you really think it's going to be test tubes? Wake up, Daphne. He'll have you on your back in no time. You'll end up pregnant and alone when this phony 'job' disappears because the 'scientist' gets tired of you."

Daphne scowled. "Ma, did I mention all the boys who applied and interviewed for this job? It's a real lab, I've seen it, and not that private. Lots of windows for ventilation, and they all face the street. And after all, have you looked at me? No one is going to be that interested."

Mrs. Delaney continued ranting as though she hadn't heard. "Why couldn't you have chosen a career—if you must choose a career at all—that's more ladylike? You could teach science, I suppose. Or you could paint or something..."

Daphne shook her head. *Sometimes I think I'm a stranger to my* *own mother.* "I can't paint, you know that, but I don't expect you to understand. I guess our desires are incompatible, but since I have the opportunity of a lifetime, and it also takes me out of your sight and away from your ugly comments... I know what I need to do. See you around, Ma... or maybe not." As she rose stiffly from the bed, Daphne's muscles ached and throbbed as though she'd been in an actual battle. She left her mother glaring at her retreating back and made her way down the hall. Outside Donny's room, her pounding heart skipped a beat. *What if he's not in there?* she fretted. Her fist trembled as she knocked. *I'd hate to have to chase all over the farm looking for him.*

The door swung inward and her brother's sandy hair, styled into smooth, shiny, and immobile dapperness with quite a quantity of Brylcreem, poked out into the hallway.

"Donny," she said, jumping right in, "you know how I asked you to give me a ride back to school next week?"

He tilted his head to one side.

"Can we do it today instead?"

# Chapter Two

New Orleans, Louisiana

Daphne stared up at the pink-stuccoed house that so closely resembled all the other row houses in the French Quarter. Though they varied by color and by the presence or absence of flower boxes in the windows, this building, with its black, wrought-iron balcony shading the front door from the strong Louisiana sun, fit in amongst its neighbors with ease.

*Home. Thank heaven.*

Drawing the key from her purse, she slipped it into the lock and let herself into the house, following the sound of voices to a small but cozy parlor. Her shoes echoed on the polished wood of the floors, drawing the eyes of several ladies, all around her age.

"Daphne?" Jeannie rose to her feet, setting aside the fashion magazine she'd been clutching and crossing the room with a speed her dainty feet should not have permitted. Next to her tiny brunette roommate, Daphne always felt like a bear about to go into hibernation... sluggish and stuffed. *Maybe I should ask her to design a slimming exercise regimen like she's learning at school.* Then she thought of how much she would sweat if she began skipping rope. *Maybe not.*

"Yes, it's me, girls. I'm back early. The farm was a bore, and I wanted to get settled back in before I start my new job next week."

"Oh, Daphne, I'm so glad to see you!" Anna cooed, also rising, but with an audible groan. Her generous curves far surpassed Daphne's, to the point of stoutness, but as she worked in a bakery, this surprised no one.

"Anna, are you back to work already? I had such a craving for your pralines. My ma is a good cook," *when she's not souring the meals with her frown,* Daphne added silently, "but she doesn't believe in sweets, especially not for me."

"I'm glad I never met her," Anna replied with a shudder. "I feel fat enough without people calling attention to thinner girls."

"You two are just silly," April cut in. The naturally slender and fashionable, golden-haired girl approached on silent feet. "Plenty of men prefer plump women to thin ones."

*Says the girl with boys circling her like flies around the pigsty,* Daphne thought, but she recognized the thought for green-eyed jealousy and pushed it away. "How have you been, April?"

The girl giggled. "I'm just dreamy," she drawled. "My Ken proposed." She showed them a chunky gold band with a heavily antiqued filigree and a square diamond set in the center.

"You look dreamy," Daphne agreed, "but then you normally do, so it's hard to tell. What's the verdict, ladies, any change?"

They turned one way and then the other, meeting one another's eyes and shaking their heads. "Dizzy April," Jeannie stated at last.

April stuck her lip out and flounced back to her chair, her perfectly coiffed hair bouncing with her movements. No matter how she stomped her feet, she could not produce a satisfying tantrum, and a moment later, a giggle escaped, destroying the image.

All the women laughed, enjoying themselves as they reestablished the boarding house's dynamics. Then, a flash of red caught Daphne's eye. She turned to see a stranger; tall, flame-haired, and stoop-shouldered, lurking near the door of the sitting area.

"Come on in," April urged. "I promise we won't bite you. Daphne, this is Mary. She's rooming with Phyllis. She's a bit shy, but ever so nice."

"Pleased to meet you," Daphne said, approaching the new arrival. "First year of college, or are you in town looking for work?"

"Both, actually," the redhead whispered, accepting Daphne's offered hand but at the same time seeming to shrink away from contact.

"Well, welcome," Daphne said cheerfully, perfectly willing to be the voice of kindness until Mary found her place. "What do you want to study?"

"I'm not sure yet," Mary admitted, twining a strand of scarlet hair around one fingertip. It held the curl, though Daphne could see no hint of pomade in it. "I thought... maybe I'd figure it out from what I study this year."

"That's a good plan," Daphne said, hoping to encourage the young woman. "I came planning to study... well, who knows what, but since my family thought I was going to marry the neighbor boy, it didn't matter."

"They *thought*?" Jeannie repeated, emphasizing the word. "Did something go wrong?"

Daphne shrugged. Her final conversation with her mother and the long car drive with her brother had greatly clarified her thinking. "Bob has decided not to return from France. He's met someone else and fallen in love. Our engagement was something that was expected of us, but the more I think about it, the more I realize I'm actually happy for him. Turns out that apart from our families, we're just childhood chums. I like him, but I've never been in love with him, so for him to marry someone else is actually best. I can't complain."

"What did you decide to study?" Mary leaned forward, and suddenly Daphne realized how much the new girl towered over her. *I'm far from petite. No wonder the poor thing is shy. She's taller than many men.*

A rush of pure happiness welled up in Daphne as she considered what the next few weeks would bring. "I discovered that I love science. Especially biology. I just got a job working as a lab assistant to a prominent researcher who's studying yellow fever. I'm so excited."

Mary shuddered. "I hope you have a good time. That doesn't sound like something I'd enjoy."

"I'm not surprised," Daphne replied. "But to each her own." She turned to her other friends. "So, all the rooms are full now?" she asked.

"All but *that* room," Anna replied with a shudder that set her plump cheeks jiggling. "But I think Miss Lois isn't intending to fill that one, ever."

"Why is that?" Mary blurted, and then blinked in surprise as though she hadn't expected to ask the question aloud.

*Uh oh. Hope we don't lose our new roommate.* "Well, um.... Not that I believe it, but..."

"It's fact, Daphne," April cut in. "Listen, there are rumors this house is haunted, though none of us have heard or seen anything scary—isn't that right, girls?"

As heads wagged, April continued. "About forty years ago, there was a man who lived in this house. He was strange and a bit unsettling, though wealthy and supposedly quite charming. People used to speculate he was a gentleman vampire. He brought a woman home with him one night."

Giggles greeted this bald pronouncement.

"A short time later, screams alerted the neighbors, who rushed into the street to find this same woman, naked and bleeding. She said the man bit her neck, and she had the wounds to prove it. She died right then and there, and the neighbors, upon breaking into the house, found bottles of wine mixed with human blood. So apparently, the man was a vampire after all. He disappeared that night and was never seen again. Maybe he turned into a bat and flew out the window."

As April spoke, Mary's expression changed from nervous tension to understanding. "Ah, that kind of story. Well, never mind. They say New Orleans is full of vampires, but since I only go out during the day, I should be safe."

As one, four heads turned, and four sets of eyes stared at the shy young woman who suddenly sounded so confident.

"You don't actually believe in vampires, do you, Mary?" Daphne demanded.

Mary shrugged. " 'There are more things in heaven and earth, Horatio, than are dreamt of in your philosophy,' " she quoted. "I'm not ruling anything out."

"Sounds like maybe literature or religion would be a good path for you," Anna suggested.

"Both good ideas," Mary agreed. With Anna, she seemed more relaxed. *I can imagine why,* Daphne thought. *Anna is such a gentle soul. You'd have to be incredibly shy to feel uncomfortable with her. I bet they'll become good friends.*

"So, what are your plans, Daphne, since you're back early?" Jeannie wanted to know.

Daphne considered. "I'm not sure. Sleep plays a large part, since the hours on the farm are so early—even earlier than here, once school starts—and I'm exhausted."

"You can give me a hand in the garden as well," another female voice cut in. Lois, their landlady, sauntered into the room, her short, pin curled hair tousled, a thin dressing gown wrapped around her fashionably slim figure.

*I wonder who she's been entertaining that she's wearing her bathrobe in the middle of the day,* Daphne thought, suppressing a giggle. "Of course," she assured the owner of the house. "I'd be happy to. Since we all get to enjoy the lovely courtyard out back, it's only fair we help maintain it."

"How do you tolerate having so little outdoor space, after growing up on a farm?" Anna asked.

Daphne pondered the question. "I'm not sure," she said at last. "Maybe because farming wasn't something I felt passionate about, and you don't do science in a cow pasture, so I prefer the city? Maybe because the farm always reminds me of everything that's wrong with me—" she shut her mouth abruptly, realizing she'd said too much.

Jeannie grabbed Daphne and squeezed her in a tight hug. "There's nothing wrong with you, Daph. Nothing at all. Anyone who said there was didn't know you. We're all here because our dreams didn't meet up with our families' expectations, but after all, whose life is it?"

Daphne smiled, but knew it didn't look too convincing. Around her, her friends all twisted their faces into similar expressions. *All of them. Amazing. Even beautiful April. Even Mary. I wonder what her story is. None of us fit into the mold we were born for, and none of us was willing to shape ourselves into it.* She nibbled on her lower lip as she pondered.

"That's right," Lois agreed, tucking a long, skinny cigarette into her mouth and lighting it. "Not one of us will be getting out of this existence alive. Don't die without having lived. Don't let your families steal your life."

She blew out a mouthful of smoke and Daphne fought to contain a grimace. *I hate that, for all that it's so common. I know how much a campfire can make a person cough, so how is it good to suck burning smoke directly into the lungs? That's another area I'd like to study, once the yellow fever initiative ends. Maybe by then, I'll be enough of a scientist to commission my own studies. Maybe the college will let me work for them. Teach a few classes while furthering knowledge through my own investigations.* As her imagination dragged her away from her friends and the smoky parlor before them, she realized Lois had made a good point. *My dreams—no, my goals—are so far away from the ones my parents had for me, there never really was a realistic way to have both. It was either live the life they chose for me and quietly suppress myself until I wither away—which is what I'm pretty sure Ma did—or cut loose of all of it, and this was my choice. Right or wrong, my future is in my hands now... and I can't wait to get started.*

# Chapter Three

Daphne ran her fingertips over a perfectly clean, completely transparent beaker. It sat on a shiny, black counter that joined up to a tall shelf stretching to the ceiling of a narrow row house, whose front parlor had been hastily converted into a laboratory. On every shelf, bottles of powders, liquids and other, less easily described substances stood side by side in perfect alignment. Daphne smiled as she read the labels and realized she knew them all. *Amazing discoveries will be made in this place.*

"Good morning, Mademoiselle Delaney," a low-pitched voice in a thick French accent broke into Daphne's thoughts, distracting her. She turned and greeted her employer with a beaming smile and a thrill of excitement.

"Good mornin', Monsieur Dumont," Daphne replied, suddenly shy. Her employer's pale-skinned handsomeness rendered her temporarily speechless. His black hair, dark eyes and sharp features were quickly becoming her favorite look. *Stop it, Daphne,* she sternly scolded herself. *If you develop a silly schoolgirl crush on your boss, it will only hurt your professional reputation. You're already in a precarious position, being a girl in a man's field. Don't ruin things by acting like one.*

After a last, longing look at his compelling face, she turned away, cheeks flaming, and regarded the equipment again. "So, what's your research plan, sir, and what will you need me to do?"

"Well," M. Dumont replied slowly, enunciating his words carefully to compensate for the heavy tones of France in his voice, "start by telling me what you know about yellow fever."

Daphne inhaled, relaxed her shoulders, and began to think aloud. "The disease has been sickening and killing people in humid, tropical and semi-tropical climates for centuries. Outbreaks are common in Africa, South America, and the Caribbean. The Southern and South-eastern United States have been hit hard in repeated waves, New Orleans especially. It sometimes moves north, but not as often. Most people show a few mild, vague symptoms. A few people get really sick with headache and body aches, high fever, nausea, and vomiting.

"Occasionally this acute phase gives way to the toxic phase, with yellowing skin as the virus destroys the liver, resulting in the patient vomiting blood, bleeding from the eyes, nose and mouth, and other severe symptoms. People with toxic yellow fever often die."

She took another deep breath and added, "It has been understood for quite some time that it is a mosquito-borne virus." She dared a glance at her employer and again found herself distracted. That is, until a strange look passed over his face. If she hadn't been watching closely, she might have missed it. "They developed a vaccine about a decade ago."

"Very good, Mlle Delaney. You are quite knowledgeable. So, we are looking specifically for a way to cure people already infected with the yellow fever virus. A vaccine does little good to the victim who is already ill."

Daphne nodded. "How do you propose we do that?"

He took another long moment to ponder his answer... or maybe the best words to express it, and Daphne dared another drooling, lingering gaze. *He looks like he's made of blades; angular cheekbones, pointed chin, and a thin, sharp nose. That combination shouldn't be handsome. I don't know why it is, but I can't look away.* He met her eyes unexpectedly and she nearly swallowed her tongue. It took no small amount of effort to school her face back to excited professionalism rather than a mooning stare.

"To start," he said, not seeming to notice her unwarranted reaction, or at least not addressing it, "we must collect samples. They say the disease is spread by mosquitos," here his face again contorted into that expression she didn't know how to interpret, "so we can assume it is in the blood, but I need to know if it's also spread in other ways—through contact with bodily fluids such as urine and saliva. To do that, we must examine samples of fluids from test subjects."

The wheels in Daphne's brain began turning, drawing her attention away from her growing crush.

"While you were away on holiday, I placed an advertisement for paid test subjects. I will need your help with the sample collection. Are you up to this?"

"Collecting saliva, urine and blood samples from people?" Daphne asked. He nodded. "I don't see why not. I mean, blood doesn't bother me, M. Dumont. I grew up on a farm. I've dispatched my share of chickens and watched the butchering of cattle and hogs. Since I grew up with animals, urine doesn't frighten me either. I've mucked stalls. Saliva... is a problem. It disgusts me, but I'll make myself get used to it."

Again, that sharply pointed chin dipped. "Very good. We will start with the sample collection tomorrow morning. Come in clothes you don't mind staining."

"Yes, sir," Daphne agreed, "and for today?"

He smiled, and the whiteness of his teeth startled her. "Today, my little assistant, you will earn your keep cleaning and sterilizing test tubes." He pointed to a messy jumble of glass crusted with dark and obscene stains. "I have developed a reagent that reacts only to the presence of yellow fever antibodies, but I don't have enough for a project of this scale, so I will be making more for our use."

Daphne regarded the sink and sighed. *No matter where I go, I never get away from washing dishes.* Her smile faded to a frown as she pushed up her sleeves and got to work.

"All right, ladies and gentlemen," Daphne said, pitching her voice high and loud to cut through the chatter of the crowd in the former parlor of the converted laboratory. The conversations subsided to a hum and Daphne continued. "Thank you all for stopping by today. We will be collecting fluid samples for our yellow fever study, so I need everyone to form three groups." She indicated an imaginary line between two groups of people. "You all on the left will start off providing saliva samples. The group in the middle will start with urine, and you on the right, make a line in front of the desk and M. Dumont will be drawing a small amount of blood. Once everyone is finished, we will switch. All right?"

Muttering greeted her words. *Looks like they didn't read the advertisement carefully,* she thought with an inward grin. "Anyone unwilling to provide all three samples is excused from the study. Please leave now."

Three women and two men shouldered past their neighbors and headed for the door, leaving about ten people in each group. The crowd quickly organized themselves into lines, each clutching a slip containing a number Daphne had given them when they entered. Reasoning people could produce urine samples without excessive instructions, she quickly handed each one a collection container and inked the individual's number onto it. The group lined up outside the necessary while Daphne addressed the saliva sample group.

"I know this might seem a bit gruesome," she informed them, "but it's vital we determine whether yellow fever can be spread this way. If so, a cough, a sneeze, a tobacco chaw—all could become a source of contagion. So, I'm going to hand each of you a small test tube, and I'd like you to, well, expectorate in it."

Heads nodded, but one toothless specimen in a despicable, once-black hat raised a trembling hand.

"Yes, sir?" Daphne asked politely.

"Whaddaya mean 'spectorate?" he demanded.

The wave of rancid breath emanating from the old man told Daphne he had more going on than just bad hygiene. *He smells like death, poor man. I think something's terribly wrong inside him.* Around the fellow, people drew back, grimacing at the foul odor.

"I mean you need to spit," Daphne explained.

A splat of tobacco-browned saliva hit the floor and oozed between the boards. A fussy-looking matron fluttered her hand over the buttoned-up jacket straining around her ample bosom.

"Into the tube, please, sir," Daphne added.

At last, the old man understood his instruction. Somehow, seeing his sputum and knowing she'd have to examine the stinking mess under her microscope bothered Daphne more than the fact that she'd have to clean it off the floor later.

"What do we do with these?" another man demanded, emerging from the toilet with his container clutched in his hand. This one, younger and taller, with a greasy slick of blond hair and a widening widow's peak, had an expression on his face that made Daphne deeply suspicious.

"There's a collection tray on the table there," Daphne replied, indicating a low table against the far wall. Instead of heading that direction, the man approached her.

"Did I do it right?" he asked, waving the container far too close to her face.

She recoiled enough to take in the contents, which, instead of the familiar yellowish liquid, contained a viscus white substance. "That is not urine," she said, raising one eyebrow.

He lurched forward again, but this time Daphne stepped to the side, leaving him to stumble.

"Is there a problem, Mlle Delaney?" her employer asked from across the room. Daphne spared a glance in his direction and caught sight of a needle poised over the arm of a young, brunette woman who had her free arm thrown across her eyes. She peeked and then sighed with relief as he stepped away.

"Just a smart alec, M. Dumont," Daphne replied coolly. "He seems to think I can't tell urine from semen. Or perhaps he's too stupid to know the difference."

The man spluttered, but before he could speak, M. Dumont had crossed the room and gripped his arm. Extracting the sample from the man's hand, he tossed it into a trash bin near the door.

Though nearly a head shorter, he handled the rude fellow with ease, maneuvering him to the door. "You are excused from this study," he said firmly. Then, with a decisive shove, evicted him from the premises. "We are doing serious and life-saving research here," M. Dumont said firmly, the softness of his tone and the exotic hints of France in his accent in no way undermining the importance of his message. "We are not playing games. So, if anyone else thinks teasing my assistant is more important than making sure we have uncompromised samples, please leave now."

Slowly letting his gaze lock with each of his 'test subjects', he induced squirming discomfort, but no one moved. He nodded once before returning to the trembling girl. She tossed her hand over her eyes again and squeaked as the needle penetrated her inner elbow.

Daphne returned to her task, smirking. *I didn't get flustered. I wonder if he was impressed. I'm a bit impressed with myself. Ma and I may not see eye to eye, but she taught me how to model cold, unruffled disapproval. I would thank her, except then I would receive that same stare.*

"Miss?" a middle-aged gentleman asked, taking a single, respectful step her direction after leaving his sample on the tray, "where do I go next."

*Wake up, Daphne,* she scolded herself. *He certainly won't be impressed if you're daydreaming.*

Dumont lolled in a red leather chair in his apartment. A radio on the table beside him yakked senselessly and he reached over and switched it off. "No matter how long I live," he muttered, "I'll never understand why people find this noisy box amusing."

Closing his eyes, he called to mind the image of the work he and his assistant had accomplished that day. "Samples collected from the general public, to compare with my control of known yellow fever cases collected at the hospital while Mlle Delaney was away. Wasn't she a force to be reckoned with, putting that dirty masturbator in his place?" he chuckled. "I knew when I saw her that she was the one. Smart, driven, and knowledgeable, but still raw enough to trust my judgment. Of course, it doesn't hurt that she's pretty as a spring flower, with those big brown eyes and that soft, huggable figure..." he trailed off, mentally stroking the soft coil of light brown hair he had noticed escaping from her tidy chignon.

"No," he reminded himself sternly. "Don't be swayed by a pretty face. You can't risk it. The work is the only thing that matters. You have to isolate V1 and learn how to kill it, if you ever want to have a normal life. Who knows if Daphne—" he broke off with a sigh. "She won't wait so long. I won't ask it of her. She has that infatuated look, but it will do her no good to become entangled with me. I must resist. I must."

Rolling up his shirt sleeve, Dumont lifted a hypodermic needle from beside the radio. Depressing the plunger completely, he jabbed his inner arm and drew a sample of blood from his own vein. A container waited nearby to receive the sample.

# Chapter Four

After weeks splitting her time between peering into microscopes in her senior-level science classes and counting white blood cells against a slide printed with a grid at work, Daphne feared the circles pressed like a raccoon mask around her eyes would become permanent. She caught herself squinting far too often as well, whether from the sun after long hours spent inside, or simply from habit, she wasn't sure. However, the mirror in the college ladies' room showed her exactly where her first wrinkles would be developing, unless something major changed in the next year.

"I guess it's a fair trade," she muttered to herself, but she couldn't resist the temptation to spread the crinkled skin with her fingertips, trying to remember how she looked before science took precedence over looking as pretty as she could.

"Daphne?"

Turning away from her foolish vanity, face flaming at being caught studying her appearance in public, she locked gazes with Jeannie, fresh from another exercise session and wearing a charming glow, her long brown hair pulled back from her face in a casual knot that served the dual function of looking stylish and keeping it out of her way. Daphne's similar coiffure proved less flattering on her round face, leaving her looking more like a washerwoman in training. *Stop it,* she told herself. *You're being vain and silly.* "Hello, Jeannie," she said to her friend, in what she hoped was a normal tone.

"Is anything wrong?" her roommate asked.

Daphne shrugged and shook her head at the same time. "Just taking a break between class and work. Why? What are you up to?"

Jeannie narrowed her eyes at the obvious diversionary tactic but responded calmly. "I'm on a break as well. How would you like to walk down to the sweet shop? I'm dying for a praline before I go on with my day. It's on your way, isn't it?"

Daphne nodded. "On the way to the streetcar, at least. Sure, I wouldn't mind." Though she spoke the words casually, the thought of Anna's expertly prepared sweets made her mouth water and her stomach rumble.

"Oh, honey, you sound hungry," Jeannie said, leading the way out of the bathroom. "Haven't you had any lunch yet? It's nearly one-thirty."

"I ate." They stepped out of the classroom building into a grassy yard enclosed by shady trees and an iron gate. The bright February sunshine tightened her eyes to another skin-crumpling squint.

"What did you eat?" Jeannie pressed.

"Well, after that huge breakfast Lois provided this morning, I wasn't feeling particularly hungry for lunch. I can wait for dinner."

Jeannie frowned. "That's what I was afraid of. Daphne, honey, you need to eat. How will you be able to concentrate on your work if your stomach is rumbling? Are you trying to lose weight?"

The comment, offered at a normal volume, set Daphne's teeth grinding. Several girls, all of them perfect and slim, turned to stare. "A bit," she admitted.

"You don't need to," Jeannie shot back. "You're beautiful, just as you are. In your case, I'd recommend a few exercises to be sure your muscles are strong, but your weight is nothing to be concerned about. You're a healthy woman with a bit of curve. Nothing serious."

Daphne drooped. "I know."

They passed through the gate and turned down Law Road toward the sweet shop. Further on, at the streetcar stop, she would catch a ride down to the French Quarter and her place of employment.

"So, then," Jeannie continued pestering as they made their way toward their goal, visions of sweet, candy-coated pecans dancing in their minds, "why are you suddenly set on slimming? You never used to worry about it, at least not that I was aware of."

Daphne shrugged. "It's the usual, I suppose."

Jeannie stopped dead, her dainty hand closed around Daphne's upper arm. "Do you mean that the way it sounds?" she demanded. "Did you meet someone?"

"Not as such," Daphne admitted. "In fact, I know I don't have any chance where this fellow is concerned, but, well, I can't stop being attracted to him. When I feel fat and dumpy, I lose confidence and start acting like a ninny. I don't like that. At the very least, I want him to notice how poised I am, but I can't do it unless... unless..."

"Unless you feel your best?" Jeannie suggested. At Daphne's nod, her friend continued. "Well, there's nothing wrong with wanting to look your best. As you say, it does wonders for the confidence, but, Daphne, you're wrong on two fronts. Nothing about your looks would make you hopeless, if the fella has any character at all. If he doesn't, you can do better. I take it he's handsome?"

"Devastating," Daphne muttered. "Sometimes I can't tear my eyes away."

Jeannie grinned. "Sounds like a huge crush."

"Enormous," Daphne admitted. "I've never felt this way before, not even about my former fiancé. It's so strange."

"Not so very strange," Jeannie contradicted. "From what you've told me, you loved Bob as a friend, but were never particularly in love with him."

Daphne nodded. The explanation felt right.

"So, since you always 'knew' you'd marry Bob, you probably didn't let your eyes—or your mind—wander, isn't that right?"

Daphne dipped her chin again. "Isn't that pitiful? Here I am, twenty-five years old and suffering from a silly, schoolgirl crush on a man I can't have. Why is my development so stunted?"

They passed under a huge and shady tree. While in summer, the patchy protection from the glaring southern sun would be welcome, in the deep winter, both girls shivered in their jackets and tucked their hands under their arms to keep the cool breeze from nipping their fingertips.

"Honey, there's nothing wrong with being a late-bloomer," Jeannie informed her. "I fell in love with a boy when I was only sixteen. It was ever so hard to behave. You won't have to worry. If you can find a good man—and I still don't know why you'd say your sweetheart isn't attainable—you can marry him and not have to suffer so long without relief."

The blunt comment brought stinging heat to Daphne's face. She bit her lip hard.

"Oho!" Jeannie exclaimed. "Why, Miss Daphne, did you misbehave with someone?"

Daphne quickly took in their surroundings. Outside the college campus, the crowd had thinned down to nothing. Only a stray dog chasing a squirrel down the street lingered to overhear her confession. "Well, we were going to be married, Bob and me. Everyone knew it. We had... some experiences." She gulped, recalling their handful of sweaty, scratchy encounters on the floor of the hayloft. Even the memory produced a riot of tingles. *Bob only wanted me because he was supposed to, but without him, will I ever taste passion again?*

Jeannie regarded her in silence for a long moment. "Well, under the circumstances, I'm not surprised. Especially as he was going off to war. But, may I ask you, Daph, why you and he didn't marry before he went away?"

"He enlisted so fast," she explained. "He didn't want to wait. We talked about eloping, but our parents had all been dreaming of huge, fancy dresses and a dance floor filled with magnolias. They wouldn't hear of it. This was the compromise. I couldn't let my fiancé go away to danger and a far-off country without something to remember me by, could I?"

"Of course not," Jeannie said soothingly, patting Daphne's shoulder.

"It didn't matter though," Daphne added, her pleasant memories fading and inciting sad darkness in her tone. "No sooner did he see the beauties of Europe, then he dropped me like a rock."

"Well, I wouldn't worry about it too much if I were you," Jeannie said firmly. "My auntie June worked as a dance-hall girl, married a rich old man, divorced him, and then met my uncle. He loves her to this day."

The twitch of Daphne's lips might have been a smile. She didn't mention that she didn't look like a dancer. What would be the point? *Jeannie would just argue again. I mean, my friends don't mind, clearly, but so far, the boys haven't been too keen.*

Sighing, Daphne turned to leave the chilly shadow. A beam of sunlight fell warm on her face. It brought hope Daphne had not expected. *Is it possible? Not only that someone might someday care enough for me that he would let me keep doing what I love, but also ignore my unfashionable weight, and overlook my lack of virginity? It seems impossible, but I do wish such a thing could be.* Again, the memory of her brief liaisons with Bob heightened the sensitivity of the delicate parts of her body. *I enjoyed that,* she admitted to herself. *I guess I'm just a robust farm girl... who happens to love science.* She smiled, a true smile at last.

Their destination appeared at the end of the block: a small storefront below another boarding house. This one sent an aroma of toasting sugar out into the street. Mouth watering, Daphne hurried the last few steps and threw open the door to a sweetened draft of warm air. "Hmmmmm," she hummed.

"Daphne, Jeannie!" Their friend waddled out from behind the counter and grasped their hands. Curls of sweat-slickened hair escaped Anna's bun and clung to her skin. She smelled like pure candy.

"Hello, Anna," Jeannie said. "Daph here is on her way to work, and we thought we'd stop by for a praline, but then I found out Daphne hasn't had lunch. Is there any of the soup of the day left, since she's watching her figure?"

Daphne elbowed her friend in the ribs. "Stop that. Okay, I am a bit hungry, but if there's no food, I'll live."

"There's plenty of sausage gumbo," Anna informed them, frowning at Daphne. "You don't need a bit of slimming, plus, it's cold out there. Let me get you a bowl."

Embarrassment and amusement warred within Daphne as she sank into a chair of twisted wires before a tiny table. "Lord have mercy, you two are determined."

"Here you go," Anna said sweetly, setting a steaming bowl in front of her friend. The delicious smell of spices had Daphne shoveling it in before she even realized what she was doing. Jeannie joined her and set a praline on the table beside the stew.

The bell above the door chimed, but the steam from Daphne's gumbo obscured her vision, and so she didn't look up. That is, until a familiar, accented voice drew her attention away from her lunch.

"M. Dumont?" she asked, not quite believing her eyes. He turned.

"Mlle Delaney," he said, a warm grin curving his thin lips and revealing his teeth. Daphne bit down on the inside of her cheek to keep from swooning. Feeling someone watching her, she broke away from the compelling lure of her employer's luscious black eyes and found Jeannie staring.

"Uh, Jeannie, this is my boss, M. Dumont."

"Please, call me Philippe," he told the woman. She beamed.

Something hot and unpleasant coiled in Daphne's guts as she watched the two beautiful creatures eyeing each other. *That just figures. Of course, all the men go for Jeannie, or for April. They're so beautiful, slim, and charming.* She sighed, knowing she was feeling sorry for herself, and stuffed her praline into her mouth.

"Can I help you, sir?" Anna asked.

"I would like some pralines, please," he replied. Turning back to Daphne, he added, "It has been a long time since I visited the city, but I've never lost my taste for them." He grinned again.

"Pralines are delicious," Daphne agreed, stirring her gumbo. Her appetite evaporated, whether from infatuation or jealousy, she wasn't sure which.

"So, Daphne, you never told me your boss was so young and handsome," Jeannie said. Though her words sounded flirtatious, her expression spoke volumes.

"Oh, I'm not so young as all that, miss," Philippe said. "You'd be surprised."

Jeannie shrugged. "We're not as young as you might think either," she retorted. "Listen, I have a class starting shortly. Daphne, will you be all right getting to work from here on your own?"

"Land sakes," Daphne hissed. "I've been making my way alone all this time without mishap. I'll just hop on the streetcar."

"That was my intention as well," Philippe said. "Don't fret, Jeannie. I will be sure Mlle Delaney arrives safely at work."

"And who will keep her safe from you?" Jeannie sassed. He raised one eyebrow while Daphne choked on a spoonful of sausage and spiced broth.

"Jeannie!" Daphne spluttered once she managed to draw in enough air to speak, but her friend had already ducked out the door. Sighing, face burning, Daphne sank back onto the chair.

"Are you all right?" Philippe asked her.

"Yes, of course," she replied. "Well, I might die of embarrassment, but other than that..."

Philippe laughed. "Your friend was merely looking out for your safety... and teasing you."

"So I noticed," Daphne said dryly. "I've had enough soup for one day. Thanks for the praline, Anna, honey. I'll see you tonight. Maybe you should swap rooms with Jeannie, or I might push her out the window."

"You have a balcony outside the window," Anna pointed out, and Daphne gave up. Rising from the chair, she coughed a couple more times, accepted a cool glass of water, and drained it quickly to quell the last of her spasm.

"Are you ready?" Philippe asked. Daphne nodded. He indicated the door and she preceded him out into the afternoon chill.

"Sorry about my friends," Daphne said, her lips twisting to the side. Philippe smiled. "I like them. They seem not to be too serious."

*Am I too serious? Is that what he's saying?* she wondered. *I've deliberately quelled my personality in order to seem competent to succeed in a man's world, and because I didn't want this crush to get in the way of work, which I'm really enjoying. If I loosen up a little, would it be all right?* "We're all pretty silly," she admitted. "I've just been trying to act professional."

Philippe turned and regarded her with an unreadable expression. "I have no doubt of your professional qualities," he said.

She nodded, not in the least bit sure how to take his comment.

They proceeded in silence along the last block to the streetcar stop, and within a short time, the cheerfully painted conveyance pulled up alongside them. They climbed aboard, but all the seats had been taken, so they stood side by side, clutching heavily fingerprinted chrome poles as the trolley made its way down the track toward the French Quarter.

"I live down in here," Daphne commented idly.

"As do I," Philippe replied.

"I figured as much." He turned and gave her an assessing look. "I mean," she babbled, suddenly nervous, "there's a whole second story above the lab. I assumed that was your apartment."

He nodded. "Good observation, Mlle Delaney."

*He called Jeannie by her name and joked with her. He's still calling me by a title. It means he sees me as a professional,* she reminded herself as a little corner of her heart died. *There are lots of researchers who choose a girl because they want to go to bed with her. He chose me because he thinks I'm a good scientist. That means more than this silly crush, which I always knew wouldn't amount to anything.*

She studied the sharp, angular lines of his profile. *He's awfully good-looking. Well worth mooning over, so I guess I'll keep on mooning... in private. The rest of the time, I'll keep on being the trustworthy assistant he already believes I am.*

The trolley rattled through the city toward its loveliest and most historic neighborhood, and the pair hopped off at Canal Street. From there, the converted townhouse awaited only two blocks to the west, and Daphne's home a further eight blocks in the same direction.

"What's our plan for the day?" she asked as they hot-footed it across the busy road toward their final destination the corner of Royal and Conti Streets.

"Today, we're going to—" he began as they reached the far side of the street safely, with only a few honks from passing motorists, and made a slight southward turn. In the distance, the Natchez released a belly full of hot steam in a reverberating whistle that echoed off the buildings and bounced along the street. Further talk would be futile until the sound died away.

At last, the echoing screech headed north, away from the river, and Philippe resumed his comment. "More of the same, I'm afraid," he said. "We must finish cataloging the white blood cells in all the blood samples and marking the chart before we move on. Since my reagent is nearly ready for use, we must hurry. Neither the reagent nor the samples will remain fresh forever."

She nodded. "That will allow us to determine if there are other methods of transmission." She schooled herself into chilly calm, the way she had at sample collection. "If it can be spread through the air, in toilets, or through intimate contact between persons—such as kissing—it's important to know that."

"Precisely," he agreed. In her peripheral vision, Daphne noticed several people within earshot shifting and squirming in discomfort.

"I'm looking forward to getting started with the second phase," she admitted, the desire to be honest warring with an innate knowledge that men found brainy women less attractive. *He isn't attracted to you,* she reminded herself, *so it's better for him to see you as a competent assistant than as a fluttery and brainless female.*

Settled again in her valuable and coveted role, Daphne turned to regard the empty, dormant window boxes and dry vines of the wrought-iron balconies of the row houses. *It's so pretty here, not like the flat, boggy farm. This city is filled with magic, just waiting for me to discover it. Silly ghost and vampire stories almost seem... plausible in this environment.*

Again, Philippe's compelling features drew her gaze. *He could be a vampire. He has the facial features for it, certainly, and those smoldering dark eyes... and black hair. He could take a bite out of me any time, and I imagine all my friends feel the same way. Alas, his skin is too healthy-looking, and his teeth appear normal, not jagged and sharp. He'd be hard-pressed to draw blood with them.* Her naughty mind conjured up an image of those perfect white teeth dragging across her skin in tingling love bites and she shivered.

"Cold?" he asked, and a fiery blush ignited in Daphne's cheeks.

"It's a bit cool," she admitted, crossing her arms over her chest and compressing the tips of her breasts, which had come alive with arousal.

"Inside the laboratory, the temperature is quite comfortable," he informed her.

"Then I'm glad we're almost there," she replied. *Especially since I'll need the microscope to distract me.*

Stepping through the door into the now-familiar laboratory space brought a rush of relief. Here, many intriguing items captured her interest. Each time she attended courses at the college, she learned new information about more of the compounds on the shelves. She had been practicing growing microorganisms in a petri dish and felt confident in her ability to reproduce the experiment in the real world. *I wonder if we're planning to grow cells and observe whether they show signs of yellow fever contamination, whether it can reproduce in that kind of setting. So many avenues to pursue, all of them fascinating.*

"All right, Mlle Delaney. Time to prepare the slides," he informed her, waving at a collection of clean glass rectangles, each marked with a grid. "Shall we begin?"

"Oh, yes, definitely," she replied, moving to the former kitchen where a sink awaited her, and she began to wash her hands.

"So, Miss... or should I say *Mademoiselle* Daphne Delaney, I think you've been holding out on me."

Daphne lifted her head, tearing her eyes away from the letter she'd just received, and regarded Jeannie with a puzzled frown. Movement in her peripheral vision revealed Lois, who sat in the corner sipping a bourbon. April, who had up to that moment been fighting a pitched battle with her messy and knotted needlepoint, also turned to look.

"What do you mean?" she asked.

"I knew you were interested in someone. Deny it's your boss. I dare you."

Daphne's eyebrows lowered further. "What?"

"Come on, Daph," Jeannie wheedled. "Tell me. You have feelings for him, don't you?"

Daphne closed her eyes. "What difference does that make?"

"Why would your feelings not make a difference, sugar?" Lois asked, sipping her drink.

"Have you looked at me?" Daphne demanded.

Lois furrowed one eyebrow. "Of course, and I'll ask again; why would your feelings not make a difference?"

Daphne regarded her friends. Both April and Jeannie—slim, lovely, and perfect, regarded her in confusion. Lois' face took on a more pointed look that spoke of both understanding and irritation. "You and Anna have the same problem. You think that just because you're fuller-figured than is fashionable right now, it's impossible for you to be attractive. That's a load of hooey, and you should treat it accordingly. Put it in the mental hog-pen and let it be trampled. Loads of men like a curvy woman better than a thin one, sugar, and loads of others don't care one way or the other. You're beautiful in your own way. Pretty face, soft figure, gorgeous hair. If you care for this man, don't assume it's hopeless. It isn't."

"It is," Daphne insisted. "One, I need to look like a professional. You don't know what an honor it is to be selected to work with M. Dumont. I can't sigh and stare at him like a schoolgirl. I have a job to do."

"Honey, it can work both ways," April told her seriously, tossing her needlepoint aside in disgust. From across the room, Daphne could see the hopeless tangle of knots. "Working closely with someone you care for is bound to make the feelings grow. But if you do good work, why would you lose his respect?"

"And two," Daphne pushed on, not wanting to hear such things. *They give me hope I can't afford to entertain,* "you didn't see him flirting with Jeannie. He *likes* a slim woman. In all the time I've worked with him, he's never smiled at me like he did the first time he met her. In fact, I think she should try to win him. I imagine he'd be agreeable."

Jeannie opened her mouth, shut it, and opened it again. "Uh, no thanks. Sorry, Daph, and no offense, but his look doesn't do it for me. He's all angles. Besides, I don't think he was exactly flirting. More like just being friendly."

"But that's just it," Daphne wailed. Clearing her throat, she continued in a more sedate tone. "He was friendly with you. He's coldly professional with me. Nothing more. Never. Since he truly sees me as a fellow scientist, I'll be content with that."

She fixed her eyes on her letter, effectively ending the conversation. Though she could feel three sets of eyes on her, she made no move to respond to their attention, pretending the missive in front of her contained something of great interest.

A warm hand closed over her shoulder. She looked up to see April's blue-green eyes staring down into hers. The empathy in her friend's expression twisted her heart. *She knows what it means to want what you can't have. Even beautiful, fashionable,* perfect *April understands.*

"What are you reading, Daphne?" she asked, and Daphne felt a rush of profound relief at the change of subject.

"My ma sent me a letter." She rolled her eyes.

"Bad news?"

Daphne shook her head. "Not bad, just dumb. She's letting me know that since my former fiancé moved on to greener pastures over in Europe, my father and the neighbor found a different way to join their farms into a single commercial production. She's also letting me know that if I want, I can start teaching in the parochial school come fall, and ... and she's found someone she thinks I should meet." Daphne sighed. "I'm so tired of my ma trying to arrange my life in ways she would approve. I mean, why can't she accept that I'm happy?"

"She doesn't understand it," April pointed out.

"Well, obviously," Daphne replied, her tone harsh and snappish, "but that doesn't make me wrong."

April touched the back of her hand. "I know."

"Sorry," Daphne lowered her forehead to the desk with an audible clunk. "I just get so sick of my family. It's like, they've never heard a word I've said in all my twenty-five years. They have plans, and I don't fall in line, so they try to force me. Drives me bonkers."

"You're far from wrong," Jeannie reminded her from across the room. "You have your education almost finished, you have a fantastic, professional job, which should lead to more in the future. I know it hurts when you realize you'll never have your family's final approval, but, honey, we're all in that boat."

"It's true," Lois added from the corner. "Women who break the mold have to face the disapproval of those who expected a certain amount of compliance, but it's worth it. Be yourself, Daphne, and be happy. If they can't be happy for you, it's their problem, not yours."

Daphne nodded with her head still against the wood, which felt strange and almost elicited a hysterical giggle. "You're right. I'll let them know that I'm happy for my father, but I'm not going back. My life is here, now. And in the future, when the yellow fever research ends, who knows where I might end up?"

"Atta girl," Lois cheered. She downed her bourbon and hauled herself to her feet. "I'm going to turn in," she announced. "Good night, girls."

"Good night," they chorused.

# Chapter Five

"Hmmm," Daphne hummed, peering through the microscope.

"Hmmmm, what?" Philippe asked, rising from his seat beside her and stepping quickly in her direction. A warm hand on her shoulder sent tingles through her body. "Did you find something interesting?"

"Interesting, yes," Daphne admitted, fighting down her attraction for the thousandth time, "but not relevant."

"You never know what might be relevant," Philippe said, his grip tightening. She could feel his hot breath on the back of her neck. "What do you see?"

"I, uh..." she broke off, blushing, and cleared her throat. "I think this person might have syphilis."

She rose from her stool and stepped back from the microscope, bringing her even closer to the firm, slim line of Philippe's body. For a moment, it almost appeared as though he embraced her, and then he retreated, circling her body and peering into the microscope.

"You're correct, Mlle Delaney," he said after an extended moment of scrutiny. "Well spotted."

She grinned at the compliment, even as she mourned the loss of his warmth.

"As you say, very interesting, but not relevant."

"Can we do anything?" Daphne asked. "This person needs treatment."

"I suspect he... or she already knows," Philippe informed her. "When someone has a serious illness, they know it. Our work here is very important, and who knows if breaking the anonymity of our study might bias our results."

"That's a pretty big assumption," she responded, daring to challenge him, "that the person would know something is seriously wrong."

"I know. I don't like it either, but we must follow protocols, Daphne. Perhaps after we finish, we could contact the person... though I don't look forward to having that conversation, do you?"

She shook her head. "How uncomfortable. Very well. We'll wait and have the awful conversation after. I hope this person seeks medical attention on their own."

"As do I." Philippe returned to his own microscope, and Daphne stepped forward, scrutinizing her sample again. *Just because this subject has one disease doesn't mean the investigation is over.* She looked in again, studying the cells.

*He called me Daphne,* she realized, and a shiver of pleasure chased down her spine.

"Well, Mlle Delaney," Philippe said, and his return to formality drew a frown to her lips, "now that you are an actual scientist, what do you think? You wanted this very badly, but I suspect it isn't as glamorous as you thought. Am I right?"

Sulking, she answered with pouting honesty. "I never thought it was glamorous. I thought it was interesting. I still do."

"You are such an unusual girl," he commented. "I expected you to react to collecting such intimate samples, but you never batted an eye."

"I'm not squeamish," she informed him. "I grew up on a farm, remember? Once you've mucked a cattle pen, spread chicken manure on the fields and examined the insides of a butchered hog, a few urine samples are nothing to get in a twist over, you know?"

Deciding the elevated white blood cells in the syphilis sample rendered the slide inconclusive, she withdrew it, made a careful note on her chart, and retrieved the next one.

"So I see," he agreed. They both fell silent and a little bubble of regret rose up in Daphne as she recalled her sulky tone.

*I wish we could keep talking. I like talking to him. It's not wrong for research partners to be friends, is it? I think it might be inevitable.*

To her surprise, he spoke again. "What drew you to science? Forgive me for making assumptions, but it is not the most common ambition for young ladies."

Daphne stared another moment into the microscope. The sample on the slide showed a shockingly low white cell count. "This one appears positive," she stated. "It might be a good one to use for cultures, if you want to go that way." She made a note on her chart. "Now as for what you were asking, I decided to attend Newcomb, as you're no doubt aware, because my parents and my fiancé's parents wanted me to be educated... for the sake of future children, you know? I think they pictured me studying art and literature and French and becoming a cultured lady, since both families have dreams of transforming themselves from farmers to 'landowners', whatever that means."

She slipped the slide out from under the clip and replaced it carefully back in its spot on the table beside her before retrieving the next one. "Turns out, I don't have an artistic bone in my body. I can't draw, paint, or sculpt. I don't mind reading literature, but it didn't seem like a goal, more like a hobby. I was about to withdraw and see what I could learn about the latest farming techniques by sitting in on my brother's classes—Ma and Pa refused to allow him to enlist and made him go to the agricultural college instead—but I wanted to complete the semester. Near the last day of classes, the dean of students talked to us about the loss of life in the war, the empty science classrooms at Tulane, and all that, and asked if any of us were interested in taking a science course."

She peered into the microscope. The cells on the slide looked completely normal. "This one is healthy. Might be good for a control."

She turned to look at Philippe and saw his dark eyes fixed on her, which elicited a shiver. That gaze had almost a palpable touch.

"Still cold, Mlle Delaney?" Philippe asked kindly.

"No," she admitted, and then added nothing more on the subject, though his eyebrows shot up. *Probably better wrap up the rambling,* she reminded herself. "So anyway, I took a science class, and loved it, and kept on. That was two years ago. If all goes well, I'll finish my science degree in the spring, and, thanks to you, have real world research experience to go with it."

"What do you hope to do with your degree?" he asked, his gaze still probing deeply into her.

"More of the same," she replied succinctly. "Not to toot my own horn, but I seem to be a bit good at it already, and heaven knows, I'm having a blast."

His serious face broke into a toothy grin that sent tingles straight to her belly. *How I wish I could kiss that smile.*

"And your parents and fiancé? What do they think of that plan?" he asked. "Sounds pretty far from what they had in mind for you."

She shrugged. "They hate it, but I don't get to back up and live twice, once for them, and once for me, I guess I'd better do what I love. I do it well, so it's better than falling in line with their plans that I be a lousy cultured lady and grow resentful. They'll have to rise without me." *No need to mention Bob. It's not like it matters anyway.*

"You're quite a determined young lady," he said softly.

"Oh, M. Dumont. You have no idea," Daphne replied. She removed the slide and reached for the next one.

"Don't forget to mark the chart," he said.

Daphne closed her eyes. *Too much chatter. You almost made a serious mistake. Focus.*

Comparing the number of the sample—7b—to the line on her paper, she noted 'c' for clean and then moved on. *I wonder what your story is, Philippe,* she thought. *I wonder why a young, handsome, intelligent man like you is single. I wonder why you're peering into microscopes instead of shooting Nazis. So many questions and no answers. Who are you, Philippe Dumont?*

But he offered her no glimpse into his mind, and so Daphne, after studying his profile for several long moments, returned her attention to the microscope. *At least these slides are willing to satisfy my curiosity.*

When Daphne walked into the boarding house parlor that evening, hungry and with a pounding headache, she found her entire adopted family gathered around an end table that had been pulled from the corner of the room and surrounded with dining chairs. A fat candle flickered, the wick nearly disappearing in a pool of wax, rested in the exact center of the table. The women held hands.

"What's happening?" Daphne asked, not sure if she felt amused, alarmed, or irritated.

"We're having a séance," Jeannie replied in an undertone. "Come, take a seat."

Daphne felt her eyebrows rise. "What?"

With a sigh, Mary, who sat at the head of the table, opened her eyes and regarded Daphne. The shy, trembling woman she'd run into from time to time had been transformed into something... different. Something that put Daphne on edge. Her brilliant green eyes seemed to bear bruised shadows beneath them, and her skin had turned from pale to ghastly. *Is that the effect of the strange lighting in here? She looks... ill.*

Mary spoke, and her voice had gone from tremulous and stuttering to low, calm, and collected. "We are conducting a séance to contact the spirit of Geneviève Paul."

"Who? And why?" Daphne challenged her, not sure why she felt belligerent, but willing to give her gut instincts the benefit of the doubt.

Mary's thin, pale lips twisted to one side. Then she slumped a bit from her powerful posture, restoring a bit of the girl Daphne recognized, but still didn't know.

"When you all told me this house might be haunted by the ghost of a woman who was bitten by a vampire, I did some research. I've always had a way with the dead, and I thought, if I could discover this woman's identity, I could help her move on to the next life; set her free, you know? I found out her name was Geneviève Paul, quadroon and soiled dove. She died in 1903 at the age of twenty-two and was buried in St. Louis Cemetery #2."

Daphne leveled an unimpressed look at the eager young woman but didn't speak.

"Only, when I went to the supposed 'grave', I couldn't connect with her spirit. There were plenty of ghosts hovering there, spirits of prostitutes. The city kept that particular spot ready for them. But of Miss Paul, I could find no sign."

"Perhaps because she went on to Heaven and didn't wait around to talk to you," Daphne suggested.

"Or perhaps because her spirit is trapped here, where she died," Mary shot back, showing irritation at Daphne's lack of engagement.

Daphne shrugged. "Did you find anything?"

"No," Mary admitted. "Though I had barely started when you got here. Now, do you intend to carry on jawing and interrupting me, or will you pull up a chair?"

"Neither, thank you," Daphne replied. "I don't think there are ghosts, but if there are, I'd rather not disturb them. I'll see you guys around." Her tone and expression cool as ice, Daphne wandered down the hall toward the kitchen, hoping to find something worth eating. Her stomach rumbled as she searched through yellowish-white cabinets and raided the icebox, still muttering to herself about the silliness of her housemates. "Séances, bah. Lot of nonsense." She dropped to a seat at the oversized kitchen table. "I would have thought students and professionals like us would be above all this superstitious nonsense." A shiver rolled through her. "And it's even worse if it's real."

"What's real?" Lois asked, meandering into the kitchen, a cigarette dangling from her fingers. The owner of the house made her way to the sink and filled the kettle with water, which she set on the stove. "Care for a cup of tea?"

"Yes, please," Daphne accepted, "and it's nothing. The girls are being silly in the parlor, having a séance or something."

Lois whirled around, her short, wavy hair bouncing. "What?" she demanded.

Not sure why this upset the landlady so much, Daphne nodded. "Mary says she's trying to contact the spirit of the lady of the evening who was supposed to have died here."

Even from halfway across the room, Daphne could hear Lois' teeth grinding. The older woman crossed the kitchen quickly, her movements faster and more purposeful than Daphne had ever seen in the four years she'd lived here. Carrying her sandwich over to the stove, she tended the water and measured out tea into the pot.

A few minutes later, Lois returned, her normally relaxed face squashed into lines of disapproval that created wrinkles around her forehead and mouth. She shook her head and released a heavy sigh. "Thank you for letting me know what they were up to, Daphne. I won't have such things happen in my house."

Daphne blinked. "It's all nonsense, though, isn't it?" she demanded, startled more than ever by Lois' vehemence.

"Oh, Daphne, if only that were the case." The older woman collected her cup of tea and sank into one of the two chairs remaining at the kitchen table. "Hon, how can you live in New Orleans and not believe? This city is full of supernatural things. It does no good to stir them up. A house can be ruined by inviting spirits in. Not to mention, you might not get what you summon."

Daphne pursed her lips. "I believe in science, not the boogeyman," she stated baldly, exaggerating.

"Well, whatever you believe or don't believe, Miss Smarty Pants, in my home there will be none of this. That's a firm rule. I don't mind if you drink a bit, smoke, or entertain a gentleman now and again, but I won't have any messing about with spirits, you hear?"

Daphne's eyebrows, which had been hovering far north of their usual position, threatened to take flight. "I swear it," she promised. "I wouldn't bother with that trash anyway, but if it's important to you, I'll say so aloud."

Lois nodded. "No séances, no Ouija boards, none of that."

"All right," Daphne agreed. "I said I wouldn't, Lois. I wasn't planning to anyway."

Lois took a sip of her tea and her tense muscles began to relax. To Daphne, it looked as though she were melting. "I'm sorry I came on so strong," she said at last. "I don't scare easy, but those things frighten me."

"I noticed," Daphne commented. "It's no problem. This is your home, so we'll follow your rules. It's only fair."

Lois nodded and then scrubbed a hand over her face. "I never would have guessed a nice, quiet college student like Mary would be the one to stir up trouble after all these uneventful years with the rest of you. No wonder Phyllis left."

"She left?" Daphne gaped. "How did I miss that?"

"Because she didn't move out," Lois replied. "She ran off. Disappeared. Stiffed me on a month's rent. Now I have to wonder if Mary didn't scare her off doing something spooky in the room."

"It's possible," Daphne admitted. "Phyllis always did have a superstitious streak. I hope she's all right."

"Me too," Lois agreed. "Hellfire and damnation, this is upsetting."

"I'm sure everything will be fine," Daphne said, patting her landlady on the arm. "Mary probably didn't realize. She's used to playing these silly games and didn't think of whether it would upset anyone. Now that you've laid down the law, she'll stop."

"I hope so," Lois replied. "I surely do hope you're right. Something still feels... off, and I wish I could put my finger on what it is."

With those unsettling words, Lois rose to her feet, gulped down her tea and meandered out of the room.

# Chapter Six

"Monsieur Dumont," Daphne called from the lab.

Philippe stuck his head in the door that led to the hallway. "Oui, mademoiselle?" he replied. He stepped into the room, wiping his hands on a thin white tea towel.

Daphne grinned. *My ma would go nuts to see him using that on his hands. 'Dish towels for dishes, hand towels for hands.' Bah. She needs a hobby.* "I finished testing all the blood samples with your reagent. You say it turns purple in the presence of yellow fever, but should not react to anything else?"

"Correct," he replied. "What did you find?" Tossing the towel carelessly onto the worktable, he drew near. His scent, compelling even over all the strange odors in the lab, made her heart pound once again, as did the warmth radiating from his body.

"Well, the samples you brought from the hospital all turned bright purple, as you can see." She waved at the table in front of her, where, in a black-lacquered wooden holder, the contents of six test tubes had turned from reddish-brown to a violent shade of magenta. "Since those are the control, they seem to confirm the first part of this hypothesis. It *did* react to blood known to be contaminated with yellow fever, so that's excellent."

"And the others?" He leaned over her shoulder, peering at the chart.

Daphne shouldered him away. "Knock it off, mister," she teased. "Don't steal my thunder."

Philippe chuckled and drew back.

"As for the samples we collected from everyday people, three also tested positive. Cross-referencing with the blood cell counts, it would seem to confirm that they have active cases of yellow fever." She pointed to three other test tubes, whose unnatural purplish hue revealed the ill health of their owners.

She turned to take in Philippe's face and found him looking at her with shivery intensity.

Allowing a heartbeat to bask in that stare and wish it meant more, she moved on. "Seven samples show a lighter reaction." The blood in those tubes had turned a paler, subtler maroon. "Their white cell counts were close to normal, so I'd say they were exposed and developed antibodies sometime in the past."

"Sounds logical," Philippe agreed.

The exhalation brought with it a puff of warm air that stirred the hairs on the back of Daphne's neck. She shivered and made no attempt to conceal it. "The rest were negative. No reaction at all. Some had normal white cell counts, and others didn't, but since many illnesses affect the white blood cells, I'd say those folks are, or have recently been, sick with something else."

"This is very interesting, M. Dumont, but our sample size is a bit small. I suppose after we finish this pilot study and publish our results, we'll need to redo the experiment on a much larger scale, you know, to make it more conclusive."

"Without doubt, Mademoiselle Delaney," Philippe replied. "That is my eventual intention. So, those are the only results?"

She glanced at him again and saw a strange look on his face that matched a curious note in his tone.

"Well, almost," she admitted. "There was one sample that came out... strange. I wondered if it was contaminated. I was about to ask you if we should exclude it."

"Why, what happened?" he demanded, his voice turning sharp.

Puzzled, Daphne lifted the last test tube and showed it to him. "It turned more pink than purple. I can't imagine why this one sample would turn a different shade, when all the others are lighter and darker versions of the same thing. Not one showed a different color." She glared at the dark pink sample. "I'm not sure how to interpret this. Is it an indication of something in your reagent we need to control for? Do you have any idea, Monsieur?"

She turned and found him staring at the test tube with rapt attention. "What number is that?" he demanded.

"B-21," she replied.

His breath caught, and he plucked the tube from her fingers and held it up in a shaft of late-afternoon sun that filtered through the windows. "Vingt-et-un," he muttered under his breath, gently swirling the contents and admiring their appearance. "Oh, mon Dieu. C'est vrai!"

"Philippe?" Daphne bit her lip as she caught herself using his first name. Though she thought of him that way, he'd never invited it, but he seemed not to notice. "M. Dumont?"

Philippe inhaled, and the breath shuddered as though some powerful emotion burned through him. With exaggerated care, he set the tube back into the holder. His fists clenched, biceps bulging and straining the sleeves of his shirt. "C'est pas possible!" He punched the air.

Daphne, startled by this display of incomprehensible emotion in a man who, up to this point, had been a study in professionalism, drew back a step. "Is everything... all right?" she asked.

Philippe met her eyes, a black fire burning in his, and slowly nodded. "Oh, yes, Daphne. Everything is *perfect*." Then, as though a dam had burst, he threw his arms around her waist and spun her, nearly knocking into the table and the stool. "Pink! C'est incroyable!" he shouted.

Still startled, Daphne allowed him to move her, using her weight to keep them on a safe path among the furniture. Then he stopped dead, dropping his arms away from her sides and cupping her face instead. "You, ma chérie, are a wonder," he proclaimed. Then he leaned in.

Daphne, expecting the kiss on both cheeks typically bestowed by the French, gasped in shock when his mouth landed on hers. Philippe's wild excitement stilled as he suddenly seemed to realize what he was doing. Slowly, he drew back from her a fraction.

Unable to react or even to understand what she felt, Daphne stared up at her employer's face. The dreams she'd had of this moment could not begin to match the firm warmth of Philippe's lips on hers, the sensation of drowning in his enticing scent. She licked her lip and found it already wet. *He kissed me,* she finally realized. *He actually did it. I can't believe it.*

She drew in a shaky breath, and another waft of cologne and clean, aroused man filled her.

Philippe's gaze skated from her eyes to her lips and back. With more deliberation this time, he leaned in again, claiming her mouth in a compelling kiss that no longer spoke only of his unexpected excitement. The bold embrace told an undeniable story of suppressed attraction.

*Dear Lord,* Daphne thought in awe, *does he actually want me?*

The slow glide of his tongue into her mouth seemed to settle the issue. Daphne's desire to remain aloof vaporized like alcohol over flame. Her arms slipped around his waist and she stepped close, so the entire front of her body warmed in his radiant heat.

Time slowed as they explored one another. Daphne coiled her tongue boldly around his, making no secret of her own desire. A tingling sensation flared in her belly and crept outward, teasing a soft moan from her.

Philippe drew back with a gasp. "Daphne," he breathed.

She remained still, biting her lip and hoping for another kiss she could now see would not be coming. Disappointment crushed the flame of desire in an instant.

"Daphne, I'm sorry, I— I don't know what came over me."

"I'm not sorry," she informed him. "I wan— I wanted that. I have wanted it."

His throat worked convulsively. "You did?"

She nodded. "Of course. Who wouldn't care for a man who... who can see past a woman's appearance, treat her like an equal? I think it was inevitable." She reached out one trembling hand and trace the stubble on his cheek.

Philippe opened his mouth, closed it again and shook his head in a short, sideways motion. He grasped her fingers and drew them away from his face.

Daphne closed her eyes, only to open them again with a start as warm, moist firmness caressed her skin. A sigh dragged itself from his belly as she saw Philippe holding her hand against his lips. Slowly, he lowered it to her side.

"Mlle Delaney," he began, trying to recapture formality.

Daphne would have none of it. "Philippe," she stated his name firmly. "No matter what, even if nothing comes of this kiss, I don't believe we can go back to titles. You'd better plan to call me Daphne from now on."

His lips smiled, but his eyes had turned troubled and confused. "Very well, Daphne," he said. "I... I have to think about this, about what it might mean. The work is too important. We must not get distracted from it."

"I agree," she informed him. "But maybe acknowledging that there's something between us will actually make things easier."

"It is possible," he said, though something about his tone and expression urged her not to get her hopes up.

Daphne poked out her lower lip, testing his resolve.

A shudder shook Philippe's entire frame, as though he had moved to draw close and turn away at the same time. She licked her lip, and his resistance crumbled.

Hauling her into a voluptuous, body-compressing embrace, he ravaged her mouth with a wild kiss. This time, Daphne laced her fingers into his hair and held him captive—a willing captive— to her passion. *You're not going to make this decision by yourself for both of us,* she told him silently. *We have to figure out together what's best for us. Make no mistake, Philippe. I believe we can be scientists and lovers, and I intend to try it.*

With an inarticulate, conflicted sound, Philippe drew away from Daphne and whirled. "Please, go home," he urged. "I can't do this, not this way. I have to think."

"All right," she said coolly. "You think, Philippe." She trailed her fingers down his back, and he shivered. *I think this is probably inevitable, but I can't tell him that. He has to know it for himself.* "I'll see you tomorrow."

He nodded, not turning to face her, and Daphne let herself out of the laboratory and into the street.

Night had long since fallen, and still, Daphne lay awake, examining a medallion in the ceiling plaster by the light of a waning moon.

"Daph?" Jeannie whispered.

"Yes?" Turning on her side, Daphne propped her cheek on one fist.

"Can't sleep?" Jeannie asked, though the answer was obvious. Daphne didn't bother to reply, so Jeannie went on. "Did you intend to interrupt the séance the other day?"

Daphne blinked at the dim silhouette of her roommate. "I completely forgot about that. I didn't set out to interrupt, but I'm not sorry. That kind of garbage is nothing to play around with."

Jeannie sighed. "I'm starting to agree with you, but... well, Mary is really mad. She blames you, and she's starting to give me the creeps. She has this hollow stare..." She shuddered.

"That shy giraffe?" Daphne asked with a giggle.

"Stop it," Jeannie hissed. "I'm not kidding, Daphne. You may be all science, but don't!"

Startled by her friend's vehemence, Daphne shut her mouth with a snap.

"Look, I don't know what to think about any of this, but promise me you'll be careful, won't you?"

Though still not sure what harm Mary could possibly do, Daphne vowed nonetheless. "I swear, Jeannie. I'll give her a wide berth, okay?"

Jeannie bounced up from the bed and removed a tiny silver cross from around her neck. "My mémé, my grandmother, gave me this. It will keep you safe, even from voodoo curses."

"Voodoo is a lot of hooey," Daphne declared, even as she hung the chain around her neck.

"Oh, no," Jeannie whispered, and Daphne could see how wide her eyes had gone. "It's real. My auntie did Voodoo. It's a religion, and most of its practitioners are okay, but every now and again one goes wrong, and then it's really bad. They have power you can't imagine, Daph."

Though she still didn't quite believe it, Daphne couldn't help but respond to Jeannie's obvious sincerity. "I'll be careful," Daphne promised.

Unsettled, she rolled over, her delicious confusion replaced by concern. *I hope Lois carefully screens who she allows to live here,* she thought. The moon shone through the window, illuminating the view of the balcony across the street. Vines twined around the wrought iron bars. *It's going to be a long night.*

# Chapter Seven

Daphne peered with bleary eyes into a cup of chicory coffee. The pungent aroma teased her with promises of wakefulness, but the punch of caffeine failed to break through her exhausted fog.

"You should go back to bed," Lois informed her over her own steaming cup, from which a scent of brandy perfumed the coffee.

"I can't," Daphne sighed. "Philippe and I are so close to a breakthrough."

"Yes, but, Daphne," Anna protested, her plump face pink and her eyes bright, "if you're this tired, how will you accomplish anything? You'll probably put cream in the samples and chemicals in your coffee."

Daphne sighed, slumping back in the chair, her eyes skating up along the red-painted wall of the dining room until they could rest on the soothing, creamy plaster of the ceiling. *I've done a lot of ceiling-staring lately. I wonder what I'm expecting to find up there.* "It's a real possibility," she admitted. "I guess I'll have to see if I can wake up enough to do a good job, and if not, let Philippe know it's best if we postpone until tomorrow. He'll understand."

"Since when do you call M. Dumont 'Philippe'?" Jeannie demanded before taking a large bite of her toast.

*Do I tell them?* Part of Daphne wanted to. The urge to boast about the wild, delicious kisses they'd shared nearly overwhelmed her. *But no,* she reminded herself. *One, it's a bit scandalous to be kissing a man alone in a lab where no one can keep an eye on us.* She thought of how much more mischief was possible and suppressed a giggle. *And two, I don't know what it means yet. Yes, he kissed me, but he never said a word about a date, a relationship or anything. As far as I know, it might have been an aberration—an unwanted one.* Settling for a partial truth, she said, "I think we're becoming friends. Hard not to when we have similar interests and work so closely together."

Jeannie leveled an assessing look on her roommate, as though daring her to come clean with more, but Daphne refused. *They've heard enough about my silly crush. Since I don't have anything conclusive to add to it, I won't.*

Daphne stretched, swallowed a mouthful of scrambled egg, and rose, draining her coffee cup as she carried her dishes down the narrow hallway and into the kitchen.

Partway there, a tall, red-haired figure barreled into the hallway and shouldered past Daphne, before whirling her around with a painful grip on her arm.

"What is it?" Daphne asked, her sleep-deprived brain struggling to grasp what Mary might want.

"You just had to, didn't you?" the towering young woman demanded. "It's not bad enough you bring your skeptical vibe in here and interrupt my work. You had to go and tattle like a little kid too? What's wrong with you?"

Daphne pursed her lips and squinted. "I didn't 'tattle'. It came up in conversation. I certainly didn't ask Lois to stop you. It's her house, so she should be able to decide what goes on in here, don't you think?"

Mary assessed her with cool brown eyes. *She does have a hollow stare, just as Jeannie said,* Daphne realized. "You have no idea," the woman intoned in a strange voice that sounded nothing like the Mary she'd been struggling to get to know, "how important my task is, how much is at stake. You should mind your own business."

Unintimidated, Daphne drew herself up to her full height and inhaled deeply. *I may not be as tall as her, but I definitely have the advantage in strength over this willow of a woman.* "I was minding

74

my own business, actually," she drawled, "I don't much care whether you play your silly ghost games or not, but if you hope to accomplish something, you're going about it the wrong way. Impressing a lot of superstitious girls might make you feel like you're something special, but unless you plan to become a palm reader, I suggest you get busy learning a trade and leave the scare-stories to the children. They're better at it."

Whirling on her heel, Daphne strode away. Again, Mary attempted to grab her, but she shook off the clinging hand and stomped into the kitchen, quickly filling the sink with water and soap suds and washing off her dishes, leaving them to drain on a towel on the counter before making her way outside through the back door. Spring had begun to creep around the city, and the early flowers poked their heads up through the damp soil, ready to turn the winter-brown courtyard cheerful again.

Opening the gate, Daphne stepped into the alley between the boarding house courtyard and the courtyard behind them, turned right, and made her way to the street.

The close-crowded buildings blocked some sunrise light, leaving the avenue shaded and cool. In the summer, it would be a welcome relief from the blistering heat, but now, on the cusp between winter and spring, it left a chill in the air that made Daphne wish she'd gone back for her jacket. *The confrontation with Mary unnerved me,* she realized, *and after that sleepless night, no wonder. I was a bit grouchy though.*

Trying once again to shake off her malaise, Daphne trudged south almost to the riverfront and waited for the trolley to take her to school. *Sitting in class is going to be brutal. Will I even be able to stay awake for it?* Though a bright morning sun scattered warmth onto her shoulders, her eyes wanted to close. She wanted like nothing before in her life to curl up in a patch of sunshine and sleep.

*Sleeping outside in the street is stupid. If you're too tired for class, then Anna's right and you won't be worth much in the lab.* She sighed. *I hate missing things I'm supposed to be doing, but I'll be worse than useless if I force myself. I don't normally miss class, but being exhausted is almost like being sick,* she reasoned. *If I let Dr. Martin know tomorrow that I wasn't feeling well, it should be fine. He'll understand. But I must at least stop by the laboratory and tell Philippe... tell him I'm staying home sick today.*

The more she assessed her condition, the more she realized she did indeed feel ill as well as exhausted. Her stomach churned, and a hint of dizziness turned her upright stance uncertain. Wanting to walk off her malaise, she left the Urselines station and walked north, passing the French Quarter Market, with its bustling trade in everything imaginable and a few things beyond comprehension. Air scented with coffee and fried seafood blew past her in a chilly rush, but she noted the cold had lessened considerably in the last few weeks. Plants growing in riotous profusion on balconies and in window boxes across the street confirmed it.

*Falling in love in the spring,* she thought, her exhausted mind rambling. *And I can't deny that I'm terribly in love with Philippe. It's nothing like Bob. Philippe fills my mind day and night. His scent draws me. The look in his eyes turns my brains to mush, and yet, I want nothing more than for him to think I'm smart—and pretty. For him to desire me as a woman and still respect me as a scientist. Dear God, I love that man, but what good will it do me? Can he love me back? Will he? Do I dare ask him after only one kiss?*

Though her heart began to pound at the thought of initiating such a blunt conversation, realizing that his kiss surely meant *something* dredged up a warm glow. *He wanted to kiss me, or he wouldn't have done it. A casual kiss from a Frenchman would aim for the cheeks, but he kissed my mouth.*

She passed under the shadow of a row house and shivered in the sudden chill, hurrying to the tiny shaft of sunlight between the building and its neighbor. *And then, once he started, it was like he couldn't stop. Maybe, like me, he's interested, attracted even, but fears impropriety. I'll have to ask. I'm willing to be a bit improper. Philippe Dumont is well worth it.* She grinned to herself. *I'll just have to be sure he's aware that I can be a scientist and a sweetheart, and it's no contradiction.*

She pondered what it might be like to be Philippe's sweetheart. *Talking science over dinner at some swanky restaurant. Going dancing until dawn. I'd be the envy of every girl in town. Long kisses in the moonlight, and that sexy accent.* She rolled her eyes heavenward and took in a bright spring sky that made her eyes ache. *He's French and might want to jump the gun a bit.* She bit back a giggle as two laundresses made their way past her, each carrying an oversized wicker basket full of soiled linens. *I might just let him, if he asked nicely.*

By now she had made her way nearly to her destination and executed a sharp right turn. A couple of blocks of dreamy contemplation brought her to the plate glass display window of the former shop turned laboratory. Inside, she could see her station, materials shiny clean and lying ready for her nimble hands and quick mind. Further down the lacquered black worktable, Philippe hunched over a microscope. His white lab coat gleamed painfully bright in the sunlight and she squinted at the sight of it. Her hands trembled as she manipulated the doorknob and let herself into the room.

So deep in thought was her employer, that the sound startled him. A sample slide slipped from his fingers and hit the edge of the table, shattering. A shard of glass jammed into his thumb. He plucked out the glass and stuck the cut digit into his mouth.

"Sorry," Daphne said.

Philippe shrugged. "I didn't expect you. Don't you have class this morning?"

Daphne shut the door and made her way quickly across the room. Stooping, she began to collect the broken bits. Philippe laid a hand on her shoulder and quickly drew her away from the mess. "I'll take care of that. Sit down." He steered her onto her stool and faced her, his injured hand tucked behind his back.

"Oh, um..." Suddenly feeling flustered, Daphne wrung her hands. "I, uh... I, um... I do have class, but... but..."

"But what, Mlle Delaney?" he demanded.

She noticed dark circles to match her own ringing his eyes. Then his words finally registered, and her awkward smile turned over. "Daphne, remember?" she said. "I mean, that's not much to ask, is it?"

Philippe sighed and took a step backward, scrubbing his hand over his face. He opened his mouth, shut it, and opened it again, mouthing like a hooked fish before finally squeezing out a word. "Daphne," he said, and the sound of her name in his luscious voice set her shivering. "Daphne, listen... I... I won't say I'm sorry. I... I wanted to kiss you, but..."

She rose and stepped close to him, crowding into his space. "But what, Philippe? I'm not a child, you know."

His eyes traced the front of her body: full breasts, soft, outwardly curving lower belly, plump thighs. "Believe me," he said, and his voice suddenly became hot and intense, "I noticed that. You're all woman, Daphne Delaney." His hand came to rest on the dip of her waist. "So many women now look like lamp posts, but not you..."

Unable to believe what she was hearing, she reached out and caressed his lower lip with her thumb. He closed his eyes and then shut his lips around it, swiping it with the tip of his tongue. Daphne gasped.

Their mouths met in a flash of unfettered desire, her hand trapped between his chin and hers. She withdrew to wrap it around his neck. "I couldn't sleep," she mumbled against his lips. "Not a wink, all night. I couldn't stop thinking about you."

"Me too." His mouth opened on hers and she mirrored the movement, allowing his tongue to delve, and meeting him there in a kiss of explosive passion. Arousal began its slow burn in her belly and spread, warming each limb and pooling at the apex of her thighs. She arched her back, bringing her pelvis into full contact with his, and to her delight, she felt his firm erection pushing out the front of his pants. *He does want me,* she realized.

"Daphne, I tried so hard not to fall for you," he whispered. "I didn't want... to be unprofessional..."

"I know," she replied. "I feel the same way. I so wanted you to see me as a scientist and not just a dolly to warm your bed."

"You are a magnificent scientist, and with practice, you'll be amazing," he breathed, "but I still want you to warm my bed."

Daphne's cheeks heated, and he pulled back to admire the rosy color.

"Do you disagree?"

Daphne's lower lip found its way between her teeth in a move that invoked both shyness and provocation. "I probably wouldn't resist you too long," she admitted.

His lips pulled back to reveal gleaming white teeth.

"Are you sure," she pressed, "that you'll still respect me?"

"Oh, yes." His fingers slid into her hair and he claimed her mouth again. "As a lady, and as a scientist."

She beamed. His approval warmed her heart, where her mother's unending disapproval had left her cold and uncertain.

Another endless kiss fused them together. Then Philippe pulled back with a sigh. "What do you do to me, ma petite? I've been awake all night, rehearsing what I wanted to say to you to make you understand that, while I desire you, like you and care deeply for you, and while this had the potential to be something amazing, I'm not a worthwhile partner."

She rolled her eyes. "I've heard that before."

"There's a lot you don't know about me." He released another lungful of air.

*Goodness, he seems upset. I wonder what's going on that I don't know.* Deciding boldness was the best route, she went straight to the point. "Tell me."

A flash of movement in her peripheral vision drew Daphne's gaze to the window—and the people passing in the street, turning to peer at her—locked in Philippe's embrace.

"Maybe we should step into the kitchen," he suggested. Daphne agreed with a nod.

Like many of the French Quarter row houses, the path from lab to kitchen wound down twisting hallways, past mysterious rooms with closed doors, most of which Daphne happened to know contained stored equipment and boxes of papers that must have represented years of research.

The kitchen oddly resembled the one on her family farm, with a wood-clad ceiling that matched the floor, a white sink, and a mint-green refrigerator. *Full of blood, not eggs and bacon,* she thought with a snigger. Then her stomach dropped as she realized Philippe had brought her here to be alone. *I hope I didn't misjudge him, and this isn't a flim-flam to get inside me. I want it all—the job, the man, all of it. I wouldn't mind letting him have a taste of me under those circumstances.*

Feeling both naughty and nervous, Daphne looked up at Philippe with wide eyes. "All right, tell me, please. What's going on? I can see that, for whatever reason, you find me appealing. I'm grateful, because I've been attracted to you from day one, but you seem more uncertain than just a concern for professionalism would account for. Especially given the Curies and other scientist couples."

"You're right to think so," he admitted. "I have to be honest with you, and there are many parts, so I beg you to listen patiently, Daphne. Can you?"

"Of course."

"I wanted to protect you, and not let you get too close to me because, for as long as I can remember, danger has followed me."

Daphne's jaw dropped. "Danger following a scientist? Philippe, you're studying yellow fever. Who wouldn't want to know more about the disease and prevent more deaths?"

"First confession," he said with a sheepish grin. "We're not actually studying yellow fever, at least not directly."

Daphne opened her mouth to interrupt, but Philippe held up a quelling hand. She noticed, for the first time, that he had thick bands of scars encircling his wrist. "Sorry," she mumbled, remembering she had promised to be quiet.

"There is another virus, I call it V1. It mimics the symptoms of yellow fever so exactly, people rarely notice a difference. I believe it is, in fact, a mutation of yellow fever. However, it has changed enough from yellow fever that it is not affected by the vaccine."

Daphne inhaled, and for once the enticing scent of Philippe's cologne, though it stirred her senses, did not capture her awareness. "That could cause an epidemic."

"Oh, yes," Philippe agreed. "As near as I can tell, it is not spread by mosquitos, but only by contact with an infected person's blood."

Daphne bit her lip as the possibilities dawned on her.

"At this moment, we have the only known sample of V1 in our lab. Remember the strange positive result you had on sample twenty-one?"

Daphne nodded. "I remember how it excited you. Is that V1 then?"

"Oh, oui," Philippe informed her. "We must see if we can develop a vaccine or cure for this virus, for reasons you already understand."

"Yes," Daphne agreed. "I do understand, but is that the danger you mentioned? You're exposed to a dangerous and barely-known virus every day, and fear contracting it?"

"Non, non," Philippe replied, his accent thickening. "I know how to be careful in the lab, and so do you. Non, the reason is that there are people—powerful, dangerous people—who want to control it rather than eradicate it."

Daphne stared.

"Just imagine the power that would result from controlling a virus that looks and acts like a known disease, but the transmission is completely under the control of the owner and that has no known vaccine? They could decimate armies, or even whole towns, and no one would know."

"Who would do such a thing?" Daphne demanded.

"Evil, dangerous people," Philippe informed her. "They have been after me for years. They—" he broke off, gulped, and when he began again, his voice had roughened and grown wavery. "Long ago, I loved a woman. She meant the world to me, and they killed her. I went into hiding after that, and I seem to have shaken them off my trail, but that could change at any moment. I was trying to protect you, should they catch up with me—which I promise you they are trying to do—by not letting myself care for you."

"Ohhhh," a comprehending, but not entirely articulate sound escaped from Daphne's belly.

"Do you understand now?" he demanded.

She nodded. "But you came to care for me anyway?"

He snorted. "You're lovely *and* your love of discovery easily equals my own. I had to think you might be my perfect match."

Daphne sucked in a noisy breath. "Do you mean that?"

"Of course." His fingers stroked over her skin. "But then, how could I expose you to such danger? How could I make you vulnerable to these monsters?"

"I think that should be my decision to make, don't you?" she asked.

"You're very smart," he agreed, "but you have no idea of the resources my enemies have at their disposal. They could end your life with no one the wiser but me. I can't... I can't bear to lose another. And you, Daphne. Your future is so bright. How could I ask you to risk it?"

"Yet here we are," she said, stroking the stubble on his cheek with her thumb.

"Here we are," his lips twisted to the side, "unable to keep our hands off each other. And yet, the research remains to be done. How can we let ourselves be distracted by passion when our task is so vital? If we can develop a vaccine before our enemies develop their weapon, we might have a chance of finally bringing them down."

"You know, if we succumb to the inevitable, we might be less distracted rather than more," Daphne pointed out. "But who are these people? Nazis?"

Philippe laughed, and it sounded bitter and harsh. "Non, not Nazis, although they do support and fund them. They also supported the Central Powers in World War I, fed the flames of aggression when the United States fought Spain, and even helped Napoleon rise to power. Whenever there is conflict, panic, chaos, and death, you can find these monsters lurking in the background, ready to incite violence for their own dark ends."

"Which are what?" Daphne demanded.

He shook his head. "Good-hearted people will never understand the dark lure of power, and no one has greater power than those who control war."

Daphne sighed. "Sounds like a nightmare. You're just one person, with no government to back you. Aren't you afraid to be so vulnerable?"

"It's easier that way," he replied. "The fewer people I let get close to me, the safer I am. But I couldn't work alone. I cannot trust myself not to see answers because I want to see them. I needed an impartial assistant, one who knew nothing and thus who would have honest reactions. That's why I needed you, Daphne. I tried so hard not to fall for you, but I failed, and now, because of me, you're in danger."

He broke eye contact, staring down at the place where his chest met hers.

"Oh, Philippe." She stroked his hair, the grease of his pomade slicking her fingertips. "And you know exactly what it's like."

He nodded. "I never want you to be hurt, Daphne. Least of all because of me. I tried to tell myself that it would be enough if I could help guide you on your path and watch you grow beyond me into the scientific community. I never planned to touch you, but once I did, once we..."

"Once we kissed," she finished for him, accepting equal responsibility for that embrace even though he'd started it, "it became impossible to stop kissing. The dam has been burst. We care for each other, and there's no stopping it."

"None."

She leaned her head against his shoulder. "I can see you're distressed, and I believe you about your quest and your dangerous adversaries, but I have a hard time grasping it. All I see is two people... falling in love. Am I wrong?"

She looked up into his eyes. The fiery intensity of his dark gaze sent shivers down her spine. "No, not wrong."

Again, his lips sought hers. This time, his kiss seemed to sink deep within her, stirring blood and arousal. She could feel him wrapping around her soul, becoming a deep and fundamental part of who she was. *Does this mean I never loved Bob?* she wondered, but the obvious answer couldn't be denied.

"Do you really think," Philippe asked, panting, "that if we succumb to this, we will be less distracted? I'm not sure about that."

"I think it doesn't matter anymore," she replied, pulling his head down to rest against the swell of her breasts. He kissed her there, and she thrilled at the touch.

"Perhaps not. So, if I were to invite you upstairs to my chambre?" he suggested. "Would you accept, or would you protest on the grounds of maidenly coyness?"

"If you invited me," she said slowly, blushing hot, "I suppose I would say yes, and I suppose if I did accept, you would find there was not much need for restraint. It's been a while since I lay with a man, but... it has happened a few times."

Philippe lifted his head, eyebrows raised at her admission. Then his face relaxed into an expression of understanding. "Ah, that's right. You have... had a fiancé. I suppose you will have to break things off with him if you go upstairs with me." He chuckled.

"Actually, he broke things off with me by letter around Christmas. Our engagement was more our families' ideas than ours. We were more friends than lovers... but we were lovers." The heat in her cheeks threatened to start a fire, but she lifted her head defiantly. "I'm not sorry."

Philippe raised one eyebrow back toward his hairline. "I've bedded a lady or two," he admitted with the coy air of a shamefully naughty secret. "How about we agree that these things are more normal than not, and don't mean anything for our relationship?"

Daphne nodded. "I like the way you think."

"So, shall we?" He stepped back and offered her his hand. She regarded it. Despite her internal eagerness, she feared appearing too bold.

"Hesitant, ma petite?"

"What about our work?"

He smiled at her attempt at prevarication. "Later. As you said, we might be less distracted then. Besides, I'm not thinking straight after a sleepless night. I would probably confuse blood with wine and end up drinking the wrong one."

Daphne shuddered. "Don't joke about such things, please, Philippe. I already have a housemate trying to conduct séances, and don't forget we live in a city of vampires. I've even heard I live in a haunted house."

Philippe snickered at the idea. Then he shook himself and extended his hand again. "Yes or no, Daphne. A no is fine, or a not yet. It's very soon, but please tell me what you want."

Daphne considered how tenderly Philippe had kissed her, how attractive he was, and how much she desired him. *It would be amazing.* Certainly, Philippe gave her a feeling she'd never had before, part convergence of interests, part hero worship, part schoolgirl crush. *Can it stand the test of time? We certainly have enough in common.* Cutting off her meandering thoughts before she could start visualizing wedding dresses, she laid her hand in his and allowed him to lead her out of the kitchen, to the wooden staircase and up to the second floor. There, she discovered a hallway lined with closed doors. At the last one, Philippe turned the knob and opened the door to reveal a brass-framed bed, dressed in a white sheet.

"Simple," Daphne commented.

"My needs are simple," Philippe replied, "and I never stay in one place very long. My scientific equipment is the largest part of what I transport from place to place."

"So I see." A glimmer of understanding regarding what a future with Philippe would entail dawned on Daphne. *Always on the run. Never staying in one place long. That means no recognition for our work, no friends...* And yet, with Philippe's compelling presence drowning her senses, she could no more resist him than she could deny her next breath.

He drew her into his arms. With the first touch of his mouth, her doubts evaporated. Perfect love and trust welled up until only Philippe filled her completely. *Well, not quite completely, not yet.* She shivered. Meanwhile, Philippe's fingers worked busily on the buttons of her plain white blouse, loosening the garment so it hung open at her sides. His eyes left hers and traced down her neck until he took in the sight of her ample breasts, straining the seams of her sharply-pointed brassiere. Daphne swallowed hard. Her figure, while appealingly generous in its overall impression, lacked any semblance of subtlety. *Jiminy, I look like a sculpture of Mother Nature.*

Philippe, it seemed, could appreciate the obvious. Without hesitation, he stepped into her space again, reaching behind her to release the clasp. Daphne's heavy breasts spilled free, the plump, pink nipples straining toward him.

Watching Philippe watch her, Daphne felt a most curious sensation. Although his admiration showed clearly on his handsome face, she couldn't quite dispel a nervous flutter. *Being nude with someone new isn't easy,* she realized. While she had gotten used to Bob's eyes and hands on her, Bob looked as young as he was—a boy at play and not a man. Philippe's aggressive masculinity made her feel different; on edge in a delicious way.

*On with it, Daphne. Don't stand there like a ninny.* Overriding her anxiety, she reached forward and shoved his lab coat to the floor before quickly opening the buttons on his tan shirt. Underneath, he wore a sleeveless undershirt, and she lifted it over his head. His thin, hairless chest captured her attention. Unlike the farming men familiar to her, Philippe's wiry muscle remained invisible. She'd seen him lift heavy equipment, but now he seemed harmless.

A movement released a cloud of his personal fragrance, which she inhaled, and her eyes slid closed. Then her lids shot open again as his hand came to rest on one full breast. His fingers closed around one tender nipple and he chafed it, sending heat straight to her core. Moisture surged, and a soft, helpless moan escaped.

"Do you like that, pretty Daphne?" he asked.

She nodded, and the touch abruptly stopped. She regarded him in silent curiosity. Philippe lowered his hands to the fastenings of his own trousers, slowly loosening the waistband while she watched, mouth dry. A pair of loose-fitting white undershorts slid into the pile of discarded clothing on the floor, revealing a nicely proportioned penis, erect and ready to introduce itself to her. She gulped.

Philippe tossed back the sheet and stretched out on the bed. "Will you be joining me then?" he asked, arms behind his head, regarding her with casual interest.

Suddenly, Daphne's generous curves again tightened down her arousal with nerves. *What if he finds me fat? Disgusting? What if he changes his mind?* She drew in a shaky breath and released it. Though she longed to say something, anything, the words stuck like dry biscuits in her throat, threatening to choke her.

Drawing air into her lungs and slowly releasing it, she worked the fastening of her high-waisted trousers and eased them over her hips. Then only her own panties remained. She'd forgone the usual waist-nipping girdle, expecting to return home to bed after telling Philippe she wasn't feeling well enough to work. *Well, I'm going to bed after all,* she thought, *though not quite in the way I expected. Ah well, on with it, girl.* She eased the soft fabric over her plump bottom and returned to an upright posture, waiting to see if Philippe would react to the sight of her naked body.

His eyes lovingly caressed every line and bend, lingering on her breasts with a fascination that shallowed his breathing and caused a visible pulse point in his throat to begin throbbing. Her waist did nip in—though not as much as fashion would have preferred, without a corset to restrain it—and she could feel his gaze like a touch on every inch of skin. Her round hips and plump thighs next drew his attention, and at last, Philippe extended one hand, inviting her to his bed for a second time.

Relief rushed through Daphne, nearly making her weep. *He still desires me.* The heat in his expression told her that her unfashionable body pleased him.

Daphne approached the bed and sat down on the edge.

"Nervous?" he asked.

"A bit," she admitted. "It's soon, you know?"

"I know. You can change your mind."

She regarded his rampant erection and considered her own disappointment if she backed down now. *It will change everything, to sleep with him,* she thought, *but if I don't take this opportunity, it might not arise again. Even if it's just the one time, I can't not share Philippe's bed this once. If he truly means what he said, I have to take that chance. I have to cultivate this relationship. It's what we both want.*

"I'm not changing my mind," she said firmly, and then stretched out on the sheet beside him.

His lips tempted her, and she boldly leaned forward to claim the kiss she wanted. It soothed her, the touch of his mouth, and she began to relax and melt into their encounter.

"So lovely," he murmured, cupping her hip in one hand. He stroked the undulating line of her body up to her breast and back down. "Come closer, mon amour, and let me feel you."

*His love? Oh, dear Lord. So soon, but I want it. I want this thing between us so badly.* She wriggled eagerly closer to him, until their bodies aligned, his thick erection nestling between her upper thighs, her breasts squashed against his chest. Tender feelings welled up. He didn't immediately grab and grope as she had expected. Instead, his fingers skated over her, drawing enticing tingles to the surface and making her shiver.

She stroked him as well, enjoying the gooseflesh that rose up on his skin. Their hands touched gently, contrasting with the heat of wild kisses that fused their mouths. At last, Philippe's wandering fingers made their way back to one nipple and delivered a firm pinch. Daphne gasped as liquid heat shot straight to her core.

*Oh dear,* she thought. *I'll be ready in seconds at this rate.*

Though her prediction proved true, as Philippe moved to caress the pouting tip of one breast and then the other, he showed no hurry to get to the main event. Instead, he layered one stimulation upon another until pleasure thrummed through her body, hot, undeniable, and wild.

Whimpers escaped her, growing in strength as he cupped and lifted the generous mounds to his lips, kissed each straining morsel, and then drew one in for an arousing taste. Daphne moaned at the suction.

"Oui, comme ça," he murmured. "Tu l'aimes."

"Yes, I do, I love it," she admitted, her voice thin with pleasure. "More, please, Philippe. More."

He chuckled at her needy pleading. "Of course, darling." He leaned down to suckle her other nipple and his hand slid down her belly. No longer shy, Daphne parted her thighs eagerly and let him explore her wetness.

No fold of her womanhood escaped Philippe's questing fingers. He stroked down to her opening and pushed inside, withdrew, and returned upward to torment the tender knot of nerves that pulsed with longing.

"Easy now," he urged as she squirmed. "On your back, love."

Daphne flopped onto the mattress and opened wider. Philippe homed in on her clitoris and rubbed a gentle circle on it.

"Like this?" he asked.

Daphne's only response was a pleasured whine.

"So eager. I like this." A few firm strokes on the pulsing bud sent her flying past the stars. Daphne fisted the sheets as the pleasure rocketed through her. Then she felt her body compress as Philippe mounted her at last.

She bent her knees, cradling his narrow hips, and he teased her clenching folds with the tip of his sex, arousing a new round of spasms before aligning with the opening and slowly easing inside.

Daphne's pleasured whimpers gave way to a deep groan as her long-neglected passage accepted her new lover into its depths. The stretch felt perfect. Her hands compressed his shoulders as he began to ease back and then surge forward again.

Daphne lifted her hips to meet his every thrust. *It's so intense, so perfect,* the thought reverberated in her head. *Oh, yes... oh yes...* "Oh, yes!" she cried as the still-lingering peak flared to new life. Her muscles locked, clamping down on her lover. His sex touched the mouth of her womb and he froze, shuddering as his own climax overtook him. The world seemed to drift. A sound like ocean waves whooshed in Daphne's ears. It gradually dawned on her that she was listening to Philippe's pulse. He lay beside her, his shoulder beneath her head. He felt warm, strong, and comfortable. Daphne slept.

Philippe regarded the woman in his arms with a blend of tender amusement and consternation. *How the devil did we get to this place? I wanted to tell her the kiss was a mistake, and instead, I compounded it by making love to her. It was like something took over my mind and heart.*

*It would still be wisest to leave her.* He recalled Geneviève and his heart clenched. *If they caught up with me—and despite changing my name I know they still search. He will never give up—I don't think I could survive it. I can't lose another woman I love. Not and survive.*

He sagged. *So many years alone. I hate it. If only he would let me be, I would let him be.*

Philippe had no way to relay such a message, and even if he could, sending it would bring about the exact outcome he'd been trying to avoid. Only this precarious, foolish plan remained to him, and only Daphne could help him achieve it.

*I cannot stop myself from loving her, so I must do what I can to keep her safe, no matter the cost. Safe and with me. Not that she'd accept anything else. She's like a hurricane. I could no more stop her claiming my heart than I could stop the wind from blowing.*

For the moment, Philippe could do nothing more. His powers of reason exhausted without any progress being made, he gave up, settled in, and watched his beloved sleep until his own fatigue dragged him down into slumber.

"Philippe?" Daphne asked as she prepared clear, viscous samples to receive a drop of reagent, "what am I supposed to be looking for here? It's pretty well known that yellow fever can be detected in blood and urine, but not saliva, so why am I studying saliva samples?"

She turned to watch him as he hunched over a sheaf of papers, pen in hand. He lifted his head and regarded her. Despite the flash of intimate awareness in his eyes, so far, her prediction seemed to have proven true. *It's easier to work now, and I feel less distracted. I know Philippe cares for me, so that painful knot of unrequited longing has dissipated. After a relaxing romp and then a long nap, I feel human enough to work hard and not let my mind wander.*

Philippe reached his hand across the small distance between them—smaller than before the momentous events of the day—and caressed her cheek. "Knowing so much about yellow fever will provide a baseline. I know almost nothing about V1, and I know more about it than anyone. We must compare everything between the mutated virus and its parent. See what has changed. This might provide clues for developing a vaccine."

Daphne nodded. "I can see the sense in that. All right, Philippe. I'll carry on just as I did with the blood."

"Good girl." He patted her shoulder and returned to his notes.

Daphne dripped one drop of the solution from a pipette into each sample, noting the lack of color changes on her chart. *Saliva still disgusts me.* "Oh, and Philippe?"

He looked up again.

"This reagent is running low. Is there any more?"

"Merde," he cursed, leaving her unsure whether to giggle or blush. "I thought I made enough. Sorry, no. I'll have to make more."

"What's in it?" she demanded. "Can I help?"

"Of course," he replied. "We'll get started tomorrow. The samples are degrading fast, so we'll have to get more soon."

Daphne shrugged. "So it goes. You know I'm willing to lend a hand in whatever you need to do."

Philippe grinned. "I really did make the right decision, choosing you—and wipe that look off your face, *mademoiselle.*" Daphne pouted, ignoring his instructions. "You're a marvelous scientist, mon amour. That's why I'm glad I chose you. That you're also quite loveable is nice, but I promise I didn't choose you for that reason."

Daphne's lips pulled to the side in a disbelieving face.

Philippe leaned over and kissed her lips. "Get back to work, assistant," he barked.

She grinned. *Much nicer now that we can relax.*

The following Friday, Philippe looked up from his test tube and met Daphne's eyes. Despite having spent their first hour of work time in bed, his intense gaze caused a thrill to flutter through her.

"Is everything all right?" she asked softly. *This whole thing is so new, I still don't quite know how to interpret it.*

"Yes, mon amour," Philippe replied. "It only occurred to me that you might be hungry. It's been a long week, and a... a busy day." He grinned wolfishly, eliciting a flushing heat in Daphne's cheeks.

"It has," she agreed.

"So, would you be interested in joining me for dinner tonight? Antoine's has a Chateaubriand for two that is to die for." He paused. "Have you been to Antoine's?"

Daphne shook her head. "That place is far outside my meager budget. Maybe something a bit more modest..."

Philippe's eyes sparkled. "Allow me, milady. I think you will enjoy it. You do like Creole food, do you not?"

Daphne opened her mouth and shut it again. Pursing her lips, she relayed the truth. "My family is Cajun, not Creole, and up until the war, we were poor as church mice. I would never have come to the city at all, if my parents hadn't suddenly decided to gentrify. But fancy dining was never part of my background."

Then, realizing she was being a bit negative, she added, "I do love to eat though, obviously, and new experiences are always fun. If you want to show me a restaurant you like, Philippe, I'll happily give it a try." Then she glanced down at her outfit. *Thank goodness I wore a skirt today for that class presentation. I don't look restaurant fancy, but it's better than trousers.*

"All right then," he said, his white-toothed grin dazzling in the sunset rays pouring through the plate glass windows. "Pack up and let's go. I want to show off my lovely lady."

Daphne beamed.

Working quickly, she settled all the test tubes back in their places, finished marking the chart and strode to the sink to wash her hands. Philippe followed suit, and then ducked upstairs, presumably to change out of his work clothes.

Feeling a bit out of her depth, Daphne examined the shelf of chemicals and compounds above the workspace. *I'm a really strange girl,* she admitted to herself. *I feel right at home in a lab full of noxious powders but eating with my sweetheart at a nice restaurant makes my stomach churn.*

The flutters had increased until they almost felt like nausea. Daphne swallowed.

Philippe reappeared, dressed nicely in brown, high-waisted slacks, a white shirt, and a red tie. Daphne bit her lip at the sight of her lover. *Lord have mercy, he's handsome.* The churning increased, and Daphne had to cough and clear her throat.

Philippe raised one eyebrow but made no comment. Approaching, he extended one arm, and she wrapped her hand around it.

He escorted her into the cool street. The scarlet light of the setting sun filtered between the close-clustered buildings of the French Quarter, to lie like streaks of blood on the streets. A chilly wind chased into the shadows. Daphne shivered.

"Do you not have a jacket, mon amour?" Philippe asked, concern wreathing his face.

She shook her head. "I forgot this morning. I had a presentation at school, and I was distracted. It went great, by the way. But don't fret, honey." She grinned at the endearment, and one corner of his mouth quirked in response. "You're putting out heat like a radiator. If I stay close to you, I won't be cold." *Won't be in danger either,* she added silently. *With Philippe by my side, no one will bother me, even at night.* The thought broadened her grin and chased the churning of her stomach down to a gurgling corner.

A few blocks of milling people brought them to a small, angled street behind the Cathedral, where, among unassuming storefronts, a green, wrought-iron balcony stood on spindly pillars. Beneath, barely visible in the growing gloom, a sign proclaimed the restaurant's name in black and red block letters.

Philippe whisked Daphne inside, where she stared in awe at dark wooden beams crisscrossing a dark ceiling. Red-painted walls glowed softly in the light of dozens of candles and some muted electric lights.

"Table for two," Philippe informed the Maître D', a portly gentleman with an oversized mustache.

"Right this way," the man responded, leading them to an empty table.

*No wait? How odd. Must be because we're a bit early,* Daphne thought, regarding the mostly empty room.

Philippe tucked her into her chair.

The Maître D' handed them each a menu printed in fancy script on cream-colored paper. Daphne perused it in silence, trying to decipher French words written in ornate cursive.

A movement right in front of her drew her attention to a newly arrived waiter, who placed a glass of wine in front of her.

"Merci, Jacques," Philippe murmured.

"You're welcome," the man replied in an accent that sounded like the south, and not the south of France either. Daphne studied the gentleman, a well-spoken man with medium brown skin and broad features, dressed in a white suit with a black tie.

"They must know you well here," Daphne commented, eyeing the glass she hadn't asked for. She lifted it to her lips and the rich complexity of flavors drove her eyes shut for a moment.

"That they do, mon amour," he agreed. "This is one of my favorite places. I eat here nearly every week."

Daphne's eyes shot open. *Yikes. If he can afford to eat here every week...* she glanced at the menu again. *Science must pay better than I realized... or he has money from somewhere else, like an inheritance, which would explain why he's able to do research independent of a university or government office.* "Well, then, Philippe," she said, "would you please be so kind as to order for me? I've never been here before and have no idea what's good." Somehow, being in this fancy place and seeing how at home her sweetheart looked in it made her more nervous. The churning sensation returned to her stomach and she chased it away with another sip of wine.

"My usual, then," he said. "Provided you like oysters, salad, and beef."

"All those are good," she agreed.

He turned to the waiter. "Oysters Rockefeller; the chateaubriand this time, since there are two of us, and at the end, two house salads."

"Very good," the waiter agreed. "How would you like the meat cooked?"

"Rare of course," Philippe replied.

The man grinned. "I should have guessed. All right. I'll be back with your oysters right away." He turned to leave.

Daphne made a face.

"Is something wrong?" he asked.

"Um, no, nothing," she stammered, not wanting to sound rude.

"Tell me," Philippe urged, leaning toward her and taking her hand.

"It all right," she replied, more firmly this time. "In my family, we rarely eat beef, but when we do, my parents prefer it well done."

Philippe eyed her. "Well done? Mon Dieu. It's steak, not charcoal, Daphne. Trust me, please. It's so much better this way."

*I've heard this about French people, that they prefer their meat undercooked. Oh well, when in Rome.* "I'll try it, but I'm not making any promises." She looked at him out of the corner of her eye with a sassy expression.

He laughed. "I predict you will be a rare steak convert before you know it."

"I predict the meal will still be mooing when it arrives at the table," she teased back.

Soon the nonsensical conversation had them both in stiches.

Later, and she would never have admitted it, but the rare steak not only tasted better than the dry lumps her mother had always served with ketchup, but somehow the mineral-laden beef finally settled her unhappy stomach.

# Chapter Eight

Six weeks passed. Winter warmed to sultry spring in the humid city strung between the lake and the river. Philippe, with Daphne looking on in fascination, brewed new reagent, and together, they gathered fresh samples.

Daphne's graduation neared, to her delight, and despite the distractions of passion and work, she had every indication she'd finish with honors. Only one slight problem—a lingering discomfort in her belly—cast a shadow over her happiness.

One day, after making sure no one loitered around the boarding house, she crept into the parlor, where a spindly black telephone rested on a tiny table and placed a call to a local physician.

"Delaney?" the male voice on the other end said, and Daphne prayed like anything no one was listening in on the party line.

"Yes, sir."

"I have your chart here."

Daphne's heart pounded fit to break her ribs, and her lingering nausea told her in no uncertain terms that she could easily vomit in the near future.

"Looks like the test is negative."

Her breath exploded in a disbelieving whoosh. "But I have all the symptoms... fatigue, nausea..."

"Perhaps you're ill," the man said cheerfully. "Drink some tea and go to bed. If it gets worse, go to the hospital, but in my opinion, your best course of action is to get married before that test result changes."

Daphne hung up the phone without any further comment.

"What was that?" a voice behind her made her jump. She whirled around to see Anna behind her. While Daphne felt slightly ill, Anna looked... awful. Her plump roundness had sunk into hollows beneath the eyes and visibly sagging skin on the arms, chin, and belly.

"I felt sick," Daphne explained, "so I went to the doctor. Say, Anna, are you all right? You look a bit under the weather yourself."

Anna nodded, loose flesh flapping. "I feel horrid. Food disgusts me, and all I want to do is sleep. I believe there's a sort of grippe running through town, and we all have it. But why go to the doctor? It's certainly not the most dangerous illness... unless you had reason to suspect it's something else?"

Daphne considered Anna. They'd been friendly enough, but not exactly close friends, not like Jeannie, so she chose her response carefully. "After growing up on a farm, I rarely get sick. I'm healthy as one of the oxen, so if I feel even a little bit bad, I take that seriously."

Anna pursed her lips. "Do you honestly think I believe that? Come on, girl. You've been staying at that lab later and later. Does the mysterious Philippe have you peering into microscopes until all hours of the night? Really?"

"Actually, yes," Daphne replied, sticking her nose in the air. *It's not a lie. Philippe and I generally make love first thing when I arrive. Then we work long into the evening.* "The research is getting to a critical point, and has to be done quickly, before the samples degrade. But, say, Anna, what are you suggesting?" Daphne glared at her housemate.

"Please, Daphne. You're not fooling anyone. First, you're all google eyes and sighs over him, and then you start glowing like a star. Now you're coming home late. If he's using you, he deserves to be horsewhipped, but you, Miss Delaney, should have more self-respect."

"I have plenty of self-respect," Daphne began, but Anna held up one hand.

"Stow it. I don't believe you. You feel all gooey because he wants you, but what will happen when he drops his secret lover and takes up with someone more 'appropriate' in public? What will happen to your self-respect then?" Anna placed her fists on her hips.

Daphne eyed the woman, from the top of her piled-up blond hair to her incongruously tiny shoes. "Is that what happened to you? I think it must, you have so much venom invested in the story."

"Never in a million years would I sell my virginity so cheaply. I may be fat and unattractive, but I have my self-respect." Anna stuck her nose in the air.

"Good for you," Daphne said honestly. "I think that's just peachy. Now if you'll excuse me, the doctor recommended tea, and I aim to make some."

She brushed past Anna on her way to the kitchen.

"What's his last name?" Anna called after her, "so I know who to go after when you're crying your eyes out."

"Dumont," Daphne replied, "and you'd best remember that name, so you can say you knew him, once he discovers a cure for yellow fever."

Anna's unladylike snort followed her into the kitchen.

As Daphne brewed her tea, her agile mind picked through Anna's tirade. *Something about what she said has triggered a thought, but I can't quite make it out. A mild illness with fatigue and nausea as its symptoms. There are thousands of those, but one of them is...* her eyes widened. "One is yellow fever," she breathed. "Is it possible the vaccines are failing?"

She clapped both hands over her mouth in horror, wishing to unsay the words. *Well, I do have the means to find out at my disposal, don't I?*

She drank her tea quickly, ignoring the unpleasant way it sloshed in her tummy, and hustled out into the warm, sunny New Orleans noon. At the lunch hour, people milled about in profusion, businessmen and secretaries rubbing shoulders with dock and warehouse workers. All seemed to be carrying Po Boys and muffulettas. Daphne's sour stomach appreciated neither the sight nor the aroma, although normally the sweet, salty, savory blend of fried shrimp, warm bread and crisp vegetables tempted her.

Her quick pace increased her already painful heartbeat, until her pulse throbbed in her head. A strange whooshing noise sounded in her ears and her breath had to force its way out through a throat that threatened to close up on her.

A man stepped into her path, staring up at the buildings until his bowler hat tumbled from his head. Daphne veered sharply to avoid colliding with the fellow and his headwear and succeeded in stepping on someone's foot. A startled squawk rang in her ears and she mumbled a half-coherent apology as she increased her pace. At last the familiar façade drew her into a space she now knew as well as her own home. The lab sat, silent and still, exactly as she'd left it late the previous night. Even the strange floral and chemical scent of Philippe's mysterious reagent still hung in the air.

*That's what I need,* she thought. She spat into a test tube and dripped the yellow fever detector into it.

"Idiot," she hissed as the precious drop fell into the container. "Yellow fever isn't shed in saliva. That's why it's not conta—" she broke off and stared at the bright pink splotch wending its way down into the tube. "Holy Mary," she breathed.

Quick as a flash, she rolled up her sleeve to the elbow and hunted around the room until she found an abandoned syringe. Taking a deep breath, she jabbed it into her flesh. She filled a clean test tube with her sample. Another drop in the reagent also showed the damning pink.

Drawing air into her laboring lungs, Daphne retrieved the saliva samples. Careless of the numbers they'd assigned, she dispensed drop after drop, but not one sample showed the slightest change of hue. Or rather, one did.

Only one.

Daphne stared at the sample in mute horror for an hour that must have lasted a half a minute, and then she carelessly tossed the sample into the holder. Turning, she dragged the book in front of her and flipped rapidly to the first page, where the samples and names had been linked. She tore several pages in her haste. Then she ran her finger down the lines until she arrived at twenty-one.

No name had been written in the box.

"I made this list," she mumbled. "I wrote every name. Nothing was left blank. Philippe must have added this... after. Which means he's concealing the identity of the donor, even from me, which probably means..." she trailed off, the full horror of her suspicion dawning on her.

Daphne's mind finally went blank. She sat staring, still as a statue, while minutes passed for which she had no recollection. Her powerful brain had finally failed.

How long she would have sat immobile, it would be hard to tell, but the familiar scrape of the front door shattered her attention. She whirled.

"Oh, hello, mon amour," Philippe said cheerfully as he stepped across the threshold, a bottle of wine in the crook of his arm. "I didn't expect you until later. Is all well? What happened to your class?"

Daphne blinked and opened her mouth, but only a toad-like croak emerged.

She watched in detached fascination as Philippe set the bottle on the table and approached, his cheerful expression reshaping itself into one of concern.

"Are you all right?" he asked again.

Daphne slowly turned her head to the left and then the right. She inhaled, a choking breath that stuck and clung to every inch of her throat and seemed to sear her lungs.

Though the arms Philippe wrapped around her warmed her body, the cold inside her refused to be comforted. "What is it, love? What has happened?"

He kissed her temple, in full view of the window.

She recoiled from his touch, and the movement seemed to free her words, so they poured out in a torrent. "What did you do to me?" she hissed. "Did you know this would happen? Did you choose me as an assistant or a secret test subject?"

"I beg your pardon?" He pulled back, staring down into her eyes, his mouth twisted in confusion.

Daphne inhaled, released the air, and inhaled again, trying to calm herself enough to speak the words. "You infected me. Sample 21 is yours, isn't it?"

Philippe's gleaming white teeth sank into his lip. He drew in air sharply through his nose. "Infected you? What do you mean?"

"Don't be dense," she snapped. "That V1 virus you're going on about? The one that turns the reagent pink? I have it all through me. I thought I was pregnant, but I'm not, so I tested my saliva and—"

"Saliva?" he said, phrasing the word as a sharp question. "It doesn't shed in saliva."

"Oh, yes it does," she replied, waving at the holder filled with clear, liquid-filled test tubes, two of them shining in tones of rose.

"Mon Dieu," he breathed.

"Yes, you see?" she demanded. "You probably infected me the first time you kissed me, and ever since then, you've added more of the contagion into my body—not to mention, we have no idea if it passes through semen. You told me this virus is only passed directly from host to victim, so if you knew you were carrying it, why did you touch me? Am I going to die?"

Philippe sagged, his body curling into hers as though seeking a comforting embrace, but Daphne's rage and fear kept her rigid. "It is unlikely you will have a severe reaction at this late time. I've had this for so long... To be honest, it's like yellow fever in that, unless you develop toxic symptoms, which will happen immediately after exposure, you will acclimate to the virus and it will no longer bother you."

"Unlike yellow fever," she shot back, "you don't merely carry the antibodies after it runs its course, do you, Philippe? You become an asymptomatic carrier, infecting everyone you touch. You become a walking disease."

The words elicited a gasp, and he shook his head. "I don't think of it that way. Anyway, once you get to this stage, it does no harm. You will be fine."

"Fine except I would never dare touch another man, for fear he would have a bad reaction and I'd be responsible for his death."

Philippe scowled. "Were you planning to have many lovers, Daphne? I... I thought you and I had something special together. It's what I want, don't you?"

Only twenty-four hours before, such a frank vow of his intentions would have sent her into a flutter of wedding bells and pink rose bouquets, but today she frowned. "Who I go to bed with is my business," she snarled. "At this point, I'm not sure I would go near you, even if you were the last man on earth, which, for me, it seems you are. Did you plan this?"

His embracing arms dropped away from her. "Non, of course not! I thought we would be safe so long as we did not exchange blood. I had no idea it transmitted through kissing. Yellow fever does not, as you know." She glared. "They are separate things, Daphne. I kissed and touched you because I love you. Curing this contagion had nothing to do with how I feel about you."

The dearly coveted words failed to warm her. "Love? Is this how you love me then? By trapping me with you for life? Might as well have bound my feet like a Chinaman." Though she knew the words were rude, she couldn't stop her mouth from spewing out the most appalling garbage.

"I told you I didn't know this would happen," he growled, finally roused to anger. "I would never have knowingly put you at risk."

"But you knew you were contagious, and you knew V1 had altered radically from yellow fever. You should have tested all your bodily fluids, not just your blood. Where's the science in so much assumption?"

"Faulty." He sighed and stepped back from her, turning away and covering his face with his hands. "I gambled with your health and lost. Sorry doesn't begin to express how I feel, though I doubt my regret matters to you."

"You've got that right, buddy," she snapped.

They both fell silent, considering their thoughts without expressing them. Daphne felt a trembling begin at the tips of her fingers and make its way up her arms and across her torso. Her ability to breathe again called itself into question as strange, shuddering gasps shattered her furious respirations. At last, great, noisy sobs tore themselves from her throat.

In an instant, Philippe had her in his arms again. She lowered her shoulder to the soft white fabric of his shirt.

Deep sobs wracked her from head to foot. *Diseased, contaminated, and incurable. Philippe says he's had it for a long time with no adverse reactions, but does that mean anything? He's clearly young, not much more than thirty, so who knows what the long-term effect might be. If it's harmless, how can it be a weapon?* Though confused, Daphne's grief had taken precedence over her need to understand. *Can I trust that it was an accident, or did Philippe take me to his bed just for this reason?* She still didn't know. *Certainly, this changes things. My dream of being a scientist couple like the Curies seems impossible now.*

Drawing air into her shuddering lungs, she pulled back from his embrace.

Regret turned every one of Philippe's sharp features into a blade. "Can you forgive me, Daphne?" he asked, his voice contrite. "I can't lose you now."

"I don't know," she replied honestly. "It may be too much. I need time to think."

He sighed. "I promise you, I did not mean for this to happen."

"And yet, it did happen, and so I have to understand how I feel about it, and about us. How can I trust a man who puts me at risk by exposing me to a deadly virus? You knew it was in you. That was reason enough to stay away."

"I tried to stay away," he reminded her. "I tried to be professional with you, more professional than I am with anyone else, because I didn't want to fall for you, but I failed. In the end, I couldn't resist you. You're like a force of nature, Daphne."

"You did *not* treat me like a professional, Philippe," she pointed out. "You left me ignorant of a very important fact, one that changed the entire picture. You let me make decisions without information. If someone knew themselves to be infected with the clap, and went to bed with a partner anyway, it would be no different."

"Actually, it would," he pointed out, lips twisting to one side. We know that gonorrhea is spread through sex. Until this moment, I had no idea V1 was."

"Semantics." Daphne shook her head. "No excuses, Philippe. You put me at risk, and I became infected because you didn't have enough information, and because you didn't share the information you have with me. That makes this at the very least, not entirely an accident." She dashed her hands across her cheeks to dispel the lingering moisture. "This is not acceptable in a professional or a personal relationship. I have to think about whether I could or should forgive you, and what this means for my participation in your work and in your life. I will let you know what I decide, when I decide it. I have to go."

Though she held her head high and stormed out the door, Daphne's insides felt shrunken and shriveled. *Is something so wrong with me that I cannot attract and keep a decent man? Bob used and abandoned me, and now Philippe is using me too, but for what end I still cannot imagine.* The early afternoon sun fell warm on her shoulders, but her internal shivering did not abate. The cityscape she normally loved passed unnoticed as she made her way back to the boarding house.

Not wanting to see anyone, she tiptoed hurriedly past the open door of the parlor to the stairs and made her way up. *Jeannie should be in class right now, Anna is at work, and Lois normally sleeps most of the day away.*

Finding her room blessedly empty, she tugged off her shoes without opening the buckles and dropped them to the floor with a satisfying clunk. Then she flung herself back on the bed and stared up at the ceiling.

*Now what? I have a disease, an unknown one, and it's probably going to live in my body for the rest of my life, if Philippe is correct about that, which he has no idea if he is, and is just assuming. I'm sick of him assuming. He needs to pull himself together and act like a scientist.*

*We've already established that, while V1 stems from yellow fever, it's no longer the same thing, nor does it act the same way. The only actual facts we know about it are that it's contagious through saliva, blood and possibly semen, and that it's possible to live a number of years without debilitating symptoms. Also, that yellow fever vaccine doesn't work on it, if Philippe did his work correctly.*

*I need to fact-check every one of his discoveries to confirm their results using unbiased methods. He was right that he needs me to verify his work.*

She rolled onto her side and stared at Jeannie's tidy, carefully made bed. *She tossed and turned all night instead of sleeping again. I hope she's all right.*

"I have to go back," she realized, voicing her epiphany aloud. "Whether I remain Philippe's lover is still in question, but if I have this virus, I have to take part in researching its cure. I don't want to carry it for the rest of my life, just waiting for it to enter a more active phase that sickens or kills me. Damn, what a mess."

Daphne shut her mouth with a snap at the sound of footsteps on the wood floor of the hallway. *Who could be here in the middle of the day? Everyone should be in class or at work, and Lois rarely ventures upstairs. Who's out there?*

Rising from the bed and cursing under her breath at the noisy squeaking of springs, she shuffled on silent stockings to the door and listened but didn't hear anything further. Sucking in a lung full of air, she slowly twisted the knob and peeked out into the hallway, just in time to see the door to the room Mary and Phyllis shared clicking into place. A soft scratching sound accompanied the sharp smell of sulfur and fire, and then a rank, ammoniated aroma floated into the hallway. Daphne shut the door again.

"I swear that woman is three-quarters a witch," she muttered. "Lois will have a hairy canary if she finds out, and poor Phyllis, if she decides to come home, will have to sleep in that stink. I wonder where she went, anyway. It's common enough for her to go on a bender with one of her customers at the bar and not come home for a week or more, but with all the weird stuff going on in here, it makes me suspicious."

Daphne sank to a seat on the edge of her bed, her thoughts rolling and bouncing like a shrimp boat in a Gulf hurricane. A throbbing in the vicinity of her left eye warned of a powerful headache brewing. *And no wonder, between the virus, my impossible decisions, and the stench of whatever hocus-pocus Mary has going on down the hall.*

Unexpectedly, the whole situation caught up with Daphne at once. Exhaustion dragged her under, and she slept.

Thick, dark clouds skidded across a full moon, round like a pregnant belly and softly golden. The clouds themselves showed no such delicacy, shaping themselves into all manner of threatening forms: skulls, ravens, and open graves.

"There are not so many graves like this here," a soft voice murmured, and Daphne turned to see Anna standing beside her. The normally robust girl looked almost gaunt, her skin hanging from her limbs, her eyes ringed with black circles. "Not so many at all. So much easier to rise when you lie on the bones of your relatives in a little brick house."

"What are you saying?" Daphne demanded. "Anna, have you lost your mind?"

The girl lowered her lifted chin and turned. Daphne gulped. Her friend's eyes glowed red in the moonlight and her jaw sagged open in a wide, ugly grin. "Oh, maybe I have," she intoned, and a foul, rotten stench emerged. "Lost so much, but then, so have you, haven't you?"

"What do you mean?" Daphne took a step back, uncertain what to think, but knowing she wanted to put space between herself and her friend at any cost.

"You know what she means," another voice chimed in. Daphne risked a glance to the left and a squeak of terrified disgust escaped her. Phyllis, her skin mottled gray and green, dragged herself naked along the ground. Behind her, an oily slick of liquid fouled the grass. As Daphne watched in horror, the girl struggled to her feet. The flesh of her belly had swollen and turned black, as though all her decayed organs only awaited the right moment to burst forth. "It's in you too. Soon you'll join us, Daphne."

"I will not," she replied, trying to sound firm, though she wanted nothing more than to vomit and run away.

"You will." *Oh no! I know that voice.* Cranking her head to the right, she saw Jeannie, pale in the moonlight, her eyes also ringed with sleepless bruises.

"Please, no," Daphne whispered.

"Oh, yes," Jeannie replied. "Soon you'll see. There's so much to enjoy, to be thankful for. It's a world we never imagined." She tilted her head to the side, as though in contemplation. Daphne could see the side of her neck covered in tooth impressions, all of them bruised and a few penetrating the skin.

Another foul aroma wafted across the scene, which Daphne now recognized as Jackson Square, though devoid of its usual bustling live-liness. No artists sketched the Cathedral, no couples strolled through the grass, chatting softly of their future plans. Deathly silence hung heavy over the gated green plaza. Silence and her friends, remade as animated corpses, and the putrid stink of rot and... something. Something that wafted from a massive iron cauldron set over a crackling fire. Behind it stood Mary, her towering body nude save smears of soot or paint in some kind of mystical pattern.

"I will banish you, foul beasts," she intoned.

All three zombies laughed; hollow, ugly laughter that made Daphne want to cover her ears. As one they turned toward Mary and began to inch in her direction.

"I'll have to banish you too," Mary said to Daphne, her tone sorrow-ful. Though her gaze remained locked on the creeping monstrosities, she didn't seem overly concerned about them, "or at least the darkness that lives inside you." She sighed. "You had to meddle, didn't you? Couldn't leave well enough alone?"

This made no sense to Daphne, but before she could ask, Mary began to chant—strange words in an unrecognizable language—and stir her cauldron with a huge wooden paddle. Daphne thought she could pick out a hint of French, a smattering of Latin, but also a great many words of which she could determine nothing.

The fire grew brighter and brighter until she had to close her eyes against its brilliance.

It grew so bright, it lured Daphne right up out of her doze and back into her body, into her bedroom, where late-afternoon sun filtered through the sheer curtains.

In the background, the soft chanting continued, but of the rest of the dream, only an unsettled feeling remained.

"I wonder what brought that on," Daphne muttered to herself. "How strange and disturbing to see all my friends transformed into zombies... into vampire zombies, I'd guess, except that the bites on Jeannie's neck looked like human teeth, not fangs." She sighed. "I wonder if the virus causes strange dreams or if I've simply overtaxed my mind."

She rolled to her back and stared up at the ceiling again. "What a terrible pickle I've gotten myself into."

From the other bedroom, she heard a splash, and a new layer of stink crept under the closed doors to tease her nostrils. "Well, that certainly doesn't help."

Giving up on the bed, Daphne rose to her feet and opened the door. In the hallway, the stench threatened to choke her. As she passed Mary's door, the other woman ducked out, gasping.

Clouds of yellowish smoke billowed out. Daphne coughed and clapped her hand over her mouth. Her belly roiled in disgust. Lips down, one eye squinted, she gave Mary a long, disapproving look.

Mary didn't even have the grace to look sheepish. She stared back, boldly challenging Daphne with a confident jut of her chin.

"That's disgusting," Daphne said at last, her fingers muffling her words. "If...when Lois finds out you're still casting spells and making potions in her house, you'll be looking for a new place to live."

"Lois is a fool," Mary said firmly. "She condemns what she doesn't understand. The darkness that surrounds us all will move against us soon, and I, for one, aim to be prepared for it."

"By summoning it?" Daphne asked, blinking as the acrid smoke stung her eyes.

Mary sighed. "I hardly expected *you* to understand, Miss Science, but you will one day, and when you do... well, I'll still do my best to protect you, but I'll definitely say I told you so."

"You do that," Daphne offered, "provided we don't both suffocate in this hallway. What on earth are you making anyway? It smells like the grave... if a cat pissed in it."

"You're better off not knowing," Mary replied.

Daphne took a few steps toward the stairwell and Mary followed. "When Phyllis returns, you're going to have a hell of a time explaining why her room smells like a public toilet for cats."

"Phyllis is no longer among the living," Mary said bluntly, and Daphne froze, one foot on the staircase's brilliant green runner, the other poised in the air.

"Horsefeathers! No dice, Mary." Daphne blurted out the slang thoughtlessly. "You can't possibly know that. Where do you get this information?"

"From the spirit world, naturally," Mary replied. She passed Daphne, who still stood frozen on the step. "Better keep moving before you fall. It's very odd though. Just like the lady of the evening who used to live here, I keep getting a message that Phyllis is no longer living, but I can't communicate with her spirit."

A whole jumble of doubts and rational arguments tumbled through Daphne's mind so fast, none of them coalesced into anything expressible. Feeling dizzy from the overload of thoughts, she set her foot down on the stair to steady herself.

Mary continued talking, as though to herself. "Something very strange is happening in this city."

"Honey, it's New Orleans," Daphne reminded her housemate, once her tongue unstuck itself and her feet resumed moving. "This city has been full of strange things from the beginning."

"I know," Mary replied with a careless laugh. "I'm one of them. However, this is a different kind of strange. The spirits tell me this darkness doesn't stay constantly, but comes in waves, at various times, for reasons they either don't know or are unable to share. Even worse, they don't follow the rules."

Daphne squinted one eye, whether from the lingering stench of the smoke, or from the strange story, she couldn't quite tell. "You're saying ghosts have rules?"

"Oh, yes!" Mary exclaimed. "Ever so many rules. Some are the same for all ghosts everywhere. The ones who break those rules can get into a lot of trouble, and you don't want to know what trouble looks like for those who have passed. There are also rules individual ghosts impose on each other."

Daphne's eyelid began to twitch. "If ghosts—incorporeal be-ings—impose rules on each other, how can they enforce them? It's not like one ghost can give another a knuckle sandwich."

Mary laughed. Opening the door to the parlor, she stepped inside and sank onto a high-backed black armchair. Daphne followed and perched on the settee.

*This is pure hogwash, but I'm enjoying the distraction. I'll think about my own problems later.*

"Ghosts are only incorporeal if they're weak. Over time, if left to their own devices, they will either fade, move on, or gain strength. Ghosts that gain strength from the negative emotions of the liv-ing—fear, rage, illness—become dark and monstrous. They can ac-tually regain a measure of their physical strength, enough to touch, scratch, throw things. Even a cold spot is a sign of a ghost that is growing in strength."

*Interesting how confidently she describes this, like a professor giving a lecture straight from a textbook.*

"These bad ghosts continue to grow in strength until they completely overtake the location they've claimed. If they can either capture another ghost to dominate or cause the death of a living person, they become nearly unstoppable. Those are rules they're not supposed to break, though many do anyway. Then it's up to people like me to banish them."

"People like you?" Daphne regarded Mary with curiosity. "What do you mean?"

Mary smiled, her freckles dancing across the pale skin of her face. A tendril of tightly curled, carrot-colored hair sprang free from her coiffure and stood like a tiny orange spring above her head. "I'm a natural medium, like my mother, grandmother, and so on, all the way back to the Old Country."

"Ah." Breaking eye contact, Daphne examined her fingernail. *My skin color is normal,* her scientific mind informed her as she observed herself in a clinical way. *So, either that's not a symptom of my illness or I'm acclimating to it.*

"At any rate, what's happening in this city," Mary continue, her tone growing more didactic with each word, "from what the spirits can tell me, is a scourge that used to come through often, about once a generation. It kills, but it seems to eat the soul as well, not like a natural disease or even an act of violence.

"It comes less often now, but it is still present, still powerful, and for some reason, it's targeting this house. I'm trying to find out what that means, what's after us, and what to do about it, but the information is hard to come by. So right now, I'm working on basic warding and protection spells, to keep out evil spirits, curses and bad intentions." She heaved a sigh that swelled her small bosom to operatic proportions before deflating it again. "But whenever Lois finds evidence of my work, she destroys it. I swear, that woman wants us to be invaded by demons."

Daphne searched through her mind for something to say in response to this lecture, but nothing came to mind. She leaned against the arm of the chair and studied the ceiling. *If this keeps up, I'll get my degree in ceiling staring long before I get my science diploma.*

"Do be careful, won't you?" Mary urged. "You have something dark that clings to you all the time. I don't know what it is, or if it's dangerous, but it concerns me."

*Can she see my infection?* The thought irritated Daphne in its irrationality. Annoyed at being made to think mystical things, she snapped, "I'm always careful."

"You are?" Mary raised one russet eyebrow. "Are you sure?"

Daphne frowned but didn't reply.

Mary smiled, but the curving of her lips didn't suggest humor. Then she leaned across the space and patted Daphne's hand. "I understand, you know, how deep the desire is to be loved by someone who appreciates you. It's not easier for me either."

The angry retort died on Daphne's lips. Her shoulders sagged. "If only the expectations placed on girls weren't so stifling."

"Agreed."

Deciding to humor her housemate a bit further, as the distraction allowed her busy mind to rest while her subconscious wrestled, she asked, "So, darkness around me?"

Mary nodded. "Around us all, and around this place. Something terrible happened here, but it isn't what we think. The evidence is wrong. The spirits are acting strangely, and they aren't who they should be. Whatever happened is still affecting this place, not in the sense of a haunting, but more like a curse, a lingering taint." She pondered. "I know that doesn't make any sense. I don't understand it myself. Now as for you, what hovers around you feels the same as the taint, or rather almost the same, but it's not as dangerous." She growled in frustration. "I hate not understanding what's happening. I can deal with ghosts, but the unknown makes me feel afraid."

"And curious at the same time?" Daphne suggested. "Untangle the mystery, find the cure. It's such a slow, tedious process, but the reward has the potential to be so great... and the problem needs to be solved."

Mary nodded. "That's it exactly."

*Maybe a medium and a scientist have certain motivational similarities,* Daphne thought. *I wonder... I wonder if the supernatural is real, and the reason I turned to science and rejected it is because I lack the ability to perceive it.* The radical thought shook her to the core of her every deeply held belief, the persona she'd spent most of her life cultivating. Somewhere deep within her, a superstitious Cajun nodded and winked. Daphne sighed. *Oh dear.*

"Somehow, I will get to the bottom of what's haunting this place, and I will set everything to rights," Mary vowed.

A soft sound drew the girls' attention to the doorway of the parlor, where Lois stood, her slender hands fisted on the curves of her hips, a ferocious frown curving grooves around the corners of her mouth. "You'll do no such thing, Miss Mary Murphy. I warned you not to do any more of this mumbo jumbo in my home."

Mary bit her lip. Daphne could see no evidence of her breathing. They all seemed to pause, poised on the precipice of a great chasm.

Lois opened her mouth and dragged them over the edge. "All my senses are fully functioning, my girl. I can smell that stink on you, and I know what it means. I can see you've ignored my rules. Renting a room in my home is not a free-for-all. I told you what would happen if you crossed me again. Get your things and leave. If you're not out by nightfall, and all your magical quackery with you, I'm calling the police."

Mary blinked, stunned.

"Well, what are you sitting there for? Get up!" Lois clapped her hands. "Get packing and get out of my house." She advanced on the girl.

Though her voice trembled, Mary showed no signs of rushing. She rose to her feet, tall and majestic as a queen. "I haven't done anything harmful. I only wanted to protect the house and its occupants from a great evil. It's all around you all the time. You're in danger, and I only want to help."

"I don't want or need your help, you charlatan." Lois took a threatening step toward Mary, who held her ground.

"I'll go," Mary said softly. "I'll go now. Don't worry." She turned to regard Daphne, who sat staring at them both. "I urge you not to linger here," she added. "You must leave at once. Without me to protect you, I feel something terrible is going to happen, and soon. None of you will survive if you're here when it happens, and you won't even have the comfort of becoming ghosts. Something dark and terrible will claim you for its own. Tell the others."

Without another word, Mary brushed past Lois and made her way out of the room. Daphne heard her shoes clunking on the stairs a moment later.

Lois rounded on Daphne. "What were you doing encouraging her?" she demanded, eyebrows drawn together in a dark and angry line. "I told you what I expected."

"It was just a conversation," Daphne pointed out, not sure where her calm came from. "I wasn't participating in anything."

Lois glared, and then shook her head as though to clear it. She sighed. "All right, all right. You'd better give me some space, Daphne. I'm a bit shook up. Go to work or something. I'll see you later."

In truth, Daphne felt a bit shaken herself. Lois left the room, and the echoing footsteps suggested she had headed out to the garden to bask in the warmth of a late spring sun.

*Well, this is a fine kettle of fish,* Daphne thought. *What am I supposed to do now? I'm furious with Philippe, so going to work is the last thing I want to do. I've missed my classes for today—not that I'd be able to concentrate under the circumstances anyway—and I sure don't want to loiter here.*

Ducking out of the parlor, she made her way to the street. The sun, glaring painfully bright over the crowded streets of the city, did indeed chase away the stench of Mary's potion, though it couldn't drive dark and aimless contemplations from Daphne's mind. *What if I'm the evil thing Mary fears? What if my infection is more contagious than Philippe realizes, and I'll cause everyone's death? What if I've already spread it to them without realizing it?* She gulped.

Turning south, she made her way to the river. There, men shouted and bustled, loading and unloading materials from boats. They gleamed with sweat, even though full summer heat had yet to take hold. To Daphne, the warm temperature felt pleasant, though the brightness of the sun stung her eyes.

She lifted her face and studied the clouds above her. Fat and puffy, they shaped and reshaped themselves in the late spring breeze, transforming for one moment into a dragon, for another into a hair ribbon.

The mindless activity helped Daphne settle her panic. *I lack knowledge. All I have is wild supposition. I need to go back to the lab, continue to study, until I truly know. If I'm going to die, I want time to prepare. If I'm contagious, I need to know that too, and limit contact with unaffected individuals.* The thought of seeing Philippe again made her stomach knot. *But he's the only one besides me who's aware this virus exists, or so he says. I need his help. He needs mine. I have to find a way to work with him.* She pursed her lips.

"Pucker up, cutie," a rough male voice said approvingly. Daphne raised one eyebrow and nailed a dockhand with a furious scowl. He backed up, hands raised. Without a word, she turned on her heel and stalked away.

*The only way to solve a problem is to confront it head-on,* she reminded herself. *You've never been timid in your life, and today is not the day to start.*

Lost in thought, she startled herself by turning toward a door, and then blinked, realizing she'd arrived at the lab. She took a shaky breath, twisted the knob, and stepped inside.

Philippe sat hunched over a table. His very posture radiated misery. At the sound of the door scraping over the threshold, he lifted his head and turned to regard her. Hope flared in his eyes. Faster than she could comprehend, he hurried to her, slipping his arms around her waist. His lips descended, but she covered his mouth with her fingertips. "No," she said firmly. "I'm not here for that. I'm still upset with you."

His lips turned down beneath her touch and his eyes grew sad.

She pressed on. "I don't know what's happening to me, and that's unacceptable. I refuse to live with this virus and not know more about it. What you've told me doesn't sound too well researched, and I don't trust you at this point, so I'm going to need to verify all your results, for as long as you've been researching them, to be sure you didn't make any other mistakes. Do you understand, Philippe? I'm here to work."

He drew his head back a fraction. "I understand, Daphne. Yes, we will work. I do hope, in time, you will come to forgive me, but I understand why you're not ready. Still, know that for me, nothing has changed." His warm breath touched her skin and she tingled, longing to turn that quelling touch into a caress, to feel the rough, dark stubble on his pale cheeks.

"Noted," she said dryly. "Where do we start?" Her fingers trembled, and she dropped her hand to her side. *Don't give up being mad too quickly,* she urged herself. *Now you have even more reason to maintain a professional demeanor.*

# Chapter Nine

Daphne's back ached. It felt like a mild flu. Her shoulders also made themselves known. *How odd. Usually, when I'm studying the microscope, I don't feel any pain. Not until I'm done.* She shifted uncomfortably, and then shifted again. *This disease is very much like yellow fever, the mild, 'acute' part. I wonder if it also has a toxic phase. Clearly Philippe didn't get it, and clearly, it lasts longer than yellow fever, since I still feel a bit off this long after the initial infection.*

"Philippe?" she said.

"Hmmm?" Daphne snapped her head to the side and found herself face to face with her boss. Suddenly, without warning, all the memories of their last few weeks flooded over her. She quickly returned her gaze to the sample in front of her, though she took in no information. *We're not just boss and employee anymore. We're lovers—partners, in life and work. He wants that. I thought I did too. Is it right that I'm doubting that dream so easily? If so, what does that mean? I loved him, but love doesn't end so easily, does it? I mean, how do couples live together for years and years without end? They must have disagreements. Make mistakes. Hurt each other, sometimes as badly as this. They get past it. The question is... did he mean to do it?*

She turned to eye Philippe. He hunched over the microscope, lips moving in some sort of silent conversation with himself. His uncomfortable posture and the harsh downward turn of his mouth spoke volumes. He lifted his head, glanced her way, and quickly broke eye contact. In that brief moment of connection, such pain burned in his shockingly dark eyes, it made her own sting.

*Well, damn,* she thought. *I guess that says it all, doesn't it? He's honestly, truly upset. That wouldn't be the case if he intentionally infected me to study the results. There would be excitement or triumph in his expression. Instead, he looks brokenhearted.* A strange, hot feeling blossomed in her heart. *Brokenhearted over losing a relationship with me? Dear Lord.* Her belly fluttered. Again, Philippe lifted his head, and this time, when he met her eyes, he remained. Their gazes locked.

*I love you.* The words rang in her head, as if they had been spoken aloud. Daphne nibbled on her lip, indecision warring with the undeniable pull of Philippe's affection.

"Do you swear to me," she said with quiet intensity, "swear, Philippe, that you didn't infect me on purpose?"

He squeezed his eyes shut and his nostrils flared. "I swear it," he vowed in return, without hesitation. "I would never have done that. Do you honestly think I wanted to cause you harm?"

She sighed. "I don't. I'm pretty sure I believe you, but I find it hard to accept you would take such a foolish risk."

"And for that, I'll never forgive myself." At last Philippe tore his intense gaze away from Daphne's face and studied the black lacquered surface of the desk.

Without conscious thought, Daphne reached out and laid her hand on his. His head shot up, his face wreathed in questions.

"Philippe, I..." she started, but then the words choked on themselves and instantly died.

His fingers closed around hers. She clung to his hand as though to pull herself from a raging sea. *Once upon a time, every part of this relationship made perfect sense. Can I return to that feeling? Can I trust him again?*

Philippe's chest loomed before her, cutting off her thoughts, and his arms encircled her back, and yet he still perched on his stool. No pressure on her hand suggested he had pulled her, but she stood before him. *Did I move?* she wondered for a fraction of a second before her mouth met his in a voluptuous kiss. The couple made no attempt at subtlety, their lips parting as one in a wild tangle of tongues.

The rational, reasonable part of Daphne's mind tried to fight against their passion, but she found herself unable. Philippe's kiss, his scent, the strength of his embrace all conspired to submerge that part of her beneath a torrent of undeniable desire.

"Philippe," she gasped against his lips, struggling to draw air into her laboring lungs. "Philippe, please."

"Please what, my love?" he asked, peering into her eyes. His own seemed illuminated with a black fire.

"Let's get away from the window," she begged. *The rest is inevitable, but let's not put on a spectacle in front of the entire French Quarter.*

Again, time seemed to bend around itself. Though she felt no awareness of moving, between one heartbeat and the next, she found herself in his bedroom, her clothing scattered, her body stretched out on familiar sheets. She blinked in surprise.

Philippe stripped off his socks. She reached out one hand and drew him down beside her. After the strangeness of the lost minutes leading up to this point, once her beloved embraced her, Daphne's senses turned from dull to hyper-aware. Every touch of his body on hers—the coarse prickle of his chest hairs on her breasts, the weight of his arm across her hip, the scratch of the stubble on his cheeks as he kissed her lips again and again—each one etched itself forever on her memory.

Philippe wasted no time on preliminaries. His fingers skated down her body, stroking one pert, erect nipple and then the other before blazing a ticklish trail down her middle.

Daphne planted one foot on the mattress and bent her knee, giving access to her aching womanhood to her only source of relief.

"Hmmm," he whispered against her lips. "So wet."

"I've always loved how you touch me." She arched her hips forward, wordlessly urging him to caress her.

His fingers delved between the slick folds until he found her clitoris. Daphne gasped, her head falling back. Philippe kissed her neck and delivered a stinging bite to her tender skin, even as he lovingly stimulated her most sensitive place. He layered pleasure on pleasure, building up in her a terrible and delicious tension, before finally easing her over the precipice of delight. A raw scream of ecstasy tore itself from her. She thrashed and bucked, but Philippe showed no mercy.

"Oui, comme ça, comme ça," he murmured. A pressure against her shoulder urged her onto her back. She flopped down gracelessly, waiting for her lover to mount her, eager to feel him filling her again.

Instead, a different spreading pressure wormed its way into her empty passage. Daphne's eyes flew open to see Philippe crouched between her parted thighs, his burning eyes fixed on her intimate parts. His fingers pressed deep, withdrew, and surged forward again.

"Philippe?" she asked in a wavering whisper.

"Hush, love," he urged. "I almost lost you. I'm so thankful you're here. Let me... let me love you."

He lowered his lips and kissed the tender bud.

"Ohhhhh," she moaned. "Oh, Philippe."

The fingers rotated, seeking and finding another pleasurable spot deep within her. His lips touched her clitoris again, and then his tongue snaked out to tease the erect nubbin.

Again, pleasure built, almost frightening in its intensity. Daphne lay helpless, unable to resist, passive against the passionate onslaught. Breathing in shallow pants, she found her knees locking involuntarily as she sought to bring about the promised peak. Stars sparked. She squealed and twisted.

The cosmos shone and glistened behind her closed eyelids. A loud pulsing sounded in her ears. Her heaving breath finally began to slow back toward normal, and she became aware of a change in the quality of the light. Her eyes flew open and she beheld Phillipe, poised above her, ready to merge them once again into a being of pure passion. Today, though, Daphne felt aggressive. She surged upward, embracing Philippe and using her momentum to twist them sideways until his shoulder hit the mattress. Then she pounced on him. No longer content to let him take the lead, she straddled his narrow hips.

"Oho," he said, and excitement replaced contrition in the set of his features. "Does milady fancy a ride then?"

"Oh, yes, mister. You'd better believe it." She shimmied her hips, making her breasts bounce and jiggle.

Philippe fisted the swollen tumescence she craved. "Ride away, then," he urged, levering the thick organ upward. Daphne lowered herself down, gasping as the rigid length speared into her hypersensitive sex. A flurry of spasms resurrected the ghost of her just-completed orgasm, reminding her that, for her, finished did not mean spent. *Dear Lord in Heaven.* Her head fell back, though for once, the ceiling held no interest for her. Not compared to the sensations raging through her. Passion, pleasure, love, and lingering frustration pulsed with her heartbeat.

She paused, fully impaled, and allowed the moment its due. *I've never felt this complete.* Warm hands cupped her hips, urging her up, and then releasing her so she could sink back down. A frisson of tingles greeted the movement, along with the promise of another foray into ecstasy.

Of her own accord, Daphne claimed the rhythm, riding her man, just as he had suggested. His stroking fingers found their way to her breasts, lifting their heavy weight. He thumbed her nipples, stroked and rolled the tender peaks. A deep groan tore itself from her.

Banked pleasure flared to new life. Flames flickered in her belly and fanned out until heat flushed her face and a riot of clenching spasms tightened down in her, from her scalp to the arches of her feet. As pleasure peaked again, Daphne lost rhythm. Philippe cupped her hips again, driving up into her as she shuddered around him, until he too froze, poised at full engagement, and moaned.

Replete, Daphne lowered herself onto his chest. His hands came to rest on her back. His lips touched the top of her head.

"Je t'aime," he whispered. "Thank you for coming back."

"I could never leave you," she whispered, the words seeming not to come exactly from her, or at least not intentionally. Fatigue, upset and the sudden release of tension dragged her down, down into restful darkness.

Red light on the outsides of Daphne's eyelids drew her up from slumber and she opened them to a room bathed in sunset darkness. Beside her, Philippe lay awake, watching over her, his eyes touching her skin with a palpable caress.

Her heart warmed and a fluttering sensation in her belly reminded her of the love she now shared with the man she had thought she'd never have. *He loves me. He said so. He'd better after everything that has gone wrong recently.*

Daphne sighed. *What happened? I went from angry to...* this *without thought.* At the recollection, a new and more complex swirl of emotions tangled her insides. "I'm still upset with you," she said, and could hear the resignation in her voice. "I don't appreciate you keeping important secrets from me. That was wrong, Philippe. It was also bad science. Whether you intended me to be a test subject or not, you treated me like one. That will stop. From now on, I expect full disclosure of anything that affects me, our work, our personal lives. All of it. I also plan to redo every experiment you've done up to this point. You've proven yourself unprofessional. I aim to rectify that. What's at stake is too important."

She shifted her position until she could look in his eyes.

A wry expression twisted his lips. "Very well, my love. Though I doubt you'll believe half of it."

"Good Lord, there's more?" She lifted her head. "More, Philippe?"

His breath released in a pained sigh. "So much more. Please, love. Give me some time to get through this."

Daphne pursed her lips. "Time? It seems to me you've taken more than enough time as it is." She rolled over and pulled herself into a seated position, wrapping her arms around her knees.

His lips twisted and pursed.

"Making faces won't save you," she added. "You're asking me to trust you with everything. My heart. My career. My future. Even my life, unless your story about dangerous enemies was fabricated to hide the fact that you're really trying to cure yourself of this disease—"

"Non," Philippe snapped. Rolling to one side, he propped himself on his elbow. "Non, nothing like that. Who do you think infected me in the first place? I didn't do this to myself, I assure you. It was *him*." He spat the word with venom that would have put a cobra to shame.

" 'Him' who?" Daphne demanded. "Who did this to you, to us, and why? Why infect a renowned scientist with a virus? Was it to motivate you to find a cure? But, no, that doesn't make sense. Before, you said they wanted to use the disease as a weapon, so what use would a cure be? I don't—"

Philippe cut off her diatribe with a hand on her thigh. "I wasn't a scientist then. I was little more than a boy. Lie down and get comfy, my love. This is going to take a long time. I beg you, try to believe me, no matter how far-fetched the story might seem."

"This isn't instilling the greatest sense of confidence in me," Daphne said dryly.

"All right, then," Philippe said, rising from the bed, heedless of his naked body. "Let us begin with a demonstration. "You've been feeling ill, have you not?"

She frowned. "Yes, a bit. At first, I thought I might be pregnant... Oh, God!"

He turned to see her staring in horror, her hand fluttering around her bosom.

"Qu'est-ce que c'est?" he asked. "What is it?"

"Well, I'm not pregnant now, but what if I do conceive? How will the virus affect the baby? The way you and I go at one another, it could happen."

Philippe snorted, smiling grimly at a personal joke she could only guess at. "I think it is unlikely, and before you ask, no, I have no empirical evidence to prove my sterility, but... it is most unlikely I have the ability to father a child. And before you demand it, yes, I will happily provide you a sample to examine."

Her twisted half-smile concealed no more humor than his. "Probably for the best." Then she frowned as her stomach gurgled and seemed to squeeze in on itself.

"Are you feeling well, my love?" he asked, laying a hand on the softness there.

She shook her head. "This is why I thought I was pregnant. I'm slightly nauseated all the time."

Understanding dawned in his face. "Ah, I think I know why. I've created a... medicine that helps deal with the worst of the symptoms. Will you let me get you some?"

Daphne tilted her head to one side. "Sounds mysterious. Care to share the active ingredient with me?"

"No, I'd rather not," Philippe replied. "Please, just trust me for once." She scowled. "Try it, see if it helps, and then I'll tell you. I don't want you to allow negative thoughts to minimize your perception of its usefulness."

"Eye of newt, is it?" she asked dryly. "My witch of a housemate cooks up less mysterious brews than you do."

He chuckled without humor and lifted a bathrobe from the corner of the wardrobe, wrapping it around his slender body. Then he strode barefoot from the room.

Daphne settled back on the bed, studying the ceiling as though the answers to all her life's wildest questions lay in the painted plaster.

*I still feel like he's trying to obfuscate me. It seems as though a huge gulf of unknown things lurks beyond my understanding. He promises to share, and yet, he holds back, always. What on earth can be so terrible that he doesn't dare tell me?*

*I mean, I love him. My doubts and concerns did not obliterate my feelings. They only forced me to examine them more deeply, but in the end, I returned to where I started. However, now I know I have to be quite firm with him and not let him hide things from me anymore. No partial answers. No sneaky evasions.*

*I'm afraid M. Philippe Dumont is going to require a great deal of train-*
*ing before he becomes a worthy partner. Well, I've broken horses. I can*
*tame him. Guess I'm going to have to.*

The slap of skin on wood drew her attention to the open doorway,
where Philippe stood, a tumbler with two fingers of some dark, thick
liquid held in each hand. He paused and raked his eyes hungrily over
her. "You're so lovely," he murmured.

"Lovely? Probably not. What I am, Philippe, is still confused. You
owe me an explanation, and I intend to hear it now."

He frowned and approached the bed, handing her a glass. She
scooted up to rest her back against the headboard and accepted the
drink with a critical sniff. The aroma of licorice and alcohol burned
her nostrils, but beneath it, another, earthier odor lingered at the back
of her throat, as though she'd already taken that first sip.

"This is medicine?" she asked doubtfully.

He nodded. "I tested many configurations before I found one that
was tolerable. If you don't hate anise, it's not too bad. Try it. I promise
it will settle your stomach." He sipped.

Daphne copied his move, cautiously, and found drinking the
'medicine' created a similar experience to smelling it. Powerful
licorice liquor burned in her throat and set her eyes watering. Herbal
and floral notes burst on her tongue, but after she swallowed, that
earthy, mineral flavor lingered. She struggled to swallow the harsh
alcohol, but once it settled safely in her stomach, she realized it did
have a soothing effect.

"That is the strongest thing I've ever tasted," she stated, "and my
family is Cajun, so strong food and stronger drinks are in our nature."

"I know," he agreed. "I prefer the taste of a balanced red wine, but
this is medicine."

Daphne made a face and sipped again. "Okay, Philippe, I've trusted
your mysterious promises again, but now you need to give me something to go on. Tell me what's happening."

Philippe sighed deeply. His face had settled into lines of extreme
upset. He slouched against the headboard beside her and grasped her

free hand in his. Then he sipped his drink and coughed, sighed again, traced lines up and down her fingers with the tip of his thumb. All this gave Daphne the distinct impression he was stalling.

"I grew up in a small town in rural France," he said at last. "Very small and very poor. We were poorer than most, as my father grew grapes to make wine, and then drank more than he sold. We lived off whatever my mother could grow in a miserable patch of garden on the edge of town. From my childhood, all I recall is being cold, hungry and sad."

Daphne tightened her hand on his, offering a comforting squeeze. *How different my family's farm is. Even in the midst of the Depression, we had enough to eat.*

"We weren't much worse off than the others," he continued, and his frown had turn ferocious. "Especially not once the fever came. Half the population died in the first month, including my mother and baby brother. My sister succumbed next. My father, the miserable sot, survived. I suppose he had more alcohol than blood in his veins by that point."

"So, people really do die of it?" Daphne asked. *Dear God, this is what I have inside me?* She shuddered.

"Yes, more often than not," he admitted. "It happens immediately. It wasn't until the worst of the carnage had passed that I realized... someone had infected us on purpose. It was a test."

The horror of that simple statement dawned on Daphne and she bit her lip. "Are you joking?"

"I wish I were, my love," he replied, his voice catching. "Non. No joke. I will never forget the day. I had gotten the illness but recovered quickly. I was in the garden trying to find usable food among the neglected plants, when *he* came into town." The venom in Philippe's voice, harsh and angry, rang like a gong in Daphne's head.

"Who was he?" she asked, her tone timid for the first time she could recall.

"Sébastien," he spat, as though the word tasted vile on his tongue. "I don't know his last name, if he ever had one, or where he came from.

He could have been a Spaniard, an Italian or an Arab. There was no way to know. He was swarthy, and his eyes looked black as night—if night had hellfire in it. He's a monster. I knew right away I wanted nothing to do with him. After all, I was only a child. Seventeen years old. I couldn't imagine how to deal with the devil incarnate. I tried to run, but I was weak from the fever and from hunger, and he caught me easily." Philippe shuddered. A gagging sound emerged from his throat. He swallowed another mouthful of his herbaceous brew.

Again, Daphne squeezed his hand, offering a comforting link to reality.

"He took me with him, back to a miserable rotting hunk of stone. Perhaps it was once a castle, but no longer. Only a ruin. And he ruined me there." Philippe took another drink. "He inoculated me with the disease over and over, kept me more or less drugged in a state of dreamy unreality and..." his voice broke. He cleared his throat. "And since I could not resist, he made me part of his harem."

Daphne's stomach clenched. *Oh, dear God, no.* "But... but... you're..."

"Male?" Philippe laughed bitterly. "To *him*, it makes no difference. He seeks to possess whatever he finds beautiful. He cares nothing for male or female, or for the preferences of his victims. He takes what he wants, and because he has such control over his victims, he can keep them compliant, almost insensible. It was over a year before I came to my senses enough to realize what he was doing, let alone fight against it. I think, by that time, my body and the virus had come into equilibrium with one another. I became as I am now... an asymptomatic carrier. It lives in me without harming me."

Daphne nodded. "All right, that makes sense. It seems that is also what happened to me, though it didn't take as long."

He shook his head as though startled to find himself in his New Orleans row house instead of a ruined castle in Europe. "True. I had no idea that would be the case either." His expression turned contrite. "I'm so sorry, my love. I swear, on my life and hope of salvation, I never meant to infect you."

*Poor darling. He looks so unhappy.* "Hush now, my love. Hush. It's done. Let's not fuss over it anymore. We're going to find a cure somehow."

He nodded. "With you at my side, how can I fail?"

The curve of her lips felt more automatic than authentic, but she bit back harsh words about his methods thus far. *He knows. Why bring it up again? No point in nagging.* "I'm very sorry you were held prisoner and abused," she said gently.

"It was a nightmare. A nightmare. I had not even truly become a man, and then to be used in that way..." Philippe shook his head violently.

Daphne cuddled close to him. "How did you get away?"

He started and stared at her, as though wondering who she might be. "I was lucky," he said at last. "For some reason, *he* fancied himself in love with me, enough to let me regain increasing awareness. I'd been more or less insensible for... I don't even know how long.

"One day I became aware. He was... he was on top of me, and I was disgusted and ashamed. I... I hid my feelings, looked for an opportunity to get away. *He* thought I cared for him, the idiot. As though I would fall in love with a man. I'm not that way."

He ran his hand along the softness of Daphne's upper arm, the swell of her plump breast, and came to rest on her gently rounded belly. "Pretending earned me a measure of freedom to move about the castle. One day, an opportunity arose, and I took it. Ran like hell.

"Everything had changed while I was locked away. The war had wreaked havoc on the countryside, and I couldn't find my way to anything I knew. Besides, I knew *he* would look for me, and if I went home, *he* would find me.

"I decided to make my way to a totally new place and start over. A week later, I boarded a ship for America. I was able to exchange simple tasks and basic assistance for my passage. I had grown stronger in captivity, somehow, and so cleaning the ship and running errands for the wealthy passengers proved no problem."

Daphne nodded. "Wise. So, you became a scientist then?"

"Oh, oui," he agreed. "I knew there was something bad in me, something *he* put there, and I was determined to root it out, but I didn't know how. I apprenticed myself to anyone studying infectious diseases. I learned everything I could, and in time, I began to work on my own projects. I discovered the link between yellow fever and V1. I had such hopes, and then one of *his* minions found me. I was living in New York then, and I had to run again, to start over. I won't go back. I can't."

Daphne squeezed his hand reassuringly. "Of course not."

"I thought by leaving New York and coming south, maybe I could get away from *him.* So much time passed, I dared fall in love, but I knew. I knew they would find me. I planned another move, but it was too late. His right-hand demon, the head whore in his harem, found me. She killed my Geneviève and sent me running again. Running for so many years. They haven't found me yet, but I've been here too long, and soon I must run again. I won't put you at risk, Daphne. I can't bear it."

*The years of his story don't add up,* she thought, musing over the information. *It sounds like he's been on the run forever. Is it possible he's closer to forty than thirty?* The light had dimmed further, bathing the room in silver light and deep shadows, but the smooth, unlined refinement of Philippe's features contradicted her theory. *If he's forty, it's the youngest looking forty I've ever seen. Even thirty seems like a stretch. He hardly looks older than me.*

His lips twisted into a wry expression. "What do you see in my face, love? Are you looking for evidence of how a man can be corrupted against his will? Am I a disgusting pervert or a weak and spineless victim?"

"Neither of those things," she said emphatically. "I doubt any woman would think so. We understand better than men how vulnerable we all are to those with evil intentions, especially when one of them thinks they care for you. These people don't realize that love and force cannot exist in the same relationship. They turn everyone to victims, while still maintaining their 'tender feelings'. Then they dare to become hurt and angry when their coercion is rejected. You bear no blame for that, and yet, for him, it's personal."

Philippe regarded her with lowered eyebrows.

"No, think, my love. He thought you cared for him, and then you rejected him."

"He was mad to think it," Philippe snarled.

"Love, listen." Daphne rested her head on his shoulder. "We can immediately know he's mad. He kidnapped a young boy—and others by the sound of things—and thought it was acceptable to keep all of you as a harem. He even believed you cared for him. He's a lunatic. However, in his mind, he's the sane one. You rejected him. As a scorned lover, he would feel an intense desire to reclaim you."

"As well as a great deal of jealousy toward anyone I might care for," he added darkly. "My poor Geneviève. But I knew that. I knew he had set his watchdogs on my trail." He gulped and muttered a string of French curses under his breath.

"Are you sure they're still on your trail?" Daphne asked. "How long has it been?"

"Long time," he replied. "Years since they last saw me. Drink, love. The elixir will settle your stomach and ease your symptoms."

Daphne sipped the last of her beverage and set aside the cup, shuddering at its powerful alcohol burn.

"Are you sure they're still after you?" she asked. He nodded. "How do you know?"

"Still checking my facts?" he asked. "I doubt you'd believe me if I told you." He chuckled at some unshared thought and rose from the bed. "Probably we need to have something to eat. It's growing quite late."

For the first time, Daphne realized how dark the room had grown. "Oh, God. Is it night?"

Philippe lifted a pocket watch that lay on a low table beside the bed and held it up to light she belatedly noticed came from a full moon hanging overhead.

"It's almost 9:30," he announced. "Unfortunately, I have nothing to eat here. I meant to go to the market today, but... distracting things have continually gotten in the way of that plan."

*If you'd told me the truth from the beginning—or at least from the time we became lovers—we wouldn't be doing this now,* she thought, but again decided not to nag him about it.

"Get dressed, Daphne. Let's go and find ourselves some dinner."

"Shall we try Antoine's?"

He laughed. "The rare steak suited you, did it? Now I'm not surprised. Yes, let's go."

With his mysterious medicine settling her queasy belly, Daphne's hunger made itself known in a loud rumble. *I wonder what he means by that. Still, hungry is hungry, and it's easier to think with a settled stomach.* "I'm ready."

# Chapter Ten

Philippe froze, staring up in disbelief at the house. "You live here?" he whispered, sounding both appalled and horrified.

Daphne nodded. "For the last four years. Why do you ask?"

He shook himself violently. "Non, this is not good. You must not stay in this place."

"I know they say it's haunted, that the New Orleans Vampire once murdered a girl in the upstairs bedroom," she replied cheerfully, "but don't worry. That room is closed off. No one stays there."

"Non, non, you must not stay here." *She does not understand. Even now she cannot take the danger seriously.* "This place is not safe," he explained again.

"Well, I think one of my housemates is a witch," Daphne admitted, trying to keep the conversation light, "but in this city, that's not the worst thing a person could be. Her intentions are good. Oh, but I think the landlady evicted her earlier today. She wouldn't stop brewing up potions in the bedroom and holding séances in the parlor."

"Daphne." Philippe laid a hand on her arm. "Daphne, listen to me. You cannot stay here. I will not allow it. If *his* minions come for me, this is where they will start looking." He swallowed hard. "*They* will know you belong to me, and you will be defenseless against them."

Daphne opened her mouth, and then shut it again.

"I need you to come with me, my love. Stay with me!" He tugged on her arm, his skin crawling at the unwelcome sight of his former home. Daphne set her heels and refused to move. *Damnation, woman. I love your curves, but you certainly could give a rock lessons in being stationary.*

"Explain, Philippe," she urged. "Why would Sébastien's minions look for you here?"

He shook his head. *Do I dare tell her the rest? She seems willing to believe up to this point, but... the rest sound so fantastical. So ridiculous. Her rational mind will name me liar and leave her vulnerable to attack.* A phantom image of his Daphne—her beauty turned ashen in death, bruised circles under her glistening eyes—floated in his mind, and he swallowed hard against a sudden burn in his throat. "Daphne, please, listen. I will tell you the rest, I swear I will, but let us get away from this place. I cannot bear to be here." She continued to stare at him, unmoving. He cursed silently. "Terrible things happened in this place." His voice dropped to a ragged growl. "This is where Geneviève was murdered."

Daphne's jaw sagged, and her rigid stance relaxed enough to allow him to lead her away. She moved woodenly, like an automaton on a too-thin string, moments from collapsing into a heap all over the ground.

Rather than wait around for his beloved's agile mind to put the pieces together and discover facts that defied logic, Philippe hurried her down the street as quickly as he could urge her leaden legs to move. *I want to get her home before the powder keg explodes.*

She made no move to pull away as he hurried her through the darkened streets, but at last, she began to speak. "My housemates already think we're misbehaving. If I stay out all night... well, I won't lose my place there. Lois won't care, but one of my housemates is already throwing a tantrum. This will only confirm her suspicions."

"Why do you care what she thinks?" Philippe asked. "Is she your dearest friend?"

Daphne shook her head. "Jeannie won't care either, as long as we're happy together. It's Anna. Remember her? She works at the bakery near my college?"

"Ah, yes... the very curvy one." Even in the dim lighting, Daphne must have seen Philippe's eyes turn wolfish. She punched his arm.

"Yes, you lothario. Stop it. She's a proud virgin and wouldn't welcome your hungry stare."

Philippe couldn't help but smirk, though his heart wasn't in the teasing. *She's a little jealous. I like it.* "*You* welcomed it," he pointed out.

She shook her head, refusing to rise to the bait. "My concern is this. She knows a good many of my classmates and professors. If word gets out that I'm behaving improperly, it will cast a shadow over my work. I can't bear it. A man could bed every woman in town, frequent houses of ill repute; even seduce a married woman and it would have no effect on his career, but let a woman put one toe out of line, and she's done, fit only for the whorehouse." Her impassioned speech drew attention from the crowds of pedestrians clogging the French Quarter's shadowy streets.

"Better hush, love," he urged. "Tell me in private."

"Oh, no," she snapped. "You're not putting me off that easily. If I go with you now, I'll be ruined. What do you plan to do to prevent that?"

Philippe froze. Someone crashed into him from behind, nearly knocking him off balance, but he scarcely noticed. "What do you mean? What do you want me to do, Daphne?"

"For a smart man, Philippe, you do and say a remarkable number of dumb things. I want—no—I expect you to preserve my reputation. You've said several things today about your level of commitment to me. Did you mean them?" She tugged his hand to get him moving again.

Philippe inhaled through his nose. His heart seemed to freeze in his chest, and then commenced hammering. *I think I know where she's going with this. Do I dare?*

She continued speaking before he could decide what his opinion ought to be. "Did you mean it when you said you love me?"

*How can I answer with anything other than the truth?* "I never thought I would love a woman again after I lost Geneviève. She was my everything. When I met you, and you were more than I'd ever dreamed of, I knew I was in trouble."

He paused in their rush through the darkening twilight back to his row house and turned to face her, once again taking in her luscious, curvy figure, pretty, light brown hair and serious face. "You made the trouble sweeter than your friend's pralines and even harder to resist. Nothing easy will ever happen in our future, and there are still many things I have to tell you, but I can no more stop loving you than I can stop breathing. You're my world now, Daphne, and if you let me, I'll never let you go."

A streetlamp flickered to life and illuminated a blush of pleasure on her cheeks. She broke eye contact, studying his shoes for a moment, before looking up through her eyelashes. "Do you really mean that?"

Heedless of the shoving pedestrians in the public street, he lowered his lips and touched them to hers. "Every word."

A faint half-smile curved her lips. "All right then. Tonight, I'll go home with you, but tomorrow, we're getting married."

The word hit Philippe like a sledgehammer to the guts. "Married? Mon Dieu."

"Of course. What did you expect? I may not be a perfect innocent, but if we're going to be life and research partners, we're going to make it official." Her sweet expression could not conceal the stubborn set of her jaw.

"Daphne, how could I do that?" he demanded.

"I dunno, buddy," a crude voice with a harsh, northern accent cut in, "but the rest of us would like to continue on our way. Can yous move it along?"

Embarrassment set Philippe's face aflame. He grasped Daphne's hand and steered her the remaining few blocks home, quickly locking out the night and all its milling humanity. Alone at last, in the lab where everything had started, he turned again to face her. "Marriage, seriously?" he asked.

"What did you expect, Philippe? I may be willing to bend the rules a bit, but why would that make you think I tend to abandon them completely? You know what you mean to me, but you also know what my reputation means to me. I don't have to sacrifice one for the other, so I don't intend to. That is, unless there's something very important you haven't told me. Are you already married? Did you marry your Geneviève? No, wait, that doesn't make sense. If she passed... you'd still be able. What's going on?"

Philippe sighed. "Non, I never married her. She was a... lady of the evening, and I'm a man on the run. We both knew marriage was not in our future. How could we post the banns without drawing *him* straight to me? And besides, there was no time. They found me the same night I asked her to be mine. But that presents us the same problem. For one, I have not been using my real, legal name. That name is a deep secret I'd rather not advertise."

Daphne's face turned to a mask of confusion. "Philippe, the banns ceased being a common tradition ages ago. How Catholic are you, anyway? Is this something they still do in France? It's wartime, love. I meant we ought to elope. Yes, you'll have to use your real name, but only the two of us and the officiant have to know it."

He blinked. "I never thought of that. Um, it's a bit of a radical idea. May I think about it overnight?"

Daphne shook her head. "Nope. First thing in the morning, Philippe. I won't accept anything else. Then, afterwards, you can tell me the rest of this story. I think... I think I might need a drink to go with it... or five... and I don't feel like being out right now."

Amusement blended with irritation and a frank admiration of her strength of will. "It appears I have no choice," he conceded.

"None," she agreed. "So, what is your legal name anyway?"

"I doubt you'd believe me if I told you," he replied. "Not if you know as much as you seem to about this town, not to mention the history of your house."

Daphne raised one eyebrow. "It wouldn't happen to be Philippe St. Pierre, would it?"

He closed his eyes, shutting out the view of her triumphant expression. "Do you believe it?"

"Believe that a man who looks no older than thirty is actually older than my Pa? It's hard to swallow, I'll admit."

He opened his eyes, nailing her with a fierce, burning stare. "You'll have to swallow much more than that, love. My age is only one of the many things that will require a strong drink to wash it down. Are you ready to face them?"

She bit her lip, amusement fading.

"Are you certain you want to join your life to mine?"

"I think... I think it's already too late," she pointed out.

Philippe wilted. "Much too late," he agreed. "Much too late and we haven't even begun. Let us retire, Daphne, and put stories and questions to rest. If tomorrow is to be our wedding day, we should face it after a good night's sleep."

"I agree," she said softly.

A fat full moon hung low over an empty field. Level ground stretched as far as the eye could see, and the low grass that tickled Daphne's feet did little to obscure the view. She turned in a slow circle, hoping to make some sense of where she was, but no landmark appeared. A hot, dank breeze ruffled her hair, which for some reason hung long and loose down her back. She glanced down at herself and gasped to discover she was naked.

Lifting one arm, she covered her breasts while her eyes continually scanned the horizon, desperate to discover something sensible out there, something she could understand. Nothing appeared. No buildings, no landforms, not even a stunted tree.

Daphne swallowed hard, and her heart thumped heavily against her ribs. "Philippe?" she called softly.

His comforting, French-accented baritone did not reply. Instead, a strange rustling drew her attention to her left, where a humped shape rose from the ground. The grass waved on top of the lump, until it split and a bare, pale back broke free of the soil.

Daphne's fingers began to tremble as she recognized the thin, willowy shape of Mary Murphy. The redhaired girl lifted her hands to the moon and a low keening wafted back to Daphne. Other humps rose and split to reveal a second figure, and then a third. One by one the entire group who inhabited Daphne's boarding house rose from the earth, turning to one another and weeping. They seemed not to notice their naked state, or perhaps not to care. They grasped arms, as though comforting one another.

Then a low laugh emerged from nowhere. A short, dark-haired woman in a flowing white dress made her way across the field. In her hand, she clutched a sort of leash or string, but the creature on the other end did not move like a dog.

"All right, enough whining," this new arrival snapped. "It's too late for all that. You belong to me now, and you must obey. You will obey. Kneel before your master."

As one, the women fell to their knees. Daphne's own feet and legs suddenly felt weak, as though she ought to follow the directives as well. "Holy Moses," she breathed, her father's favorite curse rising easily on her tongue. A direct thought strengthened her legs against the order, and she remained standing.

"You did well," the tiny woman said to the creature on the string, "but you said there was another. Where is she?"

"I don't know," a familiar voice replied.

*Who is that? I can't place it.*

Before Daphne could puzzle it out, the strange woman jerked on the leash. The crawling creature sprawled in the dirt with a whimper. "You find her. Find her now."

Another bare female figure rose to her feet, her face turning this way and that. Abruptly, Daphne dropped to her belly in the grass. *Oh, God.*

"She's near," the familiar voice insisted. "I can smell her, can't you?"

Daphne could hear the beastly woman snarling. "What are you talking about? You make no sense, you useless bitch." Another jerk of the leash dropped the woman to the ground. She swung a foot and the sprawling woman grunted at the contact.

Horrified, Daphne began to back away quietly, trying not to rustle the grass.

The woman turned, revealing a medium-toned face with sharp features. "I know you're there," she spoke confidently into the night. "I will find you soon. You will be joining us."

Daphne continued scuttling backward. *I don't know what that is, but I have no intention of trying to fight with it.*

Her friends wept and clung, and her heart clenched at the sight of them.

"I said shut up!" the woman said, slapping out with one hand and knocking Mary to the ground. As one, the rest fell silent. "Come with me. We'll deal with your friend soon enough."

"Run, Daphne," Mary screamed. "Run far and fast and never come back. These monsters will never stop."

A kick flew in from the side, hitting Mary squarely in the belly. The woman gasped and then retched into the grass.

Daphne scuttled, crab-like, as fast as she could, but the tableau of horror before her never seemed to grow more distant.

A hand clamped down on her arm and lifted her to her feet. She screamed, and then screamed again as she found herself staring into an unknown face with caramel coloring and a broad nose. The woman lifted Daphne up from the ground, directly to her face and buried her nose in her hair. Daphne squeaked in surprise.

"I know who you belong to," she snarled. Her golden eyes lit up like tiny moons and her head shot forward, right toward Daphne's throat.

Daphne sat up with a gasp, her heart pounding so hard she wanted to vomit from it. Slowly, a room came into focus—a familiar space housing a comfortable bed on which she'd rested many times. Soft breathing drew her attention to the space beside her, where Philippe slumbered, relaxed and peaceful.

"What a strange dream," she murmured to herself, though the details had already begun fading from her mind. Comforted by the presence of the man she loved, the man who would soon be her husband, she settled back down against the pillow. Philippe shifted, laying his arm across her waist, and they settled in again.

"Do you like it?" Philippe asked, pulling a length of pale-yellow fabric set with intense turquoise ribbons out of his wardrobe.

"It's so long," Daphne blurted without thinking. Then, lest another rude comment escape, she took a sip of her coffee.

"Ah, that is true," he pointed out. "The style has changed a bit."

"And I rarely wear dresses," she added, pointing out the high-waisted trousers draped over the back of a chair.

"Love, if it is to be our wedding day, do you not want to make an exception, just this once? I mean, it is true we are eloping, but should we not still enjoy the occasion?"

Philippe's sentimentality caught her off guard, though as she pondered, she realized she'd seen other evidence of it—of his tender words spoken at just the right moment, of his frank admiration of the body she'd always found unfashionable. Even his appreciation of her intelligence warmed her at key moments. "You have a point," she conceded at last. Draining her coffee cup, she added, "Where did you get that thing though? I mean, up until last night, marriage never crossed your mind, so why do you have a dress so fancy it ought to be a costume hanging in your wardrobe?"

"I bought it for Geneviève," he replied, looking sheepish, "though she never had the chance to wear it. Though it might look fancy to you, it was only a tiny bit formal when I bought it."

*He really expects me to believe he bought a gown designed forty years ago for his late lady love? It would fit with the claim he made that he's that Philippe, the one whose lover died in my boarding house.*

"Are you ready to hear the end of my tale?" he asked. "Or would you rather hurry to the courthouse?"

"How about both?" she suggested. "I'm not going anywhere until I've washed up. We had a busy day yesterday, and I can still smell you on my skin. In the meanwhile, if you want to tell me the wild final chapter of the story you've been sharing, I'll listen."

"Will you believe?" he asked, that strange fire lighting in his eyes again.

Daphne couldn't help but sigh as she rose naked from the bed and made her way down the hall to the tastefully appointed green and white bathroom. Running water into the bathtub, she retrieved a washcloth, a bar of soap and a towel. "You might consider shaving," she pointed out to Philippe, who leaned against the door jamb, watching her with unabashed fascination.

"I might consider it," he agreed, stepping up to the sink.

She giggled. "Okay, get with it, mister. Are you really sixty years old? Also, what's with that story about the house? The way I heard it, it wasn't very flattering for you." The tub reached optimal fullness, so she sank into the hot water with a sigh.

His teasing grin faded. "Far from flattering," he agreed, "but also far from accurate. I already told you what happened. If you think about it, you should remember."

"One of Sébastien's minions, was it?" she realized.

Philippe nodded. "Her name is Ragonde, and she hails from somewhere in the Louisiana swamp, from a village of mixed-race people hiding from normal society. I have no idea when *he* found her, or how, but she rose to be his second-in-command. Despite being petite, her strength is considerable. One of the side effects of V1 is unnatural strength."

Daphne regarded her soft figure. "Not likely," she responded.

"You haven't tried yet," he informed her, "but at any rate, the way you and I have it, it seems to work differently."

"Why do you think that is?" She rinsed a slick of soap from her skin and turned her attention to sponging herself off below the neck.

"You really do want the entire wild story, do you?" Philippe shook his head. "I'll tell you, though it will strain your credibility to the breaking point."

"I'll listen though," she promised, "and not make comments or laugh. Just get it out, Philippe. I need to know what you believe."

His lips twisted at her telling phrasing. "All right. To begin with, you keep mentioning my age, as though I were a young man when I took Geneviève out of the *bordel* in 1903. In fact, that is not the case. I had already lived several lifetimes by then."

Daphne choked on a lungful of air, turning her gasp into a graceless cough. "I beg your pardon?" she demanded in a hoarse wheeze. "How old are you then?"

He laughed without humor. "I was unfortunate enough to be in Paris to witness the execution of Marie Antoinette. Disgusting." He shuddered. "I was even captured in a painting of the event. That was about six months before *he* found me."

Daphne could find nothing to say, for the simple reason that her lungs had completely seized.

"Before, when I lived in this city, they called me an immortal, which unfortunately is rather close to the truth. I have no doubt one of *his* ilk could put an end to my miserable existence, but thus far they have not done so. This is why I say, since you survived your initial inoculation with V1, you will be fine, and you will remain so for a long, long time. I haven't had as much as a runny nose since the late 1700s."

"So then," she mused through numb and tingling lips, "the war you spoke of that changed your life was not World War I?"

He laughed bitterly. "Not even remotely. Let me give you a hint. That campaign of conquest was led by a man named Bonaparte. Though Sébastien funded him generously and even provided him with an advisor."

Bath water splashed as Daphne shook herself.

"I think he was attempting a hostile takeover of leadership, because his predecessors funded the Reign of Terror."

"Leadership of what?" Daphne croaked. "What is this group any-way?" She rose on shaky legs and reached for a towel, but her trembling fingers refused to close over the textured fabric. He set his razor on the edge of the sink and retrieved it for her, offering a hand to help her out of the tub.

"I'd better not say unless you're sitting down," he commented wryly. "You look like you're about to fall over."

She nodded, not really understanding the suggestion, but did manage to stagger back to the bedroom and sink onto the mattress. Philippe approached closely behind her and appropriated her towel to wipe the vestiges of shaving cream from his cheeks.

"What are they?" she demanded, not waiting for him to start on his own. "Dear God, what are *we?*"

"*They,*" he enunciated patiently, "are vampires. You see, when some-one is infected with V1 at the moment of death, they rise, and the virus becomes their life force. The person is gone and only the disease re-mains. It is a most curious infection, the only intelligent virus I've ever known. We, however, are no such thing. We are not the undead. Somehow, the V1 virus comes into a state of equilibrium with our body systems, enhancing our strength, our immunities, and our lifes-pan, but not interfering much with our day-to-day function, except that it allows us to sense other carriers of the virus, especially those of the same line. You will probably be able to recognize immediately if someone comes from *him.*"

Daphne could find not a single word to say. Her mind had gone completely blank, and in that empty place, she slowly became aware of a resonating vibration that seemed to emanate from every part of her body, and a matching pulse that reached out from Philippe and intertwined with hers.

"Is this the reason," she blurted gracelessly, "that I can't keep my hands off you, even when I'm furious with you?" *Stupid,* her rational mind sneered. *This wild tale comes straight from a dime novel. There's no truth in it.* And yet, the unmistakable pulsing from her core danced and tangled with his, fusing them into a single being.

"I believe so," he agreed, deep thought turning his expression to a considering frown. "It fits all the facts, though I have no other evidence to prove it."

"So, we're stuck together. Humph."

Philippe laughed, the first true, deep laugh he'd uttered in the longest time. "You're the one who wants to get married, Daphne."

"I... um... well," she spluttered, and then rolled her eyes upward to regard a scene painted on the plaster ceiling. A giggle rose up in her belly. She tried like anything to suppress it. *Come on, girl. Deadly diseases? Vampire consortiums? Political intrigue? Either you're in love with a lunatic or the whole world is about to fall on your head. It's no laughing matter.* But she couldn't hold it back. The giggle forced its way out of her mouth, followed by another, and then another. Philippe sank down beside her and took her in his arms. They clung weakly to each other as they wheezed and chortled hysterically.

"Dear Lord," she finally choked out. "Here I thought I was signing up for some epidemiology research. I'm in so far over my head I can scarcely take it in."

"Do you believe me?" Philippe wiped his streaming eyes.

"I'm trying to," she admitted, pressing her trembling lips together. "You can't blame me for finding that challenging."

"Nor do I," he concurred. "If you're trying, I can't ask for more, except for this: be very careful, Daphne. It's hard to say where you're in more danger, here with me or out there in the city."

"I agree," she said. "I don't want to become a victim of dark powers, especially not if one of them has some kind of false claim on you and sees me as a rival. Um... do I want to know what was in the drink?"

"Probably not," he admitted. "May vampire legends are just that; legends. However, some parts are true."

She shuddered. "Is that why the elixir tastes so strong? To cover up a tell-tale ingredient?"

He nodded.

Daphne frowned. "Okay, let's get this done, Philippe, shall we?"

"You still want to marry me, even after hearing such wild tales?" He regarded her with raised eyebrows.

She smiled. "Who else will take care of you if I don't? Besides, however long it might take me to accept vampires, immortals, and centuries, you and I both carry a virus the world knows nothing about. We have to work together to cure it, for our own sakes. You need me to keep your research honest, but that means you need my reputation to remain intact. This is the best way to ensure we're able to meet our research goals."

"Practical Daphne." He sighed. "I suppose it's the best I can hope for at this point. Up, love, and let's get ready."

Daphne bounced to her feet, pleased to discover her legs no longer trembled. "Ready, Philippe?" she demanded. "I've been trying not to imagine this day for months, but I never succeeded. This is my dream come true. I'm more than ready."

"Well, almost," he refuted, waving at her naked body. "You look lovely, but it's a bit much for public, even in New Orleans."

Daphne giggled and reached for the dress. *Jeannie would throw a fit if she found out I was getting married in a dress meant for someone else, but it doesn't bother me. I have more to worry about.* She pulled on her undergarments. "Is this meant to go with a corset? Because if so, you're out of luck. I can barely abide a girdle, which is one reason I wear trousers so often."

"I love a woman's curves," Philippe replied. "It was designed to fit a more natural shape, and I can't tell you how difficult that was to accomplish."

Daphne stepped into the dress and tugged it up around her body. Philippe stepped behind her and fastened the butter-colored fabric around her back. It fit perfectly. *Goodness, he truly does prefer a curvy woman to a thin one.* She couldn't stop a satisfied grin from creasing her lips. *Ah well. Life is interesting, isn't it? Either my lover is crazy, or dangerous undead creatures are after him, and by extension, me, but today is my wedding day, and regardless of the circumstances, Philippe loves me and also truly admires my appearance. That at least is worth a smile. It's still easy to do... in broad daylight.*

Philippe circled around her and looked her over from head to toe. "What's left for you to do?"

"Style my hair," she replied. "You should get dressed though."

"I will do that," he concurred.

Daphne's smile broadened. *I'm getting married. Happy day.*

# Chapter Eleven

Daphne rose from the bed and stretched. *Weddings don't take long, not even if you throw in a fancy brunch. Thank goodness it's Saturday. Only a few weeks left until my last round of finals. I can't let all this distract me from my original goal, especially not when I'm so close to the end.*

She turned to regard her husband. He lay sound asleep on one side, his hand resting on the mattress.

*Still, I'm glad to be married. Philippe and I should get along just fine. I've always thought we would, with so many interests in common.*

She reached for her underwear and grimaced. *No matter how often I rinse these out, it's not the same as doing a proper laundry. I need more clean clothes. One pair of trousers, one blouse and Philippe's hand me down dress aren't going to keep forever.*

She pondered what she ought to do. *I know he doesn't want me going back to the boarding house, but I wouldn't stay long. An hour at most.* She glanced at the window. *Still at least that long until sunset, if I hurry.* Decision made, she tugged on her everyday garments and tucked her hair into a simple bun. *Bet it looks like a bird's nest after such a busy afternoon.*

She crept from the bedroom, not wanting to disturb her husband, and made her way to the lab. A stack of blank sheets of paper waited in a drawer and she scrawled him a brief note. *Gone to get my clothes and let Lois know I'm moving out. Back in an hour. Love you. Daphne.*

Satisfied all would be well once she had access to the rest of her garments and possessions, and thankful she'd been too busy over the years to amass more than what would fit in two suitcases, she made her way out into the heat of a late spring afternoon. The bright sun stung her eyes and immediately brought beads of sweat to her forehead and the back of her neck. *Summer's going to be beastly this year. I can tell already, and it's only May.*

*I'll have to take Philippe home to visit my parents. At least there's open land for the wind to blow, and the proximity to the Gulf provides a few ocean breezes to regulate the temperature.* She thought of her stoic, hardworking parents meeting her dreamy, romantic French husband and grinned. *They won't have a clue what to make of each other. What a hoot.*

*I can't wait to introduce him to Donny. I'm not even sure they speak the same language.* She pondered the alignment of her brother's slang-heavy dialogue and Philippe's careful, accented precision and an indelicate snort tried to claw its way up from her belly and out her nose. She squashed it down, but having been struck by the absurdity, she couldn't release it, and the urge to giggle grew until her shoulders shook.

*I'm going to look like an idiot if I walk along laughing at nothing. I'm not loony, so I'd better think of something else, quick.* She cast about in her mind for a topic with which to occupy herself, and, unsurprisingly, hit upon her husband's bizarre tale of viruses and vampires. *I don't think he's lying,* she admitted to herself. *He seems so sincere. Plus, Philippe is such an open book. Whenever he tried to conceal something from me, I sensed it, but when he laid out this wild account—Marie Antoinette no less—he seemed completely sincere. What does that mean?*

The warm sun beat down on her shoulders and slanted into her eyes, making her squint. Movement beside her drew her attention to an alley, where a ragged young man with a five-day scruff of scraggly beard, withdrew into the shadows and peered at her with red eyes. *Looks like a dope fiend. Poor man. Maybe when we finish with yellow fever—and V1, which clearly exists despite Philippe's less than stellar research techniques—we can work on cures for drug addiction.*

The thought spurred a new idea in her mind. *I hear there are drugs that cause hallucinations. That might explain what happened to Philippe.*

*Maybe he* was *kidnapped. If the Nazis or their collaborators took his town in about 1940, and he was taken prisoner, that would fit. Though not the claim he was only nineteen at the time. He's not old, but he's got to be a bit older than me...*

*Of course, this might have happened before the war. Strange things began in Europe before the outright fighting broke out, what with the Depression and all.* The timeline tangled itself into a Gordian knot and she put it aside.

*If someone did enter the town and test out an experimental disease weapon in anticipation of conflict, maybe they did take a young man hostage. And if they were testing diseases as instruments of destruction, maybe they also tried drugs. Maybe they gave him something that altered his perceptions and caused hallucinations. Maybe he really did see Marie Antoinette—and vampires—in some sort of drugged dream.*

The explanation made perfect sense to her. *That would explain his shoddy techniques in the lab. He didn't learn from legitimate scientists, but from war profiteers. They care little for the publishability of their results.*

Soothed by her discovery of an explanation that exonerated Philippe while still dismissing his account, she grinned as she unlocked the door to her former abode.

The grin turned grim. *What a vile abuse to visit on someone. Drugged and assaulted. My poor husband.* She shuddered. *I'll have to apply a particular study to helping him recover from these outrageous abuses. No one, man or woman, should have to live with such memories.*

She mounted the stairs and one last thought occurred to her. *I wonder if anyone is actually after him, or if his paranoia is a side effect of whatever substance caused the hallucinations in the first place. That might actually fit.*

Relieved, she pushed open the door to her bedroom, wondering if she'd fine Jeannie there, resting up for a week of exercise and lessons. An empty room greeted her. Her own bed lay in disarray, just as she'd left it, and guilt sizzled when she realized she was leaving dirty sheets for Lois to deal with. *Maybe I should pay her a little extra, since I'm leaving without warning. It might take time to find a new tenant.*

Daphne proceeded to one of a pair of slender wardrobes that stood along the wall and opened its doors, revealing her life's possessions. Pulling out two carpet bags, she stuffed in her trousers and skirts, blouses, stockings, and undergarments.

As she completed her task, a strange sense of wrongness began to churn in Daphne's belly. *I suppose I need some more of Philippe's V1 elixir.*

Gradually, it dawned on her that, in addition to her queasy stomach, something felt... wrong. *What is it? What's bothering me?*

Pausing in her task, she turned and scanned the familiar bedroom with careful scrutiny. *My bed, just the way I left it. Nothing there.*

She turned to Jeannie's bed, and the sense of wrongness buzzed in her head until she nearly retched. "The bed isn't made. Dear God."

As long as she'd known her roommate—over two years—never once had Jeannie left the room without making the bed. *Even when she washes the sheets, she still pulls the covers up over the pillows. Says her mama insisted on it. 'Be tidy when you can.' She always was.*

Drawing closer, she bit her lip at the sight of a strange, brownish stain in the vicinity of the pillow. "What is that?" she breathed. Her fingers trailed over the stain. It felt stiff. *It's blood. It has to be. Could Jeannie have had a messy woman's time?*

She regarded the placement and knew her desperate hope held no truth. *It's by the pillow, dunce. Around her neck or face, and there's a lot of it. She was seriously injured. If it were a man's bed, I'd say a deep shaving cut, but Jeannie doesn't shave her face. Could someone have hit her? It's possible, but such a blow might have killed her. This is bad. This is very bad.*

Heart pounding, Daphne backed away from the soiled bed, grabbed her suitcases and hurried from the room. *Maybe Lois will know what happened. I've been gone more than a full day. If Jeannie was... hurt, she must have had her taken to the hospital. She can tell me what happened.* Reaching the main floor, Daphne slowed her mad rush to a tiptoe. *Something bad happened in this house. It must have. I can't imagine what it was, but something still feels wrong. More wrong than ever. What is it? What's going on? What's happening?* Frustrated with her inability to put concrete information together with her vague distress, Daphne opted for caution. She moved as lightly as she could, given her generous size and the noisy soles of her boots. With every step, she felt her heartbeat increase, until her ribs ached, and her silent breaths rasped her throat in lieu of nervous whimpers. She twisted the knob of the parlor door and eased it open.

The hinges shrieked, and Daphne exhaled in a whine. "Hush, hush," she urged. "No noise. Not until I know..." *Know I'm safe.* Inside the parlor, the furniture she'd used for years lay in disarray, pillows torn apart and strewn across the floor, upholstery shredded. The table lay overturned, the telephone yanked from the wall. Shattered plaster had fallen like snow on the wooden planks of the floor. *Dear God, what happened here? Philippe was right. I should never have come. I have to leave, now!* She withdrew her head from the room and turned toward the door. The last light of sunset shone through the window in it, casting blood-red light to spill and pool on the floor. *Out. Out into the busy street, away from here. Hurry. Hurry.*

She tried harder than ever to walk quietly. *Something horrible happened here. Who knows when or what? Whoever did this might still be here. They might come back. I have to get out. I have to.* She crept toward the door. Across the hall, the only downstairs bedroom lay between her and the exit, its door slightly ajar.

"Where is she?" a voice hissed. Daphne froze.

"I told you I don't know," Lois answered. "What difference does it make? You have all the others. You should be well fed. In fact, I've never seen you so greedy. What's going on?"

"I heard a rumor." Daphne noticed the unfamiliar voice had an accent. *Sounds Cajun, yet not.*

"Rumor?" Lois scoffed. "This city is rife with rumors. You know that. What do you think you heard, and more importantly, why did you listen to it?"

A resounding slap greeted the sassy reply. "Silence, slave," the voice snarled. Daphne took another step toward the door. Both voices fell silent.

"What was that?" the strange woman demanded.

"Nothing," Lois replied quickly. "It's an old house. It makes its own clunks and clanks."

*I can't get out this way, past them. I'll have to go through the garden.* She began to edge down the hallway in the opposite direction.

"I heard," the woman continued, apparently believing Lois's prevarication, "that Philippe St. Pierre has returned to the city and has been doing 'scientific research', flaunting his presence for all to see." Her voice turned to a nasty sneer.

*Oh, Lord. She's talking about Philippe, and she called him by that name. What can it mean? Who is she and why is she hunting my husband?*

"He wouldn't dare," Lois scoffed. "As if he'd be stupid enough to return to the place where his mistress died, where all the dark forces hunt him through the night. He's probably fled back to Europe, or even Africa. Anywhere to be away from you."

"From us, you mean," the sly voice drawled. "Make no mistake, my dear. You're one of us. You can't escape it. Without what I give you, you'd have aged and died decades ago."

"I'm thankful for your gift," Lois said. "You know that. You know how faithfully I've provided you with blood all these years. You've never had to hunt or go hungry since I moved in."

The strange woman laughed. "The perfect slave, panting to do my bidding. If people knew... you'd be burned at the stake. There's enough old-world superstition in this town to light the match."

"Ragonde, Master, please," Lois whined, and the childish, wheedling tone stopped Daphne's desperate tiptoe toward the back of the house.

*Wow. She always sounded so confident, so in control. What's happening? Has the entire world turned topsy-turvy?*

"Silence." Another slap rang off the polished wainscoting in the hallway, reverberating Daphne's eardrums in counterpoint to her hammering heartbeat. "I have a task for you, wench. Sooner or later she will certainly come back for her possessions. When she does, you must keep her here. Do not let her leave. She will lead me right to Philippe and I can deal with him once and for all." She chuckled, low and ominous. Daphne closed her hand around the door into the kitchen and turned it, stepping through and shutting it behind her. *Take that, bitch,* she thought, triumphant. *I have my possessions and I'm gone. You won't use me to catch my husband...This woman must have been involved in kidnapping, drugging, and infecting him. I still don't understand, but I...* her rambling thoughts cut off in a violent squeak. On the floor of the once-immaculate kitchen lay a sight that for several moments, Daphne could not fully comprehend. Colorful shapes surrounded the table and completely blocked the path to the outside. *It looks like someone has set dresses out all over the place... with shoes.*

Daphne gulped and stepped forward. *There's only one way out, and I have to hurry. Lois and that woman—what was her name? —they might head this way at any moment. Something odd is happening in this house, and I don't want to end up in the middle of it.*

Closer to the dresses and boots, she could no longer deny the shape of legs within. To either side of the wooden table set in the center of the room, where she'd eaten her meals for so many years, drunk so many cups of tea, two female forms lay side by side, taking up all the available floor space. *I really do not want to step over this, but what choice do I have?*

Gingerly, Daphne planted her shoe in the void between two thighs and stepped forward. Now she could see, though she tried not to look, the back of a head covered in messy brown hair. She clamped her teeth down on her lip to prevent herself from whimpering. *Must get out. I can grieve for Jeannie later. And for Mary,* she realized, staring at the flame of bright red on the larger figure to her right, closest to the counter. Identifying a gap where Jeannie's sprawled arm had fallen away from her body, Daphne worked her foot in to take another step forward. *All right. Halfway there. Now what? And don't dead hands look disgusting? Blue and stiff, like the cadaver in the lab.* She shuddered. *I definitely prefer epidemiology to medicine.* The tiny space under Jeannie's chin didn't look large enough for Daphne's foot. *I really ought not step on them if I can avoid it. Clearly, they're deceased, but...*

Mary's longer neck provided an opportunity Daphne couldn't help but take. She carefully stepped into the space, muttering a nearly silent apology as her shoe brushed the woman's cheek.

*One more step and I'm done.* She shook her head, realizing there was no choice but to plant her foot on one or the other woman's hair, as both chignons had been completely destroyed. On the other side of the table, two blonds had been laid out, and Daphne could recognize Anna's bulky frame. *Poor darling, she deserved better than this.*

*How did we all end up living with a killer and never know it?* April sprawled beside Anna, and an involuntary squeak escaped Daphne when she saw her friend's face in its full horror. No longer lovely and filled with ditzy animation, April's pretty, tanned skin had turned blue with lividity. Her smiling lips sneered, rigor pulling them back to reveal her teeth. Her eyes, covered in a ghastly film, stared blank and... undeniably dead.

*I'm so sorry, my friends,* Daphne thought, choking down a sob. With great care, she placed her foot on her best friend's scattered brown hair, eager to make a mad dash for the door and the freedom of outside.

Something yanked her backwards and she yipped in surprise, whipping her head around. Then a true scream tore itself from her mouth. Mary sat upright on the floor beside her, no less dead, her pale skin purple and bruised, a livid wound marring her neck. She twisted stiff lips into a parody of a smile. She clutched Daphne's trousers in her swollen, purple fingers. "Daphne. Welcome." Then the redhead frowned. She seemed to struggle to force out the words, "I told you this place was dangerous. You shouldn't have come here."

"Let me go," Daphne begged. "I have to get out of here."

"I can't." Mary sighed, and the rank stench of decomposition threatened to upend Daphne's stomach.

Movement in her peripheral vision drew her horrified gaze to Anna, who levered her hefty body upright. "Nasty bitch is going to get what she deserves." Then she shook her head. "Why did I say that? I can't remember. It's fading."

"We're all fading, idiot," Mary said, and again it seemed as though she had to fight to speak. "It's no use. No use." She whimpered. "Soon we'll be gone, and our bodies will belong to *them.*"

April also levered herself upright, examining her discolored hands. "This looks wrong. Will we always look like this?"

"Patience, ladies," a familiar voice spoke into the room, from the vicinity of the outside door. "You'll regain your beauty soon, and you won't believe how good you feel afterwards, now and forever. You're transformed."

"Phy...Phy... Damn, why can't I remember?" Jeannie gripped her hair and yanked, sending Daphne sprawling on the floor. She rose to her feet with the same graceful athleticism she'd always had in life. "I know you. I almost do. Why can't I remember?"

"You're a newborn. Give yourself time. Soon you'll know everything. You'll relearn everything." Phyllis turned to Daphne, who gawked to see the pretty cocktail waitress with the gleaming strawberry hair smile cruelly. "Welcome, Daphne. Good of you to join us. But what rudeness is this? Are those travel bags hanging on your arms? You mustn't run away. Not when the feast is about to begin. Ladies, don't let her go."

Hands clamped down on Daphne's ankles. She kicked out, but the stiff fingers held her fast, with a strength neither Jeannie nor Mary had possessed in life. She could feel bruises forming around her ankle bones.

"Now then, Miss Daphne, just where did you think you were going in such a hurry?" Phyllis demanded.

Daphne ignored her. "Let me go," she begged her friends. "I have to get out of here."

"I can't," Mary wailed. "I want to, but my hands won't obey. What's happening?"

"It's all slipping away. Slipping away!" Jeannie intoned. She burst into noisy tears, but her hands refused to let loose of Daphne's ankle.

"Soon we will be no more," Anna said solemnly.

"You are all far too dramatic," Phyllis informed them. "You're not dying. Not anymore. You've risen to a new life, a new future. It's a blessing. You don't look grateful."

"They need time to adjust," that accented voice Daphne was quickly learning to hate spoke into the room. "You were just as bad when you awakened, but no matter. By the time I present this new cadre to the master, all of them will be ready. You'll take your places in the harem with pride."

Anna choked and began to sob.

"Such a beautiful assortment. Surely the master will be pleased."

Though she in no way slowed her frantic struggles to free herself, Daphne dared a peek at the unknown enemy who had brought all this death and destruction on her home. A tiny and caramel-skinned woman, her sculpted cheekbones revealing a heritage that appeared to blend Native, African, and European in unknown proportions, stood in a scarlet skirt and gleaming white blouse. Beside her, Lois shifted her weight from foot to foot. For some reason, the hostess and second mother they'd all come to love looked hollow and sad as she regarded her five tenants. She met Daphne's eyes for a brief second before skating away in guilt.

"Ah, yes. The infamous Daphne. Glad you could join us."

Daphne whimpered and kicked out harder against her friends.

"Get behind her," the woman barked.

Anna and April groaned and hoisted themselves to their feet, taking flanking positions between Daphne and the door. Phyllis had left it open, and a tantalizing view of the courtyard and beyond it, the gate to freedom teased Daphne. *I'll never make it. Damn. Philippe was right. My poor darling. He'll never recover.*

"Release her."

The hands gripping Daphne's ankles let loose, and she sprang to her feet, the bags falling from her arms, ready to risk everything for the chance to flee. It wasn't to be. A fist grabbed her arm and spun her around.

"I am Ragonde," the woman intoned. Though tiny, her grip on Daphne's arm threatened to tear fabric and flesh. "First general in command of an army you cannot possibly imagine."

"Vampires," Daphne spat, at last accepting the inevitable conclusion. *I owe Philippe an apology.* The pointless, chattering thought nearly caused her finally to break down into hysteria.

"You might say so."

"I might also say you're a corpse inhabited by a disease," Daphne added, trying for bravado.

"You would also be correct about that," Ragonde agreed, "but what a glorious infection. Immorality, eternal beauty, and inhuman strength. You are blessed to join our ranks."

Daphne spat bitterly on the floor. "You're little more than a talking insect. I will find a way to eradicate you, if it's the last thing I do."

Ragonde laughed. Then she surged forward and clamped her teeth on Daphne's wrist.

Dull pain turned sharp as the full complement of the woman's teeth compressed and then punctured her skin. Daphne yelped and struggled. *I thought vampires had fangs.* A dry, rough tongue swiped across the wound, and then came the suction. *Dear God.* A warm, tingling sensation flared in the bite and spread upward, along Daphne's arm. It reached her shoulder and radiated outward, up the side of her neck, across her chest and down her torso. Her breasts and genitals began to throb in euphoria. Then the spreading toxin reached her brain. She cried out, and darkness closed in on her.

# Chapter Twelve

Daphne woke slowly. Bright light filtered through her closed eyelids, drawing her gently up from a dream, but at the same time calling attention to the throbbing pain in her head. The churning in her stomach had greatly increased in the short amount of time she'd been out. *Was it short? I hope so. Am I dead? Like the others?* Quickly, she tested her memory. *My name is Daphne Delaney. I'm twenty-five years old. I grew up on a farm in southern Louisiana and I just married my research partner, Philippe Dumont... Philippe St. Pierre, apparently. Nothing feels like it's fading. Good.* Cautiously, she opened one eye a slit and realized the light she saw came not from the late afternoon sun, but from a full moon beaming bright through the window. Its brilliance blinded her, and she quickly closed her eye again. *Wow, I've never had that reaction to the moon before.*

"Aren't you going to turn her too?" Lois demanded, and Daphne had to fight not to stiffen at the sound of the voice. *Damn, I had so hoped to wake up and discover it was all a nightmare.*

"I cannot," Ragonde replied. "If I turn her, she will forget. I need her alive and under my power in order to use her to find the master's prize."

"Ah." Shuffling noises seemed to suggest the landlady puttering around the room. "And when she wakes..."

"I will send her to him. She will do whatever I say. She will not be able to resist. You know quite well how compulsion works."

Lois made a snorting sound.

"The master pioneered this technique long ago, and as far as I know, he's the only one who knows how to do it. Since he took power over North America sixty years ago, he's gone unchallenged, which is unheard of. This is why. No one else controls the living. Unlike the dead, who gradually gain sentience until they only stay by loyalty, no human slave in the harem has ever walked away. No one but Philippe St. Pierre. The master will not rest until he regains his recalcitrant lover and finds out what went wrong with the enslavement."

"Odd he doesn't come himself," Lois commented. "I mean, his bond, through you, to Philippe isn't very powerful, is it? The boy keeps one step ahead of you."

"Idiot." Daphne couldn't help but shudder at the sound of the slap. Lois grunted. "The vampire king, the most dangerous undead for miles around, who controls business owners, puts presidents in their place? The leaders of men bow before his power. He has no time to hunt down one paltry human slave, no matter his personal feelings. Besides, the vampire hierarchy is a power-hungry place. If the master leaves, he will certainly have to fight for his throne upon his return. No, I will find Philippe and bring him back, and I will finally receive my master's favor. In the meanwhile, these girls will be lovely additions to the harem. Take them on the next train and present them to the master."

"You want me to go?" Lois breathed. "But my house... my business... who will collect more girls to keep you satisfied? If I go to the master, won't he... turn me?"

"He might," Ragonde replied nonchalantly. "He might also enslave you so deep you never see the light of day again. "I think you would enjoy that, you pervert, but even if you wouldn't think so now, once it's done, you'll never know the difference." Ragonde laughed. "Now," she continued in a low, serious tone, "get those girls to the train, immediately. I will be along shortly."

"Very well," Lois grumped.

"Oh, and, ma fleur," the woman added, more Cajun bleeding into her accent, "don't think of denying me. I compel you."

"Oh, please don't," Lois begged, but already Daphne could hear her shoes clumping on the floor as she dragged herself to the door and exited the room.

"Now then," Ragonde said, "you can stop pretending to be asleep, Ms. Delaney. I knew you were awake the second it happened. I can hear your heartbeat, can smell your fear."

Daphne opened her eyes. Again, the moonlight stung them. "Argh." She covered them with her hands.

"Hurts at first, doesn't it?" she demanded. "You'll adjust soon enough to your heightened senses. In the meanwhile, tell me everything you know about Philippe St. Pierre."

"Don't know anyone by that name," Daphne muttered.

"Liar." Ragonde's slight form pounced onto the bed, and a moment later Daphne's hands were yanked away from her face and pinned to the mattress. Ragonde's blade-sharp nose touched hers. "His scent is all over you. He's had you. I know he has. Tell me where to find him."

"No, I don't think I will," Daphne replied, forcing herself to speak in a casual, defiant tone. "I meant that I don't know anyone by that name, but if you think I'd give a nasty, diseased monster like you help finding my worst enemy, you're out of your mind. I think the virus has finally eaten your brain."

The blow didn't surprise Daphne. She'd been rather expecting it. However, the force the tiny woman could muster shocked Daphne to her core. Her head flopped to the side with such violence, a loud cracking sound emerged. *Ouch. I'm lucky my toes still move. Mustn't bait the beast.*

"You tell me now," Ragonde ordered, a droplet of saliva falling onto Daphne's lip. "I compel you."

Daphne could feel the compulsion. The urge to return to the lab, to Philippe, rose up, hollow and sad as a memory of the long-departed dead. As she pondered the sensation, it faded. "No," she said softly.

Ragonde's blacker than black eyes bored into hers. "How can this be?" she snarled. "How can you resist? I exposed you, infected you. You should be in my power."

"I'm a scientist," Daphne explained. "Maybe I've developed an immunity from working with the samples."

Confusion clouded Ragonde's face but rage quickly supplanted it. Without a word, she drove a fist into Daphne's nose. This time, the crunching sounded even more ominous, moments before agony drove her heels into the mattress. Blood flowed down her throat and she gagged.

"You will cooperate."

Though it hurt like hell to move her face, with her broken nose, she slowly shook her head. *Now she'll kill me, and with Philippe's virus and hers inside me, I suppose I'll rise, brainless and docile, but at least Philippe will be safe.*

This time, the fist compressed her stomach. Daphne gasped, her wind knocked completely out of her. As the pain bloomed, it brought the lingering nausea to full life. She turned her aching head to the side and vomited a mixture of blood and the luxurious meal with which she and Philippe had celebrated their marriage.

Ragonde sprang back. "Disgusting whore. Well, never mind. I'll leave you to think about it for a while and try again. Don't jump off the balcony."

She hurried to the door and pulled it shut behind her. Daphne could hear the key turning in the lock.

Philippe woke, teased from sleep by the gentle early-summer sunshine beaming through his window. He felt wonderfully relaxed, as though the tension of his recent years had finally eased.

*We'll need to move on soon,* he reminded himself. *You're far from a free man, but with Daphne along, everything seems better.* A twinge of guilt accompanied the thought.

*She had her whole future planned. Working her way into the scientific community. Showing them all what a girl can do. Forcing them to accept her. She's a far better scientist than I am. She knows things I've never imagined. I'm taking her away from all that.*

*Instead of a life among the elite researchers of the Deep South, it will be a life on the run. I'll likely never be free of Sébastien, of the fear he might be creeping up behind me. We will never be able to stay in one place long enough for her to gain a reputation, nor would we dare to try. That very goal will be our undoing. Is this right of me? Is it right to displace her entire future for the sake of our love?*

"She chose this," he reminded himself aloud. "She invited me to her bed, and she insisted we marry. She wants to be with me."

*Ah, but she didn't believe you,* the sly voice of his conscience reminded him. *She's probably even now concocting some mental gyration that exonerates you of outright lying while still dismissing your story.*

He frowned, knowing it was true.

Shaking his head, Philippe stretched out, finding the empty bed beside him. *Probably down in the lab,* he thought. *My...* a grin spread across his face. *My bride loves her work.* Despite the twinges of guilt produced by his thoughts, he couldn't help but appreciate the warm glow of pleasure ignited by naming her his. *My wife. My bride. My lady. For all time... and that's a long, long time.*

Rising from the bed, he pulled on a pair of trousers and a loose white shirt that reminded him of the long-ago past. Barefoot, he meandered from the room and down the hall to the stairs. An uncomfortable sensation in the pit of his stomach reminded him it had been too long since his last dose of the elixir. *Daphne is less used to supporting the virus. She probably needs it even more than I do.*

Stopping at the state-of-the-art mint green refrigerator he'd purchased to replace the aging icebox with which the row house had been equipped, he manipulated the handle and withdrew a bottle of dark-red liquid, which he poured into two small tumblers. Sipping the first, and grimacing at the bloody aftertaste, he padded out into the front parlor.

Daphne wasn't there.

Philippe frowned. "Daphne," he called, his voice pitched loudly so it would echo through the house.

Nothing.

"What in the world is that woman doing?" he asked himself aloud, taking another swig of his unpleasant brew.

Then his eyes fell on a sheet of white paper lying on the workbench in Daphne's habitual spot. "Ah, a note. Maybe she went out to buy some breakfast. Let's see what the lady has to say."

He approached, setting both tumblers on the bench, and grabbed the page. Reading, his stomach seemed to drop to his feet. "Mon Dieu. She's mad." He gulped. "When was this written?"

He touched the ink and found it dry. *She didn't just write this. It's been a while, but I have no idea how long.* He shook his head. *Now, what do I do?*

He sank onto her stool. "I should go to her. Make sure she's safe."

*She'll probably laugh at you if you do.* The thought deepened his frown.

"And what if she does? She has no idea of the danger. Ragonde has almost caught up with me many times. She knows that house. She's been in it. Killed in it." He swallowed hard.

*You have no indication Ragonde is here.* He reached out for the faint connection he'd once felt with the woman. Nothing. *I haven't felt her in ages. Maybe she's off my trail.*

"Or maybe the virus in me has changed enough I can no longer feel the connection with Sébastien or any of his minions. Certainly, it's been a long time since they got close."

For the first time, he intentionally reached out, using the otherworldly senses his virus supplied, and tried to feel a connection to someone, anyone.

Sébastien's oily confidence, once his constant companion, had completely disappeared from his awareness. "Mon Dieu. I'm free. He might chase me, but he no longer owns me." Philippe exhaled in surprise and relief.

Ragonde's dark desires no longer rang in the recesses of his mind either. "No wonder my near misses with her have spread out. But, wait... just because I can't feel her, does it mean she can't feel me? That sounds a bit like pretending someone can't see me because I've covered my eyes." He sighed heavily. "I wish Daphne would come home. She would probably know some sophisticated experiment we could use to prove it."

Again, he pondered going after her, though thinking of approaching the house, let alone entering, filled him with deep discomfort. He reached out again, this time seeking that comfortable presence who had so neatly filled in all his empty places. He found her easily, like the scent of lilacs in spring. Sweet and soft, with an edge that demanded attention.

She felt terrified.

Philippe's heart began to pound in tandem with hers. Pain tightened his face and nausea turned his stomach.

Unable to think or reason, he bolted from the house.

"Get up," Ragonde snapped.

Daphne moaned in pain, curled around her bruised belly as her face throbbed. Then she shrieked as a hand fisted in her hair and yanked her backwards off the bed. She collapsed in a heap on the floor.

"Get up!" Ragonde dragged her to her knees, but despite her strength, lacked the height to pull Daphne upright.

"What's happening?" Daphne asked, her voice trembling.

"The master called to me," Ragonde explained impatiently. "We must go directly to him. He will tolerate no delays." She yanked on

Daphne's hair again. Daphne resisted the pressure. *She can hurt me, but she can't move me. I won't go to him. That's nothing but a trap, and I refuse to be the bait.*

"Go yourself," Daphne said. "You and your disgusting master mean nothing to me. I'm days from completing my degree. I just want to go back to school."

Ragonde kicked out, catching Daphne in the ribs. Bone cracked. She pitched forward on the floor, curling in on herself again. "Move, bitch," the woman snarled.

"Go to hell," Daphne croaked. "You've broken my nose and ribs, and probably damaged my insides as well. I can't even get up." The words cost her. Agony rose in a red wave whose black recesses promised oblivion.

The last thing Daphne saw was a set of white teeth flashing toward her. Harsh pressure compressed her neck, punctured. Pain turned to euphoria moments before the blackness closed in again.

# Chapter Thirteen

The door of the hated row house stood open. Philippe stared at this unexpected sight. "Qu'est-ce que c'est?" he breathed. He turned to the left and right, hoping to see other doors open, perhaps to catch one of the last cooling breezes likely to bless the city before summer heat settled in. Nothing. Windows stood open in all directions, but doors remained firmly closed, denying strangers access to the dwellings within. All but this one.

For a moment, shimmering heat rose up from the sidewalk, shaping itself into a dark-skinned woman. "Beware, Philippe," Geneviève's ghost seemed to say. "They will never stop. They will find you."

"I didn't mean to harm you," he whispered. "The last thing I wanted was for you to be hurt. I thought we could outrun them."

"I know that now," she murmured, her voice hollow and expressionless. "Be at peace, Philippe. You never meant to endanger me. I do not hold you accountable. It is not wrong to want to be loved, and you had such an open heart. She will be good for you, but you should not be here."

"I have to find her," he said. "She's here, isn't she?"

"No more." Geneviève sighed, her voice rustling through the branches of a sapling growing up from a planter in the sidewalk. "She was here but no more. They've taken her. She's gone now."

"Gone where?" he asked. "Gen, where is she? Where is Daphne?"

"Gone... Gone... Gone..." the voice faded into a whispering breeze and died.

"Gen?" Philippe stared at the spot where the apparition had appeared, but now the street stood eerily empty and silent. No pedestrians passed through on their way to the riverfront or the market. No vehicles inched down the narrow space. Unheard of in the bustling French Quarter.

Whether Geneviève's ghost had actually appeared before him or had been conjured from his disturbed imagination, Philippe had no idea. He dreaded entering the house but could think of no other way to proceed. Inhaling a deep breath of the city-scented air, he strode through the open doorway.

An unnerving silence permeated the house. "There's no one here," he confirmed aloud to himself, and the empty hallway echoed his words back to him. The sound mocked his distress. Though he hadn't entered this building in over forty years, its layout remained familiar.

Opening the first door to the left, he found a downstairs bedroom, perhaps intended for a mother-in-law or other relation. He peeked inside, and his heart dropped. The feeling of Daphne hung strongly in the air. Her fear turned his stomach, as did the sour scent of vomit wafting from the bed. "Still fresh. They left recently." He gulped down bile. Blood mixed with the mess, as well as staining the floorboards in a shiny, dark-red slick.

"She bled here," he breathed. "Mon Dieu."

He ducked out of the room, turning down the hallway to the parlor, where he noted the mess without passion. *She wasn't here. No need to linger.*

At the back of the house, the kitchen held another strong trace of the woman he loved. Here, she also bled, though only a little. A sprinkling of droplets decorated the floor beside the dining table. Over her delicate scent, the heavy, perfumed stink of Ragonde hung in the air. She smelled... pleased.

Again, Philippe noted, while he could detect his enemy's presence, he could not sense her thoughts and commands any longer. "It has been fading so long. I wonder how that came about."

Shaking off the idle thought, he backtracked along Daphne's trail, a task that became easier the more he concentrated. *I can feel her presence,* he realized. *Feel her much more strongly than either Ragonde or him. What does that mean?*

He didn't know, but the image grew in his mind of his lady love, valises in hand, walking backwards up the stairs as the memory played in reverse. He followed. Found a bedroom that could only be hers, so strongly did her presence hang over it. The layers of different feelings muddled his perceptions. All the feelings and sensations of years of living. She had been happy here, sad, tired, ill. He could sense, as a dim wash overlaying it all, a feeling of startled wrongness. *This is when she became aware all was not well,* he realized.

"Why is the bed unmade?" Daphne's memory asked. "Jeannie always makes the bed."

He regarded the tangled sheets and a flutter of admiration stirred. *She never misses a detail.*

"Where are you now, mon amour?" he asked aloud. "Where have they taken you, Daphne?"

"I am in motion," a tinny shadow of her voice replied. "I am bound and hidden, but I can barely see buildings passing. I think I am on my way out of the city."

The feelings that accompanied the message resembled a pickup truck bouncing and rattling through the narrow streets of New Orleans. The sun shone warm through the window to his right.

"Are you going north?" he asked.

"Yes," her whisper floated back to him. "North to hell and perdition."

"No, love. I will find you. I swear it."

"Stay, Philippe," she urged. "Stay and work on your cures. They are taking me to *him*. By the time you find us, I will be turned, and you will walk into a trap for nothing. Then *he* will own you again. Only this time, he will turn you too. You will be his helpless slave forever."

"I would risk that for you, Daphne," he vowed. "I must. I cannot go back to the lab when you are in danger."

"I am already dead, Philippe." Her despairing whisper stretched thin as the distance between them grew. "Soon I will be like Jeannie and Mary, and even poor Anna. Brainless undead slaves of the master. I will not know you then."

"I will not allow that to happen," he spat. "Never. He can destroy me, but he cannot take my woman. Not again."

"Goodbye, Philippe," the faintest breath reached his mind's ears. "I love you. Be well. Stay..."

"Like hell I will," he said aloud. "But how will I find my way to them?"

"I will help you," a soft voice answered. Philippe whirled around to see an unfamiliar woman; slender and tall with short, slick hair—now badly disarranged—sprawled on the floor beside him. She dragged herself forward with both hands, as though her legs no longer functioned, and her face bore several vivid bruises.

"Who are you?" Philippe demanded, drawing away from her.

"I'm Lois. I own this house. I know who you are, Philippe St. Pierre."

He glared, more suspicious than ever of her intentions. "Don't speak the name," he snarled. "Why should I trust you, vermin? You stink of vampires. You're one of them, non?"

Lois sighed, then produced a squeak as her legs attempted to drag her backwards. Her fingers scrabbled on the floor and she finally gripped tight to the leg of the nearest dresser to keep herself stationary. "I am not," she said in a strained, raspy voice. "I am like you."

He sneered. "Not like me. You're still under their compulsion. Who infected you?"

"Ragonde," Lois admitted. "I thought..." her pale face pinkened. "I thought we were lovers, but..."

"But those beasts cannot love," Philippe answered for her. "They can only harm and abuse. They are nothing but a disease, and like all diseases, they deserve to be eradicated."

"If that happens, we both die," she reminded him. "Our lifespans are long since spent. Only the disease keeps us functioning now."

Philippe shrugged. "I would gladly sacrifice this miserable existence to end theirs."

She laughed, though the sound held no humor. "What about Daphne? She's why you're here, isn't she? I know you love her. What will become of her if you're gone?"

Lois reached out one hand toward Philippe and her scrabbling legs immediately yanked her backward again.

"Why should I trust you?" he demanded. "For all I know, you're one of their spies. Certainly, you're under their influence. You can do nothing for me unless Ragonde allows it."

"She'll allow it," Lois said with a sour grimace. "She wants you to follow. She believes the master will reward her if she brings you."

"And she is aware of this conversation?" he asked, his heart rate increasing to a painful pounding.

"I have no idea," Lois replied. "However, the master has compelled her presence and she cannot resist. I'm not sure how I resisted her compulsion this much, and I'm sure I'll pay dearly for it, but she crossed a line and I can no longer intentionally support her."

"I cannot save you from your fate," Phillippe informed the prone woman.

"I know." She studied the floorboards inches below her face with a sad frown. "I will reap what I have sewn. Decades of decadence come at a heavy price, and my bill is about to come due. However, I can tell you where they have taken your Daphne."

"Where?" he asked. *Idiot, why believe her? She's one of them, their slave.* Still, he listened, aware that any lead was better than none.

"Go north..." Lois choked and gagged. Swallowing hard, she forced out, "North and east into the deep bayou near Grosse Tête. There is a path. You will be able to find it, if anyone can. There, in the swamp, you will see an abandoned plantation. *He* is there, and that is where you will find your Daphne, but beware always, for he is guarded by the undead... and even worse things."

Philippe laughed bitterly. "You lie, wench. Why would Sébastien, ruler of all vampires in America—for I have heard that is now his title—hide in a backwater swamp in Louisiana? Why would he not be in a large city, feasting?"

Lois gagged again, and this time produced a foul, blood-flecked sputum, which she spat on the floor. "Idiot, you know nothing. You run and hide, and then pretend to have knowledge, but you are wrong. Cities are too exposed. He needs solitude, and for their kind, darkness and danger mean nothing. It is an ideal place to hold court, far from the eyes of humans."

Her words rang true, though Philippe hesitated to believe them.

"Ack!" The backward scrabbling of Lois' legs finally succeeded in dragging her away from the dresser. She squawked as they hurried her down the stairs, arms and head bumping with resounding cracks and thumps on each tread. In the distance, Philippe could hear her body sliding across the polished wood as her compulsion finally overcame her will and ripped her out the door.

Philippe shook his head. "She'll not last the night. By morning, only the disease will remain." Then he sucked in a deep breath. "Her words resonated. Could they be true? Could Daphne be en route to a plantation house deep in the swamp?" He grimaced. "I still can't believe *he* would hole up in such substandard accommodations, but after all, where else in this vast continent can one find glorious manors befitting upstart royalty in such total isolation?" The more Philippe pondered the story, the more sense it made. "I will head that direction," he decided. "Perhaps, if Daphne passed that way, I will feel it." Though he knew his chance to rescue her would most likely fail, he had to try. *I will not allow another person to die while I stand idly by, afraid.* "If she must die and turn, I will die and turn at her side."

A shaft of brilliant sunshine beamed through the window straight into Daphne's eyes. She squinted. Whatever she lay on felt hard and rough. A groan forced its way between her lips. "Where am I?" she wondered aloud. "What's happening?" Again, she tested her mental faculties. "The virus that causes this condition—vampirism for lack of a better term—is called V1. I have it, and so does Philippe... and probably Lois, I think. Yet none of us has turned. All the other girls turned, and they quickly lost themselves, but I still know who I am, if not where. All right, they haven't killed me yet."

Though she spoke to herself matter-of-factly, the pounding of her heart and the twisting of her stomach felt terrible and made her want to vomit. "No, no more. My face hurts and that won't help. At least my nose stopped bleeding. Goodness, that tiny Cajun woman can hit hard."

Though Daphne knew she was rambling, the pointless chatter helped keep her calm. The brightness stung her eyes as she forced them open. At first, everything looked white, but gradually, details began to emerge. A cracked wall dressed in rags of busy green wallpaper. A scuffed and splintered floor. A cracked window covered in spider webs and lined with dead flies.

"Okay, so I'm not in the truck anymore. How did I get here? Where is *here* exactly?"

She scanned the room further. Only a green and wood toned box with a window on one end and a door on the other. Not even furniture moldering in the dusty corners.

*Do I remember leaving the truck? I remember waking up on it, with my hands tied behind my back, and my head spinning from that bite.* She raised her fingers to the double layer of bruises on the side of her neck. *I thought they had fangs. I wish they did. It takes a lot of force to break skin with regular teeth.* "Okay, that might be vital information," she told herself aloud. "They bite, and it hurts because they have no fangs, but they inject something—probably the virus itself—which causes euphoria and unconsciousness... I should have woken up her slave, and I didn't. Why?"

"Because you already belong to another," a voice hissed from the corner. Daphne whirled around and faced a woman she didn't know. Dark-skinned and hollow-eyed, she stared at Daphne in naked hunger.

"Who are you?" Daphne asked. *Fool, who cares? What difference does it make? You can see she's a vampire.*

"Here, I am called Vivienne, but that was not always my name."

Daphne narrowed her eyes. "You can remember that?" she asked, her curiosity unquellable. "I thought when you turned, your old self faded away and only the virus remained."

"Sometimes, almost..." The woman shook her head. "I feel that I should know. That I should know you. You smell... familiar, but just when I reach out to take hold of the knowledge, it's gone."

"Well, I don't know you," Daphne informed Vivienne. "I've never seen you before, and no offense, but I don't much like being here with you now."

A vicious smile creased the woman's lips. "I imagine not. Do you think I will suck your blood too? I might. I'm hungry enough. I've been in here so long... so long."

"I'd rather you didn't." Daphne edged away.

Vivienne dropped to the floor and drew her knees up to her chest. Bare feet poked out beneath the ragged hem of her skirt. "Don't worry, chère. I don't eat anyone. That's why I'm here. Master ordered me to feed, and I refused. I couldn't hurt that little girl. I wouldn't. He realized he didn't have me under his spell completely, and he locked me in here."

The story confused Daphne. "So, the master... he's here? We must still be in Louisiana."

"Yes, not far from Lafayette, as the crow flies."

"And the king of all vampires lives in this?" She waved her hand at the dilapidated room.

Vivienne laughed. "Who told you he was king? Bah. He's set himself up as ruler of this land, as far north as the Arctic Circle, as far south as the tip of Mexico, but beyond those limits, he's nothing. He could not defeat the power that once upheld the crowned heads of Europe, nor of the lands so fiercely guarded by the descendants of conquistadors... and their pet vampires who made the natives weak and sick. No, he only holds North America, though he styles himself as more."

Daphne gulped. "That's power enough to make me nervous."

"Be less concerned with the reach of his arm, chère, and more with the strength of his bite. You smell of his general, but she... lacks finesse. He will make you do things you would never dream, and like every minute... until awareness brings regret. He will make you taste shame you've never imagined, and even the vampire blood you carry won't save you from it."

"How cheery." Relatively convinced her companion wouldn't suddenly spring into an attack, Daphne sank to the floor, but eyed the woman with suspicion.

"I think it will be a long, long time before you experience cheer again," Vivienne warned. "There are dark pleasures in this place, but nothing so wholesome as happiness."

Daphne frowned. "What have I gotten myself into?"

Philippe parked his brown and white Packard along the side of the highway, between some of the last closely clustered houses on the northeastern extremity. He slipped out and scanned the horizon. To his right, Lake Pontchartrain stood calm and blue. Little fingers of water slipped from it to infiltrate and undermine the land's stability. To the left, though he could not see it from this distance, he knew the Mississippi made its noisy, boisterous way to the north.

Too much time had passed while he maneuvered to the parking garage he leased—under a false name—in a less-congested part of town. Over an hour. Then, wading through traffic beside Moissant Airfield, which had just opened for commercial flights, had eaten up another hour.

At last, with the city behind him and the open road towards Baton Rouge ahead, he reached out again with his senses, hoping to feel whether Daphne had passed this way. *Are you there, love?* He searched the road, hoping to detect her presence, but nothing registered. "Daphne, where are you?" he whispered.

Having nothing to go on but the name 'Grosse Tête', received from a dubious source he hated to trust, he frowned with indecision. *Can I trust Lois, when she's so clearly one of them? Do I dare? All that strangeness might have been one of Ragonde's orchestrations, though the subtlety of it sounded more like Sébastien than his brutal general.*

*Still, I have to consider that they would want me on a wild goose chase, not to derail me completely in the end, but to slow the time it takes to find them until they have completed whatever evil they plan to commit upon Daphne and are prepared to catch me too.*

He rested his rear on the hood of his car and stared out over the brackish expanse. *What should I do? Trust the untrustworthy, or follow my instincts?* "My instincts don't leave me anywhere to start," he admitted, hating the truth.

At the reedy edge of the water, two black herons waded up to their knobby knees, searching for minnows. *I remember when life was simple. Just hunt for food with no more thought than a wild bird. A brutish existence, but one that was easy to understand. Fill the void. Live another day. Avoid danger. There was nothing more.*

He planted his hands on the metal and scanned the sky. Some kind of predator bird wheeled and circled on the hot breeze. *I learned dark refinement in Sébastien's court. The exquisite pleasure of pain and the sick ecstasy of degradation, though I didn't understand it until later. I learned to navigate a society more stratified than any monarchy could understand, where those in power can rob their underlings of more than taxes. Our very will and reason are theirs to control. It's disgusting.* He shuddered as the memories of violation and enslavement crowded into his mind.

*That is the sensibility I took away with me, and for a while, I pursued the human side of such things, until my own awareness of suffering made it impossible to live as a user, a seeker of power on my own. Until Geneviève became more real to me than my own hunger.* He sighed and spoke his next words aloud. "I've lost so much because of these monsters, but she lost more. She lost hope and life and trust all in one moment. She died thinking I only wanted her for her blood."

He swallowed the lump in his throat. Then his eyes narrowed, squinting in the bright sunlight he'd never adapted to.

A car pulled up behind his and a pudgy man in a bowler hat stepped out. "Having car trouble, Mister?" he asked in an accent that sounded more north than south.

"No, not at all," Philippe answered, hoping the breeze between them would mask the wavering in his voice. "It's a lovely day, and I decided to stop and ponder... a decision while looking at the lake."

"All righty then, Frenchy," the man replied. "Take care." He bundled back into his car and pulled into the lane, incurring an angry honk as he cut off a motorist behind him.

"Traffic is heavy, and I must move on, but without guidance. I suppose I must proceed to Grosse Tête and see what I find there." Sighing at the inevitability of his only—albeit poor—option, Philippe returned to his sedan and slid behind the wheel, waiting for a break in the stream of cars before pulling out into traffic and continuing along the northeast road toward Baton Rouge.

Heavy explosions, like cannon fire, thundered below the attic prison. Vivienne ducked into the corner and crouched, disappearing into a pile of rags.

"What's happening?" Daphne hissed.

"The master has sent his man to collect you."

"Oh, God." Daphne looked around, desperate to find a place to hide. "What do I do?"

"There's nothing you can do, except cooperate," Vivienne insisted. "He won't destroy you, probably." Then Vivienne fell silent as the trapdoor creaked open and a large, dark face appeared. The man, who looked both young and impossibly ancient, locked eyes with Daphne. Her knees began to tremble.

He entered the room more fully, massive arms and shoulders appearing, and reached out one huge, thick fingered hand.

Daphne dodged, but he caught the fabric of her trousers and dragged her forward. "Come now, Miss," he intoned in a slurred voice so deep, it sounded like rocks rubbing together. "The master calls."

"Please, don't," she begged helplessly, losing control of her mouth.

His hand released her trousers but clamped down on her wrist instead. "We're going now," he continued, ignoring her struggles. He ducked down out of the opening and pulled Daphne after him. She gawked at a rickety wooden staircase. *No wonder he walks so loudly.*

In desperation, she began to move forward, not wanting to fall. *I can't be woozy from an injury. I have to keep my wits about me.*

Fighting not to stumble, she placed her foot on each wooden tread, eliciting one loud creaking noise after another. At last, she reached the bottom—a long hallway with a faded runner covering its entire length. Lining the wall, closed doors suggested a number of bedrooms. From some, noises emerged: a leathery slap followed by a pleasured moan from one, a menacing laugh and a terrified whimper from another. As the black-skinned giant dragged her along the hallway, she heard two male voices groaning in what could only be a sexual encounter.

Daphne gulped, her toe catching on the rug. She pitched forward into the man's back. He turned with a scowl and set her back on her feet, urging her forward before she could even regain her sense of the floor.

The hallway turned sharply. Daphne's captor dragged her to the left. One door opened, and a tall, pale figure strode out. An unholy red mess stained her face. She giggled and wiped at it with her hand. "Stéphane, when the master is through with you, I need your help. I don't want this one to rise."

"Yes, Ma'am," the man replied, his voice docile. "I'll get my tools and be there when I can."

The meaning of the conversation dawned on Daphne in a flood of horror and she froze, feet rooted to the spot as a mixture of gags and sobs tried to burst from her throat.

"Come along." The giant, apparently called Stéphane, tugged harder. Daphne stumbled, her tingling feet dragging on the carpet. He tugged again, and she went sprawling on the threadbare green fabric.

"What have we here?" the bloody woman's voice asked. "Nice and soft. She looks delicious."

"This one belongs to the Master," Stéphane replied. His voice still sounded slurred, Daphne noted in a tiny, detached corner of her brain, the one spot that wasn't screaming in terror. "I have to take her to him now." He tugged on Daphne's arm. "Up, ma'am."

Daphne's trembling limbs refused to cooperate. With a sigh, the giant dropped her wrist and lifted her to her feet, but then he frowned. "Can't you walk?" he asked.

"She looks scared," the woman pointed out. "Give her to me for a few minutes. I'll have her purring in no time."

Daphne retched, but her empty stomach had nothing to yield.

Stéphane picked her up again. This time, he draped her over his shoulder and begin moving forward with fast, purposeful strides. The shadowy corner in the hallway revealed a small, narrow staircase, which Stéphane descended at an uncomfortable pace, bouncing Daphne's belly on his shoulder with each step.

A dark figure huddled on the stairs lifted its head, showing pale skin stretched thin over jutting bones, and wild, glittering eyes. It—for even Daphne's terror-filled brain could not conceive of such a creature as 'he'—hissed and swiped out a hand bristling with sharp, yellow nails, raking them down her dangling leg. She squeaked. Stéphane trudged on, not seeming to notice.

The stairs ended in a familiar, if oversized room filled with wooden worktables, a massive stove and the oldest, most out-of-date icebox Daphne had ever seen.

Five women, all plump and clad in gray dresses and white frilly caps that covered their hair, bustled around, working on various tasks.

*Almost looks like a restaurant kitchen,* she noted, until she realized the overwhelming scent in the room—a scent that drowned out the beef, pastries, and wine—was blood. Again, her stomach tried to invert itself.

Stéphane waved to the women and crossed the room in a few long-legged strides, ducking out into a broad, grand foyer large enough to host a ball. The parquet floor gleamed with wax.

He stepped out from beneath the balcony that housed all the rooms they'd just passed, revealing a sumptuous two-story space illuminated by two chandeliers glittering with candles and crystals. Directly in front of them, a small vestibule revealed the main entrance, with oversized double doors, thickly carved and sporting chunky metal hinges and handles.

More closed doors encircled the central room. Stéphane carried Daphne to the right, where a door in the corner stood slightly ajar.

*This is it,* she realized. *Now pull yourself together, girl. You won't accomplish anything by sniveling like a baby. Yes, it's scary and disgusting here, but what did you expect? You're no dainty lady to succumb to the vapors. You're a sturdy farm girl and a scientist to boot. Put a lid on your fear.*

With all the force of will Daphne possessed, she squashed terror and revulsion down into the hidden recesses of her mind and visualized locking it away, leaving her cold and emotionless. *That's it. Channel Mama. Be strong and unflappable. Your goal is to escape, and if you study the situation, you'll find a way.*

Stéphane knocked on the open door and stepped through. "I brought her, Master," he intoned in that strange, slurring voice. He set Daphne on her feet, waited a moment to be sure she wouldn't collapse, and then moved behind her and gathered up both of her wrists in one hand.

Daphne lifted her chin and stared at the scene before her. Ragonde knelt, one knee to the floor, in a gorgeous parlor of polished wood, where a dark-haired man sat on an oversized ornate chair—not exactly a throne but heading in that direction. *So, this is my enemy,* she thought, studying the fellow. His swarthy skin defied classification, as did his shiny, jet-black hair.

A longer glance revealed a strange sight. His medium-dark skin looked odd—overstretched and thin—as though the flesh beneath had withered away. He grinned, and she shuddered. It looked as though the full lips might split apart at any moment. Like Philippe, he appeared slim rather than muscular, though she knew the vision to be an illusion.

Sébastien placed together the fingertips of his bony, overly-long fingers and regarded Daphne over the top of the pyramid he'd created.

"So, this is the girl who gave you so much trouble, Ragonde?" he asked in a voice that sounded higher in pitch than it should have. "She doesn't look like much of a threat."

"I cannot explain it, my lord," Ragonde said in a voice so meek, Daphne almost couldn't believe she was actually generating it. "I bit her twice, and still she is able to think clearly and refuse my orders. It is as though my bite has lost its power." She shuddered as she said it.

The man grinned, and the effect of taut skin pulling over wiry muscle made Daphne want to... she didn't know what. Cry? Scream? Run away? *Running away seems like an excellent idea. Wish I could.* She gave an experimental tug against the hands that held her. They felt heavy as tree trunks and unyielding as carved stone. *Unfortunately, this minion won't allow it.* She frowned. Though panic tried to course through her, setting her heart pounding and her breathing into uncomfortable gasps, she forced herself to think clearly. *Like when the hurricane hit the farm all those years ago. It was scary, but I never lost my head. I won't lose it now either. So, how do I get out of this situation?* She racked her brain while Ragonde and Sébastien discussed what her ability to resist might mean.

She scanned the room, noting polished parquet floors, an expensive Persian rug, and some sort of wardrobe or cabinet set in the corner. *Might be a place to hide, though not for long since it's the only one in the room.* Two windows behind the throne admitted bright, noontime sun. *And vampires are not susceptible to sunlight, as legends say, though they do seem a bit sensitive to the brightness.*

Her thoughts spiraled uselessly. Nothing concrete came to mind. *Sébastien is the key,* she decided at last. *The head of the snake. The most dangerous part. He's the one I must be most wary of... but that's obvious, and how it helps me much less so.*

"Watch and wait," a voice murmured in her mind. "The clues to solve any problem appear eventually if you study the problem with enough care."

"So, Miss," Sébastien's voice, low and seductive with a certain sibilance, hissed so close to her ear, she jumped in surprise, and then found herself looking into black pools that wanted to drag her under and drown her, "just what brings you to my world?"

"She did." Daphne snapped, gesturing toward Ragonde with an angry tilt of her head. "I have no interest in you or your world. I came to the boarding house to pick up my things, since I'm moving, and she grabbed me, bit me, and beat me up. I'd be happy to go home and pretend this is all a bad dream."

"She's a liar," Ragonde cut in. "Smell her. She reeks of Philippe."

If Sébastien hadn't been standing so close to Daphne she could feel the heat of his body and smell the blood on his breath, she would have missed the tiny gasp Ragonde's words invoked, and the slight redness that stained the whites of his eyes. *Holy Moses, he really does think he's in love with him.* Daphne filed the information away for later but forced herself not to react.

The strange man inhaled deeply. "She does," he agreed, and Daphne's already painful pulse hammered against her ribs until she feared it would burst. "Tell me how you know Philippe St. Pierre."

"I don't," Daphne replied. "Your goon must be mistaken."

"Not to mention," Ragonde continued, "she knows a great deal about us. She called me a disease and said she was studying a cure."

Sébastien's black eyes widened. "Tell the truth, wench," he snarled. "You won't like how I force it out of you, but I will if I have to."

Daphne weighed her options for a split second and then answered with as much honesty as she felt fit the circumstances. "I'm a student studying science. I also worked as a lab assistant for an older scientist who's studying yellow fever. We isolated a mutated form of the virus. That's all."

"And your claim that she has it?" His eyes slid toward Ragonde and then back to Daphne.

"She was beating me up and frightening me. I may have said some insulting things, but you don't think I actually knew what I was saying, do you? Walking disease, monster, beast..." She turned to face Ragonde and narrowed her eyes, despite the pulling pain it generated in her broken nose. "Bitch. Because of the focus of my study, I tend to think in terms of disease. She's nuts if she's reading that much into it."

This time Sébastien turned to face Ragonde directly. In profile, Daphne could see his lips compress into a disapproving scowl. He narrowed his eyes.

"Why believe her and not me? Think!" Ragonde insisted. "A scientist studying yellow fever to find a 'cure' for a mutated version of the virus. She didn't guess that. She knows. Besides, who else could this mysterious man be? What other scientist would waste time and resources studying a disease that already has a vaccine? I believe Philippe is the scientist, and she is surely more than his assistant, she's his lover. His smell is all over her. She even smells of his virus. She's playing dumb, my lord, but you know better than to trust a smart woman when she plays dumb, don't you?"

Apparently, Ragonde's words crossed a line. Sébastien growled at her and she fell silent.

*Interesting. She challenges him. She wants to be more than his head stooge. She nags like... an old wife.* Like the sunlight streaming through a gap in heavy brocade curtains, revelation illuminated Daphne's mind. *She's in love with him, and jealous of his continuing obsession with Philippe. Now that might be useful information.*

"Well, sir," Daphne said, opening her eyes up wide, which she knew made her pretty, round face resemble a brainless china doll, "as you can see, your lady made a mistake. I don't know anyone by the name she keeps saying and she misunderstood what *I* was telling her. I know you don't mean to take away innocent people. Please, let me go home. My graduation ceremony is the day after tomorrow, and I bought a pretty new dress for the day."

Too late, Daphne realized her mistake, as Sébastien's overstretched skin tightened obscenely into a wolfish expression. "Oh, but my dear, taking away innocent girls is *exactly* what I do. Girls and boys. Pretty innocents are my favorite playthings." The wolfish expression turned considering. "Now, what to do with you? Your study of the virus presents interesting possibilities, ones I might want to exploit later. I'll have to think about it. For now, I think it's safe to say you will not be leaving any time soon. And since you're shrewder than you look, I'd better make sure you won't even think about leaving. Stéphane?"

The man holding Daphne's arms shifted, releasing her for a second, only to take hold from a different angle. Crushing her around the waist, he lifted her off her feet.

Daphne shrieked and kicked, her boots connecting solidly with his knees, but he seemed not to notice the abuse.

A table lay in the middle of the room, and he tossed her onto it. Daphne scrambled to rise, to get some sort of leverage in her baggy trousers, but the fabric slipped on the polished surface and she could find no traction. A moment later, the huge minion took hold of her arms again and yanked them over her head, so she lay flat on her back, pinned and helpless.

*Well, not helpless,* she amended, thanking her lucky stars again that despite the fear burning an acid hole in her stomach, she could still think clearly. As Sébastien approached, she kicked out viciously, aiming for his groin, all decorum abandoned. He easily dodged and then laughed, grasping her ankle in one hand. She shoved at his fingers with her free foot, ignoring the pain as his nails dug in. *I can't be helpless. I can't.*

Unconcerned with her struggles, he dug his fingers into the fabric of her trousers, where they bagged concealingly around her crotch.

She drew in a shaky breath and screamed, kicking violently, but failed to connect with him. His laugh turned frightening, but even scarier was the effortless way he tore apart the fabric, leaving her bare from the waist down.

"Stop it!" Daphne hollered.

"Of course, I will not," Sébastien replied. Dark humor turned his strange face to a grinning skull. "I want you under my power. Even if you are not connected to my lost love—which I doubt; Ragonde is correct, you smell like him, especially here." He cupped her intimately.

Daphne recoiled from the touch, or tried to, but between Stéphane pinning her arms and Sébastien's claws sunk deep into her ankle, she could manage little movement.

"Please, don't," she whimpered.

"Ah, but I will, Doucette," he informed her, leering at her exposed privates. "I will violate what he has claimed, and you will beg me to do it. I will bite you and make you my own. I will claim your sex... and your science... for my kingdom."

Daphne laughed, bitter and shaky, with a hint of a sob. "If you bite me, you'll knock me out. I won't have a clue what you're doing. How exactly do you expect me to work for you if I'm unconscious?"

His grin stretched tighter, until she feared his skin would split. "You're mistaken, Doucette," he informed her. "Ragonde is a fine general, but her bite lacks... finesse. You'll see. Once I've tasted you, you'll never doubt your loyalty to me, or your obedience to my demands. You'll do exactly as I ask, always."

In a split second, even as terror and disgust threatened to turn her belly inside out, several ideas began to take shape in Daphne's mind. Though murky and half-formed, the shadow of a desperate plan flared to life. Sébastien's hand began to stroke obscenely over her intimate parts, in an unwelcome parody of a lover's caress. *Don't think of what he's doing,* she warned herself fiercely. *You can't avoid the assault. Keep thinking only of escape.* A thick finger invaded her, and she squeaked against her will. *Damn it. Please, don't.* "Please," she whimpered.

"Begging already, my sweet?" he laughed.

*Arrogant bastard,* Daphne thought. *If he's wrong... if he doesn't subsume my will, I gain the advantage. As long as I retain my wits, I must play along, pretend obedience. Only then will I have the opportunity to escape—hopefully before Philippe finds me.*

Sébastien leaned down, his face drawing close to her groin.

*Philippe. Think of Philippe. He must never be the victim of this monster again. Never. I will not be the bait in this trap. I will endure what I must to save the man I love.*

A flash of movement, and Sébastien's teeth sank into her inner thigh. His teeth, sharper than Ragonde's, punctured the flesh with less pressure. Daphne gulped, waiting for blackness to rise.

It didn't.

Instead, the drowning euphoria of the bite radiated out through her limbs and settled in her core in a surge of wet heat. Her pulse throbbed in her intimate flesh, potent as a lover's caress. The monster between her thighs lapped at the wound he'd created, and each stroke of his tongue built her ecstasy to greater heights.

"I hope my Philippe does come after you," he murmured. "I would set you to play together as entertainment for my court. I can just picture him—slim and sexy—enjoying your lush curves."

Daphne tried to speak, to voice her outrage. *Philippe's and my passion and pleasure are not for your entertainment, you disgusting pervert,* she tried to scream, but her throat closed on the words. Her mind remained sharp as ever, fully aware of the degradation being visited upon her. Her body, however, rushed headlong toward completion, no longer responded to its commands.

Sébastien's finger slipped into her again, deeper than before, and he laid a single slow lick onto her clitoris. Daphne's scream changed from outrage to pleasure as the undeniable peak shook her body.

*Damn, damn, damn!* Her mind cursed in time to the pulsing of her intimate parts.

Sébastien rose, a knowing grin on his disgusting face. "There, that's better. Now then, my harem girl, you belong to me, body and heart. I will play with you when I wish, and you will no longer resist. How I will enjoy dismantling your innocence one act at a time. In the meanwhile, Stéphane, take her back to her room, and bring her something prettier to wear. These modern clothes do nothing for her lovely figure. Heavens, the world has forgotten how to dress a woman. Her curves beg to be adorned in lace, not hidden under such masculine.... Bah." He turned away. "Ragonde, you mentioned you had some new baby vampires for my harem?"

"Yes, milord," Ragonde replied, her pout visible to Daphne even from across the room, "and a lovely mature woman who ought to be turned in reward for her years of faithful service."

"Show me." He extended his arm and she grasped it. They left the room, Ragonde in a sulky slouch, even as her master sashayed his way out in obvious satisfaction.

Daphne's body still throbbed in the aftermath of her unwanted orgasm. The violation hung heavy on her soul and she wanted nothing more than to hide away and weep. Realizing her lower half remained bare, she looked upside-down at her captor, but to her relief, his blacker-than-black eyes remained blank, fixed on the wall. *Wow, he's far gone.*

She realized what life for Philippe must have been like all the years he'd spent under Sébastien's control, and her belly heaved in disgust. *My poor darling.*

"Come, ma'am," the man intoned, his voice hollow and his accent so heavy Daphne could scarcely make out a word. "We must find you something to wear."

Though she wanted little less than to wander through a strange house alone with a huge man, clad only in her blouse, the utter lack of awareness in his eyes reassured her somewhat.

"Very well. Release me."

His huge, dark hand loosened its hold on one wrist, and he circled the table. Daphne scrambled upright, covering herself as best she could. The bite on her thigh throbbed, but the spreading euphoria was dissipating, leaving shame in its wake. *Soon, I'll break down,* she admitted to herself. Stubbornly, she squashed the urge to weep. *Not now. The moment will come, but not now. I have to maintain control.*

With more brute force than was necessary, Stéphane dragged her from the table. Her wobbly knees gave way, leaving her stumbling, but he did not relent. The hallway loomed before her, filled with unknown threats, but she had no choice. She succumbed to the force she could not resist and allowed herself to be led away.

To keep herself from dissolving into a pile of mush and having to be dragged like a stubborn mule, she studied the walls of the hallway. They stood high and white, with ornate crown molding, and the floor gleamed in polished hardwood.

*Kind of looks like a French Quarter row house, only grander, and yet the upper floor is a shabby mess of spider webs and peeling wallpaper. Looks as though the grand vampire of North America wants to live in splendor without investing too much effort. I suppose if you have mindless slaves to sand and polish your floors for you, the work must go quickly. Maybe he left the upstairs icky on purpose, like a dungeon.*

"A dungeon for a prisoner," she whispered, and then dragged her lip into her mouth and bit down hard to stifle a sob.

"This way, ma'am," Stéphane urged, making his way to a wide, curving staircase lined with a green runner.

"How did you come to be here, Stéphane?" she asked, probing for information. *Never know what might turn out to be an advantage.*

"The master brought me," he replied. His long legs ate up the distance at such a pace that Daphne, despite her own greater-than-average height, had to scramble to keep up.

"Brought you from where?"

"From France. It was bad there. This place is better. It's ours. The bad people wanted to hurt us, but here we can live in peace."

Daphne considered the hard, muscular body, prodigious strength and broad-featured yet attractive face. *They don't match his babyish words or soft tone of voice. I wonder if he was born... a little off, or if that's part of his enslavement. None of the other vampires sound or act like him. Would a congenital birth defect of the mind affect a vampire?*

*There must be some interplay of mind and body even after reanimation. Truly, this is the strangest virus I've ever run across.*

"Weren't you scared?" she asked, pitching her voice softly and letting concerned sympathy bleed into her tone. "I'm scared and I'm only a short distance from home. Crossing a whole ocean?" she shuddered.

He stopped and turned to look at her, and his blank eyes seemed to focus for a moment. "I was happy. I didn't like my home."

"Why not?" Daphne asked, cocking her head to the side.

"They were mean there. They made us take medicines that made me sick to my stomach. They wouldn't let us go outside, and they sometimes threw cold water on us."

"That's very sad," Daphne replied. *Prison or asylum, but I'd guess asylum because of the medicine.*

"Yes," the towering man agreed, "but master takes care of me now. I can go outside and look at the birds any time I'm not busy. I like birds. They're pretty."

"I like birds too," Daphne agreed.

"And now you can look at them with me." His face softened into a white-toothed grin of simpleminded pleasure. "Master wants you to stay."

"That he does," Daphne agreed, trying to sound matter of fact, while convulsively swallowing down a gag. *Keep me and do disgusting, perverted things to me. I don't feel enslaved... but that first moment after the bite surely does strange things to me, and there's no way I can stop it from happening again.* A little sob escaped.

"Are you well, miss?" Stéphane asked.

She dabbed gently at her nose with the back of her hand. It still hurt, but perhaps a bit less than before. *Goodness, I seem to be healing quickly.* "I'm scared. I don't know this place, and I miss my husband. I want to go home."

Stéphane's dark eyebrows drew together. He scratched at his forehead, deep in thought. Then his expression brightened. "I know! Why don't you bring your husband here? Then you can work for the master together!"

Daphne sagged. *He'll never understand.* "I don't think they'd get along well," she admitted. "My husband likes being free. He doesn't want a master. But at any rate, let's find me something to wear now, can we? I don't like being this bare."

Stéphane frowned again, clearly not understanding why anyone wouldn't get along with his master. "Very well," he said, sulking.

"Can we walk a little more slowly, please?" she added as she stumbled again, her weakened knees unable to keep up with his rapid, long-legged strides. "I'm not as fast as you." To lighten her companion's mood, she added, "I'm a turtle."

He grinned at the silly joke and then continued moving up the staircase, now at a painfully slow rate. Daphne sighed. *I'll have to refine my technique for how to talk to this fellow. Being very specific seems to be the key. I'll get it right in the end.* The thought of just how much time she would have to perfect the technique depressed her. Her lips turned down as she trudged along the second story corridor. Stéphane led her into a sumptuous bedroom completely filled with dress forms. Each sported a luxurious gown, whose styles ranged from the French Revolution to the turn of the century. *I guess the 'master' isn't keen on modern fashion,* she thought, swallowing down another hysterical sob.

# Chapter Fourteen

Grosse Tête turned out to be not much of a town, mostly a collection of small, ramshackle houses clustered under huge, spreading trees.

"At least the grass is green," Philippe murmured aloud. He reached out with his senses, trying to determine if Daphne had gone this way, but found nothing. Another sensation—almost like a scent, and disturbingly familiar—teased the edges of his awareness. His stomach jumping, he opened himself to it. Memories flooded into him, images he'd tried hard to forget. Sébastien pinning him to the floor while Ragonde stood by, watching his violation and laughing. A thousand scenes of degradation and abuse. And then, even deeper, more hidden memories, ones he'd never shared, of Sébastien whispering words of love into Philippe's ear and compelling him to answer in kind.

The scent of his enemy, of the virus that had transformed them all into ageless monsters, drove Philippe to his knees and finally turned his stomach inside out. He heaved and retched into the soft grass along the side of the highway. "That bastard. He had no right."

A strong compulsion rose up in Philippe. In that moment, he wanted nothing more than to run away. To leave this place, this state, this entire country. *If* he *is here, I should be somewhere else. Anywhere else. The frozen arctic. A desert. I can live anywhere. Why am I moving directly toward the enemy who has power over my very thoughts and will?*

191

The urge reverberated so strongly, his body began to react, levering him upright and sending him back in the direction of his car. His head pounded, and the bright afternoon sun stung his sensitive eyes. The vile taste of vomit lingered in his mouth. *Run away, run away.* A voice chanted in his head. *Run away again. Always running.*

Sliding into the driver's seat of his Packard, he reached for the ignition, and then sagged. It felt as though all the energy had been drained out of him. His body went limp. "I am so tired," he admitted aloud. "Tired of running and hiding. I'm a man, but I've lived like an animal for so long, I almost forgot the difference. Feed, mate, run. That's been my life... until now."

A vision arose in his mind. Round, pretty face with large eyes and a shrewd, intelligent expression. Lush, curvy figure twining around his in unashamed ardor. Brilliant mind that could make sense out of even the most outlandish puzzles. "Daphne. My wife," he reminded himself. "I cannot let *him* have her. No matter the cost, I must try."

He reached out again with his inner senses, blocking out the scent of his enemy, though it lay thick and heavy on the town, and focused on his bride. Not her memory, but her awareness. "Are you there, love?" he murmured.

In his mind, a scene took shape. A beautifully appointed bedroom with glossy wainscoting on the walls and heavy drapes in a sedate wine tone at the windows. Clothes trees and dress forms crowded the elegant space, and inside, Daphne stood before a mirror. Though the reflection showed her curves displayed to perfection in an old-fashioned yet perfectly preserved gown of soft blue fabric, sprigged with white flowers and trimmed with pink ribbons, her face showed none of its usual confident openness. A strange look of shame almost overpowered the fear he had expected.

Behind her, a huge figure lurked, and it seemed at first as though he posed some sort of threat, but as Philippe watched the scene, it became apparent he was brushing Daphne's hair.

He pulled the top back, puffed it, and then smoothed the surface before pinning it into place. The rest hung long down her back. "There.

You look very pretty now," the man said, and Philippe noted with interest that he sounded like a simpleton. *He seems familiar, like the memory of a dream. Who is he, and why do I feel sick trying to think about it?*

Daphne turned to face him and smiled, though a pinching in the corners of her eyes revealed her discomfort. "Thank you, Stéphane."

The man's dark face broke into a broad grin.

*So, she's found an ally already. That's good.* "Daphne," he whispered.

She whirled back to the mirror and stared at her reflection, her eyes widening. "Philippe?" she mouthed, but no sound escaped. *She hasn't turned yet. Thank God. She's still living.*

"Yes, love. I'm coming. I will get you out of there."

A tiny shake of her head sent her hair tumbling, and the huge man laid a hand on her shoulder. "Don't twitch so, Miss. You'll make a mess of your coiffure."

"I'm sorry, Stéphane," she told the man gently. "I had a shiver. I'm still afraid."

Stéphane's eyebrows drew together. "Don't be, Miss. When the master sees how pretty you are all dressed up, he'll take good care of you."

Daphne frowned, but made no reply.

Scarlet rage bloomed in Philippe's guts and radiated through him until his fingertips tingled. *He touched her. That bastard touched my woman.* No longer afraid, only furious at the obvious violation his beloved had suffered, he firmed his determination.

"Don't give me away, love. There's no telling what this man might say in passing, but do not deny me. I will come for you. I will find a way. You keep working on your own solution, and we'll remain in touch. Think of me when you're alone, and I will answer."

"You mustn't risk yourself," her thoughts responded to his, though her lips made no movement. She stepped away from the mirror. "Can you take me back to my room, Stéphane?" she asked her companion. "I'm tired."

Again, the giant frowned. "That room is not nice for resting. Shall I take you to one of the bedrooms?"

"No, thank you," Daphne replied primly. "I'd rather stay in a familiar place. Besides, my friend is there."

"She's a bad girl," Stéphane informed her. "She tells lies about the master."

Daphne sighed. "Nonetheless, that is where I must go."

Stéphane extended his arm and she slipped hers through it.

"Stay away, Philippe," another thought floated his direction. "Stay away and be safe. I cannot bear to think of you in this place, at *his* mercy."

"You're mad," he sent back, "if you think for one second that I would leave you to your fate. There is no debate, Daphne. I will find a way to get you out."

Then he withdrew his consciousness from hers, not wanting to hear her argument.

The Packard reformed, solid and shiny, around him. The soft brown leather upholstery cradled his body, and yet his mind focused inward still, to the place where Daphne resided.

"How do I get to my wife?" he asked himself aloud. "She's somewhere near here, but where? There's a great deal of wilderness out there."

*The only thing to do is start, he told himself with a sigh, eying the swamp grimly.*

*How on earth is Philippe in my mind? Have I cracked up completely?* As Daphne mounted the stairs to the neglected third floor, the idea circled around and around. *This is important. It matters, but I can't quite figure out how. So many pieces, and none fit together. The jigsaw puzzle is incomplete, and I can't see the picture.*

"I'll come back soon, ma'am," Stéphane informed her as he unlocked the door to the attic bedroom. She stepped inside with a wave. The lock clicked behind her.

Deep in ruminations, a movement from the corner startled her. She jumped, blinking as a ragged shape rose from the floor.

"Vivienne," she murmured, resting her hand on her pounding heart.

"He touched you. I'm sorry. Please don't blame yourself."

Daphne swallowed hard. At last, the dam holding back her emotions shattered, leaving her weary and sad. Great, gulping sobs clawed their way out of her throat. She sank to the splintery floor, her hands over her face.

Vivienne drew near to her and pulled her close, embracing her in warm, motherly arms. Daphne let herself be comforted like a child. She barely felt the sting of teeth in the side of her neck. The relief it brought felt more like a warm hug than wild euphoria. She curled up in Vivienne's arms and let her eyes drift closed.

Dense trees surrounded him, interlacing branches hung with festoons of gray Spanish moss. Still, stagnant swamp water, frosted with a thick coat of algae, sent a rank stink into the air. The dark, muggy atmosphere lent a sense of creeping menace.

Philippe shivered in the heat, squinting to peer through thick shadows at the road ahead. *Road—ha! It's a path, and barely that.* Any moment he expected the deer track leading into the undergrowth to disappear into a wallow of invisible, waist-deep sludge. *Ground in the swamp isn't always as solid as it looks.* He tested each step before putting his full weight on it.

A strange, barking cough shattered the heavy silence. Philippe peered into the underbrush, but nothing moved. He took another cautious step forward. A mosquito whined past his ear and he slapped at it.

The coughing call sounded again, a series of staccato chirps, punctuated with gurgling sounds. Unnerved, Philippe took a heavy step forward, and a large black and red shape burst out of the bushes and hustled away.

"Turkey," he breathed, hand pressed to his aching chest. "Only a wild bird. This isn't the most frightening thing in the swamp."

As though to confirm his suspicion, a soft splashing in the watery bog to his right revealed the armored back of an alligator as it propelled itself through the water, its huge tail sweeping from side to side.

*Too close for comfort.* "Stay there, please, Mr. Alligator," Philippe suggested. "I'm not easy prey, though you might think otherwise at first sight. I'm stronger than I look."

The alligator made no response, save to draw even nearer to shore.

Philippe stepped away and immediately regretted it as stagnant water seeped into his shoes. Trapped between uncertain ground on one side, open water on the other, he froze to ponder his options.

The reptilian hunter closed in on him. Only a short stand of scrubby plants separated him from the approaching beast. In a sudden surge of movement that seemed impossible for so large a creature, it lunged in Philippe's direction. He jumped back and found himself in ankle-deep mud.

A loud squeal rent the air, and the alligator retreated into the bayou, a wild piglet squalling in its massive teeth.

Frowning, Philippe made his way back to the path and crept forward, unnerved by the swamp in all its wildness. It seemed the way forward was his only possible path. *Advance or retreat, but I cannot retreat. Daphne needs my help.* He pushed on, and the path grew narrower. Water lapped over the narrow strand of dirt. His shoes, already soaked with slime, soon became saturated. Wetness oozed out with every step.

The path disappeared into a stand of trees, invisible under the dense canopy of sparse leaves and hanging moss. He inched forward. Around him, strange noises grew in intensity. Frogs boomed, insects buzzed, and birds cackled and shrieked. A barely visible form streaked past a break in the tree trunks and skimmed the water. Philippe recognized the familiar white head of a bald eagle as it flapped away, a fat fish caught in its talons.

*Predator and prey. The life cycle played out in a drama of death before me, but am I the hunter... or am I the prey?* Though he knew the answer, he didn't like it, and turned his mind away from such thoughts. *Daphne. Remember your bride. You cannot let* him *have her.*

The path turned sharply to the left, a sudden turn he almost didn't see in time. Only the movement of a turtle as it slipped into the water warned him of the danger before he floundered in. Muttering, he executed the turn. A few more steps brought him out of the trees and into weak, patchy sunlight that revealed a ramshackle hut of sticks with a grassy roof.

Philippe sighed in disappointment. "This is not where I will find my enemy. He would never settle for such substandard accommodations."

Shoulders sagging, he turned to walk away, when an ominous click penetrated the swampy sounds. Philippe whirled to find himself face to face with a shotgun. Clutching the wood and metal stick in gnarled hands, an elderly Cajun with a long white beard squinted at Philippe. He opened his toothless maw and let loose a stream of incomprehensible gibberish that sounded like a blend of English, Spanish, French, and God only knew what else.

Philippe answered in French. "Pardon me, sir. I'm afraid I lost my way. I was looking for a friend's house, and I took a wrong turn."

The Cajun gabbled in response, gesturing with his gun. Philippe took a step backward. The man advanced and Philippe retreated, eyes fixed on the threatening stranger. Another step and his shoe came down on something wet. It shot out at an awkward angle, leaving Philippe sprawled in the slime at the edge of a stagnant puddle. Algae coated his pants and brackish water soaked into his hair.

The hillbilly broke out into a peal of cracked laughter. "Va-t-en," he drawled, at last using words Philippe recognized. "Get out, demon spawn. I see you again..." He fired the shotgun to Philippe's left, just close enough that a few pieces of shot scraped Philippe's arm and hip.

Another ricocheted off a tree branch and creased his cheek. Blood immediately began to trickle down his face.

Scowling, Philippe hoisted himself to his feet, his dignity in tatters. Casting a baleful glare at the old man, he turned on his heel and stalked away, head high, spine itching with the knowledge that the shotgun remained leveled at his back.

He hurried to the bend in the road, glad for the thick growth of trees that shielded him from view and turned back toward the main road.

"This isn't working," he admitted to himself. While he could easily find Daphne's consciousness anytime he looked, the sense of her presence did not grow stronger or weaker depending on his location. *I wish I understood how it functions. Daphne would say we need to eliminate variables to prove the validity of our theory... except I don't have a theory. All I have is a dangerous enemy, a missing wife, and pond scum in my hair.* He shuddered.

His car still waited for him where he had left it, along the narrow shoulder of the main road, near where he had spotted the trail. Philippe's scowl deepened at the thought of smearing smelly water on the upholstery.

Frustrated, he squeezed out and scraped off as much of the muck as he could, before climbing into the driver's seat, executing a complicated U-turn, and heading back to town. "I need a new plan of action... but what?"

"Come along, miss," Stéphane's voice cut into Daphne's unpleasant dreams. She opened her eyes, soothed by the moonlight darkness in the room. *Regardless of the nature of the virus, it certainly causes light-sensitivity. Perhaps that's the origin of the legend that vampire cannot come out in the sun. Clearly, it isn't true, but there's a kernel of truth in it.* The idea that she might be able to gather data soothed her fears, at least enough to make her not feel as though she was on the verge of vomiting. "You too, Miss Vivienne. The master wants you both."

The words had an immediate effect on Daphne. Her nervous nausea returned full force, and she gagged, memories of Sébastien's vile touch crowding into her mind. She shivered. "Please, no," she whispered. "Stéphane, honey, I know your master has done you some good. I'm glad he has. But I didn't like the way he touched me. Please don't make me go back."

Stéphane frowned in confusion. "You did like it, miss. I saw it."

Tears stung Daphne's eyes and closed her throat, preventing her from answering.

"You know that's not true, Stéphane," Vivienne chimed in. "You know it's the magic in our bite that makes people feel good. That's not the same as wanting it. Have you ever eaten anything that tasted good but gave you a stomachache?"

The big man nodded slowly.

"When someone touches you in a way you don't like, even if it feels good, it's like that."

Daphne swallowed down the lump in her throat and rasped, "I just got married, honey. My good feelings belong to my husband."

Understanding dawned in the broad, open face. "Oh, I get it. It felt good, but also bad, because you miss your husband?"

*Not exactly, but close enough. It's clear the idea of willingness doesn't mean much to him.* "That's right," she agreed. "So, can you understand why I don't want to see your master? He's disrespecting my husband and he's doing things that aren't right, because I'm a married lady."

Stéphane grasped Daphne's hand and hoisted her to her feet. "You explain it to him. I'm sure he'll understand. He's a smart man."

Daphne pulled against the clutching fingers, but to no avail. Stéphane had a grip like a vise, and she could in no way remove herself.

"Vivienne," she begged.

"I'm sorry, chère," the lady vampire said. "I have no ability to resist. My mistress has called me, and I must obey." *The semblance of obedience is a useful tool,* Vivienne added silently into Daphne's mind. *It builds their confidence and thus our advantage.*

Daphne fought and pulled against Stéphane's grip as he maneuvered her down the narrow stairs.

"Miss, please don't fight," he urged. "I don't want you to fall."

Vivienne took hold of her opposite shoulder, forcing her upright. "I'll help."

Daphne stared at her companion, the betrayal burning in her heart.

"You can't fight if you're unconscious, and he won't care. You need to keep your wits about you," Vivienne murmured in an undertone. "I'm sorry for what you have endured, what you will endure, but your only hope is to remain aware."

"Aware while he assaults me?" Daphne snarled. "You're torturing me."

"Do you think I've endured less from him?" Vivienne shot back, irritation showing. I've been here for decades as his plaything. I tried to fight him and look at me now. Locked in an attic." She shut her lips and a thought reverberated inside Daphne's head. *Listen to me, girl, his arrogance is his undoing. If he believes you obedient, he will trust you far more than he should. Play the slave to save your life, and you may get a chance to run to freedom before he inflicts the final, irreversible damage on you. Fight, and you'll be turned in a week.*

Though Daphne's heart clenched at the unwanted words, she had to acknowledge the truth in them. *How can I? Is it even in me to feign submission to his sexual exploitation?* She shuddered. *And how is Vivienne in my head... and Philippe? This is so far outside everything I know to be true.*

Taking a deep breath, her mind occupied with partially formed theories, Daphne's feet firmed on the stairs and she allowed herself to be led, calm as a lamb, into the lovely part of the vampire lair.

*Philippe is inside my head. I can hear his thoughts, even from a distance. We can communicate this way. We did. I might have believed I dreamed it, had Vivienne not just done the same thing. All right, this is a new scientific theorem. Under certain circumstances, telepathy is real.*

*I've observed it. Now, to determine the circumstances. If I can extrapolate the causes, perhaps I can control them, find some way to harness them.*

She thought harder. *Philippe shared his virus with me, and now we can communicate. He's human, more or less, though no longer mortal, or so it would seem. His body and his virus seem to have achieved a stable symbiosis.*

*Vivienne bit me, also sharing her virus. They must be related, yet different. She's been turned, but her enslavement is incomplete, which is why she's kept prisoner. Philippe, Vivienne, and I are able to resist being controlled. Why?*

Her memory dredged up images of Lois, compelled into obedience by the vampire who controlled her, of Ragonde, unable to disobey an order from her master. *Ragonde bit me. I can feel her compulsion, but it doesn't affect me.*

Too many pieces of information still eluded Daphne, preventing her from completing the puzzle and seeing the full picture. *However, Vivienne is right. If I want to untangle this enough to benefit from it, I must show Sébastien an obedient face, no matter how he disgusts me. He will treat me like a prisoner unless he thinks I'm helpless, so I need to act helpless. I have to observe his obedient slaves and mimic their behavior.*

The first floor lay out before her, all polished wood and lush finishes, fit for a king. *Sébastien may not have been able to make inroads into the vampire leadership in Europe, but on this continent, he's the supreme authority. Never forget that. He expects to be obeyed. I have to use that.*

At last, Daphne's pounding heart and jumping stomach distracted her from her pondering. She bit her lip and tried to firm her trembling knees as they approached Sébastien's spacious parlor, still trying frantically to put together pieces of information that might benefit her.

*This man cares deeply about aesthetics. He wants a harem of beautiful people. He wants a house befitting his status. Even Stéphane has a certain beauty,* she realized, turning to eye him. Tall, with well-formed muscles and a handsome, if vacant face. Dark skin and soft black eyes. Shiny bald head. *Maybe my pretty face will please Sébastien, or at least distract him. Maybe he's ancient enough to appreciate a curvy figure, as Philippe does.* The thought of attracting his desire sickened her.

Stéphane turned the handle of the double doors and revealed the sumptuous parlor. At one end, in a carved chair that resembled a throne, Sébastien lounged, his chin propped on one fist, regarding the new arrivals with bored indifference.

Daphne studied their enemy. He certainly didn't present an imposing air, dressed in a loose, blousy white shirt, tucked into skintight brown pants and tall boots. *Dressed up like a pirate in a romantic adventure story? Really?* Daphne narrowed her eyes. His medium brown skin and dark eyes, full lips, and an overly wide nose, did not bear identifying characteristics that suggested one racial background over another. *He could be a Moor, or an Arab, or even from Mexico or South America,* she realized. *Even one of the swarthier versions of Italian, Spanish, or Greek. He's unidentifiable.*

Sebastien's mysterious origins irked Daphne. *Another piece of the puzzle I can't fit in anywhere. Damn it, why can't I make this all make sense?* Though his ethnic background mattered little in the greater scope of her dilemma, she wanted to rage nonetheless at this further evidence of her ignorance.

*No, that's not correct. I'm raging because he touched me,* she realized. *He had no right.* Daphne pushed the thought away, realizing its futility. *Vivienne is correct about one thing. I have to remain alert and in control of myself, and that means behaving as a mindless slave. No matter what he asks, I have to obey.* She wanted to gag, but forced herself to stillness, her eyes wide as blue marbles, her expression blank.

"Ah, Stéphane," Sébastien drawled. Again, Daphne tried to place his background, using the accent in his tone, but again, she failed. *It sounds a bit Cajun, and a bit French, as though he learned English in the bayou, but even the French is accented. There's a hint of something else, something older, in that word formation.*

"Hello, Master," Stéphane said with a friendly wave. "How are you?"

"I'm frustrated, mon ami," the man replied, levering himself upright in his thronelike chair. "You see, the vampire council of Europe is coming to visit me next week. They want to see what I've built here in the Americas, but I don't trust them. I think they will try to challenge my power. I cannot let them claim my kingdom."

Stéphane dropped Daphne's arm and clasped both hands over his mouth.

"Of course, I cannot allow that to happen. Do not be afraid, Stéphane. I'm stronger than any of them realize. They will soon discover that chasing a bear into its den is a deadly thing to do. The War has ended in Europe because upstart Americans put a stop to European supremacy. I think it's about time for a vampiric world war as well. Goodness knows I have enough fighters, both human and vampire, to take them in a show of brute force, but it's not enough. My slaves have brought me rumors from the far reaches of our land, of a perfect weapon guaranteed to bring Japan to its knees. That is what we need. A perfect weapon that will destroy our enemies on contact and leave us untouched. With power like that, we will be unstoppable. You—girl."

He gestured to Daphne. Though she would rather have set her heels in a gesture of defiance... or run like hell... she forced herself to move forward in a wooden, mechanical step.

"That's better. You see, Ragonde? She only needed a firm hand to be brought to heel."

Ragonde snarled in response but made no attempt to argue.

*Good,* Daphne thought. *He believes me... or at least he believes in his own superiority. Now to keep my wits about me while pretending to have none.*

"Tell me about Philippe," Sébastien ordered.

"I know no one of that name," Daphne intoned in an expressionless voice.

"You are a scientist, yes?" he pressed.

"I am a student of science," Daphne corrected, pretending to be unable to conceal the tiniest truth.

"Who is your teacher?"

Inside her, Daphne could feel a feeble urge to obey, to spill the honest truth to this monster before her. As she considered the sensation, it grew noticeably weaker, until it faded altogether. *As though something more powerful choked off the compulsion.*

Another sensation of command, stronger, fresher, but no more controlling, urged her to lie. She recognized its personality as Vivienne's, but she had no need of it. *Stop,* she sent the silent message to the dark-skinned woman. *I know what to do.*

The compulsion faded.

"Dr. John Foreman," Daphne intoned. "Dr. Robert Johnson. Mr. Michael Reed."

"Stop, wench," Sébastien ordered, and Daphne fought a grin at the realization that his compulsion no longer whispered in her mind. "What are you doing?"

"You asked who my teachers were, Master," Daphne replied. "Did you not want the answer?" She tilted her head to one side.

"Let me try, Master," Ragonde urged. At his nod, the tiny woman surged forward, crowding close into Daphne's space. It took all Daphne's force of concentration not to pull back from the powerful, dangerous creature. "You told me you were working on the cure for yellow fever. That was a lie. Tell the truth now!"

In her peripheral vision, Daphne saw Sébastien's gaze harden. *He's compelling the truth from me.* "I was hired as an assistant to a scientist working on a cure for yellow fever. Though there is a vaccine, it is harsh, and many people become sick from it. We wanted to help people who are not strong enough to endure the vaccine. There are still too many swamps and too many mosquitos."

"And who is your master?" Ragonde demanded, interrupting Daphne's flow of chatter.

She turned fully to face the throne. "The great Sébastien, king of all vampires," she intoned. He beamed.

Ragonde slapped her, knocking her head sideways. Daphne's teeth cut into her lip and she tasted blood. "Don't be stupid," she snapped. "You know what I mean."

"Too rough, Ragonde." Sébastien rose from his seat and approached Daphne, shouldering his general out of the way. "Dear one," he said in a voice as soft as a father speaking to a frightened child. Daphne wiped the blood from her lip to hide her shudder. "Can you tell me the name of the scientist you worked with?"

"His name is Phil Peters," she murmured. "Master, my face hurts." She stuck out her bleeding lip. Too late, she realized what a mistake it was, as Sébastien ducked in and claimed it, sucking her blood and swiping the wound with his tongue. A moment later, a pulsing heat spread downward from her face and set her extremities tingling.

"You see!" Ragonde crowed. "Phil Peters. Philippe St. Pierre. It is him! I told you it was." Her harsh voice rang in Daphne's ears, but she refused to react. It took every ounce of willpower for Daphne to force herself into stillness as Sébastien ravaged her mouth.

At last, he released her. "If that is the case, he will follow. He always was a romantic fool. He will come, and we will claim him. In the meanwhile, I have an idea. Daphne, love," he said, his voice turning from casual to pointed, "Ragonde says you discovered a virus that resembled yellow fever but was not identical. Is that true?"

"Yes, Master," Daphne said. *Tread carefully, girl. This could easily backfire.*

"Did you discover a cure?" he demanded, his gaze changing in the way that suggested he meant to compel her.

"No, Master," she replied honestly. "We had barely begun to catalog the disease's similarities to and differences from yellow fever. We had not yet begun work on its cure."

"What did you discover?"

She swallowed hard. "V1 is transmitted through contact with all bodily fluids, not just blood. It is spread through direct contact between host and victim, not through mosquitos. It seems to have a strange... telepathic component."

"Well done, Miss." Sébastien sounded impressed. "Now, if you were going to cure it, what would you do?"

*No reason not to be honest.* "I know how to create a reagent that reacts to the V1 virus," she informed him. "To develop a cure, I would take samples of fluids known to contain the virus and expose them to various agents until I found one that would cause it to stop reacting to the reagent. That would be a cure, but it might be dangerous to the host."

Sébastien pursed his lips. "How so?"

"Well, Master," Daphne intoned, fighting to keep her voice empty of inflection, "vampires only remain alive and upright because of the virus. If I cure it, they will no longer have an animating force in their bodies, and they will instantly die."

Sébastien's overstretched grin grew wide and frightening. "A little injection, or a pill in their food, and they fall down dead. That's exactly what I need," he muttered.

"Since the virus seems to extend the lifespan of human victims who have not been turned, killing the virus might enforce their normal lifespan, which might kill them instantly, or age them quickly. Also, the cure might well be poisonous to the host, which would cause him or her to die, and since the virus is also dead, they would not rise."

Around the room, the four vampires gasped in unison as the implications of this outcome became clear to them.

"Mon Dieu," Ragonde breathed. "We could kill without reproducing. No unexpected revenants to contend with."

"We could infect humans for a brief time and then cure them," Sébastien added. "No need to spend resources on an army forever. Only as needed. This would be remarkable."

"Master," Stéphane said hesitantly, "promise you won't cure me."

Sébastien patted the larger man's hand. "No, mon ami. Of course not. You are a faithful servant. I would be lost without you. As long as you obey, you are safe."

Daphne heard Stéphane's relieved sigh, though she did not turn to take in his expression.

"I could finally be rid of you, bitch," he snarled, turning to Vivienne.

"I'd like nothing better," she informed him, voice filled with defiant pride. "I died long ago. I'm ready to rest beyond your reach." *Promise me, Daphne,* the woman's voice rang in her mind. *Promise me you'll use your cure to free me.*

"But, Master," she reminded him, blinking in surprise at Vivienne's unexpected request, "I have not yet developed any cure. My work was interrupted."

Sébastien focused his attention back on Daphne. "Yes, that is true. Now then, if I provide you the supplies, you will make the cure and give it to me."

"Yes, sir," she vowed. "You give me what I need, and I will provide the cure." *Like hell, I will, but this seems a good way to buy time.*

"Excellent. I expect you to have the work done by the time the council arrives next week."

Though Daphne knew it was unlikely, she responded, "I promise."

Sébastien beamed. "Good girl. Now then, before we get down to serious business, I feel the need of a bit of entertainment. Stéphane, are you feeling like enjoying a woman today?"

"Yes, Master," the man replied eagerly.

"Good. You and Vivienne shall play together before me."

He grasped Daphne's hand and pulled her back to his throne, sinking to the seat and dragging her onto his lap.

Vivienne's eyes went wild, and she turned to flee, but Stéphane's long legs ate up the distance between them before she could manage three steps. He lifted her over his shoulder and carried her to the table in the center of the room.

"Now, watch, love," Sébastien murmured into Daphne's ear. His hand came to rest on her bare chest above the deep, square bodice of her borrowed dress. He eased the fabric down, baring one breast and toying with the nipple. "See how much fun it is to be a vampire. You Americans with all your talk of rights and duties have forgotten the pure joy of decadence."

*Pure, nothing, you disgusting pervert,* Daphne thought, willing herself not to fight his unwanted touch. *I have to consent. I have to com-*

*ply. If I fight, I'm doomed. He'll know he can't control me.* Though she wanted to retch or cry, she dug her teeth into her lip and remained still.

Pinned to the table, Vivienne had stopped fighting, apparently recognizing the futility of resistance. She turned to meet Daphne's eyes and frowned. *We cannot win through outright rebellion;* her words rang in Daphne's head.

*I know,* Daphne sent back. *I hate this.*

*Hate it. Hate it like hell. Only hate will keep you sane and strong. Do not succumb to fear.*

*No fear,* Daphne agreed.

Stéphane hiked Vivienne's skirt up to her waist. Underneath, her tawny skin, bare and smooth, seemed to draw his attention. He kissed her inner thigh and then worked his way upward. Daphne closed her eyes to block out the sight of the violation.

Sébastien's teeth compressed the side of her neck, and for once she welcomed the euphoria that blocked out her will to resist and made her compliant to the touch she did not want. Daphne's skirt began to climb up her knees, but she pretended not to notice.

Philippe regarded the service station attendant in frustration. The man gnawed on a wet mouthful of tobacco and spat brown saliva onto the ground, far too near Philippe's shoe.

"Don't get no strangers 'round these parts," he insisted. "I knows everyone in this town and most who comes through regular. I don't know nobody like you's talkin' about though."

"Are you sure?" Philippe pressed. "It's very important. This is a woman. Short and thin, with a compelling presence and dark, intense eyes. You'd remember her if you saw her, I'm sure."

"Whoo-eee how you talk," his unhelpful informant replied, smoothing a strand of thin, greasy brown hair off his forehead. "Can't hardly make out a word. Where's you from, anyhoo?"

Philippe sighed. "France, sir, but that was long ago. I'm looking for a woman..." he tried enunciating more clearly in hopes of triggering comprehension.

Awareness flashed in the man's eyes for a moment, and the skin around them crinkled slightly. "Nope, don't know nobody like you's talkin' about. Say, if your dame ran off, better let 'er go. Ain't no woman worth chasing after."

*He does know,* Philippe realized. *He's intentionally blocking me.* "Very well, sir. Do you know of anywhere I can stay for a few days, until I get my bearings?"

The man drew his lips back into a parody of a grin, showing stained, brown teeth. "No, suh. I surely do not. We don't cotton to strangers much. You'd best plan to move on, if you knows what's best for ya. Anyhoo, there's no hotel or motel or any dad-blamed thing 'tween here and Baton Rouge." The grease monkey regarded him again, his stare turning baleful. "You'd better get yerself over there now. Skedaddle. 'Fore we decides you's up to no good."

"I'm not doing anything wrong," Philippe informed him, "but I consider myself duly warned. Good day, sir." He turned on his heel, intent on his Packard and getting away from this unpleasant fellow and his questionable behavior, when something warm hit the back of his shirt. Moisture seeped into the cloth, mingling with the swampy water. Without thought, Philippe whirled and nailed the man with an intense, evil glare. One that promised vile retribution. The attendant took a step back.

Satisfied, Philippe gave himself a vigorous shake and felt the clod of chewing tobacco fall from his shirt. *This town is in the vampires' clutches. That means I must be close... but not close enough. Now, what to do?*

He slipped into the seat and shut the door, his mind whirling with undefinable possibilities.

"This is what a test tube looks like," Daphne explained, hunching over a small table in the clothing room to sketch the shape roughly on a sheet of white paper. "I need as many as you can get."

"Can you write the word?" Stéphane asked. After his session with Vivienne, the simpleminded man seemed cheerful and relaxed. Daphne had noticed her strange ally seemed much less content in the aftermath of the encounter. *And no wonder. She probably feels as used and dirty as I do.* Daphne shuddered at the memory of probing fingers. No matter the pleasure she'd been unable to suppress, it still felt unwanted and wrong. *At least he hasn't attempted full intercourse with me... yet.* She shuddered again.

"I can write it, honey," she told Stéphane, forcing her mind back to the all-important task of acquiring scientific equipment. *This is the only thing that keeps me alive at this point. If he wants this 'eure', my memory must remain intact and he knows it. I likely won't discover anything useful in a week, but if I look busy enough, maybe he'll leave me alone... and I can find a way to escape. Preferably before Philippe tries to ride in like the cavalry and I have to rescue him too.*

*Focus, woman*, she scolded herself silently, then added aloud, "Can you read, then?"

Stéphane shook his head. "No, miss. But I compare the shapes. You know?"

"Ah, that's very wise of you," she replied. *He's clearly lacking a bit, but he's clever enough to compensate. If only I could count on him as an ally, but he's so loyal to the ma... Sébastien. And no wonder. Here, he's treated as important, allowed to indulge with women, everything.* Daphne sighed. *He can't understand why anyone would feel differently, and that makes him more dangerous than helpful.*

"Test tubes," Stéphane repeated, tracing his finger over the letters as Daphne formed them. "What else?"

"Beakers." She sketched the shape and word. "They look like measuring cups used for cooking. I need acetic acid to clean the glassware." *It will be a miracle if he gets this right.* "I also need a lot of chemicals.

I don't know how to describe them, but if I write the words, you can match them, can't you?"

"Yes, miss," Stéphane agreed. "I will match the shapes."

"All right then," Daphne agreed. Then another thought occurred to her. "Where will you get this stuff? Most of it is not available in the grocery store or even the hardware store."

Stéphane's grin turned crafty. "I know a laboratory," he said, enunciating the long word carefully. "I used to work there a long time ago. They have lots of these shapes." He stroked his fingers over the page.

Though Daphne wondered exactly what business a vampire's henchman had working in a chemistry lab, this didn't feel like the time to ask questions. "I see. All right then, honey. As soon as you can get these things, bring them here. I have a lot of work to do for the master." *And maybe, if I'm busy, he'll keep his hands to himself.*

"Yes, Miss," Stéphane agreed. "If I get it all right... will you give me a kiss?" He waggled his eyebrows.

Daphne couldn't help laughing, though she could hear the hint of hysteria in it. "Only on the cheek, Stéphane," she told him earnestly. "I'm still a married lady, remember?"

Stéphane's grin turned to a pout. He grabbed the list and slunk from the room.

Daphne sank onto the sumptuous—if musty—bed still residing in the middle of the room. A cloud of dust rose up, setting off a round of coughing. "I suppose I'll be sick next," she muttered. "Wait, can I still get sick?"

The ceiling above her, veiled by a thin sheet of gauzy burgundy canopy, seemed to have been made of smooth plaster. A tiny crack ran from one side to the other. "Even this level is showing its age. I hope the whole building doesn't fall apart one day...at least not while I'm inside it." She studied the crack, shuddering as a large spider emerged and marched, bold as anything, toward the corner of the room. It began busily constructing a web. Like the sticky strands, the disjointed pieces of Daphne's thoughts began to cling to one another.

"I won't get sick," she whispered. "I can't prove it, but it stands to reason. Philippe is hundreds of years old, and he says he hasn't had so much as a head cold or an allergy. On this, at least, I believe him. Something about V1 keeps other microorganisms from taking hold in the body. If one strain of V1 fights off another, that would explain why neither Ragonde nor Sébastien can control me. I share Philippe's strain. My body has acclimated to it. Now it fights off all other invaders.

"Maybe this is also why we can seem to communicate telepathically. I can hear Philippe strongly in my head at times. Also, Vivienne. Sébastien and Ragonde sound like a whisper, and even the whisper fades quickly. I still react to the initial bite, but its long-term effects are blunted, and then they disappear." She breathed slowly, willing understanding to emerge. "Is this related to why Vivienne is also beyond their control? I can hardly imagine it would be otherwise."

Daphne pondered. "I can't know that for sure. She's like them. She died and reanimated. She can't remember her former life to know if she was perhaps a voodoo practitioner whose spiritual practice lent her some kind of protection, or if she has a natural immunity, or if the virus simply worked differently on her for some unknown physiological reason. I can't draw conclusions without information, so there's no point in creating theories. Poor Vivienne."

Daphne's eyes stung as she recalled her unexpected ally stretched out on a table and forced, fully aware, to become a display of sexual degradation against her will. "I was no better off, fondled again by that disgusting germ. Lord have mercy, how do I get out of this mess? And how do I take Vivienne with me? She has no business being here."

"What are you doing?" a harsh voice snapped. Daphne shot to her feet to take in Ragonde's scowling face.

"I gave Stéphane the list of supplies I need. I was thinking through what steps I need to follow to get the result I want. It's relatively easy to develop a substance that will kill a virus, but if I'm not careful it might also kill the host."

Ragonde smirked, only half listening to the long-winded explanation. "Thinking about science after Stéphane leaves you lying on the bed? Girl, you really are hopeless."

Daphne opened her mouth to protest the unfounded supposition, but only a croak emerged. *And after all, why protest? This decadent bunch think sex and blood are the foundations of existence. Don't argue.*

"Madame Ragonde," Daphne began, eyes fixed on the floor in a parody of meekness, "would you please help me to discover a room where I can set up my laboratory—one near a powder room I'm going to need a sink—It takes quite a bit of space and equipment to perform scientific experiments."

"You're out of luck there," Ragonde sneered. "This place was built long before running water and has never been connected to any city supply. You'll have to use the swampy water from the well, like the rest of us... and that reminds me. The master says you're starting to smell. He wants you to take a bath."

Daphne sighed. "All right. How do I go about that?"

Ragonde's smile turned wicked.

"No, I don't need your help," Daphne said quickly. "Just point me in the right direction."

Ragonde's grin faded to a scowl. "Fine. There's a washtub in the kitchen. You'll have to draw water from the well and heat it on the stove, the old-fashioned way. Then it's back to the attic for you. I won't have you wandering around the house. I don't trust you."

*That makes two of us,* Daphne thought, but in the interest of feigning enslavement, she kept it to herself and followed Ragonde down the stairs and out of the room.

"Merde," Philippe snarled, banging the heel of his hand onto the steering wheel. "I hate that I was right. The entire town is under the influence of those monsters, and they're protecting them." Sadly, he acknowledged the truth. "I won't be able to find out anything helpful here. They're too tightly controlled." He slumped in the Packard's drivers' seat and leaned his head back, squeezing his eyes shut.

He reached out with his senses. "Daphne, love, are you there?"

"Leave me alone," her harsh voice hissed.

Philippe's eyes shot open in shock. "What can this mean?" He reached out again, but her awareness had been blocked as though with a steel plate, and his thoughts bounced back to him unheard. Anxiety welled up in his heart in an instant, replacing rational thought with wild supposition.

Shaken, Philippe cranked the ignition and pulled his car out onto the quiet road. "Have they enslaved her?" he asked aloud. "Has she succumbed to the decadence of the vampiric court? A woman as sexy as Daphne might be tempted by it. Does that mean she no longer wants to be rescued?"

His throat tightened, and a pulsing heat rose in his face. *There's no way she's avoided being used. Pretty as she is, knowing Sébastien, he put his claim on her within hours of her arrival. What if she liked it? Impossible not to, if he bit her. The physical sensation of the bite is overwhelming. Some humans become addicted and choose to stay.*

A stinging sensation at the back of Philippe's throat rose in response, fighting with the rage aroused by the thought of another man's hands on his wife. "Daphne," he whispered, his heart splintering into shards.

Not knowing what else to do, he turned his car around at the next intersection and headed out of Grosse Tête, in the direction of Baton Rouge.

"I need a shower," he muttered, clinging to any rational thought he could dredge up, "and a bed. I need to think about what's best to do next." Though the move made sense—the silly little town possessed no hotel, not even a cheap motel with cockroaches—driving away from where he knew his wife was felt horrible and wrong. "But I must regroup and think about my options. I must try to contact her again and get to the bottom of what is happening. Flailing about in the bayou will not succeed. It's too big and too wild. Somehow, I must find a guide, but it won't be a willing one."

All the long way to Baton Rouge, he whispered under his breath, desperate to understand the wild pieces of unharmonious information jangling in his head.

# Chapter Fifteen

The attic room looked welcoming in its shabby unkemptness, Daphne noted as Ragonde threw her through the door and left her crumpled in a heap on the floor. No longer interested in feigning calm, she curled up in a ball and let loose loud sobs of shame and fear.

Vivienne laid a hand on her arm. "There, there, Daphne."

"How does a person get used to this?" she demanded. "The fear, the casual violence, the loss of autonomy." She sniffled. "I hate their hands on me. I hate it. I would kill them if I could."

"I know," Vivienne's strong fingers slipped into Daphne's hair, loosening the pins and letting it fall loose around her face. "It never gets easier, chère. The decadence they so pride themselves in claims victims, but they don't care. They're selfish. Selfish people with power are the worst."

"Why don't they control you?" Daphne asked, wiping her eyes and sitting up. *I don't want to break down. Not now. Focus on answering questions, Daphne, on building theories. Fall apart later, when you're safe.* Though she knew she would likely never find safety again, she clung to the fragile hope. "Everyone who dies after being exposed to V1 is the slave of the person who infected them. I saw my friends. They forgot themselves within moments of waking."

"I know," Vivienne replied. "I can't imagine what went wrong in my case. Maybe if we can figure out why they can't control you, it will give me a clue."

Daphne flopped onto her back on the floor. The ceiling of this crummy little room had much deeper cracks than the second floor. Little flashes of daylight slipped through. "So, you're immune to their influence and so am I, but to what extent? Why am I? That's easier, since I have full possession of my memories." She pondered, chewing the tip of one finger. "So do all the other living slaves, so what is it? Why can't they control me? Philippe said they could control him... why him and not me? Wait! Philippe!" Daphne shot to her feet.

"What is it, chère?" Vivienne demanded, startled by the sudden movement. She watched Daphne pace with wide, dark eyes.

"I was exposed to V1 before I ran into Ragonde and Sébastien. Philippe, my husband, has it. We were trying to cure him. I was horrified when I realized I was infected." She blushed, remembering the medium through which the virus had entered her body. "But he's alive, not a vampire. Somehow, his system and the virus reached a stasis point. They're able to co-exist. He's a carrier. He infected me, and the same thing happened, so now I'm a carrier too. He also said... he said after time the monsters chasing him caught up with him less often. He didn't have to run as much. I think... I think as Philippe's virus grew accustomed to his living body, it changed. Changed enough that it is no longer subject to Sébastien's meddling. That different, mutated virus is what I carry. It's stable within me, probably acting the way it does on Philippe to keep me healthier and chase off other viruses. When Ragonde infected me, Philippe's virus fought hers off, since it didn't recognize it as the same. Likewise with Sébastien. But I can hear Philippe in my head. We're still connected.... And I can hear you too. Why?"

"Because I bit you, probably," Vivienne admitted.

Daphne shrugged. "It did me no harm. Let's experiment."

The excitement of discovery somewhat blunted her previous upset, allowing her to think clearly again. *Someday, if I survive this, I'm going*

*to fall apart completely and for a very long time, but this is still not the
moment. I still have to try to understand so I can make a way to escape...
if it's possible.*

"What experiment?" Vivienne asked suspiciously.

"Send me a thought," Daphne urged.

Vivienne's dark face settled into lines of relaxation. "Oh, all right
then." She closed her eyes. "Did you hear that?"

Daphne shook her head. "Nothing."

Vivienne frowned.

"It must have faded. Quick, bite me again."

"Easy, there, girl," Vivienne urged. "A lot of the living people in this
house are here by choice. They're not enslaved. They just like the way
the bites feel."

"I haven't seen any of them," Daphne commented.

"They're here, men and women. Didn't you wonder who lives in
all those rooms? Over a dozen willing victims, though not enough to
keep the entire vampire population fed. A lot more human slaves live
in town," Vivienne explained. "They have normal lives most of the
time, but when the vampires come looking for food, they're ready and
willing. You may not have noticed, but it's rare for a vampire to drain
a person completely to death. It attracts too much attention. This was
especially true in the past, when it was harder to get from place to
place, but even now, it's not considered wise to create too many new
vampires. It strains the local resources too badly, and the master is
responsible for the care of all his offspring."

"That is very interesting," Daphne said, pondering whether the information had any use she could apply to her escape plan. "So, how
many loyal vampires actually live in this castle?"

"This house can accommodate thirty or so, provided they share
rooms, which they usually do, but only a few stay here permanently.
The others move through, waiting on orders for where to go next, healing from injuries, and so on." Vivienne gave Daphne a disapproving
look. "Don't think about running off into the swamp, girl. You'll be

lost and eaten by alligators in minutes. No offense, but you look like a city girl, not a hillbilly, and I have a feeling you're not too athletic."

Daphne glanced at her generous curves. "True enough, but I'll take my chances."

Vivienne rolled her eyes heavenward. "Girl, if you die, you turn. Do you want to drag yourself around for thousands of years as the gator-chewed vampire with big pieces missing?"

The thought gave Daphne pause. *What a disgusting image.* "Are you sure that will happen? I mean, are vampires impossible to kill, even if they're missing parts?"

"Now that I don't know for sure," Vivienne replied. "It's common enough for a vampire to dismember a victim they don't want to rise. I suppose even if the virus lives in a body, if there's no head or limbs, it wouldn't matter much."

"Right. And as I would be dead, it wouldn't matter to me whether the virus attempted to keep my mutilated body alive. There would be nothing left of me to suffer."

"Are you so sure about that?" Vivienne pursed her lips, her head tilting to one side. "I can still almost remember who I was. It's on the edge of my awareness. Surely, I retain enough awareness to hate *them,* Ragonde in particular. I would rather fight against them than obey them, and I follow my inclinations. They know they can't trust me, and that's why they lock me in here."

"Odd that they've thrown me in with you. Do they trust me or not?" Daphne speculated.

Vivienne nibbled on her fingertip. "I'm not sure they've thought of it much," she commented. "They have a certain view of the world, and they hold it with such single-minded determination, it's hard for them to grasp deviations."

"I suppose that's how viruses think... since the evidence seems to suggest this virus can. The main goal is to stay alive. The second goal is to reproduce. We can clearly see all their decisions fit into these goals. They have some level of rudimentary reasoning—not overusing resources, for instance—but complex decision-making seems to be a bit beyond them."

"It is a strain," Vivienne agreed. "I struggle with it too, though for some reason I've got a bit more than *they* do."

"So, let's think this through again," Daphne suggested. "For some reason, the virus that lives in me fights off other viruses, even yours, though yours took longer than Ragonde's or Sébastien's—which suggests they might be similar."

"I agree with all that," Vivienne replied. "I think you're onto something. But then, why am I, a vampire, able to fight off the influence of Ragonde, my master, and Sébastien, who is hers?"

Daphne worried at a ragged spot on her lower lip. "If I am immune to other people's virus because of Philippe's, which is different from theirs because it adapted to an existence inside his living body, then it stands to reason you must have been exposed to V1 when you were alive. Not once, which your immune system would have fought off in a short span of time, but over and over until your body and the virus adapted to one another. You think it was Ragonde who turned you?"

Vivienne's lips twisted into a frown that suggested she might be ill any moment. "I know it was. My first awareness was of her beating me because I refused to obey her... the things she wanted me to do." She shuddered.

"I noticed she has some unpleasant tendencies for both seducing women and beating them." Daphne touched a bruise still aching on her cheek.

"Seduce, nothing," Vivienne scoffed. "She prefers force, you may have noticed."

"That makes sense," Daphne muttered. "No wonder she fits in with Sébastien. They have the same omnivorous sexual appetite."

Vivienne nodded. "Now you're starting to understand. Who knows if that was always their inclination, or if the virus doesn't have an interest in male or female humans, so long as it spreads to a new host?"

"Well, viruses do reproduce asexually," Daphne agreed. "Likely they're not overly aware of gender because they have none."

"I'm not sure what that means," Vivienne admitted, "but I'm willing to take your word for it."

Daphne's lips stretched in a parody of a smile. "It's not that important, really, to understand how it works. I can't see how this knowledge helps us overall."

"Me either, but you seem like a smart girl. If there's a solution hiding in this information, I'm sure you'll find it."

Daphne shrugged. "I hope I do, for both our sakes. This is a lousy place and I don't want to be here a moment longer than necessary. I'm sure you feel the same."

"Now hold on there, honey," Vivienne urged. "I may not like these vampire beasts, but I'm still one of them. Where else would I go? I would be a walking disease. I would infect people. Now you're saying if I bit the same person too many times, they would become infected. I don't want that. Oh, no." She shook her head. "Promise me, Daphne. If you do find a cure, use it on me."

"Vivienne, you do realize... your body is no longer living. If I cure your V1, you'll just die."

"Child, I died decades ago. I'm more than ready to be at rest. Mortality is part of our humanity. I'm not afraid. I'm ready. Promise me."

Daphne sighed. "I can't guarantee I'll find anything, you know."

"You will," Vivienne replied. "I know it. I think fate brought you here for this very reason. You'll find the cure."

"I hope you're right," Daphne replied, and then she shut her lips tight without promising or refusing. *I'll deal with that only if it becomes necessary.*

The motel, a small brick box in a seedy part of town, in no way resembled Philippe's preference for uncluttered luxury. However, the hot shower had helped restore his equanimity somewhat, and his freshly rinsed clothing hanging over the back of a wobbly chair would probably help more. *Got the swamp water off me at least.* He shuddered.

Flopping onto a small bed whose springs shrieked in protest of the move, he tucked his arms behind his head and watched a small cockroach scuttle across the ceiling. "So, Philippe, what's happening?" he asked himself aloud. "Daphne would demand you look at the facts and not leap to conclusions." He drew in a deep breath, willing clarity to enter with the oxygen. Then he began laying out his situation. "She's with them. I know that for sure. I know they haven't turned her yet, or at least they hadn't when I reached out a while ago. She's still alive and in her right mind. Why would *he* not turn her immediately and place her in his harem? She's lovely and sexually satisfying. He won't care about more than that—her fine mind, and her loving heart—those mean nothing to a brute like him."

Thought connected to thought. "He did not turn her, which means he needs her consciousness, her awareness and memories for some purpose of his own. It might be as a lure for me. I'm sure that plays some role, but I doubt it's more than a small portion. If he'd wanted me back so badly, he would have hunted much harder. I'm sure he'd be glad to have me back, but like most vampires, Sébastien is more interested in power and control, and those things take time and effort to amass. He must want her for something else she can give him."

Try though he might, Philippe could not imagine what his enemy's motivation might be. "Ah, well," he muttered at last. "It doesn't exactly matter. The point is not what he wants from Daphne, but that she's still alive and thus can be rescued. Which brings me to the crux of the matter."

The cockroach scuttled into the crack between the ceiling and the wall and Philippe rolled to his side, studying the ugly industrial building across the street from his window. "Does she still want to be rescued, or did Sébastien enslave her?"

He recalled the firm rebuff he'd received, and again the thought tortured him that she might have decided to throw in her lot with the vampires. "Those bites are powerfully erotic. If I know Sébastien, he had no second thought about pairing his bite with touch."

Philippe's heart clenched, but at the same time, a red rage flared in his heart. "He touched my wife," he snarled, glaring at the pale brick wall across the street. A truck rumbled along, obscuring the view, and with it, a new thought crystalized. "I'm assuming," he realized. "Daphne would have my head. I have no idea why she shut me down. She might have been in a tense situation and needed her wits about her. I should not give up so easily."

The blank yellow bricks reappeared, and Philippe stared at them without taking them in. He opened his mind to his wife's consciousness and found himself in an unfamiliar, shabby room. "Daphne?"

"Philippe," came the soft-voiced reply. "Oh, thank God. Are you all right, love? What's happening?"

Relief rushed through him. "I'm still trying to find my way to you. The swamp is dense and hard to navigate, and the people of that town…"

"Are all infected," she agreed. "So I've heard. Philippe, this is a terrible place. I want to get out of here, but I don't know how. If I go wandering in the swamp, I don't think I'll make it out."

"No, stay put, love," he urged, "since *he* is not in too large a hurry to make you his."

A ghostly image of Daphne pursed its lips. "He thinks he already has." She made a sound in her throat that resembled a gag.

"Don't worry about that," he reminded her. "It can't be helped. Do you know why he's not trying to turn you?"

The ghost nodded. "He wants me to continue working for a cure. I think he wants to use it to impress the European vampire council. They're coming to visit him soon. Lovely piece of work, isn't he?"

"He's a beast," Philippe stated. "An absolute beast. If you find a cure, use it on him, won't you?"

"Yes, and that disgusting Ragonde as well," Daphne agreed, "but I can't do it. How can I come up with a cure in only a week or two?

We've barely isolated the virus and begun to catalog its symptoms and behaviors."

"Well, love, it's a Gordian Knot for sure," Philippe agreed. "Keep in mind... the goal is not to save the patient. Kill the virus any way you can. Later, when we're both free of this mess, you can teach me to do science properly, and we'll continue our research. For now, develop any advantage you can. I will find a way to get to you—do not ask me not to—and somehow we'll get away."

Daphne nodded, though he could see the doubt in her shadowy face. "I love you, Philippe. No matter what happens to us, never doubt it. You are the love of my life."

"I love you as well, Daphne. No matter what he's forced or manipulated you into doing, I know your heart belongs to me. I will never blame you for what you could not help."

Her eyes sparkled as tears gathered in the corners. "I hate that. I hate him. *Hate* him."

"I know, and that will make you strong and crafty. Be safe, my love, no matter the cost."

The tears fell, pale on her transparent cheeks. "I have to go back to thinking, love. There's never a moment to spare."

"I know," he agreed. "I will talk to you often, to be sure you are all right. Can you... if you're busy, can you give me a different signal than 'leave me alone?' "

Daphne laughed bitterly. "That wasn't addressed to you." She shuddered. "Ragonde was trying to be handsy with me while I was bathing. Disgusting creature."

Philippe frowned. "I understand. I'm sorry, my love, that I exposed you to this."

"I am too," she agreed, "but I will never regret loving you. Let's just make it stop, okay?"

"Yes, certainly," he agreed. "Farewell, darling."

She nodded and shut down the connection.

Much relieved by the communication, Philippe resumed his sightless scrutiny of the wall beyond the window while pointless and unanswerable questions stirred his mind to restless confusion.

A strange sound shook Philippe from a deep slumber. He rubbed his eyes and rolled his neck, trying to shake off deep grogginess. "What the devil was that?" he muttered to himself.

As though in answer, the sound came again, a sort of quiet scraping and rustling.

"Probably a rat, and nothing more," he muttered. "I've hardly slept in days, worrying about my wife, and now a sneaky rodent wakes me?"

Irritated, he rolled to his side, away from the window, and sulked. "Every moment that goes by makes it less likely I'll be able to find my Daphne before they do something horrible to her that she'll never recover from, and yet here I sit, in Baton Rouge, miles from where they've taken her, with nothing to go on, no ideas, not even a hint of a plan. This is intolerable and I'm useless."

The rustling continued.

"Stupid rat. Quit rooting in the dustbins and let me sleep."

The rustling continued unabated. If anything, it grew louder. A loud scraping jolted him straight out of the bed. He whirled, peering out the window to see the door of the unknown warehouse across the street standing ajar. A hulking shape crept in.

"There's something familiar about this man," Philippe whispered aloud, not sure what he was seeing.

Almost without thought, he rose from the bed, tugged on his pants and shirt, stepped into his shoes, and crept out the door.

Night closed in around him, but his virus-heightened vision cut through the gloom with little effort. Silent as a cat, he slipped through the door and froze, jaw dropping in surprise. The warehouse he'd noted and dismissed proved to be filled with long rows of black tables.

At each one, a microscope waited, sided by boxes of slides, test tubes, pipets, and other familiar apparatus.

Along one wall, huge floor-to-ceiling shelves housed boxes labeled with familiar names like isopropyl alcohol, dilute hydrogen chloride and distilled water. A row of top-of-the-line refrigerators stood opposite the shelves. The heavy aroma of chemicals hung in the air. Philippe stepped into the shadow of the nearest refrigerator and went still, hoping to remain invisible as he observed his quarry. A huge, dark shadow of a man stood stock-still—unnaturally still—in front of the boxes, his hand extended a short distance in front of him, his head cocked to one side.

*I know this shape*, Philippe realized. *I know this man. Why?* The thought produced a wave of anxiety he could not fully understand. *He isn't safe. Who is he?*

In his mind's eye, an image formed, of lolling, half-insensible on a luxurious bed. A shape passed between him and the window, blocking out the moon, and a huge, dark hand grasped his arm and levered him to his feet. "Please, don't," Philippe had muttered in semi-coherent revulsion.

"Master is calling for you," the man replied, tugging Philippe from the bed and urging his stumbling feet down the hall.

"I don't want to go." More awake, Philippe began to struggle, feebly, cursing his own weakness.

"You should want to," he insisted. "Master is good to us. You should be proud to do whatever he asks. It's better in here than it is out there."

"It's not," Philippe had insisted, but to no avail. The man would hear no arguments. Instead, he forced Philippe forward.

"Stéphane," he breathed, and then clamped his hand over his mouth to silence himself. *Stéphane is simple-minded and loyal to* him. *He's not able to reason beyond following orders, and the last I heard, he only hears orders from my enemy. Daphne would say not to read too much into it, but right now, my instincts tell me there's no better opportunity to find my way to my enemy than to follow his flunkey.*

Decision made, Philippe drew deeper into the shadows to await the other man's next move. As he watched, his busy mind continued contemplating his surroundings. *This is surely a chemistry laboratory. What could a simpleminded vampire's slave want in such a place?*

Long moments passed as Stéphane studied the boxes, occasionally grabbing an item and shoving it into a bag hanging from his arm. *He seems quite confused. What are you up to? I can't imagine, but I aim to find out.*

# Chapter Sixteen

Despite the stress of her situation, nothing fired Daphne's blood like the sight of shiny new lab equipment. Beakers and test tubes of unspotted glass glistened in the morning sunlight. Against her will, a hint of a grin curved the corners of her mouth.

"Did I do good, Miss?" Stéphane asked. She turned to him and saw his eyes pleading like a child's.

"Just a minute, honey, and let me check everything," she urged.

Stéphane's wide grin faded to a showy pout, but Daphne turned back to her loot, nodding at the various chemicals she would need to recreate Philippe's reagent. Box after box, stacked neatly against the interior wall of an unused bedroom, matched the names she'd written on her list exactly. *I didn't expect this to come out so well,* she thought to herself, surprised at the man's resourceful overcoming of his handicaps.

Then she reached the last box and frowned. *I asked for acetic acid—vinegar—to clean the glassware. He brought salicylic acid—aspirin—instead. I can't clean with that. Ugh.* Not wanting to cause a scene, however, Daphne said, "Yes, you did a very good job, Stéphane. Thank you. Now, can you do me one more favor?"

"Anything, Miss Daphne," he said, nodding eagerly.

"Can you get me some vinegar?"

He blinked. "Are you cooking? I thought this was science."

"Of course, honey. It's surely science, but vinegar is good for cleaning up. Haven't you ever heard of using it on windows? Makes them shiny and takes off fingerprints."

Stéphane regarded her, his brow furrowed, and his lips turned down.

"Never mind why, sugar," Daphne said at last. "I just need it, okay?"

He nodded, brightening, and hurried out of the room.

Daphne shook her head. "What am I going to do with salicylic acid? I don't have a headache, and it won't help a bit with my sour stomach... guess my system needs more of Philippe's magic elixir." She shuddered. "Even if I wanted to use it as a painkiller, it's much too concentrated and I have nothing to cut it with." She sighed. "Oh well. Here it is. Might as well not fret about it. It doesn't hurt anything just sitting there."

Daphne broke out a shiny new beaker and set it onto a table she'd appropriated from the lower floor. Then she set to work opening the boxes.

Philippe stared up at the towering mansion. Two broad stories of Creole elegance reached toward the moon with a row of gables. Columns like teeth sank into the ground. Philippe squinted at the top of the structure. Shadows obscured the view, but he thought he could make out cracks and rotten eaves. Some extended onto the second floor, disappearing into the frames of windows. The ground floor appeared pristine, white paint gleaming in the darkness. Only one large fissure made its way all the way to the ground, encircling several windows along the way.

Against a backdrop of naked trees festooned with Spanish moss, the entire building presented an ambiance of twisted, ugly luxury. Of decadence fading to decay. Philippe frowned. *A fitting home for a brute like Sébastien.*

Movement in the vicinity of the front door sent him scuttling into the shadow of a tree. Stéphane emerged again, returning to the narrow road out of the bayou. Philippe stayed behind. *No need to follow him any longer. I've found my quarry. But how on earth do I get inside? And where are they keeping Daphne?*

"My love?" he whispered into the wind, letting the sound flow away into the bayou to blend with the songs of bullfrogs and crickets.

"Philippe," the beloved voice whispered in his mind, "are you safe?"

"Yes," he assured her, even as he admitted to himself that to date, he'd not been in so much danger as he was now. "And you, Daphne? Are you still safe?"

"He keeps touching me," she wailed. "They all do. I don't want them to, but I can't stop them... and then..."

"Hush, love," he urged. "I know. There's nothing you can do. You can't fight it, so don't try. I know you don't want this, but if you fight them, they'll end you."

"They won't," she replied, wavering voice firming. "They want me to continue my work. They want the cure. I think *he* is planning to assassinate the European vampires."

Philippe rocked back against the trunk of a dying cypress. "He's an idiot. A lunatic. Even if he destroys a few of them, there are more. So many more. He'll never defeat them all."

"But this is Sébastien," Daphne reminded him. Philippe flinched as she voiced the hated name. "He doesn't seem to have a firm grasp on reality. I think... I think he's spent so long alone with his flunkeys in the swamp, he's begun to believe his delusions of grandeur are true."

"That sounds right," Phillipe admitted. "I recall such things, and that was when he had a small, city-sized holding surrounded by enemies. Now, it seems, he has all of North America at his disposal. No doubt all his new freedom and power have gone straight to his head."

"What do you want?" Daphne asked.

Somehow Philippe felt she no longer addressed him, as though he were listening in on the party line to someone else's conversation.

"All right, all right, but you can't rush me this way. Scientific research takes time." She paused. "No, I don't know how long. I was trying to map the symptoms and characteristics of the virus before. I'd barely begun." Another pause and then she sent him a soft message, delicate as a kiss. "Goodbye, Philippe."

He hung onto her awareness, to her presence. *It has been so long since I dared love anyone, and this connard and his minions have interfered again.* Philippe ground his teeth in frustration. "This is impossible. I will *not* lose my wife."

A wave of euphoria rolled through her and into him, hardening his sex and turning his stomach at the same time. Wanting to roar with rage, Philippe shut down the connection. It felt like an abandonment, like leaving her to her fate as unwanted hands caressed her body. *Calme-toi, idiot,* he insisted. *If you make a commotion and get caught, you'll be useless to help her.*

Snarling, he ducked into the swamp and, from the dim light filtering between the trees, began examining the building for weaknesses he could exploit.

Daphne lay gasping on the floor of her makeshift laboratory as the memory of Ragonde's bite burned her skin. Disgust roiled through her. "Nasty, degenerate bitch," she snarled. "Keep your filthy mitts off me." Though far too late, the small act of rebellion strengthened her resolve. "I will not remain here, a passive victim of these vile creatures. I *will* find a cure, and then, I will use it on them."

"Be careful how loudly you say that," a teasing voice pronounced from the doorway. Daphne whipped around in surprise, and then sagged to see Vivienne leaning against the wall.

"You startled me. How did you get out of the attic?" Daphne hoisted herself to her feet, annoyed when her knees sagged. *How many times did Philippe leave me weak-kneed? Not nearly enough, and yet I enjoyed it every time. Enjoyed him holding me afterward. This vile parody of love will not weaken my knees.* And yet, the weakness and nausea remained.

"I picked the lock," Vivienne explained. "I do that every now and again. They get angry, of course, but they don't actually stop me. I can't leave, and everyone knows it."

"Why can't you?" Daphne asked, forcing herself to talk normally.

"I'm not sure," Vivienne replied. "It's such a strong knowledge, I might almost think it's a compulsion, but they can't compel me." She sighed. "I can't leave. I can't explain it, as this is the last place I want to be, but there's some reason I have to stay. Some fate I haven't completed yet." She shook her head. "Anyway, enough about that. I brought you something." She drew a golden chalice out from behind her back, took a sip, and extended it to Daphne. "You won't be able to do your best work if you're distracted. Drink."

Daphne sniffed the cup and gagged. The rich aroma of red wine barely masked the rank mineral stench of blood. "I can't drink that."

"You must," Vivienne insisted. "The virus needs to be fed, no matter whether the host is living or undead. You will become ill otherwise, and then incapacitated and finally feral. It's vile, but there's no choice. Besides, if it makes you feel better, the donor is a willing participant. He's one of about fifteen humans who live with the vampires by choice, because they enjoy the lifestyle."

Daphne frowned. "I'm not sure if that makes me feel better or worse."

"Feel better," Vivienne advised, extending the cup again. "They weren't assaulted or harmed. They chose this life."

Daphne, seeing the wisdom of the suggestion, shrugged and retrieved the cup, taking a sip. Though the bloody flavor made her shudder, the strong wine did blunt its impact somewhat, and the drink settled her roiling stomach and left her calmer than she'd felt in the days since her capture.

"So," Vivienne said, "how's your progress?"

Daphne bit her lip. "I've begun concocting the reagent Philippe invented. It differentiates V1 from regular yellow fever, but it takes several hours to prepare. Despite the delay, I need it. If I can develop a treatment, I can use the reagent to determine its effectiveness. I'm not sure I need it, though. If I manage to find a medication to kill the virus, the cure will almost certainly kill the host, which would be a much more dramatic than a vial of bodily fluid turning pink."

"So why did you make it then?" Vivienne asked.

Daphne pursed her lips and turned toward her worktable where a fat candle heated a beaker of liquid, reducing it to a thick syrup. "I didn't know what else to do. I have no idea where to start. Studying a virus is not the same as killing it."

"Well, what would you normally use to kill a virus?" Vivienne asked. "No matter its qualities, this vampiric infection is a virus, as you've told me. A mutation of yellow fever. Start with what kills yellow fever and work from there. If you want samples of infected fluids, I volunteer."

"Thank you; that's helpful," Daphne agreed, brightening, "and of course, you're right. Instead of focusing on how V1 is different from other viruses, I should focus on its similarities. How would I clean up a spilled sample? How would I sterilize contaminated glassware?" Blinking, she returned to reality long enough to mutter, "Thank you, Vivienne." Then she dived back into her work.

Philippe circled the building, scrutinizing it in the blinding light of midday. *No point in creeping around at night, when my enemies are most active.* Though many cracks and rotten places marred the division between the second floor and the attic, none was big enough for him to wriggle through. *If only I could actually turn into a bat. That would be beneficial.* He grinned grimly at his inappropriate joke.

In the style of many plantation homes, a covered porch surrounded the entire front and both sides of the house. Only the back had a plain, flat façade. There were also narrow, high windows he would never fit through. *All right then. Waltzing up to the front door like a houseguest is a recipe for suicide, but what else can I do?*

He circled around the far side and fixed his eyes on a broken rail. *Out of sight of the front door, so of course,* he *wouldn't notice. It's a way to get onto the porch, but then what?* He scrutinized the side of the house until he found what he wanted: large windows—a matched set of them—that extended nearly to the floor of the room within, shaded by heavy maroon draperies. With a glance around the yard, he stepped into the shadow of the porch roof and made his way to the window, where he peered through a gap in the drapes, holding himself perfectly still in hopes of remaining invisible.

A luxurious room filled with sumptuous fabrics and ornate furniture met his gaze. Directly in front of the window, a thronelike chair held a person whose slick dark hair seemed familiar, though thinner than Philippe recalled. *Do vampires grow bald in time? Perhaps the virus only slows, but does not actually stop, the aging process. Hmmm.* With his heightened hearing, he could make out the familiar voice, and it knotted his stomach with anxiety, until he realized it, like the hair, had changed in quality. *He sounds higher, thinner, like he's lost some of his strength. Interesting.*

Hoping for a clue, Philippe strained to hear the conversation.

"The delegation will be here tonight… any time now. Do you think our 'welcome' will be ready by then?"

"I hope so," a female voice replied. Movement in the vicinity of the throne revealed Ragonde. Philippe hissed softly in rage. *Evil bitch. I wish the sunlight really would burn her. I'd break through this window right now and the consequences be damned.* "I checked on her earlier and she had a lot of messy things bubbling and stinking, but nothing I could identify, let alone use."

Sébastien snickered. "Checked on her or distracted her? I know you, Ragonde. Perhaps you should let me keep tabs on our little scientist."

"As if that would make a difference," the vampire woman sulked. "You just want her for yourself."

Sébastien's snicker turned into a full-bodied laugh. "What if I do? She's mine to take, as are you, and Vivienne and Stéphane. All the vampires, all the human slaves. They're all mine. You're all mine. Never forget that, Ragonde." He surged to his feet, and even from the back, dressed in a baggy shirt, Philippe noticed he had lost weight. He'd gone from hale and muscular, as were most people living in that time period, to a stringy whip of a man. *Something is not right with him. He's unwell.*

Philippe concentrated harder, to combat his pounding heart and sweaty forehead. *I will not be intimidated by this man. I am no longer a helpless youth. He's strong, but so am I, and I have more to lose this time... Hang on, Daphne.*

"Of course, Master," Ragonde placated, laying a hand on Sébastien's bony arm. "You are my lord, and you will be in control, not only of the Americas, but of the world. I will help you see to this. You are powerful, the most powerful vampire of all time, and I am strong and loyal. With me by your side, how can you fail? You will succeed, starting with these European minions. Your new toy will create a powerful poison that will destroy them, and we will send their ashes back to their masters as proof that a new power has arisen, and their time is growing short."

Sébastien nodded, displacing his hair so that patches of skull showed beneath the greasy strands. "You are so right, my pet. All will be well. You did such an excellent job finding this little treasure... do you think I should turn her when she's done with her work?"

Ragonde shrugged. "That I cannot decide. She would be more controllable—though she's not hard to control now—but then she would forget her work. After all, who knows what kind of amazing discoveries she could make, and we could keep for ourselves, for our armies, with our own pet scientist."

Sébastien nodded again, more gently this time. He sank back into his chair, groaning like an old man. His knee popped. "Very good. And if, as you say, she is in love with Philippe, perhaps in the end she can draw him back. The family will be complete. With her under our control, he will never leave again." His lascivious words brought to Philippe a flood of images of himself, pinned down by two guards as this disgusting monster violated his body... again.

Sickened, he stepped back, exiting the porch and melding into the woods. He staggered to the trunk of a towering cypress, leaned against the rough bark, and took slow, deep breaths, trying to control the urge to vomit.

"I will rescue Daphne," he vowed, "and you will never touch me again. Blessed Virgin, let it be so."

Slowly, his disgust faded to determination and he sank into a cross-legged pose, pondering what his next move ought to be.

"Have you discovered anything yet?" Sébastien's oily voice interrupted Daphne's intense concentration, making her jump.

"No, sir," she replied, hand fluttering on her heart, biting back her sarcastic reply. "I've only had a few hours since my equipment arrived. I've barely begun formulating the reagent I need to test the effectiveness of the cures. I'm quite a long way from creating anything new."

The man tutted, shaking his head, which did strange things to his too-taut skin. "Much too slow, my pet. The council's representatives arrive tonight. They only plan to remain a few days. We must be sure their welcome is ready. You must work faster."

"I'm doing the best I can," she insisted.

"Are you?" the question in his voice brought Daphne's head around and she regarded him closely, suppressing a shudder at the lascivious gleam in his overly bright black eyes. "Do I need to give you an incentive?"

Daphne inhaled, expanding her bodice to epic proportions, and took a chance. "Master, please. I don't need incentives. I want to work. I love this kind of work. What I need is fewer distractions. If you and your lady continue to pop in and break my concentration, I might never get anything accomplished. Please, let me carry on for now. When we have something to celebrate, we can celebrate." The words, though voiced in a tone of false adoration, stuck in her throat, but she forced them out as best she could. Then she bit her lip and waited, hoping her request would not strike him as a sign he lacked the control he so coveted.

Sébastien's expression turned considering. "I see your point," he said at last. "Very well then, my pet. You keep working. Develop your cure. When the delegation arrives, you can present it to them. They won't suspect a thing, as you will be part of the entertainment." He laughed.

Daphne echoed with a weak giggle. *Part of the entertainment? Not on your life, you beast.* With a nod, she turned back to her worktable, shielding her face so her enemy wouldn't see her expression.

Behind her, the door of the bedroom creaked open. She heard his shoes thudding on the wood of the floorboards. Daphne forced her wandering mind back to her work. *What do I need to do? Samples, first.* She spat into several test tubes and set them aside. Then she regarded her supply of chemicals and sighed. "Where do I even begin? What if the combination I need is not even here? I can't possibly get anything new before tonight. I have no idea where Stéphane has gotten to."

Frustrated, she found herself chewing on her fingernail and quickly tucked it under her arm. *Don't do that. No telling what you've touched. Keep it out of your mouth.* Daphne crossed the room in a few long-legged strides to the ewer of boiled swamp water she kept handy for a quick wash.

As she scrubbed her fingers, she regarded the stacked boxes of chemicals against the far wall. *All the ingredients for the reagent and nothing else. If I could figure out which one specifically reacts to the virus, it would be a place to begin, but that would take quite a lot of time. No, I need something stronger. A sword to cut through this Gordian knot.* Her eyes fell on the box she hadn't requested—the salicylic acid—and she squinted at it. *Hmmmm.*

# Chapter Seventeen

"Daphne?" Once again, an unexpected voice cut through her concentration, though this time Daphne felt no resentment. She lifted her eyes from the syringe in her hands and met Vivienne's intense stare. "It's time to dress for the party. *He* says I may attend, if I promise to behave and if I help you get ready. Are you at a place where you can get dressed? What do you have there?"

"I'm not sure," Daphne replied. "It may or may not be what I've been searching for. Only time will tell, but it had a powerful effect on the samples. I'm not saying it's a cure, but it certainly will kill the virus."

"What is it?" Vivienne asked.

"The simplest thing," Daphne replied. "Concentrated salicylic acid. Just aspirin, really."

Vivienne frowned. "Aspirin? What's that going to do?"

"It thins the blood, first of all," Daphne explained. "It's good for people with blood clots. In a vampire's body, it should cause the blood to spread more freely through the body, carrying the acid with it. It's also a powerful antimicrobial agent. This dose so strong it's capable of killing viruses, which I've seen it do in several experiments. The virus no longer triggers the reagent, whether in blood, urine, or saliva. The problem is, it's so concentrated, I have no idea what it will do to the host's body. A solution weaker than this is used to kill warts. It can burn through skin." Daphne shook her head. "I've had too little time. I can't do this the right way."

"It will be enough," Vivienne said, staring at the syringe with the most intense expression on her face. "Sometimes you have to take a chance, Daphne, and trust that fate will bring about the right conclusion."

Daphne rolled her tense shoulders. "Fate and science are not the best of friends, but I have no choice other than to try."

"Fate is real," Vivienne insisted, "only you 'so-modern' children have forgotten. You think your science tells you something, and it does, but it doesn't tell you what is meant to be."

"Well, that's certainly philosophical," Daphne said, trying not to drawl sarcastically. "At any rate, this may or may not be the 'cure' these vampires are demanding. It's bound to do something, but I have no idea what. My only hope is that it's dramatic enough to create a diversion, so I can get away."

"That sounds like a good plan. Better give me some of it too. I would love to make sure a few key members of this household have a dramatic reaction." Vivienne grinned wickedly.

Daphne giggled and drew the viscous liquid into a second syringe. "Be careful," Daphne urged. "This isn't particularly safe, with the hypodermic needle on the end. I don't want you accidentally to stick yourself."

"I'll be fine," Vivienne promised, tucking the needle into a pocket in her skirt. "Now let's get you dressed, and by the look of things, you'll need a pocket as well."

"I guess I will," Daphne agreed.

"Now then, with your coloring, a pale blue will really suit you. Oh, and I have express orders that you're not to wear any undergarments except perhaps a hoop, if your dress requires it."

Daphne scowled at Vivienne.

"They're all vampires, sugar. They like their debauchery. You and I are to be part of the 'entertainment,' which means they're making our bodies available to the guests for their use. Or they may decide to have one or both of us perform sexual acts in front of everyone."

"These people are disgusting," Daphne snarled with a shudder. "My body belongs to me, not to *him*."

Vivienne made a face. "I can't remember a time when my body belonged to me enough to make a choice of a partner. That was never a privilege I had. Not even before." Then her brow creased. "I don't know how I knew that."

"Sounds like something came back to you. Maybe vampires don't lose themselves entirely when they turn," Daphne suggested.

"Maybe," Vivienne agreed, "but what a thing to remember, that even before I was a slave, I was a whore." She frowned, but then her frown faded. "Or rather, not always. I feel like there was a time, maybe a brief time, when a man was special, and his touch made me feel cherished instead of used."

"I'm sure there was," Daphne agreed, "and if he was a vampire, or even a human infected with the virus, it may be the reason you didn't turn fully."

Vivienne nodded slowly, but Daphne's heart sank as a theory that explained the whole situation flashed into her mind. Grimly she shook it off. *There's no way to know for sure, and right now, we have bigger things to worry about.*

"If I do manage to get out, where do I go?" Daphne asked. "I'd rather not flounder into a swamp."

"I trust you'll find your way," Vivienne replied, contradicting her earlier warning. A strange light shone like black flame in her eyes. "Somehow, I just know you will."

Daphne sighed. "Well, fate isn't something I know much about, but I'll take your word for it. Say, Vivienne, let's go get dressed, shall we?" Then she muttered, "No underwear? Honestly? What a pervert."

Vivienne laughed, the sound no longer strained, and the two women walked the three doors down the hall to the room where all the dresses were stored. Despite her resolve, the likelihood of disaster hung heavily on Daphne's heart and set her belly churning. She reached out in her mind to Philippe. "I love you." Then she shut down the connection, wanting her full concentration fixed on the task at hand.

Alarmed by the brevity and tone of his wife's message, Philippe reached out again. "I'm here, love. I'm right outside. I know the way back. If we can get you out of there, we can get away." His words reverberated off the iron plate again. "Merde," he muttered. Then he sighed. "So, Daphne is clearly plotting something that frightens her. She doesn't know I'm standing by to help. I have no idea where she is inside the house, and the most likely window enters into the busiest, most frequently occupied room. How do I get inside unseen?"

From his shadowy spot near the back of the porch, he contemplated his options. Other windows surrounded the manor, just as long and low as the one he'd discovered, but all felt more exposed, closer to the front, where he'd already noted patrols of three to four vampires fanning out into the woods, always in sight of the front door. "Odd that *he* never thinks to guard the back of the house," Philippe muttered. "Must assume any enemy wishing to harm him will waltz up to the front door in a direct attack. Foolish."

The layout of the interior made entering through the back quite risky. The kitchen always bustled with activity, indicating at least several of the residents were human enough to need food to survive. Another room, barely accessible through high, small windows, had proven to be a pantry. *It's a possible entry point, though it will still leave me inside the kitchen and likely to be discovered.*

Around the other side, various parlors and sitting rooms generally housed groups of humans who lolled about, intoxicated by wine and strong bites. They gossiped and fondled one another, waiting for their next fix of the virus, but he had no doubt they were all aware enough to raise the alarm if a stranger suddenly jumped in the window. "So, that only leaves the throne room," he admitted to himself. "If I can ever find it empty, I can hurry in and find a hiding place." Though the plan didn't delight him—thus far he'd only found the room completely empty for a couple of moments before either Sébastien or Ragonde returned—it was still his best bet.

Philippe settled in, his ears straining to detect the stillness that meant even vampires had left the room. He could hear Ragonde and Sébastien chatting, their words punctuated by laughter, but their tones strained. *They're more worried than either one wants to admit,* he thought, *and rightly so. These European vampires are much stronger and saner. If they catch one whiff of deception, heads will roll, literally.* Though he wanted to grin at the thought, he didn't quite dare. Though letting the vampire council deal with his enemies had a certain appeal, Philippe knew they'd take a dim view of human slaves, especially ones who knew all the secrets of vampire society and would set to work turning them all as quickly as possible, Daphne included. Her scientific aspirations would mean nothing to them.

"Their arrival will make the whole rescue even more urgent... but perhaps easier as a house full of strange and suspicious vampires will certainly be distracting." The fact that all of them might turn on him crossed Philippe's mind. "Non, don't think that way. I will get to Daphne. One way or another, I must."

Movement swept past the front of the manor, and Philippe drew back further into the shadows. Seven tall shapes, shrouded in dark, hooded cloaks, emerged from a limousine and approached the front door. A loud knocking reverberated.

In the parlor, the voices stilled. A hush fell over the room.

The knock sounded again, louder than before.

"Well, my dear," Sébastien said, "shall we go meet our guests?"

"Of course," Ragonde replied. "Come along, Stéphane."

"Yes, ma'am," the towering guard slurred. The parlor door creaked open and then softly clicked shut.

*This is it,* Philippe thought, hurrying to the window. *Hope they didn't leave anyone behind.*

He peered through the glass. The deepening twilight cast shadows over the furniture, but the room stood empty. Easing the window away from the casement, he stepped inside. He pulled it shut again. Heart pounding, he arranged the drapes to hide any evidence of his passing and scanned the room. A wardrobe stood in the corner, and he raced to it, opening the door and praying it would work as a hiding place. The drapes he didn't trust not to betray him.

The inside of the wardrobe had been converted into several shallow shelves on which bottles of wine, their corks displaced, stood upright. A strong, bloody smell emerged. *These are for the human slaves,* he realized. *Vampires drink directly from the source, and there is no way he will offer bloody wine to his guests instead of their pick of his sexiest harem girls and boys.* Secure in the knowledge he'd found the safest hiding space, Philippe stepped into the wardrobe. There was barely enough space for his slender body between the shelf and the door. He closed himself in so only the tiniest shaft of light fell along the seam.

*Now, I wait.*

Dressed in an ice-blue gown that resembled fashions of the Victorian era, with a wide, ruffled skirt, a fitted bodice and long, narrow sleeves, Daphne reluctantly followed Vivienne down the stairs. The doors to all the rooms on the first floor stood open, revealing similarly clad vampire revelers, drinking wine and laughing as they awaited the festivities.

Daphne's stomach churned, and her head pounded. A buzzing noise like a thousand bayou mosquitos sounded in her ears. She could feel the weight of a syringe in the pocket of the carefully selected garment. The needle had no cap, and a wrong move could easily plunge the sharpened metal into her skin.

Time drew out thin and taut, like the blade of a rapier. *One wrong move and I die... and rise as a slave. Lord, help me.* Terror pulsed in her bloodstream, and her virus provided no defense. She swallowed hard against a wave of nausea. *This is it. In the next few hours, I will take action against my enemies in hopes of freeing myself from them... and almost certainly die in the process without accomplishing anything.* She bit her lip. *I have no choice. I have to try. I refuse to live this way a moment longer.*

Stiffening her spine, Daphne trailed after her companion.

Vivienne's own shoulders, left bare by the cut of her red satin gown, looked painfully tense. Her respirations grated in her throat. Her thick, dark hair, pulled back into an elegant coil, seemed to vibrate with every step. *If fear had an electric charge, I swear the two of us could power the entire French Quarter.*

They paused on the threshold of the throne room, as instructed, and Vivienne raked red-lacquered fingernails down the wood of the open door.

Alerted by the soft sound, Sébastien's head shot up. The movement displaced his carefully arranged hair, showing pale scalp beneath. Daphne suppressed a shout of wild laughter. He looked like a mostly bald man who had combed his remaining hair over the empty spot. His bony face split into a grin that threatened to shatter the crepe-thin skin, and his dark eyes shone with a wild brightness. Daphne shook herself, desperate to retain every shred of her awareness despite the fear pounding through her insides.

"Gentlemen and Lady," he intoned, and his voice had a shrill note to it, as though age had cracked it, "you were wondering what all I have accomplished during my sojourn overseas. Rest assured, I have not been sitting idly by, drinking wine and debauching innocents... at least, not entirely." He laughed.

At his side, Ragonde gave a false and sycophantic giggle, though she looked no less tense than Daphne felt.

"Not only have I amassed an army that easily rivals yours. It is composed of both my own vampiric offspring, and my specialty. Look, friends," he waved with false indolence at the collection of eager humans who awaited their fix of tainted saliva. "Living slaves who follow me willingly—and make no mistake; their loyalty surpasses that of even my most loyal children."

He extended a hand to Daphne, and she moved forward reluctantly, a false smile pasted onto her lips. He grasped her arm and drew her onto his lap on the throne. "I have also ventured into the realm of science. That's right, you see before you one of my most prized possessions; the jewel of my harem."

One of the hooded figures standing in the center of the room regarded her askance and a sound like a snort emerged from beneath his cowl.

"Yes, I realize she might appear to be any ordinary plump and pretty farm girl, but make no mistake, gentlemen. This woman is a brilliant scientist, whose work on diseases will elevate me to levels unheard of in Europe. With her by my side, I can create epidemics that will bring entire cities to their knees. But she's also done the impossible. She's developed a cure for vampirism. I now have control over who does and does not rise. Just think of the possibilities. No more accidental or undesirable offspring. Complete authority over who lives and who dies."

The hooded heads turned toward one another, eyes meeting, and Daphne could see the doubt on their pale faces. No sound emerged from a single mouth, only the soft sighing of fabric over flesh, but she sensed they must be communicating telepathically.

"Well, that is very impressive," the vampire at the head of the line stated. "We would see your 'cure' in action this evening. It would be a most valuable piece of information to take home to the council, and certainly a worthwhile means to plead your case for membership."

"That is most gratifying," Sébastien said, his voice betraying no emotion, even as his arms tightened around her, until her ribs creaked. She let out a soft squeak, and he loosened his grip. "Shall we go to dinner?"

"Yes, please," the hood in the front agreed. "We're quite parched. Do you have something lovely for us to enjoy?"

"Yes, naturally," Sébastien replied with a lascivious giggle. "A rainbow of beauties for every taste. Come, let us view the harem, and you can make your selections." He rose to his feet, dragging Daphne along with him.

"What about that one?" one of the hooded vampires asked. "She looks like quite a tasty ride."

"Sorry," he replied. "She's too new. I don't dare offer her up just yet. Besides, with the work she's doing, I can't afford to have her loyalty waver. But come now. Why not take a look at the selection?" He indicated the door.

Stéphane, who stood guard, leaning against the wall, sprang into action, leading the way back into the hall. Sébastien brought up the rear, his arm still tight around Daphne's waist. Ragonde fell into step beside him.

Daphne could hear the echoes of their telepathic conversation, though she couldn't make out a single word.

*The beasts are plotting their mayhem. If only I knew what they had it mind, it would be easier to exploit it.*

Philippe ground his teeth in frustration. Rage set his blood pulsing hard in his veins. *So close, and there's still nothing I can do. How can she endure his touch with such calm? I can't contact her, but I can feel her fear, taste it. She's near to hysteria, but her smile never wavers.*

Philippe slipped from the wardrobe into the empty throne room and peeked out the door. Once ensuring the large central room was clear, he crept along its edge, to the far side, where he could hear the sounds of revelry. *Whatever is going to happen will happen there. Lord, give me strength.*

The large, central area contained several open doors to smaller rooms crowded with eager victims. Three European vampires glanced at one another and one stepped forward. The others, obviously guards, remaining in formation. *Nervous, aren't they, and well they should be,* Daphne thought.

"Come now, friends," Sébastien urged, "surely you see something to delight you. I have a lovely harem, and all so willing. Partake and enjoy."

A naked woman with thick, nubile curves stepped forward and trailed her fingers down a cloaked arm. The vampire turned in her direction and Daphne could see the heat flaring in his eyes. "How different this is from back home," he commented.

"What do you mean?" the woman asked, stepping closer.

"I'm not used to eager meals. Normally, when we feast, a single victim feeds us all."

"Doesn't that kill them?" Daphne demanded. "Do you just use it as a way to make more vampires?"

The man turned to her with a sharp glower and Sébastien gave her arm a little shake.

"Normally, once the 'feast' is mostly dead, we give them to the babies."

She twisted her face in confusion, so the strange vampire continued. "The freshly turned ones. They're a bit... messy in their feeding. There's rarely enough left to rise."

Daphne scowled.

"They're cattle, ma petite," Sébastien explained. "Do you feel pity for the cow or the chicken, or the pig? My dear, we are predators and you are our prey. At least here, the prey is willing and unharmed." He turned to the visiting group. "This might be worth your attention, don't you think, gentlemen? Here, feeding is more like milking a cow than slaughtering it."

*Keep your wits about you, chère,* the dark-skinned woman urged silently, her voice echoing inside Daphne's head. *The chance will come. I know it, but it will be subtle. Be on your guard, or you might miss it.*

*I know,* Daphne sent back.

"Definitely worth considering," one of the other European vampires said. Tossing off his cloak, he stepped into the room and extended a hand to a delicate-looking young man with livid bruises on his neck and shoulders. The youth approached eagerly.

All the vampires threw off their robes, revealing six men and one woman. Some retained a healthy color and appearance. Others looked thin and overstretched, similar to Sébastien. *Surely this is how vampires age,* Daphne realized.

One by one, they selected victims, all of whom acquiesced eagerly to the invitations, and received their bites without protest. As Daphne expected, the bloodletting quickly led to passion. One dark-haired vampire shoved a blond woman forward against the wall, his teeth worrying at the side of her neck as he lifted her skirt to the waist. She thrust her hips backward in eager anticipation.

The naked woman urged her partner, who turned out to be a freckle-faced ginger, to the floor. He straddled her, sinking his teeth into her thigh. Daphne turned away, knowing what would follow.

She could find nowhere to look. All around the room, vampires and willing slaves fornicated as they shared blood. Once the Europeans had selected their meals, Sébastien's own entourage chose from the remaining humans. Even Stéphane cuddled up on an ornate sofa with a young, brown-haired girl, nibbling her neck as he fondled her breasts. Only Sébastien himself, and Ragonde at his side, took in the scene without participating. Again, Daphne could hear the echoes of their silent conversation, but still, she could make out no details.

Desperate for something neutral to look at, she managed to lock eyes with Vivienne, who leaned against one wall, not participating in the debauchery.

"Aren't you going to partake?" The vampire on the floor asked Sébastien. A groan overtook the question as his victim's eager mouth worked his manhood. "Come now, even the host may join in the feast."

"True, true," Sébastien conceded. He whirled Daphne around to face him and laid his lips on hers.

The unwanted kiss disgusted her, as did the sour taste of old blood on his mouth. Daphne struggled in his grip.

"Modest, my dear?" he mocked, laughing. "There's no place for modesty in my domain." He tugged on her bodice, trying to free her breasts.

Daphne jerked backward. Lifting her chin, she glared at Sébastien. Her heart pounded, but her tolerance had reached its breaking point. It snapped, releasing the angry Cajun she'd been squashing down for so many days. *I can't do this anymore. I won't.*

Waves of telepathic noise rebounded off her mind as he tried to compel her.

*This is it,* she realized. *Come what may, this stops now.*

"Go to hell, Sébastien," Daphne snarled.

His eyes widened. Another wave smashed into her, until she felt compressed by it. This time, Daphne retaliated, sending a pulse of her own will back at him. Though she had no idea what result, if any, would follow, she had to try it, had to defend herself.

Sébastien rocked back as though she had physically shoved him. He gasped, the sound swallowed up by the moans and cries echoing through the room. His face showed slack-jawed shock for a moment, before rage turned his eyes red and set his nostrils flaring. His fists clamped down hard on Daphne's arms, and he dragged her closer to him, his teeth flashing toward her neck.

Memories of wrestling with her brother, of him instructing her how to deter unwanted attention, awakened in Daphne, spurring instinctive action. She brought her knee up hard into his unguarded genitals, and when his fingers fell away from her arm, she slammed the heel of her hand into his nose. With her free hand, she dug into her pocket, fumbling for the syringe.

He croaked, hunching over, but recovered faster than he had any right to.

"Little bitch," he snarled. Lunging forward, he grabbed her by the throat and squeezed hard. Sharp metal pierced her fingertip, and she grabbed, trying to drag the syringe out, even as black spots began swimming between her and the hated face of her enemy.

"What the devil?" Ragonde's voice shouted into the mêlée. Another set of hands gripped Daphne's arms, immobilizing them.

*Help me,* she shouted with her mind, as her voice had been completely cut off.

"Get off her!" Vivienne approached from the side, barely visible through the growing darkness clouding Daphne's vision. The pressure on her arms yanked sideways.

"Get away, slut," Ragonde shrieked.

"No, you get away." The carefully pronounced, French-accented voice rang like music in Daphne's ears, even over the buzzing. "You will not harm her, neither of you."

The pressure on Daphne's throat eased, though the grip remained strong. "Ah, Philippe," Sébastien cooed. "I knew you wouldn't stay away forever, my love."

"I am *not* your love," Philippe snarled. "Now take your hands off my wife."

Gasps rippled through the room, though from her position, Daphne could not see what was happening behind her.

"Your *wife*," Sébastien sneered, "has been thoroughly enjoying my attention for days.

"Liar," she shrieked. "Your touch disgusts me. You're nothing but a rapist."

Sébastien glared and tried once again to compel her.

"That won't work," she informed him coldly. "It never has. You have no power over me. None of you do."

The hands crushing her arms shook her, hard. "Show some respect, slut."

"I'm not the slut here, Ragonde," Daphne snapped. "Not by a long shot. Now let me go."

The woman laughed. "Look, Master, the entire party is here. Now we can be rid of all of them at once. After all, our little scientist was good enough to create a cure. Let's use it, starting with these two. Vampires!"

Reluctantly, Sébastien's soldiers rose from their revels and approached, taking hold of Philippe and Vivienne. Movement from behind Daphne suggested the European vampires had risen and were now watching the show.

"Excellent notion," Sébastien agreed. "I think it might do my rebellious little beauty some good to see what happens to those who cross me. Vivienne." The vampire woman lifted her head. "Do you have it?"

With a nod, Vivienne withdrew the syringe from her pocket and held it up to his inspection.

"I've had reason to question your loyalty in the past, woman," Sébastien informed her. "You've never shown proper respect. This is your last chance to demonstrate obedience, or I will destroy you as I should have done in the beginning. Do you understand?"

"Yes, Master," Vivienne intoned.

Daphne's jaw dropped. *What are you doing?* she sent to the woman. *Trust me,* came the reply.

It occurred to Daphne, in that moment, that she had no particular reason to trust Vivienne. *She might have been in league with these two all along, and only trying to gain my confidence in order to manipulate me.*

"Now then," Sébastien said in an oily, condescending tone, "here we have the worst sort of betrayer, a faithless lover. Once, Philippe here was my entire world. I would have moved heaven and earth for him, brought down the moon for him to keep in his pocket. I showered him with love and pleasure, and how did he return my affection? By abandoning me and running away, only to fall into the arms of one woman after another. I say, for such infidelity, he should pay the highest price, don't you?"

Sébastien's toadies murmured in assent.

"And the ultimate price is to feel the sting of betrayal himself. First, he will watch me have his 'wife', watch her writhe in helpless pleasure. Then, I will end him, by the hand of the woman he never could protect."

Philippe gasped, turning to look fully at Vivienne. "Geneviève," he breathed. "You lived."

She tilted her head to one side. "Do I know you? You seem familiar, but I can't remember."

Daphne sucked in a breath that sounded much like a sob. *That's what I feared. She* is *his lost love. Dear God.*

"I knew you once," he explained. "Before you became... this. You meant a great deal to me." He lowered his eyelids.

"He's the reason you're not a slave," Daphne burst out. "You loved each other. His love, his virus, protected you from Sébastien and Ragonde. They cannot control you because you belong to him, but because he's human, he can't control you either."

Another considering expression crossed Vivienne's face. "I have no recollection of this. Proceed, Master, if you please."

Tears clouded Daphne's eyes. *So, this is how it ends.*

*Stay sharp,* Vivienne's voice rang in Daphne's head. *Their guard is lowered. This is it.*

Startled, Daphne stared, wide-eyed, as Sébastien approached her. "You're so naïve," he murmured. "There's so much you don't under-stand, but never mind. All will be well. Soon, you will be free of Philippe's influence and belong wholly to me." His head shot forward and his teeth compressed her neck. As always, the warmth of his bite spread through her body, setting her nerve endings on fire, and mak-ing her yearn for the release he promised.

This time, she refused to succumb, forcing herself to remain aware. Aware of Ragonde's hands loosening their grip on her. Aware of Philippe staring at her, his face a mask of despair. Aware of her hand, still clutching the syringe inside her pocket.

Again, Sébastien began to fiddle with the bodice of her dress. She moaned and shoved her body forward, aligning herself with him, and using the movement to mask the retrieval of her weapon.

Sébastien chuckled. "That's better." His hand slipped inside her dress and began to toy with her breast.

"You never learn, you arrogant bastard." In one quick, fluid movement, she drew back and bent her elbow, aligning the syringe with his heart. She had a split second to take in his confusion before slamming her fist forward and depressing the plunger with her thumb.

Sébastien's otherworldly reaction time didn't save him, though his quick twist did prevent the needle from entering his heart. Instead, the full dose of undiluted acid poured into his shoulder.

Sébastien roared, clutching his injury. He staggered backward and sat down hard.

Taking advantage of his distraction, Daphne dodged to the right, away from the grabbing hands of his henchwoman.

Several words in a language Daphne couldn't understand poured from his mouth.

She backed against the wall, facing the room and brandishing her only weapon, the spent syringe.

"What did she do?" the ginger vampire demanded. "What was that?"

"Concentrated acid," Vivienne replied calmly. "You see, while we have no problem in theory with this group of willing slaves," she waved at the naked humans huddled around the room, "some of us are not here by choice. They held us—Daphne and me—against our will, as prisoners, and they molested us. We did not ask for this, nor did we choose to be here. We would have left in peace and never bothered them again. They knew this, but yet, they restrained us. It is the duty of all prisoners to escape, and Daphne is a scientist. It was only a matter of time before she came up with a solution. Besides, they asked her to do this, as a 'surprise' for you. None of you were expected to leave here alive."

As one, the European vampires turned to face Sébastien, but it quickly became clear no answers would be forthcoming. He sat whimpering, clutching his arm. They turned to Ragonde.

The woman's face passed from shock to rage. She lunged toward Daphne, but Vivienne got there first. Fisting a large handful of Ragonde's shiny black hair, she jerked the woman off balance, dragging her against her chest. Lifting the syringe, Vivienne stabbed backwards, driving it into the woman's chest and slowly depressing the plunger, unloading the full dose between Ragonde's ribs, right beside her heart. Ragonde screamed, and Vivienne threw her to the floor. She writhed.

"In her way," Vivienne informed them, "this one is worse than him." She gestured to Sébastien with the needle. "She's his enforcer, and not even half as crazy. She harms and molests because she enjoys it."

"What is happening?" Sébastien asked, voice shaking. "What have you done to me?"

Daphne inched along the wall in his direction. "You didn't give me a chance to test this properly, so I'm not exactly sure, but at a guess, the aspirin thinned your blood. This allowed it to spread quickly through your body. Now, it's killing your virus, the only thing that animates your corpse."

Sébastien opened his mouth as if to answer, but only a croak emerged. Above his collar, a black line appeared, spreading upward. Everywhere the blackness touched, tissues seemed to collapse. His throat sank inward. His jaw sagged, blackened tongue lolling to the side. His teeth fell from rotted gums in an ivory shower. Sébastien choked and gagged before falling silent. Still, the blackness spread, until his nose collapsed and fell from his body. His eyeballs shriveled in their sockets and went blank, staring at nothing.

A vile gagging drew the attention of the room to Ragonde, who lay convulsing on her side as rank, brown ooze poured from her mouth and nostrils and seeped from the corners of her eyes.

Several individuals crept from the room in silence. In one corner, a young man vomited into a potted palm. The vampires, American and European, remained unfazed by the gruesome scene.

Daphne feared her ribs would shatter from the force of her pounding heart. *Any moment now they're all going to rush me. It will be horrible.* Beside her, Vivienne stood, calm and secure, regarding the vampires without expression.

A hand slipped into hers and she jumped.

"Easy, mon amour," Philippe murmured. Overcome, Daphne sagged against him, and he wrapped his arms around her, supporting her.

"Seems a bit weak," the ginger vampire commented.

"She's been through hell," Philippe pointed out grimly, "and she's not used to this sort of treatment. After all, before this happened, she was a young college student. She had no idea vampires even existed."

"I'm not sure that's very reassuring," Ginger replied. "Good leadership requires strength and experience."

"Leadership?" Daphne forced her head upright. "What are you talking about?"

"Whoever defeats the leader takes up his throne. You are now the vampire queen of America."

Daphne turned and hid her face against Philippe's shoulder, wishing she could block out the sound as well. "No," she muttered into his shirt. "There is no way I can do that. I refuse. I've had enough of vampires for a lifetime. Please, just let me go."

A chilly hand landed on Daphne's bare shoulder. She withdrew, tucking her body closer to Philippe, not even willing to find out which of the European vampires had touched her.

"She's not a vampire, though," Vivienne said into the murmuring conversation. "She's closer to a human vampire hunter. Remember how they sometimes got a little bit infected and developed greater powers? Only, she's not going to make a career of hunting us down, are you, sugar?"

Daphne shook her head against Philippe's shirt.

"There, you see?" Vivienne asked calmly. "When she destroyed Sébastien, it was not an act of vampire politics. It was a kidnapped girl looking to escape."

"That may well be," Ginger pointed out, "but her actions still leave a vast number of vampires without leadership. It is unwise to allow such a thing. Chaos will break out. Eventually, someone from Europe could be chosen, but with our lack of familiarity with the culture and situation here, it would be a rough transition."

"It would be no better," Philippe pointed out as he rubbed gentle circles on Daphne's back, "to put a twenty-five-year-old human in charge. She's only been here a few days, and she's young and ALIVE. Rather than leading, she'd immediately become food to one of the more aggressive ones."

"And you, sir?" The ginger asked. Daphne could only assume he addressed Philippe.

"Same problem. I'm not actually a vampire. It's an odd life I've led, trapped between the worlds, but I'm learning to appreciate it. Still, I'm not an appropriate choice. I've been abused too badly, sometimes by the people before me, and I do not trust myself to act out of anything other than revenge."

"Purging the ranks of your enemy's loyal servants is a normal thing to do," another accented voice behind Daphne pointed out. A soft swishing of fabric suggested some of the vampires in the room drawing away.

"And they might flee as well," Philippe replied. "Go out into the world and hide somewhere. Create another unruly nest and, as Sébastien's group did for a while, seem to cause an epidemic. This increases the risk of discovery, which is something I think we can all agree we don't want."

"Basically," Vivienne added, "it makes no sense to ask humans to lead vampires. You don't put cattle in charge of wolves, no offense, friends."

"None taken." Philippe seemed to be struggling not to laugh at the metaphor. "Are you feeling stronger, love?" he whispered to Daphne. "Can you turn around and face them? I'm right here with you, every moment."

Daphne raised her head and focused on Philippe's eyes. Beautiful dark eyes filled with love for her. Slowly, she nodded. Staying close in his embrace, she turned to face the room.

The European vampires, their hoods lowered to reveal a dizzying array of complexions and hair colors, had drawn close to each other, standing almost in formation. The rest of the room's occupants seemed uncertain. The humans had huddled in the far corner of the room. The fear on their faces showed Daphne they recognized how their fate would depend entirely on the outcome of this conversation.

"I have a suggestion," Philippe said. "Why not make Geneviève the leader? She killed Ragonde, which is understandable. That woman..." he shook his head. "If there was a way to kill her for each person in this room, it would not have been enough. I'm sure Gen would happily have taken out Sébastien as well, if only she'd been close enough. Since she's a true vampire, she is the most likely candidate."

Shock contorted the woman's face. "Sir?"

"Who is Geneviève?" Ginger demanded.

"He..." Daphne's voice broke and she swallowed hard. "He means Vivienne here. He knew her before she turned, when she used another name." Daphne paused a moment and then added, "He has a good point. She's very strong and independent. Never once did she let either Sébastien or Ragonde control her. That's why they kept her prisoner. And she's a fair-minded person, for a vampire. She respects the rights of the humans who choose to stay, but she hates kidnapping."

Vivienne turned to regard Daphne with wide, bright eyes.

The slaves in the corner all stared at the dark-skinned woman, their expressions pleading.

"Hmmmm," The ginger-haired vampire hummed, regarding the woman consideringly.

"Vivienne, would you be willing to lead?" *Remember how you talked about dying? Are you set on that?* Daphne added, shooting the thought directly into the older woman's mind.

Vivienne pursed her lips and her forehead crinkled into lines of consternation. *That's a fair question, Daphne. Up until now, this has seemed like a cursed existence.* "I do not know," she said at last. "I've been a prisoner, a victim, for decades. My body belonged to Sébastien, and he used it without thought of my preferences. I've been used by many of the people in this room. Will they respect me as leader?"

"If you were, you could use them," Ginger pointed out. "Remind them who's in charge. Take control of them. To lead, you must take their blood, and they yours. Then you will own them."

*They know*, Daphne sent to both Philippe and Vivienne. *They know they're contagious. They know their bites infect people.*

*Of course, they do*, Philippe replied. *This is why they think they're better than others. A tiny exchange of fluids, and you're a slave. It's vile.*

Vivienne shook her head. "I am not a slave driver. I will not subject anyone to my will, but there is no other way they will accept me. It would be better for a leader to arise naturally from among them, and I will depart."

"Please," a softly slurred voice begged. "Please, don't leave us." Stéphane approached on his knees, hands clasped in an attitude of contrition. "Please, don't leave me alone with them."

For the space of a dozen heartbeats, pure rage flared on Vivienne's face as she regarded the man. Daphne could recall Sébastien ordering him to assault her, and it surely had not been the first time.

"Why do you want me?" she hissed. "I could kill you now. I would like nothing better. You were loyal to *him*. You hurt me on his orders, and never gave it a second thought."

"Kill me, then," he countered, his face open and guileless as always. "You are my master now, and I will always obey you." He extended one arm to her and bowed his head, ready to accept whatever end she chose to bestow upon him.

Philippe hooked an arm around Daphne's waist and exerted a subtle pressure. She moved with him, not sure what was happening, but willing to follow his lead.

Another local vampire, one Daphne had seen inside the house, also approached. Vivienne regarded the newcomer with an unreadable expression. He knelt, eyes on the ground, and extended his arm.

As one, the other vampires approached, knelt, and willingly submitted themselves to her. The European delegation turned to regard the scene, faces twisted in lines of curiosity.

Philippe stepped backward through the open doorway of the parlor room and brought Daphne with him. As though summoned by an unseen force, vampires and humans moved, zombie-like, down the hallway toward the room Philippe and Daphne had just left. He drew her against the opposite wall, and the throngs trudged past, seeming not to notice them. Philippe edged along the wall, back toward the throne room.

*What are we doing?* Daphne asked, not daring to speak aloud for fear she might attract the attention of some dangerous creature.

*Leaving. There's a large window I used to get in. We can go out that way. I think the front door might be occupied for quite some time.*

*What about Vivienne?* Daphne demanded. *She might need our help.*

*The vampires are begging her to be their queen. She's going to be fine.*

They reached the throne room. Philippe dragged Daphne inside, and she froze at the sight of the location where so many horrible things had happened. Her hands began to tremble, her knees to shake, until she feared she might topple over.

"Come on, mon amour," Philippe urged. "Don't fall apart now. Not yet. Once we're out of here, out of the swamp, we can go somewhere safe, and you can let go. Hold yourself together a bit longer, Daphne. Let's move." He tugged her over to the window. She stumbled, righted herself and stumbled again.

At last, Philippe lifted her into his arms, seemingly unaffected by her weight. He circled the throne and drew near to the window. Pushing against the casement he swung the glass panel wide, which easily allowed him to set her through into the night. She leaned against the wall of the manor, listening to the croaking of bullfrogs and the droning of mosquitos, her mind blank.

"Philippe clambered through after her. "Can you walk?" he asked.

Out of the hated house, her pounding heart began to slow, her rapid breathing to return to normal. The dizzy feeling that had left her shaking eased and she sagged against the boards for a long moment. Then, slowly, she straightened herself to stand. "Yes, I can walk."

"Good. It's a long way through the swamp, but I've marked know the path. At the other side, I have my car. We can be miles away in an hour. Shall we?"

Daphne nodded and reached for Philippe's hand. He led her toward the back of the house, off the porch and into the night, on a narrow, boggy road under dying oaks festooned with Spanish moss.

Light flared in the darkened bedroom in the far corner of the second floor. The contained females hissed and withdrew into the shadows. *Poor beasts,* Vivienne thought. *It will be quite some time before they gain enough independence to be allowed out of captivity.*

"It's all right, girls," she said gently.

"What happened?" the dark-haired one wailed. "I feel so strange."

"The beast who spawned you is dead," she explained. "I am called Vivienne. I will be in charge here now."

The girls looked at one another. "What does that mean?" the red-head demanded, rising to her towering height and glaring down at Vivienne, rage twisting her features.

"No more men, unless you want one," Vivienne replied, "nor women either."

The plump blonde shuddered, relief creasing her features.

"You are still undead. You must still feed, but I will help you, so you don't harm anyone. I will teach you how to feed without killing."

The athletic brunette whimpered.

"However, before any of that can begin, we must share blood. Then you will be mine to protect. Please, will you come here?" She extended her bruised and bitten wrist, where blood had already begun to coagulate.

The women looked at one another, and one by one they crept towards Vivienne.

# Epilogue

A warm bed in a tidy, neutral hotel room cradled Daphne and her husband. For a long time, she'd been insensible, finally giving in to the hysterics she'd kept at bay for so many days.

Philippe embraced her, his own tears falling hot onto her forehead, until the storm passed.

Daphne struggled to draw air into her laboring lungs, while trying to melt into the warmth of her husband's embrace.

"Are you well, darling?" he murmured.

Her lips struggled to form words past choking sniffles and lingering sobs. "For the moment, though I doubt the worst is behind me."

"I know," he replied, his arms tightening around her. "You were so brave, my love. So strong."

"It made no difference." She retched as images of unwanted and degrading touches crowded in on her.

"It did," Philippe insisted. "You kept your head. You destroyed that monster and left the rest of the colony with a chance for a brighter future."

"They're beasts, all of them," she snarled, then sagged as Philippe's fingers smoothed through her hair.

"They are," he agreed. "Another species of wild animal, abused and tortured and kept in cages. Perhaps in time, with Geneviève's help, they will become better."

Daphne tried to contemplate such an outcome, but her mind went blank. *I suppose I don't care about their future, so long as they leave me the hell alone.*

She recalled how the vampires had knelt before Vivienne and offered their loyalty. "What happened?" she asked. "Why did all those vampires suddenly give their allegiance to Vivienne when they treated her like a *thing* before? They all raped her. I'm sure of it."

Philippe drew in a deep breath. "I saw this once before, back in the old country. One master vampire killed another. Those minions that belonged to the dead vampire suddenly had no one to lead them. They had no idea how to get on without their leader. They immediately pledged their loyalty to the victor, without a second thought. I think it took a series of bites over the course of a month or so to complete the transfer."

"So, they voluntarily infect themselves with the victorious vampire's virus, effectively replacing their existing life force with another? Why?"

Philippe shrugged. "Who can say? Perhaps some of the more mature ones don't. I'm not certain. Perhaps this is one way independent vampires are created. Honestly, Daphne, I'm not that interested in their politics. I'd mostly prefer to stay out of their way."

"Will they let you?" she asked. "We know who they are and where they are."

"Yes," he agreed slowly, "though I lack a blood tie to any of them. Whatever vestiges of my enslavement died with *them*, I believe, so the others will have no means to track us."

"You're wrong," Daphne said.

Philippe paused and turned to look at her, the moonlight filtering through the window to reflect in his shiny dark eyes. He raised one eyebrow.

"Vivienne has a tie to both of us. She bit me, so we could communicate, but her tie to you is stronger. You created her, Philippe. She is your lost love, isn't that right?"

He closed his eyes, his head bowed, and at last, nodded. "Yes, mon amour. Your Vivienne was once my Geneviève. I thought Ragonde had killed her. I didn't know... I didn't *think*. But she doesn't remember me."

Daphne refrained from pointing out that he *should* have known. Of course, a fatal bite from a vampire would not have led to death, but to awakening as a new creature. *He knows, and to make him say the words now, so many years later, would be cruel.*

A slow, burning pain flared in Daphne's heart and spread heat outward to her fingertips and toes. Her face heated. "Are you sure you don't want to return? Being the human lover of a vampire is something many people seem to desire. You loved her once. You love her still, I can see it. Not to mention, she's a fair and honest creature. She won't harm or abuse you. Would you rather return?"

Philippe's eyes flew open and he stared at Daphne. "Return... Daphne what are you talking about? I never wanted to be a vampire's whore, remember? I ran from that ages ago."

"You didn't love Sébastien. You do love Vivienne. Doesn't that make a difference?"

Philippe drew Daphne closer to him, until their bodies touched from shoulder to knee and their feet tangled together. "I *loved* her, mon amour, in the past. Decades ago. It was interesting to see her again, and I'm glad to know she's thriving, but the feelings I once had are only a memory. A memory she does not share. Vivienne and I... we were good together, but you must understand that at the core of our relationship, all we had in common was need. She needed to escape the whorehouse and I needed not to be alone anymore. With you and me, it's different. We are like one soul in two bodies. Same dreams. Same plans. No, I would never go back to that decadent vampire lifestyle, no matter that it is my former sweetheart in charge of it. *This* is where I want to be."

"In a hotel?" Daphne quipped weakly, relief spawning a lame joke.

"As long as you are with me, alive and safe, then yes, anywhere," he replied. In the filtering moonlight, she could see his eyes shining with hope. The virus inside Daphne responded to his feelings, bringing a mirroring sense of peace. Shutting her eyes, she leaned forward and claimed his lips in a tender kiss. *He will help me heal,* she realized. *We are bound together, and I wouldn't have it any other way.*

# Author's Notes

The legend of the Comte de St. Germain, the gentle immortal, is common in New Orleans. It's well known that a man who called himself Jacques St. Germain attacked a woman in New Orleans in the early 1900s. While that legend inspired this tale, I never could accept that St. Germain, after centuries of peaceful interaction, would suddenly turn to a killer. To me, it seemed there was more to the story. Clearly, a vampire attacked that woman, but was St. Germain the vampire? Could it have been a case of mistaken identity? And thus, a new novel was born.

I hope you have enjoyed this tale of disease, science, passion and the undead. I'm considering whether to write a sequel, featuring Vivienne/Geneviève and the newly turned roommates, and I would love feedback from my readers whether such a novel would be appreciated. Feel free to send me an email at simonebeaudelaireauthor@hotmail.com or contact me through my Facebook author page, and if you could please head over to Amazon and leave a review, I would greatly appreciate it. Even something as simple as "I liked it" or "Good read" would suffice.

# About the Author

In the world of the written word, Simone Beaudelaire strives for technical excellence while advancing a worldview in which the sacred and the sensual blend into stories of people whose relationships are founded in faith, but are no less passionate for it. Unapologetically explicit, yet undeniably classy, Beaudelaire's 20+ novels aim to make readers think, cry, pray... and get a little hot and bothered.

In real life, the author's alter-ego teaches composition at a community college in a small western Kansas town, where she lives with her four children, three cats, and husband—fellow author Edwin Stark.

As both romance writer and academic, Beaudelaire devotes herself to promoting the rhetorical value of the romance in hopes of overcoming the stigma associated with literature's biggest female-centered genre.

# Thank you

Dear Reader,

Thank you for taking time to read *BLOOD FEVER*. If you enjoyed this book, please consider telling your friends and posting a short review. There is nothing more valuable to an author than the praise of their readers. Your time and support are greatly appreciated!

# Other Books by Simone Beaudelaire

When the Music Ends (The Hearts in Winter Chronicles Book 1)
When the Words are Spoken (The Hearts in Winter Chronicles Book 2)
Caroline's Choice (The Hearts in Winter Chronicles Book 3)
When the Heart Heals (The Hearts in Winter Chronicles Book 4)
The Naphil's Kiss
Blood Fever
Polar Heat
Xaman (with Edwin Stark)
Darkness Waits (with Edwin Stark)
Watching Over the Watcher
Baylee Breaking
Amor Maldito: Romantic Tragedies from Tejano Folklore
Keeping Katerina (The Victorians Book 1)
Devin's Dilemma (The Victorians Book 2)
High Plains Promise (Love on the High Plains Book 2)
High Plains Heartbreak (Love on the High Plains Book 3)
High Plains Passion (Love on the High Plains Book 4)
Devilfire (American Hauntings Book 1)
Saving Sam (The Wounded Warriors Book 1 with J.M. Northup)
Justifying Jack (The Wounded Warriors Book 2 with J.M. Northup)
Making Mike (The Wounded Warriors Book 3 with J.M Northup)

You might also like:

Devilfire by Simone Beaudelaire

To read the first chapter for free, please head to:
https://www.nextchapter.pub/books/devilfire

Blood Fever
ISBN: 978-4-86747-036-7

Published by
Next Chapter
1-60-20 Minami-Otsuka
170-0005 Toshima-Ku, Tokyo
+818035793528
20th May 2021

9 784867 470367